Raised on a farm in rural Canada afforded Jessica Tonn with a love for stories and a very vivid imagination. Jessica's father read books to the family on the long winter evenings, fostering the love for written stories. She began writing as a teenager, starting with poems then filling notebooks with story after story. During college, then university, academic papers replaced the stories. But the stories begged to be told and soon, Jessica was back to writing. She self-published two children's stories based on life on the farm and this is her first novel.

To Annette,
A dear friend who asked me to write a story about Queen Esther.

Jessica Tonn

THE GOLDEN SCEPTER

AUSTIN MACAULEY PUBLISHERS™

LONDON * CAMBRIDGE * NEW YORK * SHARJAH

Ordering Information
Quantity sales: Special discounts are available on quantity purchases by corporations, associations, and others. For details, contact the publisher at the address below.

Publisher's Cataloging-in-Publication data
Tonn, Jessica
The Golden Scepter

ISBN 9798886939163 (Paperback)
ISBN 9798886939170 (Hardback)
ISBN 9798886939187 (ePub e-book)

Library of Congress Control Number: 2023912967

www.austinmacauley.com/us

First Published 2023
Austin Macauley Publishers LLC
40 Wall Street, 33rd Floor, Suite 3302
New York, NY 10005
USA

mail-usa@austinmacauley.com
+1 (646) 5125767

I will always thank my parents for encouraging me, reading this book in its infant stage, and loving it right from the start.

Nikki, a dear friend, who spent many hours poring over the first rough copy and wrote so many penciled notes in the margins.

My husband, who lets me be me.

Clara, my best friend, and artist extraordinaire.

SANDROCK Boutique for working with me to provide the illustrations, thank you!

Table of Contents

Chapter 1

How God Answered a Desperate Prayer

Once upon a time, a very long time ago, a time when thrones rose and fell within a moment's notice, lived an orphaned girl named Hadassah. Her parents both died, only hours apart, of the terrible plague that ravaged the dirty streets of the poverty-stricken slums surrounding the Persian city of Susa.

Sickness reduced her parents to servants of servants, one of the lowest dregs of society, hungry, helpless, and oh! So alone. Her father's health declined so suddenly, the little family was impoverished in a matter of months, destitute and homeless, trying to scratch out a living on the streets. Her mother crumbled under the emotional grief, her own body helplessly withering away around her bony frame, all laughter and joy gone from her exquisite eyes. Her last breath whispered the name of her beloved daughter as her soul tore away.

Hadassah sat helplessly beside the bodies, a bleak future stretching ahead of her. Her dress was ragged and stained. The stench of urine and rotting garbage enveloped her as she tucked her dirty bare feet under her. She rocked back and forth on her underfed legs, her grief swirling around her in a stifling cloak of utter and total helplessness.

Her striking blue-green eyes swelled with tears as she raised her beautiful, childish face toward the rising moon.

"Great God of our Father Abraham," she prayed, copying the words her father had used when he prayed.

She vaguely remembered the happy family suppers around a candlelit table, plates full of food, a smiling mother. Only six months ago, this had been her reality. Now she was friendless, kneeling on the dirt floor of a one-room, tattered tent. The blanket the family owned covered the bodies of her parents, waiting their final resting place in the hot earth of a foreign land.

"Save me!" Her prayer tore from her very core, her parched lips whispering the words of desperation. "I will be yours forever. I will be your servant till the day I die."

Exhausted from crying, the little girl curled up beside the deathbed of her parents. She knew the burial crew would come in the morning and carry them away. The bodies had to be buried quickly to stop the spread of disease. She would be thrown out of their little house, left to fend for herself among the perilous streets of one of the busiest cities the world had ever known. She had seen it, heard it, morning after morning for the last month.

There was nothing she could do to wake from this terrible nightmare. She was stuck, frozen, hopelessly drowning in vulnerability with no chance of anyone saving her. If God did not hear her prayer, no one would.

It was early morning when a firm footstep sounded at the tent entrance, startling the little girl. She sat upright and swung around to face the intruder. She looked up into the kind face of a middle-aged man stooping over to get in the small opening. His brown eyes swelled with tears as he took in the sight.

The smells of death and poverty stung his lungs with every breath. He squinted against the pain, laughter lines appearing around his eyes as he struggled to adjust to the dark, odorous interior of the tiny tent. His athletic frame shuttered with the intensity of his emotions. His cloak slipped back off his wavy brown hair, graying around the temples. His simple white kippah seemed to glow in the dusky twilight.

The little girl stared at the man, her eyes wide with fearful curiosity.

"What is your name, child?" asked the man gently. He squatted down to be closer to her height. Even in a terrible fright, covered in dirt and tearstains, the girl's beauty was undeniable. Her rich creamy olive-color skin accented her enchanting blue-green eyes, unbelievably large in her small, childish round face. Her head was covered with a thick mane of kinky black hair. Never had he seen such a beautiful child.

"My name is Hadassah," said the girl bravely. Her large eyes never left his face.

"Who are you?" she asked, slowly rising to her feet curiosity giving her small body the strength to question.

"I am your cousin, Mordecai," the Jewish man said gently.

"You may remember your father speaking of his uncle who lived in Susa. I am his son; God rest his soul. I received a letter from a friend of your

12

mother's. She told me of the terrible plague here, and how sick your father was. She begged me to come and find you, as she feared your mother was dying as well."

He paused to glance at the two figures lying still and silent under the blanket. He sighed as he blinked back a sudden wave of emotions.

"I am willing to take you home with me, if you like." He said this softly, almost timidly.

"So, your parents are dead too?" For the first time the girl's eyes turned to the lifeless forms covered by the blanket. A large dark stain grew slowly, as the smells of death and decay again shrouded the tiny tent.

"Yes, sadly," Mordecai nodded. "Both my parents have passed on to the Promised Land." His voice trembled slightly as he shamelessly wiped tears from his cheeks. The sight of such human desecration broke his heart as he struggled, remembering the smiling face of his uncle, an identical twin of his own father.

The girl was silent a long moment, watching as Mordecai wiped tears from his cheeks using the sleeve of his robe. Her eyes never left his face as if trying to read a deep secret kept there. Suddenly, the slightest of smiles lit across her face, a flash of joy leapt in her eyes. She lifted a hand toward his.

"Will you take me home with you?" The question was whispered, fear and hope shimmering in her voice.

Caught unexpected, Mordecai sobbed with emotion. He quickly composed himself and nodded. He reached out his hand and took her little one in his. He noticed the long, graceful fingers curled trustingly around his muscular palm.

"Let's go home," he said gently.

Hadassah glanced back.

"I must say goodbye," she said. Mordecai nodded.

Letting go of Mordecai's hand, she covered the distance to the lifeless forms. Carefully, she lifted the blanket to show the faces, white and wax-like in the moonlight. Her lips moved silently in a heart-wrenching farewell to her parents, the only life she had known. With a finger, she carefully traced the outline of each face, trying to draw them forever in her mind. Then, slowly, she covered over the faces again with the corner of the blanket. Rising, she turned, and together without another backward glance, the man and child walked out of the tattered tent.

They were just in time. The sun's first rays painted the sky pink and orange. A dog barked suddenly, startling them. The burial crew rounded the corner; the daily march from house to house, door to door, tent to tent, had begun.

Onlookers, bargain hunters and looters gathered at a curious distance, ready to pounce on anything of value. A couple of men looked up and saw Mordecai with Hadassah. One shouted and pointed. A group began running toward them.

Wisely, Mordecai scooped up the silent child in his arms. He quickly covered her head with a fold of his robe. He flicked his hood over to hide his own head. He turned and, clutching his precious burden close, he ran for her life.

Hadassah snuggled into his robe, quiet and grateful. The noise and yelling told her all she needed to know. Mordecai turned the corner and the street she knew was gone.

She stifled a quiet sob, her heart pounding in her chest. She did not know why men would run after them. She did not understand this world. She was only five, how could she know. Yet fear coursed through her body. She clung to her cousin as he ran, his breaths coming in short gasps. Around corner after corner, he darted, quickly losing the men chasing them.

At last, with beads of sweat on both their brows, he finally slowed to a fast walk. The streets were getting busy now, and they were easily lost in the hustle of people moving here and there. The burial crew was nowhere to be seen. He uncovered her head, knowing she was hot too. She could feel the pounding of his heart in his chest as it heaved with the effort of running and carrying her. He smiled reassuringly down at her as they continued to move.

The sun was halfway up in the sky when he stopped at a booth and bought them each a loaf of bread and a skin of warm camel's milk. His eyes softened watching the child hungrily gulp down the warm, rich fluid. How long she had stayed beside her parents without eating or drinking, he did not know. A lump again rose in his throat, but he swallowed it. How far his people had fallen for their sins!

How long, Oh Lord, will we languish so? His heart cried out. The child turned and looked full into his face, a slow dribble of milk creeping down her chin. She captured him with the intensity of her gaze.

"The God of Abraham heard my prayer," she said, her voice steady with certainty, a light sparking in her blue-green eyes. "He is the One who sent you to save me." Awe crept into her voice. "Those bad men would have hurt me, but God sent you just in time."

"So He is still with His people," Mordecai finished his thought out loud in humble reverence. The girl nodded. She stood up and reaching out her hand, she smiled up at him for the first time.

"I promised Him I would obey Him for the rest of my life." She said, her beautiful childish face alight with hope. "Can you teach me more of Him?"

Mordecai's heart swelled within him. Childless himself, God had now blessed him with an eager, intelligent pupil. He smiled down at her as he gently squeezed her hand, his heart swelling with a fierce love for this little soul before him.

"Yes, my daughter," his words were a soothing balm to both of their wounded hearts. "I will teach you of our great God, the God of Abraham, Isaac, and Jacob."

The two continued their walk from the sprawling slums of the dry, impoverished plateau. The road they followed slowly began to climb the ridge that cut through the countryside, dividing the plateau from the rich river valley, well-watered and fertile. The wealthy gathered along the riverbanks in deluxe estates, overshadowed by the citadel of Susa, the king's winter palace.

Mordecai slowed his pace for the little girl as they walked along, hand in hand. The air became fresh and warm as the stench of dirty streets and crowded living quarters fell away behind them. Hope glistened in Hadassah's eyes. She gasped as they finally crested the ridge, a physical barrier dividing the rich from the poor, the slave from the free, and the citizen from the captives.

The great river looped lazily through the wide lush valley. Orchards and vineyards striated the landscape. Great grey and white mansions peeked between lush gardens of deep green trees and flowering bushes of every color imaginable. Rich purples, yellows and reds painted color over the rolling countryside in generous splashes.

Lavender swayed gently in long, purple rows. Cherry, apple, apricot, and almond trees waved branches, laden with blossoms, scenting the breeze. Grape vines hung rebelliously over stone walls and morning glories draped ornate gates in rich blue and white blossoms.

The reddish dirt roadway twisted its way down into the valley, and lazily ambled along beside the river. Boats, with billowing white sails, flags and colorful banners flapping cheerfully in the wind, slowly cruised up and down the deep blue river. The air was fresh, laden with the scent of the blooming lavender, jasmine, and shimmered with happiness.

Hadassah breathed in a deep long breath. Mordecai stood watching her, a smile playing around his lips, moving his beard. She did not even look up at him.

"Wow!" was all she said after a long moment. The scent of the valley washed over her, clearing her lungs. The stench of the tiny tent began to disappear. The cold darkness was a distant memory. How bright and hopeful the world suddenly looked.

"What is the name of this river?" asked her eager little mind. And before Mordecai could even answer another question tumbled out.

"How far is your home from here? Can we see the river from your house? Do you have trees in your yard? Can I grow a garden?"

"Ohhhh! The flowers smell so good! What is that smell, Cousin? What makes the air smell so good?" She looked up at him, eagerly squeezing his hand.

Mordecai laughed at her delight.

"Well, my little Hadassah," They began their descent down the winding road toward the river.

"The river's name is the Shuar. We are about a two-hour walk. We can't see the river from our house. There are too many houses on the streets around us to see the river. There are several large trees in our garden. A big oak shades the side of the house your bedroom window will look out on. The lavender and jasmine are blooming this time of year, after the spring rains, making the air smell so fresh."

"You may plant whatever you like in the garden. Adinah will love to share her knowledge of plants and herbs with you. Oh, how you will bless our home."

The pair walked along the river for a long while then slowly the road began to wind its way up onto the ridge again. The landscape changed. The vineyards fell away as house after house lined the street. Once again, the two found themselves in the bustling city. Camels laden with all kinds of goods strode along. Wooden wagons heaped with cloth, spices, dishes, and other merchandise creaked passed pulled by donkeys or oxen. Everywhere there were people.

Hadassah's eyes grew wider and wider as she surveyed the hustle and bustle about her. She received many curious stares herself. She stood out from

16

among the clean, richly clad people around her with her bare feet, tattered dress, and dirty skin. But she paid them no attention. Mordecai on the other hand, gripped her hand tightly and pulled her close to him, very aware of the judgmental looks shot his way.

Women passed on foot dressed in colorful clothes, gold and diamonds shimmering around their necks, on their ears, and decorating their fingers. Each wore jeweled leather slippers, soft and comfortable, to protect their feet from the hot roads. Litters passed, carried by four giant men, naked to the waist, perspiration gleaming on their muscular backs. Richly dressed women lounged lazily on the platforms, sleepily surveying the streets around as their servants carried them along. Noble men rode by on great horses, golden tassels decorating the saddle pads and chest straps.

Hadassah's little head turned quickly trying to capture all the beautiful sights and sounds around her. Mordecai slowed his pace. He had never stopped to enjoy the familiar sights around his home he just took for granted. Watching Hadassah's head and eyes follow every move reminded him of what a fantastic view the main street leading into Susa really was.

At last, they reached the great square. Hadassah laughed as she held out her hand, letting the water from the fountain splash over her fingers.

"Not far now, dear one," he encouraged. "Adinah will be so eager to meet you."

Hadassah nodded. She was nervous of meeting this woman she did not know. Already she was comfortable with Cousin Mordecai. Her heart hurt with the thought of another woman other than her mother teaching and guiding her. But as the pair walked slowly across the square, her little heart purposed to like her cousin's wife as best she could.

The Great God sent Mordecai to save me. He will give me the ability to love his wife and to serve her well. I hope she wants me just as Cousin Mordecai does. This thought hovered in her mind causing a small wrinkle of worry to appear on her forehead.

At the fountain Mordecai turned onto a street, gently sloping up, with large, brick houses on each side. The front gardens were fenced and gated. Trees shaded the street giving it a quiet, calm atmosphere compared to the hustle and bustle of the main street. He stopped and opened the latch to one of the decorative gates.

Hadassah looked down the path that ran up to a bright yellow door. This was her new home, but she had very little time to admire it. The moment the gate clicked closed behind them, the yellow door flew open. A woman burst out. She must have been watching for them.

Her tichel was a beautiful rich blue, smoothing over her greying, brown hair. Her rich brown eyes sparkled, and she greeted her husband with a kiss. She quickly turned her attention to the little form hovering behind him.

"Adinah, this is Hadassah, my cousin." Mordecai said softly, his eyes misting. It sounded so formal, so final.

Adinah bent down and opened her arms. Tears already formed in her kind eyes and her face shimmered with joy, love, and yearning.

"Come, my little one, come!" She encouraged her fingers gesturing in her eagerness.

Hadassah hesitated only a moment. She recognized the pain behind the joy of the woman. She walked into Adinah's hungry arms. Her own little arms twisted around the woman's neck. The soft silkiness of the tichel slipped against her cheek, like the loving brush of her mother's cold fingers. The smell of Adinah's skin and clothes encircled her.

Hadassah sighed with relief. Her little heart opened, and she knew she was wanted, deeply wanted. God had cared for her after all.

A younger woman, draped in a deep green tichel, hovered at the door, her hands anxiously twisting in front of her, unsure of what to do. When Adinah finally released Hadassah from her long embrace, she smiled up at the waiting woman.

"Hadassah, meet Ruth, my constant companion and helper," Adinah explained. Hadassah looked up at Ruth curiously. Ruth smiled and opened a little napkin she held. She offered out a small dainty cake to Hadassah.

"I do most of the baking and cooking," explained Ruth. "I made this little cake to welcome you home, child. I hope you will find great happiness, in this home, just as I have."

Chapter 2

Hadassah's First Day in Her Cousin's House

The next morning, Hadassah woke with a start. She sat up quickly looking about her in amazement.

Where was she?

Slowly, the events of the past day settled back into her mind. Her skin and hair were clean. She had been scrubbed from head-to-toe last evening before bed by Adinah. Ruth had wrapped her in a soft towel while Adinah oiled and combed her hair. She had been so tired by then her head bobbed with exhaustion.

She vaguely remembered Mordecai's strong arms carrying her to her new bedroom. Adinah had tucked her in and hovered over her till she fell asleep tired from her long emotional day, full of Ruth's delicious cooking, clean and safe at last.

She smiled slowly and threw back the silky covers. She slipped out of bed; her bare feet lost in a thick Persian rug. She quickly pulled the coverlet over the bed and tidied it. It was all so beautiful she dared not leave anything disorganized behind her. She walked softly to the window. She stood on tiptoes to peer out at the courtyard garden.

The tree branches waved her a greeting. The flowers and herbs met her gaze with their rich deep greens and purples. The gentle breeze, still fresh from the night, blew the sweet fragrance of jasmine, mint, pine, and cinnamon into her nose. Her senses tingled with delight.

Overcome, she knelt by the window, her little face turned up to the sky. She looked up into the deep blue expanse, the silky wisps of clouds, driven by the wind moved slowly across the great sky. Gratitude, deep rich gratitude bubbled up in her heart, washing over the aching of her hurt.

"Great God of Abraham, Isaac, and Jacob," she prayed. "Your servant thanks you for saving me and bringing me to this beautiful place. Thank you for giving me a new home with my cousin Mordecai and thank you for giving me love for Adinah." A single tear shimmered on her upturned cheek.

"And thank you for Ruth!" she gasped out around her emotions.

A noise from downstairs startled her. It was time to begin to explore her new home. She rose hastily looking around for her dress as she wiped any traces of tears from her face.

A robe lay on the table. It looked like it had been made hastily from a larger article of clothing. Her old, tattered dress was nowhere in sight.

She smiled as she slipped the new robe over her head. A piece of ribbon lay beside it. She picked it up and tried to tie it around her as a sash. She had never been taught how to tie a knot. She saw others do it, but she did not know how they twisted the ends together so quickly. She struggled for a long moment. It was no use. Her knot just kept untying and falling off.

She heard the hum of voices and curiosity overcame her. With the ribbon trailing beside her, she hurried out into the hallway. Down the wooden stairs she hustled, only quickly glancing around. She wanted to see Mordecai before he left for his day's work at the palace.

He was standing by the door, his hand on the handle, ready to leave. Adinah was beside him. His face lit up as he turned, hearing her bare feet on the tile floor of the living room.

"My little girl is up!" he exclaimed. Her shyness gone; Hadassah ran toward him. Her little feet pattered on the tiles, the sound echoing through the room. Mordecai scooped her up in a long embrace. He dropped a gentle kiss on her cheek. She giggled as his beard tickled her.

"Now I can go to work at rest; my girl is safe and sound," he said tousling her black hair. "Watch for my return when the afternoon sun begins to fade."

Hadassah nodded her head, her eyes wide as she watched him leave. Adinah comforted her with a hand on her shoulder. Hadassah leaned up against the older woman as together they watched Mordecai exit the gate and disappear with a wave down the street.

Hadassah sighed, suddenly feeling lonely.

"Don't worry, dear one," comforted Adinah brightly. "Let's go find Ruth and get you some breakfast."

At the mention of food, Hadassah smiled. Her stomach rumbled in her and she quickly laid a hand over it to silence it. The ribbon fluttered in her hand. Adinah's sharp eyes noted it quickly.

She knelt.

"Let's teach you how to tie your sash, shall we?"

Hadassah nodded grateful the older woman seemed to read her mind. After Adinah showed her how to twist the two ends of the fabric around each other and it stayed, Hadassah bravely tried. With Adinah's gentle guidance, she tied her own sash around her waist.

"It stayed!" Hadassah finally breathed out her first words of the day to Adinah. Adinah laughed.

"It sure did! If it does come undone at any time, you now know how to retie it."

With this the two walked across the large living room. They passed the open archway that led out to the garden. Hadassah's eyes followed the inviting white stone path as it twisted its way between trees and around beds of flowers and herbs.

Adinah saw her long glance.

"We will go into the garden as soon as we have had our breakfast," The older woman assured her. They passed through into a hallway and turned toward the kitchen. Ruth squatted over the fire pit. Delicious odors curled from the pot along with little clouds of steam. Ruth looked up as they entered beads of perspiration on her forehead. She smiled at Hadassah.

"I have hot tea ready for you, my dears!" she said happily. Hadassah watched her every move. Ruth rose and went to the shelf. She collected two mugs from there. She returned to the fire and using a ladle, she carefully filled both mugs almost to the top with a creamy spiced tea.

Usually breakfast was served somewhere cooler, but both women noticed Hadassah's interest in all the new things around her. Adinah sat down at the little table in the corner of the kitchen. Ruth smiled and carried the mugs over to the table.

"Come Hadassah, taste my tea," she encouraged. Both women were at a bit of a loss as what exactly to do with their new charge. Yesterday the house was empty of children. Today Hadassah watched with huge curious eyes every aspect of their lives. Neither fully understood where the child had come from as Mordecai did not expound on the conditions, he had found the child in. Some things were best left unspoken although never truly forgotten.

Hadassah jumped onto the chair and carefully lifted the steaming mug to her lips. The sweet rich fluid was delicious, unlike anything she had ever tasted before. Her eyes lit up as she savored the spicy drink. Ruth smiled, pleased.

"I'm baking bread today," Ruth explained as she turned the milling stone, grinding fresh wheat into fine flour. Hadassah watched curiously. Her little legs kicked happily as she ate the oatmeal given to her in a bowl. The two women chatted casually with each other, each stealing glances at the child, unable to contain their delight at her presence.

Hadassah did not remember much about a house other than the decrepit tent her parents had died in. Food there was scarce and usually very bland or salty. Here the rich smells, the variety, the structure of the entire kitchen fascinated her. It was a comforting place. It smelled of plenty. Ruth's love for cooking was evident in the foods she prepared. Hadassah's stomach bulged as it had never bulged before. At last, she pushed away the empty bowl, scraped clean by her spoon, her mug empty but her stomach full beyond description.

Both Adinah and Ruth exclaimed over how much she ate. Hadassah looked up at their delighted faces, awareness slowly dawning in her heart of just how much they loved caring for her.

Once the bread was set aside to rise, the women took Hadassah on a tour of the rest of the house. They showed her the bathing room and how to use the facilities. Hadassah was delighted with the smooth silken coolness of the bright blue tile that lined the entire bathing area.

They took her back to the main living area and across the room and down another hallway. This hallway ended with a large bedroom overlooking the garden. This was the master bedroom were Mordecai and Adinah slept. It had a smaller bathing area and facilities built onto the large square room. Both women watched with enjoyment as Hadassah explored every space thoroughly, impressed with how big it was. Her little hands touched the smooth linen coverlet of the bed, enjoying the beautiful bright Persian embroidery on it.

Never had Hadassah imagined such cleanliness or comfort. The stark contrast of the tent she came from to this luxurious home fascinated her. Everything was done in that one small tent. Here there was so much space, so much room, and so much beauty. She smiled up at Adinah.

"I like this," she said pointing at a tapestry decorating the wall. Adinah nodded.

"It is a favorite of mine too," she said fondly. "It was a wedding gift many years ago."

All three examined the other two rooms of the house. One was a guest room and the other was Mordecai's study. Hadassah's face pulled into a smile as she looked around at the shelves full of scrolls and papers and writing stones. Mordecai's desk had an ink well, with feathered pens and writing utensils of all sorts on it. It smelled wonderful to her.

"This is a room you should never enter alone, my dear Hadassah," Adinah instructed gently. "This is a room I dare not enter too much myself."

Ruth chuckled at this.

"I only enter it once a week for its cleaning myself," echoed Ruth. "It is best left undisturbed. It is his world, his work, you know."

Hadassah nodded. She understood it was of great importance she did not enter this room or interrupt in any way. She noted this in her mind. She did not want to upset Adinah or Mordecai in any way. She must remember to stay out of this room.

Both women noted the slight frown on her forehead and the intensity of the way she looked.

"What is it, child," asked Adinah kneeling. "Have we said something to upset you?"

Hadassah shook her head.

"I must remember to obey." She said nodding her head with each word. "I must be obedient to you as I would my mother and father." The simplicity of her words struck Adinah.

"What a blessing you are child!" she exclaimed and drew in the little girl for a long hug. "Now, let's get on with getting proper clothes for you, shall we?"

The women measured Hadassah and planned to make clothes that would fit her properly. What she wore now was an old robe of Ruth's quickly cut to fit her little frame. Hadassah did not see the need for new clothes right away, but the women were very adamant on this subject.

Hadassah's eyes wandered out the archway into the garden again. Adinah noted it.

"Ruth, you finish in the kitchen. I will go and show Hadassah the garden. I know she is excited to run and play." Ruth nodded and hurried off.

Adinah turned and pointed out toward the garden.

"Let's go exploring!" she invited.

Hadassah needed no further invitation. Her little feet pattering on the tiles, she hurried out into the sunlight. She had never been allowed out of the tent alone. There was no place to go other than the dirty streets anyways.

But here, here, she lifted her arms and twirled with delight. The dancing shadows made by the sunlight falling through the leaves of the great trees around her seemed to share her joy. The gentle breezes pulled her along, down the white stone pathway. She giggled with delight, smiling up at Adinah.

Adinah laughed with her. After they had explored every inch of the garden, admiring the blooming lavender and jasmine, examining the intricate throats of the Morning Glories, Adinah showed Hadassah the bed of herbs, used to flavor the foods in the kitchen.

"The vegetables are not very beautiful, but their usefulness and taste make up for that," she said with a smile. Hadassah nodded. Not all beautiful things were useful and not all useful things were beautiful. She did understand that.

Adinah disappeared in the house to collect a project, leaving Hadassah alone in the garden. She just walked slowly around, looking at the trees, letting her head fall back to follow them all the way to the sky. The smooth yellowish bark of an Arbutus tree growing up against the garden wall caught her attention. It was so inviting, her little body instinctively swung up into the branches. A particularly large branch leaned out a cross the stone wall toward the neighboring garden.

With a sigh of contentment, the little girl sat down, her legs kicking happily. She looked at the trees of the other garden. A butterfly sailed by on feathered wings. Hadassah whispered a greeting, wondering at its ability to fly. A dragon fly followed, its shimmering wings moving so fast they only glistened. It was headed to the water garden. Hadassah's turquoise eyes followed the bright blue body as it dipped and turned in its sporadic flight path.

She did not see Adinah re-enter the garden and look about hastily, her sewing basket slung on her arm.

"Hadassah!" Adinah called out worriedly, turning this way and that to see where the little figure had disappeared to. Hadassah turned quickly.

"Here I am!" She smiled down at Adinah from her perch in the tree. "I am right here."

Adinah followed the sound of the cheerful voice and looked across the garden and up, over the wall. There sat the little child, happily perched on a branch.

A look of displeasure flashed briefly over her face. She quickly caught herself and smiled again.

"What a lovely place you have found to sit, Child," she said and walked down the path toward her. "I was afraid I had lost you for a moment."

"There is no place I would want to go other than here with you and Cousin Mordecai," the child explained solemnly.

At this, Adinah caught herself. She set her basket on the stone bench and lifted her arms. Hadassah hurriedly climbed from her perch and ran to her. The two embraced for a long moment.

The rest of the morning passed happily. Adinah sat on the stone bench and worked on her sewing, leaving Hadassah to run and play in the garden freely as she pleased.

Adinah was careful to never let the little figure out of her sight for long. Hadassah tried to remember to stay in sight, but her curiosity always got the best of her, and everything was so beautiful and so interesting. She ran after the dragon flies as they zigzagged through the trees and flowering bushes. Butterflies danced here and there, and every flower called her name. She danced along with them, waving her arms.

She discovered there was room between the wall of the house and the garden wall for her little body to slide easily through. She was playing under the fruit trees in the front of the house when Adinah's voice called her name.

Quickly she ran through the small passage and through the trees toward the archway leading into the house. Her little feet pattered on the stones of the pathway as she hurried to obey.

"There you are little one!" Adinah's face spread with a smile watching her charge bounding toward her, hair and eyes were shining. "Ruth has lunch ready. You must be hungry from all your play." Adinah tousled the mass of waving curls bouncing on Hadassah's head.

Hadassah nodded. In a flash, she was off to the kitchen. Adinah's mouth opened to tell her something then closed with a sigh. The little figure was just too fast for her.

Adinah decided to just head for the table in the cool shade of the living room. It was a few moments and Hadassah reappeared carrying a bowl of steaming soup. Her face was set in a focused frown, careful not to spill a drop on her way. She set the bowl triumphantly on the table before Adinah. She hurried back toward the kitchen. In this way, Hadassah set all the food out on the table then sank down into the spot allotted to her. She smiled happily at Adinah and Ruth, before trying a spoonful of the soup in her bowl.

"We have an eager little helper," said Ruth with a laugh. "Hadassah insisted on carrying everything out for me."

"God has blessed me with an energetic daughter," Adinah stated proudly. "I thought our garden was small but even so, I could not keep up with this Little One's play!"

Ruth laughed along with Adinah. Hadassah smiled into her bowl.

"I think we have lots to get used to, Mistress," said Ruth with a smile. "Hadassah is going to change our lives."

Once the noon meal was over, Hadassah stifled a yawn. Her play was catching up with her, but her little mind and hands would not be stilled. She rose quickly and as the older women planned a trip to market to get cloth for her gown, she began gathering the dishes and carrying them into the kitchen. The older women watched her. They were deep in their conversation.

Hadassah struggled to remember how Ruth had washed the breakfast dishes. She went to the bucket that was only half full of water.

I must refill the bucket, she noted to herself as she emptied it into the large dish tub. She looked about till she found a soap bar on a shelf. She carefully soaped the cloth just as she had seen Ruth do and set about to clean the dishes.

Minutes later Ruth hurried into the kitchen.

"I found her, Mistress Adinah!" she called smiling. Hadassah looked up from her task startled. Adinah hurried in. She took one look at the shocked face of Hadassah. Her hand covered her eyes for a long moment.

She came to Hadassah and sank down, laying her arm around the child's shoulders.

"I'm sorry we get so worried about you every moment," she explained in a gentle voice. "Ruth and I are not use to having a little charge such as yourself to brighten our days. You have been nothing but busy, happy, and helpful and here we are being worried nags." She laughed at herself and squeezed Hadassah's shoulders.

"Just promise me one thing, Little One," she asked. "Don't leave the gated yard without telling me." Hadassah looked into the deep brown eyes of the older woman. They brimmed with concern and fear.

"I promise I won't," she said solemnly. Then she remembered the empty water bucket.

"Can I get water? Where do I get water? Do I need to leave the gate to get water?" her voice rose with concern. Adinah sighed gently.

"Hadassah, you are my daughter. You don't need to serve me like your mistress. You are accepted and loved here no matter what you do. We will not keep you only if you are useful to us. Do you understand, child?"

Hadassah slowly nodded a great weight beginning to roll off her heart. She had not realized it was even there, but Adinah had calmed an unspoken fear. Together the woman helped Hadassah finish the dishes. Ruth showed Hadassah the well in the corner of the garden where they could draw water from. Hadassah so enjoyed learning this, that all agreed it should be her job from now on. With the water bucket full in the kitchen, Adinah prepared Hadassah for a trip to the market.

She combed out her hair and tied a bright ribbon in it. Hadassah enjoyed watching this through the mirror the older woman let her hold. Adinah's hands calmed the energetic curls and soon Hadassah barely recognized herself. The little girl staring back at her had a ribbon in her hair and a clean fresh face and bright happy eyes. Adinah sighed and shook her head as she looked at the makeshift robe that draped Hadassah's little frame.

"Well, my dear Hadassah, let's go get some cloth to make you some proper clothes." Hadassah was eager to go out into the streets again. She had so enjoyed watching the hubbub yesterday with Mordecai. And this time they would stop at shops and look at all the pretty things hanging from the doorways.

The streets in the slums had been dirty sad places, with stained clothes hanging haphazardly from makeshift clothes lines strung up in a hurry. The dirt streets were uneven, and brown water ran along both sides. Most of the wooden houses opened right onto the streets, leaving no room for venders of any sort. Children sat in the water, splashing, and making mud paddies. By noon the water was all gone, and the street was dry and dusty, scorching in the hot sun. There were no trees to be seen. All were long cut down and used to patch up a decrepit structure somewhere. But here in Susa it was all different.

"I must be home in time to greet Cousin Mordecai when he comes home!" she said walking over to Adinah. Adinah smiled.

"We will be home in plenty of time, Child." With this reassurance, they walked out the gate and down the street toward the square and the fountain. Hadassah was careful to stay close to Adinah as not to cause the older woman to worry about her. It was so hard to enjoy all the sights around her and keep up with Adinah.

At last, Hadassah grabbed Adinah's tassel on the end of her sash and held on tightly. Adinah smiled and gently touched her shoulder to guide her through the busy streets to her favorite merchants.

Bolt after bolt of cloth got placed up to her chin as the merchant exclaimed repeatedly about the exceptional color of her eyes. At last, Hadassah looked up at Adinah in desperation.

"Where did you find this exquisite child?" the woman asked, her yellowed teeth flashing. "She looks Babylonian, very rare these days to be sure. Such beautiful skin tone as well…Let me see, OH! I have just the piece for you."

At last, Adinah was satisfied and the two headed back home. The hot sun glared down on the streets. Hadassah looked forward to dipping the water bucket into the well for a long drink of cold water. They were on their street, almost home, when a group of women and girls came into view.

"Adinah!" one called and waved.

"Oh, I have been spotted." Adinah almost groaned. "Come Hadassah, time to meet the neighborhood." Suddenly shy, Hadassah moved behind Adinah, holding her hand. She peeked up at the women all chatting away, staring at her. They exclaimed over and over, some even reaching for her chin to try to get a better look at her eyes. For the first time in her life, Hadassah felt very uncomfortable in her uniqueness.

"Goodness Deborah!" explained Adinah, placing her hands protectively on Hadassah's shoulders. "She is a child, not a horse."

Deborah withdrew but still stared shamelessly.

"At least finding a good husband will not be hard." Someone chimed in. "Your charity will be well-paid."

At this, Adinah bristled and her face flushed with anger. Her brown eyes snapped.

"Hadassah," she said turning. Hadassah was right beside her. "Let's go, child. We have plenty to be doing." With this Adinah marched away, her back straight and her head high. Hadassah walked beside her in silence. Hadassah remembered the lesson she had learned in the garden that very morning. She was beautiful she was beginning to understand that. But could she not be useful too?

"Those women know not the meaning of charity," Adinah snorted. "Don't you mind them, Hadassah. The God of Abraham is good, and He knows what He is doing."

With this, they arrived at the gate. The latch was too high for Hadassah to reach. Adinah smiled as she noted this.

"You have some growing to do before you can escape my care." She smiled. Hadassah nodded. As soon as they were in the bright yellow door, Hadassah hurried to get Adinah a glass of water.

"Ahhh my girl! How thoughtful of you." She exclaimed as she turned from laying out the cloth on the table. She took a long drink of the refreshing fluid.

Ruth hurried over to exclaim over the beautiful colors. After they finally agreed on a pattern and Hadassah's measurements, Adinah smiled at the little girl eagerly hopping from one foot to the other looking longingly out at the garden.

"Go and play Little One," she encouraged. "You have been patient long enough with us."

Hadassah flashed a grin, and she ran out through the archway and into the garden. She danced around twirling up and down the pathway. She ran with the dragon flies and flapped with the butterflies. Adinah and Ruth sat in the shade of the living room and watched her happy figure as they bent over their work. It was not going to take the determined women long to make a wardrobe fit for their new little charge.

It was late afternoon, and the sun was throwing its long fingers of hot light as far into the archway of the living room as possible. Hadassah's little feet pounded across the ornate tile floor. Adinah laughed and gestured toward the door.

"Go wait by the gate. He should be here soon."

Hadassah hurried down the path to the gate. Her little black head could see down the street if she pressed her face up against the bars. She waited and waited, scanning the street. At last, his form came into view. He walked up the street not looking up till he was quite close to the gate. His face looked thoughtful.

"Hadassah!" His face lit up with delight to see the little face, pressing through the bars of the gate, smiling eagerly up at him. Too little to open the gate, she bounced eagerly from one foot to the other waiting for him to release the latch.

"You remembered to come and greet me," Mordecai joyfully called opening his arms to embrace his little charge. Hadassah jumped into Mordecai's open arms. She laid her small head against his chest, smiling into his robe, comforted by the deep thumping of his heart. The man and child embraced for a long moment. Then, hand in hand they walked up the pathway to the yellow door, standing open, with Adinah smiling in the doorway.

While Ruth and Adinah prepared the last of the evening meal, Mordecai and Hadassah walked slowly through the garden. Hadassah pointed out her favorite flowers.

"What is its name, Cousin?" she asked. "It is beautiful but is it useful too?"

This question touched Mordecai. He stopped walking and looked down at the eager face looking up into his.

"What an interesting question you ask," he said solemnly. He sat down on the bench. Hadassah pressed up against his legs to hear his answer.

"The flower itself is called The Star of David and it produces a fruit called okra. It is very tasty and delicious. My father planted the seeds from his father who brought them with him when the Babylonians took him captive from our land."

"So, to answer your question it is both beautiful and useful."

Hadassah nodded happily.

"I want to learn to be useful too, not just beautiful," she said solemnly. "I need to be useful so the God of Israel can use me as His servant."

"What a beautiful heart you have, Child," Mordecai said. He laid his hand on her head. "The most useful thing you can learn is obedience. Be obedient to God and He will use you mightily. And," he paused and looked up into the sky. "He is using me to teach you. May He give me wisdom to guide you rightly."

Adinah called and the man and child headed into the house in the growing dusk. Ruth helped Hadassah light the candles. The family gathered around the flickering candlelight.

Mordecai spoke in solemn reverence, recounting a story about the history of the Israelite people. Hadassah listened intently. Mordechai was an elder among the Jews and had a deep understanding of the history of the Israelites. His soft rich voice resonated with passion as he told his eager young pupil story after story of her rich heritage.

Her head bobbed and her eyes closed no matter how hard she tried to keep them open. The stories were so interesting, and she was so full and happy and safe. She wanted the moment to last longer but Mordecai again scooped her up in his arms and carefully carried her up to her bed, Adinah right behind him. Adinah kissed her cheek and gently brushed back her hair. Within moments of them leaving, she was fast asleep.

But suddenly she was all alone again in that tent. Her mother's lips moved slowly, and the color drained from her face. The overwhelming grief washed over Hadassah, and she threw back her head and screamed. She heard shouting and men were running, running down the street after her. She had to choose. She could not carry her mother; she was too heavy. She had to let go but her mother's hand suddenly grabbed her arm holding her down. Hadassah screamed again, trying to get loose, the men coming closer and closer, their hands grabbing at her.

"What exquisite eyes!" they repeated, their teeth yellow, their eyes glowing reddish.

One of the hands grabbed her, shaking her, shaking her hard.

"Hadassah!" Adinah's voice cut through her dream. The glaring faces, red eyes and yellow teeth disappeared, and Adinah bent over her shaking her awake.

Hadassah sobbed with relief and flung her arms around the older woman. Adinah scooped up the child into her lap and rocked her back and forth. Her hand soothed her hair as she rocked. Gradually the nightmare faded.

"I will exalt you, Lord," Adinah began to sing softly in Hebrew. *"For you lifted me out of the depths and did not let my enemies gloat over me. Lord my God, I called to you for help, and you healed me. You, Lord, brought me up from the realm of the dead; you spared me from going down to the pit.*

Sing the praises of the Lord, you his faithful people; praise his holy name. For his anger lasts only a moment, but his favor lasts a lifetime; weeping may stay for the night but rejoicing comes in the morning."

Hadassah listened to the song, her sobs quieting as her fear settled. She never wanted to let go. She wanted that voice to go on and on. The fear from the nightmare slowly faded. The psalm of David washed over her. The loving arms around her made her feel safe once more. She blinked then blinked again. Her black head rested against the soft chest of Adinah. And then she fell asleep, exhausted. This time, the gentle voice of her cousin's wife sang the dreams away, and it was only restful darkness that engulfed her.

Chapter 3
Hebrew Lessons Begin

The sun streamed in the window and the gentle breeze played with a black curl when Hadassah woke the next morning. She jumped out of bed, already hearing the low hum of voices downstairs. She wanted to say goodbye to Mordecai again. She quickly smoothed the coverlet and reached for her robe on the table. Again, the ribbon sash seemed unable to stay tied, so she ran down the stairs with it trailing behind her.

Mordecai was at the door. He turned and his beard parted in a wide smile as her little feet pounded across the tile floor. He swung her up in his arms right over his head. Hadassah squealed and giggled with delight, her ribbon fluttering around her. He dropped a gentle kiss tickling her with his beard as he did so. Then he was gone, out the yellow door and down the path to the gate. He turned and waved after carefully closing the metal gate.

Hadassah sighed and leaned up against Adinah's legs as they watched him disappear. Adinah gently stroked her hair. Adinah turned to speak to Hadassah, but the little girl was already gone.

Determined, Hadassah hurried down the hallway to the shower room. There, she picked up the comb and turning to the polished silver mirror hanging on the wall, she tried to tame the curls as Adinah did so effortlessly. They just kept bouncing and tangling and the comb snagged and pulled. At last, Hadassah was satisfied it was presentable although it did not look as good as yesterdays.

She pulled back the hair and tried to tie the ribbon, but she could not. Then she decided she should at least get her sash tied. Slowly she tied it as best she could, remembering how Adinah had showed her yesterday morning. She had just succeeded when Adinah stepped in.

"There you are, Little One!" she exclaimed.

"I can't get my hair to tie," Hadassah explained and handed her the comb and hair ribbon. "I need to hurry so I can help Ruth. I need to make sure the water bucket is full. Cousin told me about the flowers, The Star of Bethlehem. It is useful and beautiful. I like that."

Adinah smiled as she quickly combed out Hadassah's curls. In no time the ribbon was secure, and Hadassah bounded down the hallway and across the living room to the kitchen. Ruth was stirring a large bubbling pot.

Hadassah quickly looked in the bucket. It was still almost full of water. Then she hurried over to the shelf holding the dishes. She grabbed a bowl and cup and set Adinah's place. Then she hurried to set her own.

"Good morning, Hadassah," sang out Ruth. "Bring over your bowl and I will fill it for you." Hadassah hurried to obey.

"Bring over your mug but I will pour it for you. I don't want you to burn your hands." Hadassah watched as Ruth filled the mug with the rich steaming spiced tea. She sprinkled some cane sugar over it and dusted on a pinch of spices. The sweet odor filled the room and Hadassah took a deep breath.

"What is that spice you use, Ruth?" asked Hadassah eagerly.

"That is called nutmeg." explained Ruth, enjoying the moment to teach.

Adinah watched from the table, a smile playing about her lips. Hadassah was so much more open today. There seemed no memory of the nightmare that had woken the entire household with her agonizing screams.

With her questioning, Mordecai had described how he found the child as they lay side by side. Tears slid from Adinah's cheeks onto the pillow as he described how gently the child had traced her parent's faces one last time before leaving. He told of the men, yelling and running after them.

Adinah sobbed openly. Her heart breaking for the desperation the child must have felt. Mordecai wrapped her in his embrace, and she slowly cried herself to sleep listening to the beating of his heart. It was a comforting sound.

"I think nutmeg is the smell of happiness," beamed Hadassah. She looked up at Adinah and smiled as she carefully walked toward the table carrying her steaming mug of spiced tea.

"I think you are right, Hadassah," said Adinah leaning forward to take the cup from the child and place it on the table. Hadassah hopped up into the chair. She was just going to lift her spoon to begin eating when Adinah stopped her.

"Bow your head and say thank you to God for the food He has given you," she instructed. "This will remind you to be grateful no matter the meal."

Hadassah nodded and folded her hands. Her little head bowed, and she solemnly thanked the Lord for her food.

"Was that right, Cousin?" she asked intently looking up in earnest.

"It was very lovely," assured Adinah.

"What song did you sing to me last night? Can you teach me that language?"

"That was the thirtieth psalm of David," said Adinah. "And yes, it is time you learned to speak Hebrew as well as Persian."

From that moment on, Ruth and Adinah told Hadassah the Hebrew name for everything she pointed at or asked about. Hadassah practiced relentlessly. She ran after the dragonflies, calling their name. She flapped with the butterflies, singing their name. She practiced the psalm till she had memorized a good portion of it. Both Ruth and Adinah quickly noted how well she learned.

The day passed quickly for all three. They enjoyed each other's company more and more. The three sang the psalm together as Adinah and Ruth sewed.

"Today is Thursday," explained Adinah. She was discovering how hungry Hadassah's mind was. "We must finish a dress for you, so you are ready for the Shabbat."

"What happens on the Shabbat?" asked Hadassah breathlessly. She was sitting on the floor, holding her knees, rocking back and forth.

"On Shabbat, we go to the Synagogue and hear Mordecai teach. He reads Scriptures from the scrolls brought from Jerusalem. We rest on the Shabbat as the law commands given to Moses in the desert as the Israelites left Egypt from the Promised Land."

Hadassah nodded solemnly. She was so eager and curious about every aspect of her new life. Her father had thought her too young, and too feminine to learn. He had not taken the time to teach her much about the traditions of her people, leaving that to her mother. But then sickness had taken hold and Hadassah did all she could to nurse them. There had been little time to ask questions. All the energy of the little family was spent on surviving and sticking together.

Now with a full stomach and boundless energy, Hadassah's mind began to explode with curiosity. She helped as much as she could all day so Adinah and Ruth could concentrate on their sewing. Ruth showed Hadassah how to begin to make the spiced tea much to Hadassah's delight. Hadassah learned so much just by watching. The women gave her a small piece of cloth and she began to learn how to stitch. This did end quite quickly in a pricked finger, a drop of blood, and permission to go and play in the garden.

Again, as the shadows lengthened into the living room and the sun glowed orange as it neared the horizon, Hadassah's little feet pounded across the tiles. She pulled open the yellow door and dashed down the pathway to wait by the gate.

Mordecai looked up the street as he turned at the square. Sure enough a little black head poked from between the rails watching for him. He waved and smiled. A little arm popped out and waved back and the little head bounced excitedly. Mordecai's steps hurried and he smiled as he fingered the little gift in his pocket. He chuckled out loud to himself as he thought of how much Hadassah would delight in the shiny little box. She could fill it with her treasures.

He lifted the latch and the gate swung open. Hadassah stood perfectly still looking at him with a big smile on her face, her arms folded behind her. He stopped waiting.

"בן דוד, ברוך הבא הביתה (Cousin, welcome home)," she said happily in Hebrew. She smiled triumphantly waiting for his reply.

"הבת שלי! (My Daughter!)" Mordecai sang out. He knelt and opened his arms to her. She ran to him then for a long embrace.

"Did you just learn that today, Little One?" he asked. Hadassah nodded.

"I have been practicing all afternoon." She explained. Mordecai stroked his beard thoughtfully.

"You learn very quickly, my Hadassah. I need to begin to teach you, I see." He smiled then and rose. The man and child walked hand in hand down the path toward the yellow door standing open with Adinah smiling in the doorway.

Hadassah was bursting to share with Mordechai all she had learned. She pointed to everything in the garden she knew the name of. Mordecai listened closely. Occasionally, he helped her with her annunciation but once she had exhausted her knowledge, he praised his little pupil.

He sat on the stone bench in the cooling twilight and Hadassah leaned up against his leg, listening intently as he shared about the Shabbat and why it was important to the Jews. He taught her about the Torah, given to Moses by God on the Mount Sinai. He told of the great sin of the Israelites when Arron made the people the golden calf.

"Obedience, obedience is what pleases God the most, my daughter," Mordecai explained. "We came here as captives in this foreign land far from our homeland because of the disobedience of our people. Even here, among our captors, we must obey the Torah. On Friday afternoon, which is tomorrow, I will leave the palace early. I will return home and wash. At sunset, your first Shabbat with us will begin. It will be a special day."

Hadassah nodded. She was eager to learn of all that happened on the Sabbath. She was delighted to hear Mordecai would be home early. This pleased her greatly.

Mordecai reached into his pocket and pulled out the little box. He handed it to Hadassah almost shyly, hoping she would like it.

Her eyes got big, and she lifted them to look up at him.

"For me?" she breathed.

"For my princess," smiled Mordecai delighted with her reaction. Hadassah held up her arms and embraced him. He lifted her to sit on his leg.

At last, Hadassah reached out and dared to take the little box in her hands. It was small and light. It was shiny, covered in little pieces of colored glass. She opened it, and then closed it, smiling.

"My very own treasure box," she said happily. Then she suddenly grew serious.

"How do I say it in Hebrew?" she asked. Mordecai chuckled and spoke the word slowly. She repeated it after him, turning the box in her hands, watching the light of the fading sunset shimmer off the cut pieces.

Adinah called and the two headed into the house for supper. Hadassah ate with the little box sitting next to her plate, watching the light of the candles dance off the colorful pieces. Ruth and Adinah exclaimed over the beauty of the little treasure.

That night Adinah sang to Hadassah the psalm of David as her eyelids fluttered closed in blissful sleep.

"...When I felt secure, I said, "I will never be shaken. "Lord, when you favored me, you made my royal mountain stand firm; but when you hid your face, I was dismayed to you, Lord, I called; to the Lord I cried for mercy:

"What is gained if I am silenced, if I go down to the pit? Will the dust praise you? Will it proclaim your faithfulness? Hear, Lord, and be merciful to me; Lord, be my help.

You turned my wailing into dancing; you removed my sackcloth and clothed me with joy, that my heart may sing your praises and not be silent. Lord my God, I will praise you forever."

Friday passed in a hurry. Ruth showed Hadassah how she prepared for the Shabbat by making double on Friday so it would all be ready with minimum work for tomorrow. Hadassah helped as best she could. She ran to the well and drew water. She checked multiple times to be sure the pail was as full as possible. She ground the grain by turning the milling stone with both hands till Ruth assured her it was fine enough for even the king of Persia to eat. She danced in the garden and chased the butterflies, practicing her Hebrew words. She carefully practiced the annunciation Mordecai had taught her the night before.

She swept the kitchen and living room then thought she better sweep the pathways too. Adinah found her by the front gate, carefully sweeping the paving stones, so it would be ready for the Shabbat. Adinah had to stop and laugh at the eagerness with which Hadassah embraced her every task. She hurried her upstairs to her bedroom to try on the completed robe.

"How refreshing it is to see all our traditions, what we do on a weekly basis, through your eyes all afresh," she said to Hadassah. Hadassah smiled but it was lost in the cloth of her new dress as Adinah pulled it on over her head.

"There! It fits perfectly!" Adinah smiled happily at her handy work. The blues and turquoise of the patterned cloth highlighted the unique coloration of Hadassah's large eyes. Her childish cheeks glowed with happiness and the love she was experiencing. Gone was the gaunt look of mourning.

Adinah caught her breath as Hadassah spun happily, flashing a big smile, her eyes dancing with laughter. This little girl was so beautiful and so sweet. Overwhelming emotions caught in her throat, and she suddenly stifled a sob.

She opened her arms and Hadassah walked into her embrace. Adinah clung to the little girl for a long moment.

"I am so grateful God gave me you," she whispered against her hair. "You needed a mother, and the Lord knows just how I needed you. The joy you bring to my heart in just these three days you have been here. You bless me more than seven sons!"

A huge smile covered Hadassah's face and her heart filled with joy and love, even as tears stung her eyes. She was beautiful but she was useful, very useful in bringing great joy to the people she now loved the most on earth. God had heard her prayers and He was teaching her just how to be His servant. Her arms tightened around her cousin; her little heart unable to find the words to express all the emotions in her heart.

Suddenly a voice sounded from the gate.

"Where is my little girl?" Mordecai was home and the Shabbat was soon to start.

With a delighted squeal, Hadassah ran down the stairs. Her little bare feet pattered out the familiar music on the tile floor of the living room as she darted for the yellow door. Ruth opened it hearing her coming, with a laugh. Down the path she ran and right into the arms of her Cousin Mordecai. Adinah hurried after her, wiping the tears and smiling at the joyful sound.

"There's my princess!" he exclaimed as he lifted her effortlessly off the ground and threw her up into his embrace. Hadassah squealed with joy.

"Don't ever forget this moment, Ruth," said Adinah as the two women watched from the doorway. Ruth nodded, tears shimmering in her eyes. The two women squeezed each other's hands. One had a husband but no children, the other had no husband or children, but together, together they had Hadassah.

Chapter 4
Hadassah's First Shabbat

That evening, minutes before the sunset, Adinah lit the two tall, white candles set in the two golden candle holders. Hadassah watched with wide eyes as Adinah leaned in over the candles and scooped the air around them toward her then covered her face with her hands. When she removed her hands, her eyes shone brightly with unshed tears as they rested for a very long moment on Hadassah's face. Ruth sighed gently to herself remembering her brief married life when she too would light the Shabbat candles.

Mordecai came to Hadassah and laid his hand on her forehead. For the first time in her life, Hadassah heard the Aaronic blessing spoken over her. Her eyes closed instinctively, and she focused on the sound of the Hebrew words as Mordecai spoke them in his rich deep voice. The words themselves felt powerful. A shiver ran up and down her spine and her stomach tightened. Momentarily her fingertips tingled with the energy the sounds created around them.

When she opened her eyes once again, she looked up into her cousin's kind, solemn face. She did not understand the words, but she knew he would help her to understand.

"This is how Arron was taught to bless the children of Israel as they wandered in the desert, homeless and tired. The words hold great promise to all who hear and receive them in faith."

"You, my darling Hadassah, will learn to treasure this blessing for the rest of your life. May it be with you always, adorning your forehead forever."

He cleared his throat gently and continued.

"I will say the words in Persian so you will understand. The words I say are this. *"The Lord bless you and keep you; the Lord make His face shine on you and be gracious to you; the Lord turn His face toward you and give you peace."*

The beautiful words washed over Hadassah like healing oil. Her little heart burned in her. How she missed her parents, how she missed their love, but oh! How she loved her cousin Mordecai and his wife, Adinah and Ruth and the garden and her new home. How she loved learning about the great God of Abraham, Isaac, and Jacob. The same God who stooped down to hear her desperate cry and sent her Mordecai to save her.

As she gazed into the bright flickering blaze of the candles, she whispered that blessing repeatedly. God had blessed her. He had caused His face to shine on her. He had taken her from the very brink of utter desolation and filled her life with peace, joy, hope, and goodness.

Her gaze returned to Mordecai as he lifted a silver goblet filled with wine and blessed it. The Hebrew words rang off his tongue. Hadassah listened intently, the words running through her mind like music. She loved how the words raised and lowered, the force ebbing and flowing. She waited knowing Mordecai would repeat the words in Persian so she could understand and learn.

Then Mordecai turned to the bread Ruth had made. It looked like a bubbling braid. It was the most beautiful bread Hadassah had ever seen. She had not been watching Ruth make it as she was being scrubbed and dressed by Adinah. She hoped to watch Ruth make it next Shabbat to see how she formed the beautiful, braided look. Mordecai carefully folded back the ornately decorated white linen cloth. He spoke a blessing over the bread and then expertly broke the bread and gave a piece to each of the members gathered around the table.

Hadassah took the piece handed to her with reverence. She looked at the smooth interior of the bread, smiling as she remembered Ruth teasing her at how finely she had ground the flour.

"Fit even for the King of Persia," she had said with a laugh. Hadassah took a bite. The bread tasted delicious as did anything Ruth made. With a long sigh of utter contentment, she finished her piece. How grateful she was that she was a Jew, sitting here around the table with her new family learning of what pleased God.

She thought again of her desperate prayer, only days ago. Her eyes lifted and she met Mordecai's. His brown eyes softened as he looked at her, seeming to know what she was thinking. He smiled at her reassuringly.

Hadassah snuggled into her bed later that night, thoughts of candles and bread dancing through her mind. Her little heart purposed to love and obey the God of Abraham, Isaac, and Jacob with all its might. Her mind cast about to try to remember if her father had taught her anything about the Shabbat. She remembered an image of her mother, her eyes dancing with happiness, leaning over to light a candle, a white silken headdress covering her dark curls. It was one of the most beautiful images Hadassah had ever seen.

She smiled even as sleep overtook her and the image in her mind shimmered. Adinah was there suddenly too. All too soon it was a muddle in her mind and darkness swirled through her thoughts as she drifted to sleep.

She woke with a bolt of excitement. She threw back the coverlet and jumped out of bed. Her new robe was laid out on the little table. She tried to slip it on as Adinah had, right over her head but somewhere she got stuck. Where was the head again? Or was that an arm hole? This was much smaller than the repurposed robe she had been wearing.

In her struggling she bumped up against the wall, making a thumping sound. Ruth rescued her with a laugh. With her gentle fingers, she quickly gave it a tug and Hadassah's head popped through with a mass of unruly curls. Hadassah's arms found the sleeves and suddenly all the holes lined up perfectly. Ruth smiled as she tussled Hadassah's hair.

"Let's slip down to the shower room and get this under control," she said gently. Hadassah nodded, grateful for the help. She turned and headed for the stairs at a fast trot.

"Today we do everything with purpose," Ruth instructed gently. Hadassah stopped. She had unknowingly done something wrong on this Shabbat. She looked back at Ruth; her large eyes troubled.

"It does take practice, Little One," encouraged Ruth. "But it reminds us to be depended on God for everything. Think of every movement your body makes when it walks. Think of every muscle and bone working together, like all the ingredients in bread to make it rise and taste so good. This will help you slow down and master the Shabbat walk."

Hadassah watched Ruth slowly and purposely walk past her and down the wooden staircase. She concentrated on lifting one leg than the other, slowly placing one foot on the ground and transferring her weight onto it while she lifted the other. She made it down the stairs and halfway across the living room before she heard Mordecai's voice calling out.

"Happy Shabbat, my Hadassah!" Her head popped up and a smile spread across her face and danced in her eyes. Her little feet picked it up and in no time, she was sailing across the room and into his arms. Ruth turned and looked at her employer with failed disapproval.

"Oh dear, my Hadassah!" Mordecai laughed as he gently turned Hadassah toward Ruth.

"I interrupted your Shabbat walk and Ruth is giving me the eye for it." He dropped a gentle kiss on the mass of dancing, shining black curls. "Love makes the Shabbat a beautiful day, don't forget that. It is not just obedience, but obedience in love."

He could not help but chuckle under his breath as Hadassah slowly walked across the tiles toward Ruth, her black mass of hair bobbing back and forth in her concentration.

"How dull life was without her," he murmured softly to Adinah as she walked up beside him. "God knew how much we needed her."

"My thoughts exactly, husband," said Adinah. She watched Hadassah walk around the corner after Ruth. "Why is she walking so funny?" Adinah asked a worried frown on her face.

"She is mastering her Shabbat walk," said Mordecai with a loud chuckle.

"That is one of the cutest things I have ever seen!" laughed Adinah. And so began Hadassah's first Shabbat.

After a breakfast of leftovers, the little family rose and prepared to go to the Synagogue.

In her excitement, Hadassah could not help it and her body hopped a few times in excitement. Mordecai carried a scroll under his arm carefully draped in a white silken embroidered cloth with a golden tassel on it. The family walked slowly and reverently to the large building the Jews of Susa used as a synagogue.

It was merely a large open room, the women kneeling on one side with the children, and the men on the other side. All sat in hungry silence as Mordecai, draped in a tallit, slowly unrolled the scroll, and read a portion of scriptures.

The Jewish community was no longer held in the Persian Empire by force. Cyrus the great, the conquering founder of the great Persian Empire had freed the Jews to return to Jerusalem, a welcomed relief from Babylonian captivity after seventy years. But, after those seventy years, many knew there was not much to return to. Why make the dangerous journey back to Jerusalem, a burned broken city when one could stay and live well, comfortably, and safely here in Susa and around the Persian Empire? Family, friends, and work were all in plenty. Life was good.

Hope drew them back together week after week, year after year. Hope that their obedience in comfort was good enough. Hope that one day they would indeed return, but not yet. Hope that their beloved homeland would be more established once they returned, safer, more productive.

Hadassah sat in awe listening to Mordecai's rich voice rise and fall as he read from the scroll. She struggled to understand as much of the Hebrew as she could. Her mind surprised her as she understood more and more. The musical lilt of the language again drew her mind, even as the garden path drew her dancing legs.

Once the final prayer had been said, the community rose and mingled, cheerful chatter filling the room as friends greeted one another and caught up on the past week. Hadassah hung close to Adinah, unsure of what to do.

A girl came up to her, very close in age.

"I'm Sima." The girl smiled, her brown eyes dancing. "Come play with us?" With that Sima grabbed Hadassah's hand and the two girls ran off to the group of children gathering outside under a big sprawling Elm tree.

In moments, the children were laughing and chatting away. Hadassah struggled to string the Hebrew words together as most of the children spoke effortlessly. None of them hesitated a moment when she spoke in Persian. She found that the more she tried to speak Hebrew the easier it became.

All too soon Hadassah heard Adinah calling her. Hadassah bounded toward her, excited to share about her new friends. Suddenly Hadassah slowed. Standing beside Hadassah was Deborah, her dark, critical eyes watching her every move.

She felt uncomfortable, but Sima was right beside her pulling her along. It took only a moment for Hadassah to realize with a shock that Deborah was Sima's mother. Her mind reviewed how upset Adinah had been with Deborah's comments.

Hadassah walked slowly beside Mordecai and Adinah as they made their way back toward their house. She thought of Sima's joyous, friendly nature, an opposite to her mother's hostile coldness.

"My Little One has either mastered her Shabbat walk or is deep in thought," Mordecai gently prodded.

Hadassah looked up at him a long moment.

"What is a charity case, Cousin?" Her eyes noted his surprise. "Is it a bad thing?"

"Where did you hear of this, Child?" he asked with a sigh. Adinah suddenly stopped.

"I know," she said. "I thought nothing more of it really. But the other day when Hadassah and I returned from the market we met with some of the women of the community." Adinah looked down at Hadassah with a look of concerned guilt.

"One of the women mentioned something about charity," Explained Hadassah, a frown wrinkling her forehead. "It upset Cousin Adinah."

"Now I have met Sima and she is my friend. She is kind to me. I don't know what to think of her mother. I want to like her too."

Mordecai stooped down to be level with Hadassah.

"Remember, Dear Child," he said gently but firmly. "You told me that the God of Abraham, Isaac, and Jacob had heard your prayer and sent me to find you?"

Hadassah nodded.

"I remember Cousin," she said solemnly.

Mordecai gently cupped her chin and lifted her face, looking into her eyes with deep intensity.

"Orphans are seen as unwanted in many parts of this evil world," Mordecai carried on gently. "An orphan is one whose parents have both departed this realm."

"So, I'm an orphan," said Hadassah slowly, understanding dawning.

"By the definition of the word, yes, you are." Here he smiled. "But you are never unwanted. Even as our God heard your cries, He also heard our prayers," he smiled up at Adinah.

"We don't have children of our own, Hadassah. We prayed and prayed, but God never answered our prayers. We had totally given up and then suddenly, I got the letter begging me to come and find a cousin I barely knew existed. I came and found you in the nick of time."

"So, Little One, you will be called many things in life, but know this always!" he laid his hand on her little chest, over her heart. "You are a daughter of Abraham, loved deeply by God, and by Adinah and I and Ruth. We need you so much, Hadassah. Don't let the joy in your heart be soured by the unkind words of others."

"Sima will be a dear friend to you. Don't let the indiscretions of her mother spoil that friendship. Often others are going through trials that you may not see or understand. Their bitterness may spring from these battles and have nothing to do with you at all. Now, let's get going. Ruth's Shabbat dinner awaits us!"

Her little heart put to rest, Hadassah walked along beside Mordecai, her hand safe in his. A butterfly fluttered by, and Hadassah gave a skip of joy.

"פרפר!" she called out the Hebrew name as it skimmed its way across the road, looking for a tempting hibiscus flower.

Her cousin laughed his deep, joyous laugh and Adinah joined them. From that moment on, Hadassah never doubted the love of Mordecai or Adinah or Ruth. Each loved her dearly as their own daughter.

Chapter 5

Happenings around the Empire

Hadassah came into the home of her cousin Mordecai and Adinah during the fourth month, just as spring began to creep up the Shuar river-valley, causing the rich land to bloom with hope. It was also the month kings began to prepare for war.

The warrior King Darius died suddenly in the month of Tishrei of a severe and sudden illness, much like Hadassah's parents had died. Many speculated the king contracted the terrible plague from training relentlessly with his soldiers. After a great funeral and a period of deep mourning, the empire prepared for a new king.

His son, although not his eldest son by birth, Xerxes, was crowned in the month of Kislev. King Darius had named him his successor, his crown prince. Queen Atossa was Xerxes mother and daughter of Cyrus, the founder of the Persian Empire. The queen was greatly loved and respected by her husband, King Darius. Xerxes was the first child the couple had together as king and queen of Persia. To most, this was the perfect successor to the throne. Those who disagreed where quickly and quietly dealt with or bribed with coveted titles or positions. Any discord quickly folded seamlessly into the inner workings of the great palace.

Mordecai described the coronation event in detail much to Hadassah's delight. Adinah and Ruth listened intently although they denied any interest in the subject. Hadassah's beautiful eyes took on a dreamy look; never leaving Mordecai's face as he described the long richly decorated carpet that paved the way up to the great marble staircase.

"This carpet leads right up to the great marble steps, jet black with veins of gold streaking through them, rising up, and up, and up, to the top. Here, the great golden chair throne of Persia sits. Crown Prince Xerxes slowly climbed those steps, his deep purple robe trailing behind him. He turned, dramatically flicking his cloak over the golden chair, and slowly sat down, a resolved look set on his face."

"The powerful Achaemen, brother to King Darius, uncle to the new King, lowered the heavy crown, his hands trembling slightly, mixed emotions playing over his face. One can only imagine what must have been going through his mind, brother to the former King, crowning his own nephew King."

"It was whispered in a corridor here, and behind a door there, that maybe, just maybe, Achaemen would take the throne for himself. Why not? He was rich, powerful, and controlled a large portion of the army."

"But he lowered the crown and set it on the great brow of the King, his nephew, the Crown Prince, just as his brother, King Darius had requested. The crowd erupted in cheers and shouts, wishing an eternal reign upon their new King. The newly crowned King of Persia stood up and waved to his supporters. He turned to his uncle and embraced the older man. The crowd went wild, cheering this display of unity and harmony between the two generations."

Mordecai waved his hands dramatically. Adinah smiled and shook her head.

"Way too much drama for a little girl that is preparing to go to bed!" she announced.

Hadassah groaned softly even as Mordecai caught himself and quickly lowered his arms.

"Come, come!" he said holding out his arms. "Every princess must sleep, and my dearest Hadassah is no exception. Come; kiss me good night my dearest child. There will be more stories tomorrow if God wills."

Hadassah rose obediently and kissed her cousin's cheek lovingly.

"Promise you will tell me more tomorrow, Cousin." She begged hopping from one foot to the other in her excitement. Mordecai looked deeply into her sparkling eyes.

"Promise, my child!" he said. "And if I forget, you will remind me." He lovingly stroked her cheek with his finger as he chuckled at her excitement.

Hadassah nodded and darted across the floor and up the wooden steps. Adinah shook her head as she followed the little girl.

"You fill her mind too much with images of a pagan court, my husband. What of her dreams? Now she will only see kings and crowns!"

Mordecai gently laughed off the concerns of his wife.

"Let her dream of kings and crowns. Every time that crown changes brows all the Jews hold their breath. Let us just pray this King is as gracious to us as his father, Darius, was." The playfulness of his voice changed to a sad, serious tone.

Adinah's smile fell away, and she sighed gently.

"Always politics," she murmured at the base of the wooden stairs. "Always changes."

Hadassah dreamt that night she sat beside her cousin. She was holding a pen. She could smell the ink. But she could not take her eyes off the king as he sat on that throne.

Hadassah had been in her cousin's care for only a few months when Mordecai began to teach her how to read and write the Persian and Hebrew alphabet. Suddenly the music she felt inside materialized into figures she could copy into the sand, onto clay tablets, and into the flour as she helped Ruth kneed the bread. Mordecai noted the gift Hadassah had with languages.

Other scribes from the palace came to the house to speak with Mordecai in the garden during the long, comfortable summer evenings. Many languages were spoken as the men gathered discussing the rumors of wars and Egyptian rebellions. Adinah and Ruth served flavorful drinks and sweet treats then retreated to the comforts of the living room and each other's company surrounded by endless sewing projects.

Hadassah sat cross-legged on the cool white stones of the courtyard beside her cousin enjoying every moment. The men all noted Hadassah's curious mind. The scribes delighted in teaching her and praised her accomplishments. A letter or two in Arabic, Greek, Turkish or Egyptian were scrawled in the sand of the garden.

The next morning showed the entire area around the fountain covered in the letters as Hadassah relentlessly practiced everything she learned. Mordecai praised her dedication with enthusiasm. Winning her cousin's praises motivated Hadassah to work harder, learning and practicing.

Although surrounded by the culture and court life of the great palace, the family clung fiercely to their Hebrew heritage. Each Shabbat, they walked slowly and thoughtfully to the synagogue. Week after week, month after month, year after year, Hadassah listened intently to the Shabbat readings of Scriptures.

Mordecai diligently taught his young cousin the history of the Hebrew people from the calling of Abram out of the nations, to the disobedience which led the people into Babylonian captivity. He recounted the warning God gave the Babylonian King, Belshazzar through His prophet Daniel. Belshazzar foolishly did not heed the words of Daniel, as his uncle, Nebuchadnezzar, had learned to do.

In one night, the great city fell to King Cyrus without a battle to show for it. Working relentlessly, the soldiers of Cyrus had diverted the water from the great aqueducts, opening a tunnel under the huge stone walls. While the Babylonians partied in the great hall, silently, hundreds of thousands of soldiers entered the city with no challenge and spread out through the streets. The Babylonians realized their terrible mistake as Cyrus strode into the dining hall and sat in the king's chair, beginning the reign of the Medes and Persians. God used Cyrus to free the Jewish people from the Babylonian captivity. Cyrus declared them free to return to Jerusalem, back to Israel and the Promised Land, but few left.

"Every kingdom has the choice to seek the great God Jehovah or to pursue the gods of greed, idolatry, and power. Every kingdom is judged on how it handles the Jewish people in its care."

"We have been a great blessing to these empires, my Hadassah. God is faithful to His people even in times of exile and captivity." Mordecai said, the setting sun casting long shadows across the garden. "Always remember His faithfulness, my child."

Evening after evening found the two deep in discussion, Mordecai on the stone bench in the garden, Hadassah sitting cross-legged, as twilight fell around them. Here, with the fountain splashing in the background, the leaves whispering in the gentle evening breezes, Mordecai tirelessly trained Hadassah.

Adinah spoke to him quietly in the privacy of their bedroom.

"I don't think you should teach Hadassah so much of the world," she said. They rarely disagreed.

"I think she should be more interested in keeping a house and learning how to cook. We must prepare her for life, not fill her head with dreams and languages."

Mordecai sighed. He took his wife gently in his arms and cradled her against his chest for a long moment.

"But my dearest Adinah, can you not see her gift? Can you not see how quickly she learns? I feel compelled to teach her all I know. Who knows, maybe God gave her to us because we are the best to prepare her for her life calling?"

"You go ahead and teach her all you know. Prepare her for the life of a wife and mother. But let me also teach her what I know. Let me feed her mind and help her learn languages. It may be the greatest gift given her someday, the gift of reading and writing."

So, with gentleness the argument was resolved. Adinah taught Hadassah the ins and outs of running a household. Ruth taught her how to cook, but Mordecai opened her mind and filled her soul with a deep love of learning, reading, writing, and exploration. Within a couple of years under his careful tutorage, she was fluently speaking, reading, and writing in multiple languages. These years rolled by happily for the little family, living under the shadow of the great palace of Susa, undisturbed by the politics of the kingdom. And Hadassah bloomed under the loving care she received.

During the third year of his reign, the great King Xerxes hosted a massive feast. The king was finally established in his reign and wanted to display his great wealth and power to his subjects. He was also preparing to proclaim his successor and march his great army upon Greece. Princes and nobles from provinces near and far were invited to attend the festivities.

The massive stone palace rose imposingly over all the other city structures, one of the most magnificent palaces in the world. The king delighted to show off its ornate carvings, colorful artworks, and engineering genius. Everyone in the city always referenced it. Even if they had just seen the outer courts, it was held as the highest beauty standard. Those who had ventured deep inside described tapestries, marble hallways, courtyard gardens, and golden columns of immeasurable beauty.

Months and months of feasting began. Anyone who was anyone or knew anyone was dressed in their finest, rushing to the palace to join in the merriment. Everyone clamored and pushed for a glimpse of a great prince or maybe even a flash of the queen or the king himself.

Hadassah discovered she could climb out her bedroom window onto the roof of the porch leaning out into the garden. From there, she climbed up to the tallest point of the rooftop. The roof was perfectly flat over the main portion of the house. There was plenty of room for a curious girl to sit cross-legged looking down the sloping street to the square.

She delighted in sitting on the rooftop of the house to watch camels, horses, and carts loaded with all kinds of colorful things roll past the fountain at the bottom of the sloped street. Many of the travelers stopped to water their animals from the troughs around the fountain. She saw a convoy of Norsemen, with pale white skin and flashing blue eyes pass on horseback. She saw princes and princesses of incredible diversity with skin color and dress from around the entire known world.

The streets of Susa became a hub of international diversity and language. The constant parade entertained Hadassah enormously and she spent hours sitting and dreaming on her roof top. Noble men and women, foreign envois of ambassadors and exotic gifts poured through the great city gates filling the streets with all sorts of wonderful and exotic experiences.

Adinah wisely accompanied Hadassah on any trips about the city to the marketplace or the synagogue. Hadassah enjoyed her constant companionship and learned much from the older woman who recalled different palace parties and events. The entire city was abuzz with all news from the palace.

These days were endless for Mordecai, busy with all this political intrigue. The king, following in his father's footsteps, meticulously documented every day's proceedings. He was gone deep into the dark, starlit nights, only to come home tired. With the first hint of daylight, Mordecai hurried off again, with a quick kiss on Hadassah's forehead as she walked him to the gate. She watched till his figure walked down the sloping street. At the fountain he always turned and waved, smiling as the little arm pushed through the bars of the gate and waved him a goodbye. Hadassah watched till his familiar figure disappeared into the crowd, already pushing its way toward the palace gates.

Adinah, Ruth, and Hadassah missed him. Hadassah worked hard on her Hebrew and Persian letters, writing with the most care and beauty she could. She hoped her hard work would please her cousin, her teacher.

After six months of this extensive feasting and merrymaking, the king opened the outer palace, inviting all the citizens of Susa to come, eat and drink and discuss matters for ten days with their king. It was a holiday of course and no free man was expected to work during this time. The city of Susa was cloaked in happy excess of every type.

Although Hadassah longed to go and see the palace, Adinah flatly refused to take any child of Abraham near that place. Ruth attempted to slip her out for a walk through the gates, but Adinah was adamant a girl should never set foot near the palace.

On the evening of the tenth day, merry with wine and good food, the king ordered his most beautiful queen, Vashti, to walk before him with the group of princes, ambassadors, and advisors all looking on, the most powerful men in the world. The king wished to display the fantastic beauty she possessed, the completing jewel of his kingdom. All the citizens gathered cheered loudly and banged on any object that would make noise, demanding to see the beautiful queen.

Many a noble woman had been asked to do this for gatherings of men of power. Vashti had done this deed before to the great pleasure of all who had seen the sight. She would present herself in a great robe, glittering with gold and diamonds, wearing the most beautiful crown upon her flowing hair. Halfway across the room, her eyes ever fixed on her lord and husband, she would drop her robe in the most alluring of ways, and walk herself to her husband, wearing precious little but the crown.

Any educated woman of the Persian Empire was acutely aware of this tradition and the trouble it often caused. Wars were fought over a woman's body. Most Persian women would have given anything to be in Queen Vashti's position. They would have gladly shown off their physical endowments to all who would have been present. It was seen as a great complement, a great triumph of the feminine totally mastering her lord and husband with her charm, grace, and beauty. What better way to excite the imagination than to show off what only one man, the husband, could truly enjoy?

The news was whispered in the streets, around the marketplace and at every street corner. What caused the great uproar was the fact the queen refused to appear before the king at his request. Why? Why would one disgrace their husband so by refusing his request? Yes, there was a law forbidding a wife to be seen by strangers but who dared deny the king when HE asked? The city, the empire, waited in breathless anticipation.

King Xerxes rose from his couch, his face red with rage. Here, in his own palace, his own house, he was to be humiliated before his entire kingdom! His huge muscular body shook with rage as he stormed out of the banquet hall and disappeared into the inner palace. Nobles, princes, ambassadors, and the men of Susa sat in stunned silence for a long moment, trying to fully digest the evening's events.

The fingers of the scribes scratched out the evening's event in unforgiving, eternal written language. The great King Xerxes, king of the known world, had been refused by his own queen, his wife, a woman! The entire city fell oddly silent in shocked horror and anticipation. Yet again, global history hinged on the actions of a single woman.

Suddenly the wine was not so good, the company not so distracting, and one's bed at home seemed the best place to be. What would happen now? What would happen to their queen? The banquet hall quietly emptied, the citizens of Susa subdued, each eager to find one's own wife.

Rumors swirled as the king did not appear at his royal court the next day. Noble men and princes paced in hallways, muttering quietly with each other. One by one, only those closest to the king dared to enter his presence.

Mordecai embellished this part of the story great to Hadassah's delight.

"Whoosh! The golden goblet that was in the King's hand only moments earlier, whistled past Memucan's ear and crashed against a marble column. Poor Memucan ducked and grabbed at his head. If the cup had hit him, it probably would have killed him; it was thrown with such great force." Mordecai's left hand covered the left side of his temple.

Hadassah's eyes were huge as she listened intently to his dramatic recounting of the story.

"As a scribe, I was grateful I sat off in the corner, around a column, silent." Mordecai chuckled, stroking his beard, his brown eyes sparkling with humor as he remembered the incident.

Hadassah nodded, her black curls bouncing in her agreement. Adinah sighed and shook her head.

"Unbridled gentile," she muttered under her breath and her needle mercilessly stabbed the cloth.

A strange uneasiness replaced the marry atmosphere that had enveloped the city only hours before. The streets were strangely quiet, and the marketplace strained. Hadassah and Adinah felt the distinct shift in mood as they carried on their daily chores, grateful for each other's company.

Mordecai did not return at all from the palace the next evening. Hadassah longed to go and serve him, and her tender heart burned with his anticipated exhaustion. She ran back and forth to the gate to stare down the street till it was too dark to see anything.

"Can't I go find him, Adinah? He must be so hungry! What if they don't feed him?"

Adinah trembled visibly when she verbalized her fears.

"My dearest child!" she cried. "That palace is no place for a girl at this time!"

Ruth looked up sharply from her sewing. It was not often Adinah's voice carried such earnest passion. Grabbing Hadassah by the shoulders she looked earnestly into the little girl's wondering eyes.

"No daughter of Abraham should be around that place." She sighed and shook her head before proceeding with a terrifying prediction.

"I feel great change afoot, my dearest child." She kissed Hadassah's head, still bare from any headdress due to her age. Her hair glowed with health and love as Adinah gently stroked its silky softness.

"Come, my dear one, "she comforted. "Let us sing a psalm and go to bed. We should take our God-given rest, so we are ready to serve again tomorrow. Something must be happening at the palace. We will hear about it soon enough. Mark my words! Tomorrow afternoon, the royal messengers will ride from the palace, and we will know the happenings of that heathen place."

The three gathered around the lit lamps and raised their voices together.

"Contend, Lord, with those who contend with me; fight against those who fight against me. Take up shield and armor; arise and come to my aid. Brandish spear and javelin against those who pursue me."

"Say to me, 'I am your salvation.' May those who seek my life be disgraced and put to shame; may those who plot my ruin be turned back in dismay. May they be like chaff before the wind, with the angel of the Lord driving them away; may their path be dark and slippery, with the angel of the Lord pursuing them." Psalm thirty-five, verses one through six. That night Hadassah dreamed the angel of the Lord winged over the dark and silent streets of Susa. He rushed right up to the gates of the palace. He walked unchallenged right into the inner courtroom and surrounded Mordecai with His great wings. Peace settled over her and she woke rested and restored in the morning.

It was mid-afternoon when Hadassah began pacing the living room as Ruth and Adinah sewed. She frowned as she paced, unable to concentrate on her reading or writing. The royal riders had not yet been dispatched. There was absolute silence from the palace. Her young heart trembled within her.

"You can make me a cup of tea," Adinah offered, after watching her pace for a long minute. "I am sure Ruth needs one too."

Hadassah lifted her beautiful face, a smile quickly replacing her frown. Her slight form hurried to bless her elders as fast as her feet could carry her. Now as a nine-year-old girl, Hadassah was a great help to Adinah and Ruth. She was becoming more and more independent and capable. Adinah cast her eyes toward heaven. Her lips moved in silent praise to the great God of the Hebrews, thanking Him for giving her an obedient, honoring child.

Hadassah was back shortly, holding a steaming cup. Adinah investigated her earnest face and her heart melted. Hadassah flashed her pearly white teeth in a wide smile before hurrying off again to collect a delicacy that Adinah loved to eat with her tea.

Ruth received a cup with a treat as well. Then Hadassah poured herself a cup. She sat down, cross-legged on the floor as she sipped her tea, looking over the scrolls Mordecai had most recently brought home for her to read. They were all about the history of the Persian Empire and described the exploits of the King Darius in great and exciting details.

So, the afternoon passed in peace. Hadassah bent over her studies while Adinah and Ruth sewed in quiet contemplation. Soft words were spoken between the two women, careful not to disturb Hadassah, her dark head bent over her work in deep dedication. It was three o'clock by the official fenjaan or water clock when the clatter of hooves and a blast of trumpets announced the arrival of a messenger released by the palace with a royal decree.

Hadassah's head looked up with shining eyes. Adinah smiled and glanced at Ruth.

"I think I better accompany Hadassah to see what the messenger has to say." Ruth laughed as she laid down a half-finished garment.

"I will stay and finish supper. Mordecai will be hungry when he returns. Besides, Hadassah will tell me everything in detail. I won't miss a thing!" she laughed at this.

Adinah and Hadassah rushed to join the throngs of people spilling out of houses and homes all along the narrow streets, streaming down toward the fountain. A large crowd quickly gathered. Hadassah clung to Adinah's arm in excited anticipation.

Again, the trumpet sounded. The white Arabian horse, the royal crest on the brow band, tossed its delicate head and snorted, ready to run again. Its nostrils flared, flashing blood red as the beautiful animal sucked in great gulps of air. The rider expertly settled the excited horse.

The gathered crowd trembled with excited anticipation. Hadassah flashed an excited look at Adinah's face. Adinah seemed oddly strained, mixed emotions flashing over her face. Hadassah turned back, her breath coming in excited gasps.

At last, the messenger unrolled his scroll. Perfect silence fell over the crowd. He took a deep breath, his eyes darting over the written lines. His small frame sucked in a deep breath and his massive voice bellowed out over the crowd.

"By royal decree, Queen Vashti is no longer queen, never to come before the King again due to her disobedience. This has been done so all subjects under the Great King Xerxes may know and understand that women will honor their husbands, regardless of their rank; from the Queen of the great King himself down to the least of his subjects."

Adinah's sharp intake of breath startled Hadassah. The girl broke her concentration to look at her face. Adinah looked pale. Beads of perspiration appeared on her forehead. She trembled slightly, her strength suddenly failing her.

"Hadassah," she whispered weakly. "Get me home, my child."

The two turned and jostled their way through the excited throng. Hadassah struggled to support the older woman with her small frame. They finally pushed through the crowd and Adinah sank to the cobblestone street.

"Water!" she gasped, her lips the color of grey marble. Hadassah left her reluctantly and ran as fast as she could toward the fountain. She darted around the few people still busy about their own business, undisturbed by the palace news. She grabbed a cup and hurried back, her heart pounding. She saw a few figures bent over the form of Adinah. Hadassah pushed her way through and knelt beside her. Adinah lay very still.

"My mother," Hadassah said softly. "I have water for you."

Adinah's eyes flickered, and her face turned toward Hadassah.

"My child," her voice cracked. "Always obey...my Child!"

Her eyes burned intently into Hadassah's soul.

"Trust the Almighty," she gasped. "Always trust the Almighty."

Her eyes glazed and clouded as her life spirit whisked away in a breath. Hadassah was left kneeling beside her lifeless form, shock freezing her body. In the distance, the Messenger read out in his great voice…

"A new queen will be chosen, and the crown given to one more worthy…"

Somehow Hadassah found herself back in the house only hours ago a happy refuge. Now it was filling with women dressed in dark veils. She stayed beside the couch Adinah was laid upon. She could not bring herself to move from her side, the cup still clasped in her hand, the water long since spilt. Ruth hovered over her, lost in her own grief, yet terrified by Hadassah's icy calm.

Mordecai rushed into the house and found her, still frozen, her beautiful face clouded with confusion. Hadassah looked up into his red-rimmed eyes. Her eyes suddenly filled, and she finally left Adinah's side. She ran to Mordecai and buried her face in his robes. Sobs racked her body as his tears fell freely onto her shining black hair. Mordecai and Hadassah clung to each other for a long time, lost in grief.

Adinah's body was buried the next morning as is the customary practice of the Hebrews, even done in exile. A body had to be buried within twenty-four hours of death as the Torah specified. The mourners were gone, leaving Mordecai and Hadassah sitting side by side on the floor. The house seemed cold and quiet without Adinah's warm presence. Ruth retreated to her bedroom after supper, kissing Hadassah on the cheek unshed tears shining in her deep brown eyes.

Without any prompting, Hadassah rose and gathered the Holy Scriptures from the shelf and carried it to Mordecai. He smiled as he received the scroll from his daughter. She turned and collected the tallit from off the mantle. Lovingly she laid it over his head. Mordecai looked up at her. He captured her hand with one of his.

"You are more of a blessing to me than seven sons," he said softly, repeating the praise of Adinah. Hadassah sank down beside him, turning her face to him, smiling even as tears stood in her large eyes. Likeminded, the two turned to the Scriptures. The Psalms of David swirled through the mists of pain, tears, and suffering soothing the souls of the two hearts, united in love.

At last, Mordecai reverently rolled the scroll closed. Hadassah rose from where she was seated and respectfully laid the scroll back on its shelf, a place of honor in the home.

"Well, my dear daughter," Mordecai spoke once she was seated again on the floor, leaning up against his leg. "You and I must go on. At least we have each other, my dearest Hadassah. I could see no reason to live on if I did not have you at my side, my daughter." He laid his hand on the mass of black curls.

"The Lord giveth and the Lord taketh away, blessed be the name of the Lord."

Chapter 6
Hadassah Enters the Palace

Time gave Hadassah's heart relief from the sheering pain caused by Adinah's death. Never a day passed when Adinah's name was not mentioned, or her dear presence missed. Many a night found Hadassah, tears rolling down her cheeks, her arms wrapped around her legs; singing the psalms of David in Hebrew to comfort herself. Most bedtimes found Hadassah and Ruth, together in the same bedroom, comforting each other as they mourned.

Hadassah busied herself more and more with the workings of the house. By the time her twelfth birthday neared, she carried much of the domestic duties around the house. Life settled to a lonely norm as she lovingly cared for her cousin when he was home.

Mordecai buried himself in his work and his friends among the Jewish community and his work colleagues. Most evenings brought a group of well-educated men around the table, speaking of the politics of the nation and the history of the Hebrew peoples. The news of the king's campaign in Greece and the results of the latest battle were discussed in great and colorful details.

Hadassah threw herself into learning. The scribes loved helping her with her languages and often she carried on a separate conversation with individuals in Egyptian, Turkish, and Persian over the evening meal. Mordecai praised her letters, marveling in her artistic skills as she mastered the written language of Persian and Hebrew.

Ruth shook her head and served the rambunctious group evening after evening. It was here that she caught the eye of an unmarried Jewish man. The gatherings became an excuse for Ruth and Joshua to court in a very respectful manner. This brought great joy to both Mordecai and Hadassah.

Many evenings after the house lay still and Hadassah crept into Ruth's bed for comfort. She lay quizzing Ruth on the feelings of love. The two whispered and laughed together, finding ever increasing comfort in each other's company. Ruth whispered her regret of leaving Hadassah and Mordecai. But Hadassah insisted she could learn everything and care for her cousin all on her own.

"Maybe you can keep helping with the sewing," she admitted. Ruth giggled at this with Hadassah joining her. Both knew of Hadassah's dismal sewing skills. When Hadassah's thirteenth birthday neared, it was Ruth who explained the intricate and complex workings of the female body to Hadassah.

Late in the fall of the sixth year of the reign of King Xerxes, news of the fall of Athens to the Persian army broke over the city of Susa. Great was the rejoicing of the city and the citizens prepared to greet their conquering hero when he returned. But it was a silent fleet of ships that sailed up the river under cover of the falling night. A defeated and humbled king slipped off the ship in the soft folds of twilight and made his way silently into the great gates of the palace totally unannounced.

The discussion was very lively among the group gathered around Mordecai's table that night. Many of the men sorrowed over the great loss of Persian life, describing bodies piled on each other in the battle fields.

It was near midnight that cries, and wailings woke the inhabitants of Susa that slept at all. Women, daughters, wives, sisters, and mothers began mourning the losses, as household after household received the terrible news. The wailing sent chills down Hadassah's spine. Ruth's gentle voice began to sing, cutting through the dark night with a ray of hope, as she stroked Hadassah's black mane.

It took the king a couple of weeks to regain his composure. All too soon, Susa had a more ordinary hustle and bustle about it. Ruth prepared for a spring marriage to Joshua, his house being readied for his bride. Love filled the house of Mordecai and Hadassah as they watched the romance bloom. This love seemed to fill the city and soon it was whispered that the king longed for his queen. He was very fond of Queen Vashti and with the romance of war over, he longed for a queen again.

"Have you heard of the idea Memucan has placed in the King's head?" One scribe asked over the evening meal.

"Yes," said Mordecai. "Rumor has it Memucan has a candidate already picked out, his niece."

"Good political move, I suppose," said another, reaching for more bread. "This bread is great, Ruth!" he exclaimed with a smile.

Ruth shook her head.

"Compliments to Hadassah," she said with a smile. "She made the evening meal all by herself."

Mordecai nodded toward his cousin, his eyes sparkling with pride.

"So, what is happening?" asked Hadassah after returning a smile to Mordecai. A slight blush dusted her cheeks under his silent praise.

"There is to be a gathering of virgins at the palace for the King to choose a queen from among them." The scribe who began the conversation explained.

"It is a traditional method of keeping the harems full among these Persian kings," Joshua joined in from his place beside Ruth. "The Babylonian kings did it as well, very politically unifying in a great sprawling empire as this. There are people that move to Susa waiting for just this time to get their daughter into the court of women. It is then up to the girl herself to succeed in being presented to the King."

The conversation carried on and the group dispersed. Hadassah rose to ready for bed when Mordecai called her over to him.

"Come, my daughter," he motioned to her to sit in front of him.

"It is laid on my heart, my dearest child, to speak to you of something of great importance," he continued in a soft but firm voice.

"The King has decreed that all the beautiful young women of Susa are to be gathered to the palace to be presented to the King one by one. You, my daughter, are of exceptional beauty. Not just of physical beauty, but richly blessed with a loving and gracious spirit. You are a daughter of Abraham, crowned with the beauty of Sarah, blessed with the intelligence of Rebekah, and graced with the spirit of Rachel. Never forget from whence you came."

"But, my dear Hadassah, when you are called to the palace, as you surely will be in time, we must protect you. The court of the King is not a kindly place for Jewish women. You will know the extent of it all in due time. You must hide, my dearest Hadassah. You must never reveal your origin, your people, or your faith."

"No longer shall you be called Hadassah but let us call you Esther. For the Lord our God will guide you as a star in the night sky. You will shine brightly for Him all the days of your life. You will bless all you touch even as you have blessed my dearest wife, Adinah and me, more than seven sons." His eyes misted over as he mentioned the name of his dead wife, the sorrow still fresh in his heart. He blinked quickly and after a long pause, he carried on, the intensity of his words burning in the heart and mind of Hadassah.

"Hadassah!" he spoke her given Hebrew name. "Obey my voice all the days of your life. You have obeyed me as a father. May our God bless you for your obedience, Child. May He protect your going in and you're coming out."

He adjusted his prayer shawl lifting a corner and laid it over Hadassah's head. She bowed in humble reverence as Mordecai laid a hand on her head. He lifted his face to the Almighty and he prayed a prayer ripped from the very center of his heart, too intense, too raw for words. He then rose and collected a vase of oil that sat on the shelf near the Scriptures. He stood before Hadassah.

She knelt at his feet and reverently lifted her face. Gently he anointed her forehead with oil.

"You now wear a crown more priceless than any in the world," he spoke softly but boldly, with power and strength. "This crown is more valuable than any the King of Susa can bestow on his queen. You are anointed as a child of the Almighty, the Great God, the King of all Kings, and the Lord over all other gods, the One and Only true God in this world. You are His Princess, covered in His Greatness and Truth."

"Remember, who you are, my dearest Hadassah, even as you hide it from the evil of this world in which we live, in this land far from our own. We were brought to this nation as slaves due to the disobedience of our people. May your obedience atone for our people."

It was late that night, Hadassah finally laid her head on her pillow and slept, comforted in the blessing of her cousin. Next morning Hadassah dressed hastily. She hurried into the kitchen to make tea for her cousin before he left for her days' work.

When he appeared, Mordecai had one of Adinah's tichels in his hands.

"Come my sweet Hadassah," he said a slight smile on his face. "Now that you are the woman of this house you are honored with the distinction from child to woman. Wear this with honor, my daughter." With these words, he lovingly laid the blue silk head scarf over Hadassah's mass of shining black hair, the very scarf she had been wearing the day Hadassah came to their home. Hadassah turned her shining face to his, the scarf flashing the deep blue in her eyes.

"Thank you, my cousin!" she burst out, wrapping her arms around him. "I will wear it with pride." She hurried to fix his tea just as he loved. The scarf veiled her head glinting in its silken smoothness. Hadassah felt as if Adinah was right with her, smoothing her hair lovingly, embracing her in one of her long hugs.

The commandment came, delivered to every household in Susa. Every young virgin between the ages of ten to fourteen years of age must present herself in the courtyard of women for inspection. Only the most beautiful virgins would be considered. Every suitable girl, regardless of race or peoples, would have the opportunity to present herself. Every girl, regardless of skin color or language, would be given the chance to woe the heart of the king, capture his imagination, and be crowned the queen of the most powerful empire the world had yet known.

Mordecai's hand trembled as he read the official notice, sealed with the king's ring, an undeniable law of the land. Hadassah watched him carefully, emotions seething through her. Fear revolted against the unknown but, swirled in it was the breathless excitement of the possibility of being chosen.

After a very long moment Mordecai turned to Hadassah.

"Hadassah," he said with gentle authority. "Let us prepare you to meet Hegai, the eunuch in charge of the court of women, as decreed. For surely you will be chosen to be brought before the King. With your education, your skills at reading and writing, and your undeniable beauty, you will be afforded this great honor. Any man would be a fool not to choose you, my princess, even out of thousands!"

Hadassah hurried to prepare. She brushed and oiled her hair and carefully veiled herself with Adinah's blue silken tichel. She dressed herself in her best dress, smiling softly in remembrance of seeing it on Ruth's lap for so many evenings as she bent her head over her work.

Hadassah said farewell to Ruth in her bedroom. Ruth could not bear to watch her leave. She also knew Mordecai would need time alone to say his farewell to Hadassah.

"I will miss your wedding, Ruth," Hadassah squeezed her hand one last time.

"I am so glad Adinah did not live to see this day," sobbed Ruth. She covered her face in her hands as Hadassah left, turning at the doorway for one last long look.

"Sing for me every night, Ruth." Hadassah's words hung in the air as the older woman nodded.

She descended the stairs from her bedroom for the last time. Mordecai gasped when he saw her. Wordlessly he extended his hands to her. She approached him silently, obediently. He looked at her for a long moment then he turned and disappeared into his room. He reappeared shortly afterward, a velvet pouch in his hand.

"I was saving this for a wedding gift," he said. "Adinah got great pleasure in dreaming of the day these jewels would adorn our gracious Hadassah on her wedding day." With these words, he carefully drew out a necklace of myrtle flowers. Little blue sapphires glistened in the center of each flower.

Hadassah's mouth dropped open. Never had she seen anything so beautiful.

"They are from the homeland of Israel, made in days before the captivity. This necklace was part of Adinah's dowry. I took it to a jeweler and had them put in the sapphires to make it more modern. It suits you perfectly, Hadassah, my princess." Mordecai explained. "The blue brings out your eyes perfectly."

Hadassah wordlessly lifted her hair and veil and turned so her cousin could dress her as a bride preparing for her wedding day. He reached back in and drew out a pair of matching earrings. They were little myrtle blossoms budding out between two golden leaves, a matching sapphire dangling from her earlobe in the shape of a tear drop.

She turned back to face him; her eyes fixed on his face. Emotions flashed across his face in soundless thunder. Joy, pride, sadness, and admiration danced in his eyes.

"Oh, that Adinah had lived to see this moment," he softly murmured his eyes full. But his expression changed. "She would never have let you go to that palace. She always hated it so. It was almost too much for her that I was there every day."

"Oh Lord!" the words tore from a deep, silent pain in his heart. "Must our captors take our children from us as well?"

"I go in His Name," said Hadassah softly, laying her hands on each side of his face. "I go as a daughter of Zion. The myrtle blossom is a symbol of God's promises to His people. In His love and by His promises, I will be established, even into the great unknown that I am called to enter into."

The tears spilled out of Mordecai's eyes at the words of faith coming from his cousin. The pupil became teacher, her words, wise and gentle, full of emotion and faith. His tears rolled down Hadassah's hands even as her delicate fingers tried to brush them away.

"Let us go my child," said Mordecai at last. "Let us go, my dearest Hadassah. Never again will I call you by this name. From now on, you are my dearest Esther, a rising star of her people."

As she crossed the threshold, Esther turned and let her eyes roam over the life of Hadassah, an orphaned Jew, who found great comfort in the home of her cousin, sent from God to save her from her pitiful plight. Evenings sitting around reading the Holy Writings danced in her mind, times of prayer, the stories of her people. They were there branded in her memory and heart forever.

Esther would remember even if she must hide. Esther would always be a Jewish girl at heart. Esther would always remember Hadassah, hidden but present, veiled yet shining through in all she would do and say, in every moment, till the day she joined her ancestors.

Esther stepped out over the threshold of her past life into the great unknown. Just as Sarah stepped out with her husband Abraham, and Rebekah agreed to leave her father's home and travel with a servant to marry a man she did not know, and as Racheal waited in faith for seven years and one week to marry a man totally in love with her; so, Esther stepped over the threshold of her Jewish home willingly, headed for the great palace of Susa, prepared to present herself to the king of the known world.

For a second time, the man and the child exited a house that was a home, into the unknown, together, hand in hand. This trip across the marketplace was strangely silent. Each gathered their thoughts, struggling to process the emotions raging through them. This was the closest Esther had ever been to the palace. She passed through the great gates gaping open, swallowing the entire street in their huge expanse. Guards stood silent and stern on each side, great swords hanging from their sides. She was excited even as her heart hammered in her chest.

The street narrowed as they entered the outer extremities of the palace itself. Colorful murals decorated the stone walls. Statues of great winged cats with heads of men, wearing crowns glittering with gold rose imposingly over them. Palace guards were lined along the street only a few feet apart from each other, dressed in dark blue tunics, with an undercoat of white cotton against their skin. They stood with their legs spread wide, a drawn sword gleaming in the sun, the tip resting on the ground, the huge handle inscribed with family crests.

Gold glittered everywhere. The street was suddenly crowded with women in the most beautiful of clothes. The air filled with the sound of laughter and excited voices and golden bells on bangles and anklets.

Once through the narrow portion of the gates, Mordecai and Esther found themselves in the huge courtyard of the palace. Esther looked to the right at the huge black columns of polished stone, supporting the palace roof, made of cedar wood, flashing reddish in the sun. Esther could not see far into the dark interior of the buildings as people hurried in and out, ever busy with palace duties.

This was her first glimpse of the famous palace of Susa, and it satisfied all her imaginations with its huge expanse, grand presence, and towering stone structures. The roadway itself carried on toward the river, all kinds of trees and flowers peeping over the high stone wall on the side opposite the palace. The roadway finally sloped away out of site.

"Cousin, where does the road go?" The question bubbled out of her. She caught herself and switched to Persian.

Mordecai smiled and looked at her lovingly. Little wrinkles crinkled around his eyes and across his forehead. His brown hair was heavily greyed.

"Ever a curious mind," he chuckled. "That goes down to the river's edge, my dear one. The ships, if not too large, can sail right up the river and dock there. The palace was built with strategy and beauty in mind. As you can see," he pointed toward the palace. "It is built up high on the ridge overlooking the river. It was originally a fort and built with defense in mind. From the inner palace, home to the King himself, one can look out over the river and the city. It is a beautiful sight, I am told."

"A portion of the river is cut away and flows freely into marble aqueducts that flow right through the palace. This provides an abundance of fresh water for baths, gardens, and acts as a cooling system from the hot sun as it pounds down relentlessly. It is truly a great work of architecture."

The two lingered as Mordecai pointed out the layout of the palace and where he went every morning to work, neither wanting to say the inevitable goodbye. They clung to these final moments together; the hustle and bustle and noise of the area giving them a sense of privacy. But all too soon they arrived at the entrance to the court of women, accessible only through a long, long dark hallway under a roof of cedar wood, heavily guarded with soldiers. At last, the hallway opened into a small, sunny courtyard, walled on three sides with high grey stone walls.

The gateway leading to the court of women was made of wood and painted bright blue. It stood out of the high stone wall, a pop of color in the otherwise bland area. Very little was done to make these walls beautiful or attractive. It stood out from the otherwise decadent and rich decorations of the palace.

"Why is the entrance so bland, Cousin?" Esther asked, curious.

Mordecai looked way up at the tall, grey stone wall that would forever separate him from Esther. Little windows offered the only break as it towered up, a couple stories high, strong, thick, and imposing.

"It is guarding some of the most beautiful women in the entire kingdom." Mordecai said. "It is dull to discourage looters and sightseers. The windows are so high and small as not to offer any way into the building, no matter how determined one is to try."

Esther nodded and swallowed hard. She knew this was indeed farewell.

A large colorful crowd was gathered around as eunuchs dressed in rich red robes, tied with golden cords of silk hurried about to organize the excited throng of participants all jostling for their chance to get into that blue doorway. The women and girls were being separated into groups that were always trying to remix in a colorful dance. The eunuchs hurried about, back, and forth, calling out to keep the groups separate.

A few girls passed Esther and Mordecai as they stood watching at the entrance to the courtyard, their tearstained faces telling all. They had been rejected by the eunuchs, denied entrance through that blue door. Many of them had an obvious physical impediment. One sobbed loudly as she used her wooden crutches to move her twisted, body away.

A noblewoman emerged out of the hallway, dressed in shimmering silk, a crown of golden leaves fluttering about her brow. Maids carried bundles in bright colored sacks on their shoulders. Her father walked proudly beside her, a robe of rich blue and gold, trailing almost to the ground. His belt was heavily crusted in colorful gemstones, and he wore a purple sash indicating a position of power and royalty.

The poor girl was looking down. She did not see the noblewoman and the poor crippled girl walked right into her path. The noble woman let out a terrible scream and kicked at the girl, hitting her crutch, and causing her to fall hard onto the white rocks that covered the courtyard.

Esther gasped out in horror. None of the maids stopped to help the poor girl lying there bleeding, her crutch kicked out of her reach, her twisted body struggling to rise. The noblewoman laughed cruelly, and her father smiled and patted her hand comfortingly. The eunuchs hurried to greet them, as they headed for the bright blue door, the other girls parting to let them through, unchallenged. Everyone ignored the struggling crippled girl.

Esther let go of Mordecai's hand without a second thought and ran over to the girl's crutch. She picked it up and hurried to the girl's side. The girl looked up at her, startled, cowering as if expecting her to hit her with the crutch.

"Oh no!" Esther hurried to bend down. "I'm here to help you. I won't hurt you!" She cried out upset the girl would think her capable of such evil.

The girl stared at her a long moment, her dark eyes slowly beginning to soften, and a shy smile flirted about her mouth.

"Thank you, my lady!" she said her head bobbing in respect.

Esther laughed and shook her head.

"I'm no lady," she said, helping the girl to her feet. "I'm an ordinary Persian girl, just like you."

She supported the girl till she had the crutch straightened under her.

The girl turned and looked at her in wonder.

"You are truly a lady!" she said. "Thank you for your kindness. I will never forget you. I hope the King chooses you. You are a real queen." And with that, she hobbled away, her twisted pelvis wobbling as she expertly maneuvered the next group of girls coming along the hallway. Esther watched her go, a small sigh escaping her.

"You will indeed do this place much good," Mordecai said, moving up beside her. "I must let you do the rest alone, my Esther. I am dressed like a Jew, and you must not be connected to any people." His voice began to break, and he leaned over and dropped a kiss on her forehead, like a seal of his love for her.

He moved away quickly, Esther's hand dropping to her side as it fell from his. Once she passed through that gate, no man was allowed to follow except those in the king's service. She had never known a day without Mordecai's presence beside her or around her to guide and comfort her. Suddenly the huge stone structure of the palace seemed cold and hard. What would life hold for her in its long, dark corridors?

A eunuch moved up beside her and offered her his arm. She reached over to take the arm offered her, the familiar numbing pain enveloping her heart. The eunuch smiled at her when she finally tore her eyes away from Mordecai's retreating form. She turned, gracefully and peacefully to face her future.

"I am here to take you into the court of women. Hegai will want to meet you," he said, his thick speech accenting the 'you'. "That was very kind of you to help the crippled girl up. I saw that. Nothing is not seen here in the palace of Susa; remember that and you will do well."

Mordecai stood with a smile on his face even as tears stood in his eyes and splashed down his face into his beard. He raised his right hand in farewell, his lips moving silently. Esther knew he was reciting the Aaronic blessing.

Her heart stilled in her chest. The words swelled in Esther's heart, mind, and soul. She closed her eyes briefly, drinking deeply of the Hebrew words, remembering the rich resonance of Mordecai's voice. Her lips formed into a kiss as she moved away from him toward the door.

"Your name, your origin and your age?" The scribe did not even look up, his wooden tool poised to record the answer to the questions, demanded not asked. He sat at a table set up on the outside of the blue door. The eunuch paused waiting for Esther's reply before pushing the door open.

Esther took a deep steadying breath. She felt Mordecai's presence behind her, his words of warning and instruction lingering in her mind.

"My name is Esther," she said with calm certainty. "I am of Susa, and I am thirteen years old."

"Who are your people?" The voice repeated with no change in tone or demand.

Again, Esther took a deep breath and spoke it out loud.

"I am Esther of Susa," she said.

The scribe looked up from his page at the girl. The look of boredom erased from his face as a slight flush reddened his cheeks. A look of impatience suddenly swept across his face.

"Young lady," he said with marked pronunciation. "Do you not understand the question I ask of you?"

Not once did Esther hesitate. A lifetime of chosen obedience is not erased at first questioning. She knew who she was. She just chose to obey the words of her cousin, guardian, and teacher.

"I will be known as Esther of Susa," she said gently but firmly looking the scribe straight in the eye.

The scribe looked at her for a long moment, and then he shrugged, glancing at the eunuch. He bent over and carefully wrote the words, "*Esther of Susa, age thirteen*" on his clay tablet expertly cupped in his left hand. He then dipped his head to her in a nod of respect.

"Esther of Susa," he said rolling the words over his tongue as if tasting them. "Welcome to the palace. I see you already have your escort ready to take you to Hegai."

"Thank you," said Esther graciously, dipping her head in return. She turned and flashed a wide smile at Mordecai who stood on tip toes straining for one last glimpse of her. Their eyes met and held for one moment. She turned and Mordecai watched as the slender figure of his dearest child was ushered through the wooden door, the blue silk scarf identifying her out of hundreds of other women.

"God go with you," he whispered after her vanishing form. He stared after her for a long moment wondering how the time could go so fast. It seemed only a few short years ago he carried that beautiful child tucked in his cloak, held safely to his chest. Now here she was stepping out into the wide world of global politics, with a smile on her face and an Aaronic blessing hanging over her.

What could God want with her? What could a sweet, innocent, Jewish girl entering the dark world of pagan politics, gods, and wars do? What could God want with his dearest Hadassah? Stifling a sob, he turned and headed back toward the gate of the court of the king.

Chapter 7

Life in the Court of Women

Esther swept along the marble hallway, silently, her feet making no sound on the cold hard floor. She would have loved to stop and admire the gorgeous tapestries that hung over the small windows; the sunlight shifting through gave them a magical quality. Pottery stood silent and untouched in small indentations built into the great stone walls, brightly colored symbols and images dancing across them, representing gifts from around the empire. Esther recognized the designs as Egyptian, Asian, and Ethiopian, glimpses of different worlds and foreign lands.

Her guide was silent and unimpressed by the immense beauty and history they were passing at a hurried walk. Esther's blue silk scarf fluttered behind her, and her hair rustled on her shoulders as she hurried to keep up with the pace.

She tried to memorize the way but with each turn and twist it got harder and harder. After three flights of stairs up, one down, five hallways all leading in seemingly totally different directions, she lost count. They hurried down yet another flight of stairs. They were walking swiftly toward a doorway with light streaming from it.

Once through the doorway, a garden more immense and beautiful than anything Esther had ever seen in her life, opened before her. In her awed, unrestrained enjoyment of the beauty around her, Esther paused, frozen, her eyes expanding with delight to drink in the beautiful site. The eunuch hurried down the flight of stairs leading down into the garden area, not caring that Esther had stopped, dropping his arm.

"Esther of Susa," the eunuch announced to Hegai. Hegai's face was unreadable as he looked at the girl stopped mid-stride on the staircase, her face a washed in delight. Hegai did not even look at the eunuch as he continued.

"She is thirteen years of age."

"Who are her people?" Hegai asked his eyes never leaving Esther.

"She has none."

At this, Hegai looked sharply at the eunuch beside him.

"Everyone has people." He stated flatly. "Hum…. She is choosing not to say, although she looks as if she could be Babylonian." He cracked a slight smile.

"I like her." He stated simply.

"I figured you would," said the eunuch. "Also, she comes with a recommendation."

"From whom?" Hegai asked looking at the eunuch this time.

"From me," the eunuch said bravely.

"From you?" The eunuch now had Hegai's full attention.

"Yes, master Hegai," continued the eunuch. "I saw this young woman go out of her way to help a poor girl, kicked down by a nobleman's daughter as she struggled to leave the courtyard. Her body was marred and disfigured. She was in no way fit to come before the King. But she tried, poor dear."

Hegai turned and looked with fresh eyes at the girl on the staircase.

Esther sensed his presence after a long moment and looked down the stairs, her large, blue-green eyes meeting his dark ones. Hegai had seen many beautiful women in his day. He was the head custodian of the entire court of women after all. He had seen the world's most beautiful, talented, and gracious women but this girl, with the blue-green eyes, and the blue silk veil, fascinated him instantly.

"Esther lifted that poor girl off the ground and helped her back onto her feet," Continued the eunuch. He paused so long Hegai turned as if to go, thinking the story was over.

"But what she said when the girl greeted her as a lady stood out." The eunuch continued. "She referred to herself as just an ordinary Persian girl. She lifted that girl up to her level with her speech and conduct, not just physically."

Hegai cast a side glance at the eunuch.

Kindness was not often conveyed in the palace, especially among servants. These men had been captured, torn from their families, mutilated in the most de-masculine of ways often under horrific circumstances, and now lived to serve, to be seen but not understood, spoken at but never to. This girl's kindness had obviously shaken the eunuch.

"Thank you, for telling me this," Hegai said softly. The eunuch nodded and hurried off, his mission complete, the slightest of smiles hovered for a lingering moment around his mouth.

Hegai lifted a large hand toward the girl.

"Esther, welcome to the court of women. I am Hegai, the chief custodian for the entire court of women of the Great King Xerxes. Your life will forever change from this day on."

Esther smiled and quickly descended the rest of the staircase. She gracefully raised one of her slight, delicate hands and laid it trustingly in his. With a gentle nod of her head, she showed him respect.

"I am welcomed, Hegai." She said in perfect Persian, no accent or slur noted. "And I am here to serve you." She smiled gently up at his face and Hegai's last defenses crumbled. This was a woman!

He was struck with the deep sense that this girl would teach him more than he would teach her. Excitement gripped him as he gazed into the beautiful face of possibly the next queen of Persia. What a great honor he had to work with her!

"Esther," he asked curious. The two began to walk across the garden side by side. "Tell me, what all can you do?"

Esther halted and looked up at him. Hegai stopped too, surprised that this question had stopped her in her tracks.

"What do you mean?" asked Esther curiously.

Hegai smiled. Most cultured young women could not stop talking about what they could do and would have entertained him twice around the garden without really making him any the wiser. Here was a girl who spoke perfect Persian with a cultured, gracious air surprised by this simple question.

"Esther," he asked even more curious than before. "What all can you do?"

"Whatever task is given me I will do to the very best of my ability," answered Esther. She turned to him; her large eyes full of questioning intelligence. "It is the reason I am here, is it not?"

Hegai contemplated his reply.

"Do you sing, dance, or play a musical instrument?" Esther shook her head.

"None of those, Master Hegai," she replied. Again, she began walking. Hegai noted the grace with which she bore herself.

"What then, Esther of Susa, do you do?" The 'do' was accentuated this time. Esther noted it and smiled. She looked up at him hoping her reply would not upset him in any way.

"I read and I write," she said simply. "I ran the household since my aunt's urvan departed to the underworld."

Esther chose to speak of Adinah's death as a Persian would. Urvan was the name for a soul departed from the physical body that wandered three days on the upper earth. After this time of isolated grieving, the departed soul dove down to the dark depths of the underworld to whatever fate lay awaiting it.

Hegai's eyebrows shot up. She was much more interesting than even he had anticipated.

"I will need to get your skills properly assessed," he explained to her. "For now, Esther, relax and take in your new life. We will speak more on this matter tomorrow."

"Thank you, Master Hegai," Esther said simply, suddenly feeling very tired. It had been an emotionally charged morning and she was hungry. Tomorrow sounded like a wonderful time to begin anew. Hegai nodded his departure and moved on, more women arriving one by one.

Esther moved about the great garden in awe of its beauty. The other girls stood off in small groups and whispered quietly to each other. Everyone seemed a bit dazed and out of place. It was like one had suddenly stepped out of the real world into a dream.

Sunlight filtered through the billowing white curtains covering the open areas, giving the light a mystical quality. The air smelled rich and heavy with delightful scents of rose, lavender, incense, jasmine, and sandalwood. Birds fluttered about from tree to tree, oblivious to the people around them. A male peacocked suddenly shrieked, making Esther jump a little. He shook himself dramatically and fanned out his beautiful tail, turning a slow circle exaggerating the sunlight flickering off the iridescent blues, greens, and purples of his rich plumage.

The sun was high overhead when a great table was laid out, groaning under the weight of the shear abundance of food loaded upon it. Esther ate her fill, sitting cross-legged on a rug laid out under a tree. Use to a solitary life, she contented herself to watch the other women move about the garden while she ate. It gave her time to reflect on what had just happened. She, an orphaned child of a Jewish servant was suddenly in the court of women, waiting to be brought before the king to be considered for the position of his next queen.

She gave her head a slight shake and smiled. A sunbeam broke through the curtained roof and shone directly on to her, bathing her in a warm glow of golden light. She looked up and closed her eyes. *God does work in mysterious ways*, she thought enjoying the sun on her face.

That was all the time there was to muse. A eunuch began hitting a huge bong and the sound reverberated it's rich, deep tones throughout the entire compound. The girls all began to gather around into a huge hallway. The floor was deep green marble and so cool and smooth on the feet. All along the sides lay hundreds of carpets, pillows, and couches. Huge, polished columns towered up along the walls, holding up the great high ceiling of cedars. At the far end of the hallway, a huge flight of stairs led up into a large passageway, lined with small, open archways.

Hegai stood on the steps, his great voice carried easily through the hallway, silencing the hundreds of girls all gathered, watching him. He raised his hands, gesturing for silence.

"Welcome to the court of women," he began in thick Persian. He was a large man despite his condition. His muscles bulged as his arms moved. Wide gold bands decorated his arms and wrists. His skin was a rich dark color and shimmered in the soft light. His teeth glowed white. His face was kind but strict. He commanded attention when he spoke.

"This will be your home for the next year. Here, you will prepare for your meeting with the Great King Xerxes. All you need will be provided for you."

"Every morning and every evening the baths will be prepared. There will be music, dance, and singing for all of you who want to join in. There is food, comforts, and provisions. There are clothes, jewelry, and shoes. This is paradise. Behold the splendor and generosity of the Great King Xerxes!" his voice thundered the praise of the king, echoing through the hallway sending chills down Esther's spine.

"Use this time wisely. Enjoy this time. The goddess Anahitak has smiled upon you. You are given the opportunity to woe the heart of the greatest King on earth. Prepare well! If you listen and follow our instructions, you will succeed."

Here he gestured to the eunuchs lined up on either side of the staircase. They all stood tall and proud; their arms crossed over their chests. Their rich red brown robes tied with a brilliant blue silken rope.

"Here you are all equal, regardless of birth or rank." His dark eyes surveyed the group of girls all staring back at him.

"Here, you are all given the same opportunities, the same lessons, and the same privileges. Welcome to the court of women!"

His speech was so stirring the girls could not help themselves. Esther found herself swept up in the excitement of his booming voice. There was clapping and cheering. Esther turned to look at the girl on her left. She looked back at her, her dark eyes dancing with excitement. The girls laughed and embraced then turned to their neighbors and did the same.

The hall echoed with laughter and excited chattering. The eunuchs broke out of their lines and led groups of ten girls up the stairs and down the hallways. It was Esther's turn to gather with the girls around her in a group of ten. They climbed those stairs, hearts pounding with excitement.

Their guide led them through an archway. It led into a long white, washed hallway with ten openings each covered with a tapestry, five on one side and five on the other. Each girl was ushered into her room.

Esther smiled as the eunuch gestured to a beautiful red tapestry with lotus flowers blooming in deep crimson on it.

"Thank you," she said as she lifted the tapestry and entered her new room. It was small for sure but comfortable. A bed lay on the ground, draped in cushions and tapestries. A wooden chest lay open, with clothes of all colors spilling out of it. Everything she would need to live comfortably lay out in front of her.

Movement startled Esther. A maidservant stood beside the entryway, her back to the wall. She moved out into the open area and bowed low.

"Welcome, my lady," she said in a slow soft voice. "To the court of women."

"I am welcome," Esther nodded at her.

"I am at your service, my lady. You have only to ask, and I will meet your every need." She bowed low again. Her perfect skin was as dark as Hegai's. Her eyes were very dark and saw little joy. Her beautiful face was frozen. No emotions played about her lips or danced in her eyes. She was all business.

Esther suddenly felt nervous. Never had she been waited on, especially by someone who did not choose to be there. Was all she did to be monitored and watched, just as the eunuch had told her?

A feeling of panic swept through her. She could walk back out through all those long twisting hallways and be free again, right? Or was the generosity of the great king a price, a bribe for her life?

But even with the uneasiness came the questions. She could not contain herself for too long. Esther rose off the bed she had tried to sit down on to relax and approached the girl standing at the ready beside the door.

"Please tell me your name?" she asked. The girl did not make eye contact.

"Arjana," was the reply. "But you can call me anything you like." The reply was curt and to the point.

"Arjana," Esther repeated the word over again. "What does it mean?"

The girl looked up at her eyes quickly for a moment before again staring at the wall.

"It means paradise." Her face darkened as she shrugged suddenly. "Some paradise I have found here."

"What do you mean? Are you not cared for well here?" At this Esther was surprised. It seemed a place dripping with plenty and happiness.

Arjana's dark eyes finally met Esther's. Her face was grave, very grave.

"I just came from the slave market," she said coldly. "Who do you think will serve all of you women? There are ten of us for every one of you and this court of women holds four hundred girls. There is room after room after room." She paused for dramatic effect. She gestured at her own chest.

"I will be with you till you die. You will never leave this palace of your own free will again. Your chances of being chosen are slim. Look around you!" bitterness drenched the girl's voice as she spoke. A dark sparkle reached her eyes at last. She moved from her place against the wall, slowly walking toward Esther.

Esther was frozen in place. The daydream trembled around her. She remembered yellowed teeth and red eyes, hands, groping, reaching, trying to grab her, to drag her down. Her heart pounded and her breathing grew shallow and quick. The walls seem to close in around her. The tapestry over the door suddenly looked heavy and weighted.

"You will never be chosen. What if he chooses the one right before you? Your only chance is to get pregnant if you even get to see him at all. Then at least you will never be alone. You will have a child with you in the harem. But woe to your heart if it is a male. They will tear him from your arms on his thirteenth birthday just as you were torn from your family."

Tears gathered in Esther's eyes. Sheering pain tore through her as her eyelids slid shut. Never had she met with such despair and rage in a fellow human being before. She had faced sorrow before, immense sorrow. She remembered the feeling of falling after Adinah's death. But Ruth and Mordecai had caught her. They had lifted her up with their love.

"What is gained if I am silenced, if I go down to the pit? Will the dust praise you? Will it proclaim your faithfulness? Hear, Lord, and be merciful to me; Lord, be my help."

"You turned my wailing into dancing; you removed my sackcloth and clothed me with joy, that my heart may sing your praises and not be silent. Lord my God, I will praise you forever."

The psalm of David danced through her mind, burning a lighted pathway through her dark thoughts. Her brow cleared. Had her God, the God of Abraham, Isaac, and Jacob, the Lord God, the Jehovah, the Creator, brought her here to the bowels of the greatest palace on earth only to discard her like a dirty rag, using a slave girl to destroy her joy?

She shook her head.

"No!" she said the words out loud. Hope flooded her heart. Her feet stepped out on that lit path she saw so clearly in her mind. She would hope when there was no other hope. Had not God shut the mouth of the lions in the den for Daniel when King Darius the Mede threw him in? Had not God freed His people after seventy years of captivity in one night when King Cyrus overthrew the undefeatable Babylon without even a fight?

Esther's eyes opened and she smiled at Arjana. The maidservant stared at her, a look of anger and fear on her face.

"No, Arjana," Esther said softly. She moved back over to the bed and sat down, looking around her.

"My God will care for us. Look at how He has provided already? Did you not say you will stay with me now my entire life? Come," she reached out her hand. "Let us be friends and help each other through whatever trials lie ahead."

Arjana stood looking at her for a long moment. At last, her hand reached back and stooping quickly, she kissed the back of Esther's hand.

"Thank you for not punishing my indiscretion." She said and then she was back at her post, her back to the wall.

Esther sighed. Exhaustion overwhelmed her. As much as she wanted to explore her new surroundings, she felt so tired from all that had transpired. Her mind drifted over the events of the day. She remembered Mordecai's voice. She missed him already. Ruth would be getting ready for bed. She would sing a song for her as she had promised.

It seemed a lifetime ago already. Her life flashed before her eyes. She was once again a child, leaving that tattered tent holding the hand of a man, the man God had sent to save her from a life of misery and hopelessness. He had led her to a home, a family, a people.

Now she lay on a bed in the palace of Susa. She waited to meet another man. A man, that if he gave her his hand, she would be queen of the world's greatest empire. She had promised to be God's servant all the days of her life. And here she was, with a bitter maidservant, in the women's quarters of the great palace of Susa, in the harem of the most powerful man on earth.

What exactly was it that had sustained her all this time? What gave her heart hope to go on day after day? She smiled in the gathering twilight. She needed to pray. She needed to get to that beautiful garden. She needed to look up into the starry sky and talk to her Creator, for it was He that sustained her in every trial and hardship.

She sat up and looked over at Arjana. The poor girl had laid down, fully dressed, right where she stood, waiting for a word from her mistress. Respect stirred in Esther's heart. Had not her people come to this very country as slaves? Here she was, a Jewess, in a position to help one bound in slavery.

Esther pulled off a thick tapestry decorating the end of the bed and quietly walked over to the sleeping girl. She must be exhausted to sleep so on the hard cold floor. Carefully Esther laid the tapestry over the slender form. Arjana stirred and sighed but she did not wake.

What had her day been like? Esther wondered as she straightened. She turned and quietly slipped out of the room. The hallway was lit by a single torch, flickering in the soft evening wind. The palace was quiet. Esther followed the hallway to the passageway leading to the staircase into the huge hallway.

Grateful no one was in sight, she hurried down the great marble stairs. They reminded her of the story's Mordecai told her of the king's coronation. A smile flirted across her face as she remembered. She walked across that great hallway her feet making no noise on the gleaming green marble. The sheer number of girls gathered began to sink in as she studied the size of the great building. Four hundred girls in all this place could accommodate!

It had not dawned on her childish innocent mind exactly what this meant when she listened to the scribes' description of this event. Now, as Arjana had explained, it meant hundreds of lives changed in a moment. It was a huge financial expense on the palace to gather all these women, house them and feed them. Maybe this was why Adinah had been so adamant this place was no place for a girl. What exactly did the king require in return for his generosity?

Esther stepped down off the marble floor onto the lush soft grass of the gardened area. The leaves on the trees rustled a soft greeting. She smiled again looking up at the starry sky through the silken linens. The soft sound of running water drew her along as she explored the garden. The water ran through in a bubbling stream. A small series of waterfalls tumbled down into a large pool. Fish shimmered in the greying light, curiously swimming about her shadowy figure reflected on the water.

This was a perfect place to pray. She dropped to her knees and the Hebrew words swirled through her. Her lips moved silently as she poured out her heart.

"Oh Lord God," she whispered, looking up. "Help me find my joy even here. There is a purpose for me. Help me, Lord God, help me."

Peace swirled through the night, lingering over her heart and mind. It felt like hours later when she rose and made the quiet journey back toward her bedroom. She felt a sense of relief as she turned down the passageway and carefully lifted the tapestry with the lotus blossoms on it. It was her room! Arjana lay on the floor, covered under the blanket, a look of peace at last on her face.

Esther stood looking at the face of her sleeping maidservant a long moment.

"Help me, my Lord, to restore joy to this fellow person," she whispered. She remembered her deep friendship with Ruth, foraged through heartache and grief. She and Arjana had each other in this great palace. And tomorrow would begin a new day.

Chapter 8

Esther Begins Palace Studies

Esther woke with a start. Arjana was standing over her.

"Mistress! It is time to rise, my lady," Arjana had a very meager, silken robe laid out already. Esther sat up. She was still fully dressed, necklace and all.

"The baths are drawn. Let me help you undress, Mistress. I will take you to your first bath."

Esther nodded. She lifted her arms to unclasp her dress, but Arjana's hands stopped her.

"That is my job, Mistress. I am here to help you."

Esther turned and Arjana's nimble fingers soon had her gown undone. Slowly she stepped out of her clothes, her last link to her old life. She smiled as she held the necklace in her hands, remembering Mordecai's words as he clasped it about her neck.

"Can I keep them," Esther almost whispered, afraid of the answer, as she clasped the necklace to her bosom. Arjana nodded.

"Oh yes, my lady," she was pleasantly cheerful. Esther was glad for her guidance. This was all new. She did not even know where the baths were.

Esther took the blue silken tichel that had belonged to Adinah. She lovingly wrapped the necklace and earrings in it and tied them into a neat bundle. She lifted her pillow and laid the bundle underneath. She carefully placed her pillow overtop. Arjana watched her silently.

"Now my dreams will always be sweet," Esther said.

She smiled at Arjana. Arjana nodded and held open the tapestry for her mistress to walk through. Girls met them in the hallways, all dressed in colorful silken robes. The morning sun sifted softly through the linen and lattice screens. The peacock called loudly from the garden. Birds twittered and sang to each other as they busied themselves about the abundant trees and flowering bushes. The scent of lavender hung in the air so richly Esther could taste the floral flavor on her tongue.

The hallway led to a balcony overlooking five huge marble pools standing side by side. The entire area was made of white marble. Long tables stood along the baths, crowded with brass, silver, and clay bowls of every shape and size. The girls gasped as they looked over the ornate railing at their new bathing quarters.

Slave girls hurried around the pools, sprinkling flower petals over the water and pouring in potions and oils. The fragrance rising from the pools was intense. It was a mixture of myrrh, roses, and many fragrances Esther had never experienced before. Esther breathed in deeply.

Arjana guided her down the wooden steps. She silently held out her arm expectantly. Girls were all around, pulling off their silken robes and handing them to their waiting maidservants. The girls laughed and splashed as they waded down the steps and into the warm rich waters of the bath.

Esther looked at Arjana a moment. Then she shrugged and untied her gown.

"I have never bathed like this before," she admitted a bit shy.

"Go on Mistress," encouraged Arjana. She smiled suddenly, trying to be reassuring. Esther nodded and handed her the robe. The water was surprisingly warm and tingled against her skin as she waded in, deeper and deeper. The girls spread out, each soaking in the rich warm scented water.

Soon Esther found herself talking and laughing with anyone around her. They washed each other's hair. Foam danced on the water's surface, iridescent bubbles reflecting one's face back. Combs lay in great silver bowls around the pools. Girls lounged naked on the sides; others sat cross-legged chattering to a new friend or two. The maidservants moved about the merry crowd magically following their assigned mistress, meeting her every need.

Esther watched from her place, enjoying the joyous noise as the girls exclaimed over the beauty around them, the delightful smells, and the wonderful experience. A great bong from the garden announced breakfast had been served.

In a flurry of giggles and happy chatter, the girls all exited the pools. They were quickly dried and robed. They exclaimed over the colorful silken robes, each tied with a golden cord. Esther's long black curls shone with the scented myrrh oil, Arjana combed in. Every girl was provided with a ration of beauty products ensuring each one was treated equally.

It was a colorful happy crowd of girls that hurried down the huge staircase into the grand hall. The great tables were again loaded with fruits and breads of every kind imaginable. The smells that met them on the steps was tantalizing.

The girls spread out across the garden, sitting on tapestries, and lounging on couches, or walking about in groups, talking. Esther filled her plate and walked down the stream to sit beside the pond again. She watched the fish, swimming about as she ate her morning meal. Arjana brought her a steaming mug of spiced tea. Esther smiled, remembering her first experience with spiced tea, so long ago, in the kitchen with Ruth and Adinah.

Once breakfast was completed, the girls broke off into smaller and smaller groups, each going to classes, specific beauty routines, and attending to needed toiletries. The court became a little city all unto its own, each group moving symmetrically, yet individually, the eunuchs expertly moving through, organizing, and guiding as they went. The result was a sense of busied purpose with lots of fun and laughter mixed in.

Esther was directed to sit on a cushion. There were several other girls there too, all sitting in a row on a quiet porch overlooking a narrow garden. A group of men walked in, each carrying an armload of scrolls and papyrus sheets. They wore long robes of dark brown velvet. Their waist was buckled with a beautiful bright blue silk with ornate gold, silver, and purple embroidery. They were advisers to some of the most powerful men of the empire.

A shiver of excitement rippled through Esther. She had heard Mordecai and the scribes speak of the learned men. They were all eunuchs of course, cut so they would only focus on their studies. These men were some of the most brilliant minds, taken from every tribe, country, and culture the Persian Empire had captured.

Daniel and his three brave friends had been just such men for the Babylonian king, the great Nebuchadnezzar and his wicked nephew, Belshazzar. When King Cyrus entered the king's chambers, it was Daniel, holding a scroll of the Holy Scriptures that met him there. Daniel showed the conquering king what God had written about him hundreds of years before he was even born. Cyrus had been awestruck. He was so moved he gave the edict, freeing the Jewish people from their captivity. He even gave a generous gift to assist with the cost of relocating back to Jerusalem.

King Darius the Mede, the general who conquered the great impregnable city of Babylon for King Cyrus, had run to the lion's den, and called out to his dear friend, Daniel, concerned the hungry cats had torn him to pieces. It had been the jealousy of the wise men and magicians that had flattered King Darius the Mede into declaring the law that trapped Daniel into the death sentence for praying to his God. Daniel had called back to the king. When they pulled Daniel up, the king himself embraced him passionately as a man embraces a brother.

Mordecai's wise words rang through her mind. Not only had the Jewish people blessed these great empires but He had used His people to shape the very fabric of history through them. Not because of their faithfulness or obedience, but because of His promises and His faithfulness. With every generation God raised up those obedient to Him, eager to do His will and seeking out His purposes to influence history. And now, the little orphaned girl, Esther, sat before these very men to be quizzed on her skills of reading, languages, and writing.

Out of respect Esther rose. She was the only one. She bowed to the men as they solemnly filed into the room and sat in theirs spots before the girls. Each man returned her bow with a deep nod. Each one made eye contact with this beautiful girl before them. The other girls looked at her in surprise. Some half-rose but most just sat waiting, having no knowledge of the power these men could wheeled.

Esther sat down once they were seated and waited. Hegai was standing in an arched doorway. He oversaw all the happenings of the court of women. He was deeply interested in the talents of his candidates. It was his responsibility after all, to present the worthiest of women to the great King Xerxes.

His eyebrow rose in surprise to Esther's reaction. Curiosity began to swell in him. Exactly who was this Esther of Susa anyway? What would move a young woman like her to show such respect to these learned men? His interest was perked, and he watched her closely.

The learned men began their questions, and the girls answered each one as they knew. The hallway was silent except for the questions and answers passed back and forth between the men and girls. Eunuchs of the court of women carefully documented how each candidate did.

Esther answered each question carefully. He quizzed her in Persian about the poets, famous readings, and the history of the empire. Esther found the questions very simple and broad. It was basically ensuring she had read a few scrolls or poets or spoke with a learned person or two. He continued, question after question.

Esther suddenly smiled slightly and answered a very basic question in Egyptian. The learned man startled a bit and looked sharply at her. He asked another question this time in Egyptian and Esther returned his answer.

The learned man switched to Aramaic. Hegai noted the wise man's interest in Esther. Another wise man rose, his candidate leaving. He heard Esther conversing and asked a question in Sumerian. Another wise man rose to join them, his candidate too gone.

Someone gave Esther a piece of papyrus to write on. She wrote in Persian, Median, Sumerian, and Egyptian. This delighted the wise men greatly.

"You write very well, lady," said the learned man. "You are a very good student."

"Thank you," Replied Esther.

"Your grasp of the history of the Babylonian and Persian Empire does your teacher great credit," he continued. The others gathered nodded in agreement. "One would think you have had a great number of teachers."

At this, Esther smiled remembering the happy gatherings in the garden and around the table.

"Circumstances gave me many instructors, but I had one very faithful teacher," she smiled. "And a very curious mind."

"It has served you well, my lady," the learned man nodded his head to her and turned to look at Hegai.

Hegai joined the group around Esther.

"This young woman you have here in your care, Hegai, is a very talented one indeed," The learned man gave his report, Esther blushing at his praise. Esther rose as the men prepared to leave the hall, all the other girls long since dispersed.

"Please, Learned One!" Esther stepped forward and laid a gentle hand on his arm. Surprised by her touch he turned back to her quickly.

"Please give me more to study and learn. While I am here in this court, preparing, please help me learn what I should."

Her direct request obviously touched the man. His hand covered Esther's on his arm.

"Yes, my lady," he said. He paused a moment and looked at the others around him. He glanced at Hegai.

"Any objections, Master Hegai?" he asked. Hegai shook his head.

"None at all!" he exclaimed looking at Esther. "If you would really like to study, you are free to do so. But you must make all the required classes and beauty treatments. This will ensure you are ready to be presented to the King at the appropriate time."

Esther nodded.

"Thank you, Master Hegai!" she exclaimed breathless with excitement. "I will be sure to do all you ask of me."

The learned man smiled.

"I will send you some study material from my personal library tomorrow. Who, pray tell, do I have the honor of tutoring?"

"Esther. Esther of Susa." Esther smiled at him. "I thank you for this honor, Teacher." The men left and Hegai looked at the young woman standing before him for a long moment.

"Do you really want to continue to read and learn, Esther of Susa?" he asked slowly, the words seemed to be hard for him to pronounce in his amazement. "You seem to have filled your head sufficiently already. I do not understand what more you could possibly need to learn!"

"Oh yes, Hegai, I do!" exclaimed Esther, grabbing his arm with both her hands in her enthusiasm. "There is still so much more to know."

"Then," said Hegai with his slow smile touching his lips, "My Esther of Susa shall read till her heart is contented."

"Wonderful!" Esther exclaimed. She could not contain her excitement and twirled in her delight. At this, Hegai laughed a great bellow of a laugh. It was a delightful sound and Esther joined him.

"Walk with me, Esther," he said. Esther tucked her arm through his and together they headed back to the garden were lunch waited.

Once again, the meal was served on the great tables. Arjana seemed glad to see Esther as she approached on Hegai's arm. She hurried over to her mistress.

"Do you like your maidservant?" he asked. It was an innocent enough question, but Arjana froze.

"I like Arjana very much, Master Hegai," Esther said, smiling up at the eunuch. She glanced over at Arjana. "She has already taught me much about the court of women and the workings of the palace. I am grateful for her service."

"I am pleased to hear this," Hegai glanced at Arjana briefly. "She is new to her service here, as many of the maidservants are." Here he sighed in a tired sort of way.

"You have to train the maidservants too." This was a statement, not a question.

"Why yes, yes, I do." He nodded a bit uncomfortable with the direction of the conversation suddenly.

"Master Hegai," Esther exclaimed. "You are a very talented man indeed! I am grateful to learn from you."

Hegai's defenses crumbled. He blushed and nodded. He did not know what to do with praise. He patted Esther's hand then hurried off to other duties awaiting him.

"Thank you, Mistress," Arjana said.

"It is true, Arjana," Esther said looking the maidservant full in the face. "I have learned lots from you and I am grateful for your company." Arjana smiled and it finally reached her eyes. She hurried off to ensure her mistress had refreshments to drink, a spring in her step and a purpose to her movements.

The afternoon was busy for the girls. Hegai kept them moving, learning, growing. He took his responsibility seriously. He could lose his life, not just position, if he did not produce worthy candidates for the king. These women had to present with a certain level of civility, dignity, and knowledge of palace decorum, in addition to physical beauty.

There were lessons in dance, song, poetry, music, and dining. The girls had to please in all manners, be gracious, and pleasant. They would be concubines at the least, queens at the greatest. All had to become a princess, fit for the king.

After the evening meal, the girls hurried back to their rooms. Again, they made the trip to the great baths. They soaked in the rich scented waters, the beautifying potions working their magic, erasing all signs of poverty, excessive sun, or injury.

Esther's body tingled with the comforting sensation of the rich bath. Her hair was again anointed, scented, and combed by Arjana's experienced hands.

She was wrapped in the silken robe, sitting on the bed when a eunuch arrived at her tapestried door. He smiled as he handed a flask to Arjana.

"From Master Hegai for Esther of Susa," the eunuch explained and disappeared. Arjana looked at Esther, her eyes large with curiosity.

"What is it?" asked Esther equally curious.

Arjana uncorked the vile and smelled it. She smiled then and picked up the comb.

"It is an extra allotment of beautifying products, Mistress." She said as she prepared to comb Esther's hair again.

"You have found favor in Master Hegai's eyes. This is a compliment indeed, so I am told." Esther smiled at this as she turned and let Arjana comb out her curls.

It was twilight when she was free again to slip out to the garden unaccompanied. She knelt by the pool and looked up at the stars twinkling down at her. She breathed deeply of the perfumed breeze. The fish splashed and played in and out of her shadow. The peacock rested on his roost, listening to the soft singing of the psalm of David, a shepherd boy made king, as Esther poured out her heart to her God.

Gratitude flooded up into her heart. Just as she had knelt that first morning in the house of her cousin Mordecai, overwhelmed with gratitude for how God had cared for her every need, she again poured out her heart to the great God Jehovah for bringing her here to the palace. Once again, she was surrounded with people who respected her and cared for her every need. One day she may even find love in this great and busy place, full of hurting and lonely hearts.

The next day dawned, and the girls were prepared for the routine. New girls had arrived the day before and they were swept along in the happy morning rush to the baths. Groups began to form. The little groups of ten, created by the outlay of the rooms, began to spend time together, sharing meals, sitting around, and chattering happily.

Esther discovered that one of the other girls in her group spoke Kassite. Feray was the daughter of a general stationed at Susa. Feray described the beauty of the Zagros Mountains as Esther's eyes stood wide with wonder. Towering over the desert, these mountains were tipped with white during the cooler months. Flowers of immense number and beauty covered them with color with the spring rains.

"I wish I had a map to see exactly where those mountains are in relation to Susa." Feray sighed, homesickness suddenly clouding her eyes. "At home, in our living room, my father has a huge colorful map. I loved to study it, dreaming of far-off lands and wonders. I was so young when we made the journey. I don't remember all I could, as I spent hours in an oxen cart or howdah watching the countryside roll by."

Esther told her excitedly of the learned man's promise to deliver study materials.

"I am sure there will be maps in what he sends me. Maybe I could request he send me one."

"Can I come to your bedroom to study?" Feray begged, excitement filling her eyes.

"Please do!" exclaimed Esther. The two were inseparable for the rest of the day. That evening, right on cue, the eunuch called out at the doorway. Arjana smiled and got up quickly to pull back the lotus flower tapestry.

The eunuch produced another bottle of myrrh treatments. This time it was a perfumed oil to be rubbed all over, softening the skin, enhancing the effects of the purifying baths. Arjana held the bottle triumphantly, but it was the scrolls that Esther reached for.

"Thank you so much!" she exclaimed, her eyes shining with excitement. The eunuch returned her smile and bowed.

"I will convey your pleasure to Master Hegai," and with that he was gone. Arjana made a move to open the bottle, but Esther was already looking through the scrolls eagerly.

"Can you call Feray, Arjana? She really will enjoy this!"

Feray was quick to join Esther and the two girls sat on the rich rug using the bed as a back rest. They searched through the scrolls for a map but soon were lost in a story, sitting silently side by side. Feray's maid looked over at Arjana and shrugged.

Time began to slip by in a happy routine. Every couple of nights the eunuch delivered a package of scrolls to Esther's room. Feray was usually there waiting with Esther. Study sheets arrived with the scrolls delighting the girls. They worked hard on answering the pondering questions. They sent back their answers and waited with anticipation till the next delivery to see what the teacher would say. A map was delivered on request and a eunuch helped carefully secure it to the wall.

Within a week, another girl joined the study group. Soon, a group of ten girls were all crammed in Esther's room, sprawled across the bed, carpet, and sitting up against the wall, discussing history and economics, philosophy and legends together in a happy huddle.

One evening, as Arjana readied Esther for bed, she began to hum a strange tune. Words rolled off her tongue, unlike anything Esther had ever heard before. The song was haunting, sad, and happy at the same time, Arjana's usual thick, forced speech gone in a vibrating clear song of her people.

"It is all I can remember from my childhood," Arjana explained softly once she was done. "It is the only thing I can remember of my parents and my people."

"It is a beautiful song," Esther said softly. The conversation that had begun the first day the girls met suddenly stood sharply in Esther's mind. The room was silent.

"What happened to you, Arjana?"

The maidservant sat back on her heels, her hands idle in her lap, the comb still. Esther listened, waiting.

"I was little, so little," Arjana began. "I remember the wooden floor of our hut, situated on the banks of a river. My mother told me never to go to the water's edge alone. She was afraid I would be eaten by some crocodile or giant fish."

"But the pathway stretched before me, so inviting. I danced along it, chasing a bright blue butterfly. Before I knew it, I could see the water's edge, lapping up onto the riverbank, tempting me."

"Oh, if only I had looked up! The canoes where right there watching, waiting. I only saw the tempting mud. I ran to it and pushed my feet into the soft silken coolness of the rich black African mud."

"Next thing I knew I was being lifted roughly by large hands under my armpits. I screamed and kicked but the hands did not let me go. I could hear my mother screaming my name. I saw her form crumpled on the water's edge; her head thrown back as she screamed in agony to the river god to hear her cries for help."

"But no help came. I was placed in a sack and thrown to the bottom of the canoe. They captured other children that day too. We had no food or water. We soiled ourselves were we lay, unable to move."

Arjana sighed. Some was too painful for her to recount. Esther turned to look at Arjana.

"I was passed from canoe to canoe to canoe. I was fed at last and given some necessities. I don't remember much, only traveling a lot. Finally, I arrived at a slave market and was bought by slave dealers."

"They brought me here to Susa. There are homes they put us in. They teach us Persian and how to serve, and dress and act. They prepare us for life in the palace. I faithfully prayed and prayed but no one came to help me."

"I began to rely on myself and learn my skills to the very best of my ability. It is how I got here. Now, I am a maidservant in the palace of women. And I found you, Mistress. You are so kind and good to me. I feel that someone may have finally heard my cries."

A psalm rose in Esther's heart. The words bubbled out of her mouth for a long moment before she caught herself. She hushed herself, rolling the comforting words over in her mind.

"What did you say, Mistress?" Arjana asked in a hushed respectful tone.

"I sang a song of my people," Esther said in perfect Persian. "I will tell you the words. It goes like this, '*Give ear to my words, O Lord, Consider my meditation. Give heed to the voice of my cry, my King and my God, for to you I will pray.*'"

"Do you believe your God hears you?" Arjana's voice was thick with suppressed emotions.

"Yes," whispered Esther. "I do."

"Even here?"

"Especially here."

"I hope you are right, Mistress."

A long sigh sounded from Arjana.

"I am sorry I was so blunt to you that first night. I hope you are chosen. I have never hoped for much since my capture. Since meeting you, Mistress, a great hope is beginning to well up in me as never before. I promise to do all I can to help you succeed. It just seems so hopeless at times."

"The former Queen Vashti was so cruel. I never served her myself, but I met a few of the maidservants that did. What they described terrified me. I was so afraid of you when you appeared in that doorway. I was sure you would be as cruel as you were beautiful."

"Among the maids, we hope for the not-so-beautiful girls. It is believed that the most beautiful are also the unkindest. I was terrified when I saw your beauty. You are the most beautiful woman I have ever seen."

"Yet, you are so kind and caring to all around you. You share all you are given with those around you. You are so different than all the other women here. Your God must smile on you. Out of hundreds, you have even gained Hegai's favor."

Esther smiled. God had heard her prayer whispered into the twilight of her very first evening in the court. Arjana was beginning to soften and change! God was restoring hope to the servant girl's heart using her, Esther. Arjana once again began to comb out her mistress's long black locks unaware of the tears of joy shimmering in her mistress's eyes at her words.

God had surely blessed Esther even here, in the great palace of Susa, far removed from the loving home of her cousin Mordecai, far from the evening readings of the Scriptures. Here she hid her people, heritage, and language from all around her, even Arjana. But her God, the same God of Abraham, Isaac, and Jacob, the God of Daniel, was able to use her to bring hope, joy, love, and peace to those around her. What else could this great God have in store for her as she humbly and obediently followed Him?

Chapter 9
Room Change

As the weeks passed into months, Esther began to develop a great awe for Master Hegai. He was always busy yet available. He appeared exactly when needed the most and always had a solution. He was well-respected by all the eunuchs in the court of women as well as with most of the women gathered there.

Hegai watched closely over his charges. He knew many of the girls by name. Esther found herself learning a new skill all on its own. A skill she had never been able to practice before. That skill was diplomacy. Speaking a person's name and remembering it later at a vital moment proved to be a powerful tool in connecting with people. Esther watched Hegai expertly resolve a disagreement or overt an argument as he used the girl's names while calmly diffusing the disagreement.

Esther discovered Arjana knew many of the eunuch's and maidservant's names. By using the name of a servant instead of treating them like a faceless personality, Esther's popularity grew. Kindness created a boomerang effect and came back to surprise her in the most unexpected of ways.

The life of the women was not without its challenges though. Esther discovered the noblewoman who had kicked down the poor crippled girl was soon trying to do the same to any girl around her that threatened her chance of success in any way.

The evening meals began to take on a feast-like atmosphere. The eunuchs set up couches and cushions in the great hallway and the women were served much like a grand dinner in the court of the king.

Maid servants and eunuchs coached the girls on how to always present themselves in a pleasant manner, regardless of the situation. Hegai was careful to place a different girl in the position of honor, at his right hand, each evening where he personally tested their skills.

Girls of wealthy families, such as noblewomen, daughters of generals, government officials and merchants, had an advantage to be sure. But the luxuries of the palace paled even their wealth.

The noblewoman was Ashraf, the niece of Memucan, one of the king's most trusted advisors. It was on her father's arm that she had arrived at the court of women. Her father already held an official position of power in the city.

Conflict arose when those of the privileged class wanted to be in positions of honor all the time. The girls all realized this opportunity would change their lives and futures forever. Each worked hard to please Hegai and learn all he encouraged them to learn. One meal proved to be very dramatic as the nobleman's daughter rose from her couch and shouted at Hegai, demanding a place more honorable.

"Do you not know who my uncle is?" Ashraf screamed, rage making her dark eyes flash.

"Do you know in whose presence you are in?" Hegai challenged back across the table. "You are pointing fingers at the world's most powerful King. Sit back down, girl. Behavior like that will get you nowhere. Do not try the King's generosity!"

With that, he calmly turned back to the girl sitting at his right hand and carried on his testing. Ashraf had no choice but to sit back down, her face flushed with shame. Now the entire court of women knew who she was.

Many of the girls gathered about her in the bath that evening, asking for any tidbit of advice on what the king liked or how he acted. The noblewoman flushed with triumph, her ego swelling with pride. She told stories with great drama, holding a court of her own.

Esther realized that although this noblewoman knew some about the king, it was Master Hegai that really knew what exactly Xerxes liked. It was Hegai who worked tirelessly day after day, preparing candidates for the king that would please and delight him. Maybe even woo his heart to the point of being chosen and crowned queen. The noblewoman's behavior only encouraged Esther to listen and learn all the more from Hegai.

Esther found herself trying harder and harder to learn, gleaning any information she could, practicing walking right, and speaking right in any and every situation. She found herself following Hegai either physically or with her eyes, studying his every move. Hegai had no idea how talented he really was and often flushed as Esther admired a quality in him. She also discovered he could not write. When faced with this obstacle, as he always did, he looked up and his eyes met hers.

"Esther, my dear," he said calmly, always solving an issue in a calm, intelligent manner. "Can you write something for me? Your writing is exquisite."

Esther hurried over to the table to assist him. The waiting eunuch watched in surprise as Hegai requested the assistance of one of the women.

"Very good! Very good!" exclaimed Hegai as he picked up the piece of coarse papyrus. If he was at all ashamed of his limitations, he hid it with the same quiet grace he did most things. An idea sparked in Esther. She thought of it over lunch.

"Arjana," she asked as the maidservant served her.

"Yes Mistress!" Arjana had changed so much from the cold, hard, girl Esther had first met in her room. She was now a smiling, humming girl, eager to do anything for her mistress.

"Can you read?" Esther asked her. Arjana stopped in surprise.

"A little," she admitted then shook her head.

"No, Mistress, I can't. That was not seen as mandatory in training a maidservant."

"So, you can't write either, I assume?" Esther prodded gently not trying to shame her maid.

Arjana merely shook her head.

"You are an extremely intelligent girl, Arjana," Esther encouraged. "I could teach you if you want to learn. I can teach anyone else who wants to learn too!"

"Learning through reading has been so important all my life. I can't imagine life without it. It will help you so in your services. You can learn all kinds of things. You already know so much about the beautifying oils and baths."

Arjana's large dark eyes widened as Esther spoke. A dreamy look came over her face.

"I could write notes," she whispered almost afraid to admit it out loud.

"Arjana," Esther was serious. Arjana stopped and looked at her.

"I will teach you. Tonight, after the last bath, we will start."

Arjana smiled and nodded. Lunch was over and Esther was off to palace etiquette lectures. The two girls parted company as the maidservants did chores such as laundry and cleaning while the girls were in lectures. Esther caught up with Feray and whispered her idea in her ear. Feray turned to her, her vale green eyes getting large.

"Is it allowed?" she whispered back.

"I assume so." Esther said after a thoughtful pause.

"Should we ask someone?" Feray wondered out loud.

"Who could we ask?" asked Esther, gently poking her friend. "The King?"

Feray giggled at this. They turned back to the task at hand, each turning the idea over in their minds.

During the evening bath, Feray walked through the milky water toward Esther and Arjana, her maidservant with her.

"Kadri cannot read or write either," Feray said bluntly, looking at her maidservant. "She wants to learn too."

Esther smiled up at Kadri standing on the marble surrounding the tub, holding her mistress's robe, towel, comb, and hair oils. The maid's dark sable brown eyes lifted and met Esther's. A hope began to sparkle in them lighting the dark emotionless depth. She was quick to look down again but the slightest of smiles played about her lips.

Esther smiled and looked at Arjana.

"Can we begin now?" Esther asked almost breathless with excitement.

Arjana shook her head.

"No Mistress, you must remain in this bath for at least twenty minutes, or it will do nothing for your skin. It must have time to penetrate deeply and exfoliate any dead skin. You must remain in it for the allotted time, or it will be wasted. We must not let this affect your purification. Once this is complete, you must let me rub the oils on or your skin will continue to dry out and your complexion will suffer."

Esther sighed.

"You are right, Arjana. See how much you know about these baths. You amaze me with all you know, and Master Hegai would not be pleased if I waste the baths."

Arjana nodded; a slight coloring of her cheeks disclosed the pleasure she felt under her mistress's open praise.

Feray and Esther began to discuss the latest topics the teacher had sent them. Interested, both maids listened to the conversation. Bravely, Arjana asked Esther a question. Willingly Esther explained the answer to her and Kadri. A few of the other girls joined in from the study group. A lively conversation erupted between the girls and their maids and time passed in pleasant discussions.

The bong sounded and the girls looked up startled.

"Let's go!" exclaimed Esther and the girls exited the pool in a flurry of excitement. Esther was looking down, not paying too much attention in her excitement to find Arjana and her robe. She bumped into someone. She turned to apologize. To her horror, it was Ashraf, Memucan's niece as she herself had announced. Ashraf met Esther's gaze, arms crossed over her breasts, a look of conceited distain twisting across her beautiful face.

"Watch out, other girl," she challenged. "Future queen coming through." Her entourage of girls and their maidservants twittered at her comment. She turned to go but, a thought stopped her. She turned slowly; a perfectly shaped eyebrow raised.

"Who's your father anyway?" she challenged, her head slowly bobbing in unrestrained contempt.

When Esther did not immediately reply, she continued with a wave of her hand.

"Exactly! A nobody! Out of my way!" Ashraf flicked her chin at Arjana who had come up beside Esther with her robe on her arm. A maidservant stepped forward and pushed Arjana hard in the back. Arjana stepped sideways almost falling over. In her unbalance, she stepped on Feray's foot.

"Ouch!" gasped Feray. Arjana cowered back, her face crumbling as she looked up at Esther.

An icy courage washed through Esther as rage coursed through her. She felt her hands clench at her side. She stepped forward shielding Arjana and right into Ashraf's path.

The two girls stared at each other. Out of the corner of her eye, Esther saw Hegai on the balcony overlooking the baths. The great area was suddenly hushed as girls strained to see what was happening.

Ashraf's dark ebony eyes squinted. She began to laugh loudly.

"What is it, girl?" she taunted. "Or are you just too scared to say anything?"

A eunuch made a move to step in, but Hegai halted him. Even this was a test.

Esther smiled suddenly and took a deep breath.

"Generosity got us here, Ashraf," she began, gesturing with her hand to the beautiful surroundings the girls found themselves in.

"How do you know that it will be genetics that matter once we are asked to return the King's generosity? Do you not think that all the lessons Master Hegai teaches us day in, and day out will not come into play? Do you not wonder if kindness and gratitude may be a better way to present yourself then wrapped only in your father's connections and position? Improve on yourself and stand in your own merit, not just that of your father or your uncle."

With that, Esther turned and put an arm around Arjana. She was still quite naked, never bothering to take the robe Arjana held across her arm.

"Come on, my dear Feray," Esther encouraged. "Let's go and start our school of maids."

With that, the girls followed Esther down the hallway, toward their rooms. Arjana lifted the robe around Esther's shoulders. Esther smiled at Arjana. Feray forgot all about her sore foot and giggled with delight.

Ashraf gasped. She was shocked speechless for a long moment. Hegai grinned and turned away down the hallway. Esther was officially his favorite girl, ever.

It was the next evening a eunuch showed up at the doorway.

"Follow me, my Lady." He said mysteriously.

Arjana and Esther followed the eunuch obediently. He led the two down the passageway and across to another area of the living quarters. Here there was only one doorway. It was a brightly painted wooden doorway on great brass hinges hanging in the middle of the smooth stucco wall.

The eunuch opened the door and stood back, gesturing for Esther to enter. Esther led the way in, and Arjana followed. The two entered a large living area with a long couch along one wall. A small table with a chair pulled, stood in one corner. A shelf was on the wall, filled with scrolls. A huge pottery vase stood in the corner, brightly painted, and trimmed with gold.

An archway opened into another room. Esther looked at Arjana, her eyes wide. The two walked over and into the next room. There was a moderate sized bedroom with an archway draped in silken white curtains.

"Oh!" gasped Esther as she walked through an archway onto a small balcony overlooking the garden. She turned back to look at the eunuch.

"I must go thank Hegai!" she exclaimed, tears shimmering in her eyes. "He did this didn't he? Oh! I must thank him." The eunuch smiled.

"Go back out onto the balcony, my Lady. He is in the garden. He wanted to watch your reaction from there."

Esther rushed out and looked around. Sure enough, there was Hegai looking up from the garden below, his huge white smile visible in the growing twilight and flickering torches. Esther waved and blew him a kiss. His great laugh was heard booming through the garden. He turned then and hurried off, Esther watching his departing form in the growing darkness.

Praise bubbled up in her heart. She looked down at the garden, watching the fish splashing, the peacock roosting, his great tail streaming out behind him, the sunset casting the last of its vibrant colors over the rolling hills. It was beautiful, so very beautiful.

A gasp from Arjana startled her, making her turn quickly.

"Mistress, come quickly!" Esther hurried in to see what had excited her so much. She crossed the bedroom and entered through a small doorway. She found herself standing in a small, private bathing room with a marble tub inlaid into the floor. The tiles on the walls were all bright royal blue. The entire room was trimmed with white tiles boasting a scarlet lotus flower in full bloom. It was the most beautiful shower room Esther had ever seen.

A small table set beside the bath was filled with bowls and flasks. Arjana was on her knees opening lids and smelling the flasks.

"Myrrh treatments, lavender oil, rose water..." she babbled happily recognizing each by smell alone. She looked up at Esther, standing there watching her.

"You will be the most beautiful of all, Mistress!" she burst out. Esther laughed and moved toward Arjana. Arjana rose and suddenly the two girls embraced. Arjana was the first to pull back, shaking her head.

"So sorry, Mistress. I don't know what came over me. I was just so excited." Her words tumbled over each other in her desire to be understood. "It will never happen again."

"Arjana!" Esther spoke sharply through her maid's hurried apologies. She looked up startled. Esther never spoke to her sharply.

"Can't you see it, Arjana?" Esther asked. "We are friends, you and me. In this great place we have found each other, forced together by circumstances, but friends by choice. Will you…" she paused a long moment. "Will you accept my friendship?"

Arjana's eyes grew wide. She was silent for so long Esther began to wonder if she would answer at all. At last, she nodded, and a smile slowly spread across her beautiful face. It melted her icy eyes and seemed to flush over her entire body. Gone was the cold, angry maidservant Esther had met the first evening. Before her stood a girl with shining eyes and a merry heart, excited over her mistress's new living quarters and beauty products.

"I accept your friendship, my mistress." Arjana's voice was solemn.

"I pledge to serve you till the day I perish." She covered her chest with her hand. "I will tend to you with the devotion of a mother, the passion of a lover, and the faithfulness of a husband. I will never leave your side and if you lead me, I will follow you to death itself."

Love, overwhelming love, bubbled up like a fountain in Esther and she wrapped her arms around Arjana, gathering the servant girl against her, cradling her in her arms. She had saved a life. She had given hope to a helpless heart and in return that heart loved her with a fierceness that surpassed all explanation. It was a long time before the two girls parted.

The girls finally wandered back into the living room area. It was then Esther noted the six maidservants, all dressed in long dark blue silken robes with purple and gold trimmings standing three on each side of the doorway.

Esther turned to the eunuch.

"I'm assuming they come with the room too?" she asked. He nodded.

"Six maidservants from the King's very own palace, for you, Esther, favored among the women. And these are the best quarters in the court of women. Master Hegai wants the rest of your stay here in the court of women to be some of the best days of your life."

"He also wants me to inform you he knows about your school and how many girls have been cramming into your room each evening. He hopes this space will be enough for you all, to open your minds and explore the world."

The eunuch finished off his speech with a flourish of his hand. He hurried out of the room; his mission completed. He rounded the corner and almost collided into Master Hegai, leaning up against the wall, smiling as he listened to the happy chatter and laughter from inside. The eunuch gave him a nod and smile.

The next morning as soon as Esther saw Hegai, she hurried up to him. Slipping her arm through his, she kissed him gently on the cheek. Hegai blushed. He patted her hand with his large one and chuckled nervously. Affection was guarded and rarely given or received here in the palace. But Esther's kiss on his cheek was one of the most precious gifts he had ever received.

Esther had been in the palace of women for seven months when she turned fourteen. The evening meal was a feast as usual, and Esther was placed in the position of honor beside Hegai. The girls sang and clapped when the desserts of sweet cakes appeared.

Esther smiled at Hegai and assured him it was one of the best birthdays she had ever experienced. But that evening she crept out onto the balcony and sat with her legs through the railing watching the fish swim lazily in the pond. She thought of birthdays past, sitting around the small but loving table of cousin Mordecai. Adinah's eyes sparkled with joy and Ruth smiled as Esther raved about her birthday cake.

Mordecai prayed a prayer of blessing over her every year. She could still feel his embrace, the brush of his beard against her face as he kissed her forehead, and the rich tremble of his voice as he said, *"Good night my princess."*

The Lord God had blessed her so much!

How could she be ungrateful? How? But despite her best efforts a sob burst out and tears shimmered their way down her cheeks.

Hegai stopped dead in his tracks. He looked up and saw the figure of a girl sitting on the balcony, her face buried in her hands. He knew it was Esther. His heart burned with the desire to comfort her in some way, but he did not know how. He had no daughter of his own, or even wife, thanks to his physical circumstances. He felt quite lost in this area.

A sudden memory, a snippet of a conversation a eunuch mentioned in passing flashed in his mind like a starburst.

"Esther of Susa is well loved by someone," the eunuch had said lightly. *"There is an aging man that comes to the gate every day and asks after her by name. Every single day for the last seven months he has come by."*

A language Hegai had never heard before washed over the garden. Esther's face was lifted toward the moon, a smile on her face despite the tears on her cheeks, singing in a strange language.

So, there was more to this Esther of Susa then met the eye. Hegai nodded. He would tell her of the man that asked after her every day tomorrow. For now, she found comfort in a song from her people, from her past. He turned and disappeared into the shadows, content to listen and wait. It was a long time before the girl rose and disappeared into her room, the silken curtains folding around her form as they fluttered in the evening breeze.

Hegai came to Esther's quarters in the morning. In the privacy of her living room, he told her of the man that came faithfully every day to ask about her welfare. Tears filled her eyes and she struggled to maintain her emotions.

"I understand this man means a great deal to you," Hegai said. Esther nodded.

"Could I, Master Hegai, could I get a letter to him? Is that allowed?" Her voice trembled with hope.

"Yes, we can get a letter to him. Have one of your maidservants run the letter to the eunuchs that guard the entrance. Be sure to give it to Tamerlan. He will remember who Esther of Susa is."

Esther smiled remembering the eunuch that had brought her into the court of women. He had seen her help the crippled girl back to her feet and had spoken of her kindness. He had been correct. Everything was noticed in the palace.

Esther sat down and wrote out a note for Anatu, one of her maidservants, to run to the front gate. She sealed the letter with a kiss and watched longingly as Anatu hurried across the garden and up the flight of stairs leading through the maze of passageways to the bright blue wooden door she had entered so many months ago.

It was the next morning when Anatu again ran to the eunuch, Tamerlan, that a letter arrived from Mordecai. Esther's hands trembled as she carefully opened the rolled-up piece of paper and read the familiar strong Persian writing of her dear cousin. He described Ruth's wedding and expected baby. But he did not use Ruth's Hebrew name. He chose instead only to call her "a friend" but Esther knew. Mordecai encouraged her to remain strong. Remain steadfast. *And remember, shine bright my rising star.* The words rang with unsaid devotion.

Every day, letters flew back and forth. Esther's joy increased knowing her cousin was well. So, the months passed and time marched on.

Esther watched firsthand the power of education. She saw understanding light up the faces of her dear maidservants. Arjana delighted in reading, her sharp mind and curious nature blossoming under Esther's tutorage. Esther discovered Anatu had the voice of an angel, her sweet soft tones lulling them all to sleep evening after evening. And so formed a little family of eight women, all brought together under loathsome customs and circumstances, but banding together, seeking comfort in each other's company and friendships.

Esther obediently hid the origin of her people, as she had promised to Mordecai. No one in the palace outside of the women's court considered Esther or cared to know her name. There were moments Esther longed to speak of her people, share her language, and communicate her heritage proudly as those did around her. But her love and promise to Mordecai, although she was separated from him physically, held her back. She swallowed down the desire and honored her cousin as she would a father.

Hegai carefully watched his charge, enjoying her progress as she grew in beauty, knowledge, and power. Esther was undeniably his favorite. She blossomed under his expertise. Her hair shimmered in any light and her skin glowed. She carefully followed his instructions and excelled in all the classes.

Daily letters flew between Mordecai and Esther. Mordecai shared sections of Scriptures and psalms in every letter. Esther's bundle, carefully tied in a silken ribbon, grew. She had the bundle of scrolls, her most precious of possessions, wrapped in the blue tallit, with the necklace and earrings, hidden deep in the plush pillows of her bed.

Her faith was strengthened, and she enjoyed her times of prayer. She could not share too much with her maidservants for fear of revealing her Hebrew heritage but slowly, one by one, each maidservant asked to join her in prayer all save Arjana. She shook her head and crossed her arms proudly, refusing to acknowledge a god that would care. But Arjana's loyalty to Esther was undeniable. Esther hoped she would never be presented with the choice as she, undoubtedly, would preserve Esther's life over her own.

The final month began. Esther's turn to come before the king was approaching. Night after night found Hegai in Esther's chambers.

"My Lady," he began. "You must remember to always approach the King on his right side, preferably with a pitcher of wine. He loves his wine, poured by his women. His goblet is the way to his heart. Of course, the cup bearer will be present to ensure the wine is fit."

"And always be gracious regardless of the tone of his voice. He likes yellow by the way. It is one of his favorite colors. Not sure why. Must be a story behind that! I will find out."

"Master Hegai," Esther laid her hand on his arm. "Are you stressed, Master?"

Hegai looked down into her turquoise eyes, wide with concern and merriment. He sighed as he contemplated his response.

"Esther of Susa," he began covering her hand with his large one as she still held his arm. "These days with you, caring for you as you prepare to go before the King, have been some of the most meaningful days of my life. I have found myself thanking Zorvan for giving me this past year. My only sin is having loved you too closely as a daughter of my own. I have taken pride in your achievements and find my heart has become tied up in your destiny."

"I find my soul trembles with fear for you even as you leave my care and enter the palace of women, among the concubines and princesses of our great King. Their envy will be aroused by your great beauty. Angra Mainyu will stir up strife, as so often is the case, and I fear for you. I fear you will be troubled by the unkindness and injustices of women who are not as generous as you, with their words and actions."

"If you are touched by Anahitay and are found in child by the King, even greater will be the jealousy of your fellow women of the harem. I wish I was present to spare you all this, my dear Esther." He covered his brow with his large hand in a hopeless move as if to try clear the thoughts that crowded his mind.

"Master Hegai," began Esther, her voice portraying a sense of urgency for him to understand her fully.

"Friendless I came to this palace, placed under your masterful care, and given every privilege granted to all the girls present. But here I am now, preparing to leave, blessed with your friendship and personal tutorage, served by seven palace maidens."

"You, Master Hegai, wish to protect me and I thank you. But I belong to another, the Almighty God. He cares for me and will walk before me. He is greater even then the Great King Xerxes, of who I am destined to be presented to. He will protect me even in the bedchamber of the King. He has the power to open the heart of the great King Xerxes, even so I may find favor in his Majesties' sight."

"I will be honest. My heart does tremble with anticipation, but it does not despair. I know He will care for me and give me favor even in the harem. Even there, I will find friends and teachers to help and shield me. If a child is given me, even in this I will find comfort and purpose."

Hegai sighed and smiled gently.

"Your faith does you credit, my Lady." He said patting her hands as she held his arm. "Shaashgaz, of course! It is into his care you will be set under after coming before the King. Shaashgaz is a friend and will care for you well, upon my recommendation."

He smiled broadly, his white teeth flashing in the lamplight. Suddenly he laughed his great bellowing laugh.

"Are you not the same girl that stood up to that spiteful Ashraf, even the niece of the great Memucan, trusted advisor to the King? And naked no less! Every inch a lady. You have restored my spirits once again, my precious charge. Now where were we, oh yes! Your hair! The King loves hair. Yours is exquisite!"

He snapped his fingers and Arjana was instantly at his side.

"Let's find a hair style we like then we must decide on a head piece."

A pleasant hum of unity covered the chambers as everyone worked together to prepare every detail of Esther's wardrobe.

Esther's mind was left to wander over Mordecai's letter she had received from Anatu's hand this morning. It contained the words of Solomon penned to his beloved.

"How beautiful your sandaled feet, O prince's daughter! Your graceful legs are like jewels, the work of an artist's hands. Your navel is a rounded goblet that never lacks blended wine. Your waist is a mound of wheat encircled by lilies."

"Your breasts are like two fawns, like twin fawns of a gazelle. Your neck is like an ivory tower. Your eyes are the pools of Heshbon by the gate of Bath Rabbim. Your nose is like the tower of Lebanon looking toward Damascus.

Your head crowns you like Mount Carmel. Your hair is like royal tapestry; the king is held captive by its tresses. How beautiful you are and how pleasing, my love, with your delights!"

"Remember, my daughter, in whose power you go before this gentile King!" Mordecai's exhortation reverberated in her mind even as she watched Master Hegai working with Arjana to master the perfect hairstyle.

"Your hair is like royal tapestry; the king is held captive by its tresses." How fitting was the portion of Scriptures Mordecai penned her. She smiled even as her heart pounded with anticipation.

Tomorrow she would go before the king, in the evening, after supper. She would leave her maidenhood behind forever. Her life would be forever changed, and she would face this king at last, face to face. No matter the outcome, the great God of Abraham, Isaac, and Jacob went before her. Her heart belonged to Him and Him alone.

Chapter 10
Esther Goes to the King

It was strangely quiet in the room. The setting sunlight poured in through the archway. Hegai's hand trembled for a moment as he lowered the jeweled headpiece onto Esther's head. His dark eyes were expressionless as he watched the maids clasp the necklace and settle the jeweled belt.

He dismissed the king's messenger when he arrived requesting the next girl to be brought before the king.

"This girl I bring myself," he said proudly. The messenger nodded and peeked up at Esther trying to catch a glimpse of her without being noticed. Esther took Hegai's arm. She turned to her maidservants, all lined up watching her with great eyes full of fear, wonder, and love.

"Thank you, girls," she said softly. "I will see you on the other side. Till then, I go in His strength." She looked Arjana square in the face at this. Arjana suddenly stepped forward toward Hegai.

"Let me come too Master Hegai!" she pleaded. "What if my Mistress has need of something during the night?"

Hegai shook his head. He laid a hand on Arjana's shoulder.

"There will be plenty to serve your Mistress with any of her needs," he said gently. "The King's chambers are no place for a maidservant. Await your Mistress's return. You will have plenty to do, in preparing her new quarters in the court of women."

Arjana nodded. Esther suddenly let go of Hegai's arm and hugged Arjana. The fierce little maidservant hugged her back in return.

"May your God go with you, Mistress," she whispered huskily in her ear. "May your God open the heart of the King to love you as no other woman in this world! This will be the prayer upon my heart till you return to me."

Esther's heart and eyes filled. Turning, she took Hegai's arm and without a backward glance, they left the room together bravely facing the future.

A great peace filled Esther as she walked down darkened hallways, past curious onlookers, and silent, armed guards. All strained to see the woman, veiled in a soft blue veil, rather plain for one of the girls going to see the king. But the way she moved, her hair peeking out from under the veil assured all she was very far from plain.

At last, the man and the girl stood before a curtained doorway.

"This is it, Esther of Susa," said Hegai turning to look at her face. "You enter this door as a maiden; you leave this chamber as a princess."

Esther looked long and hard at the curtained doorway. She nodded, not trusting herself to speak at that moment. She took a deep breath and stepped forward, slowly, reluctantly letting go of his arm. She turned as she drew back the curtains with one of her delicate hands.

"Thank you Master Hegai," she whispered. "Thank you so much for everything!"

Hegai bowed toward Esther.

"Go my daughter," he said, the depth of his love spoken in that moment. "You are already the Queen of my heart, my dear Esther."

Esther nodded and flashed him a smile, and then she slipped behind the curtain and disappeared from his sight.

Her heart pounded in her chest as her feet silently carried her down a short, carpeted hallway and into a dimly lit, small room. The room opened onto the roof of the palace.

Suddenly there was no cloth between her and the sky. The city of Susa rolled out in front of her in a beautiful sparkling spread. With a gasp, she glided out into the open air. The breeze hit her, toying with her veil. Esther could not contain herself. She lifted the veil and freed her face fully.

She took a deep breath of the fresh air gently blowing around her. It had been so long since she had felt this free, this open. The view from the rooftop was fascinating. Streets stretched out before her. Her eyes ran down them longing to see something familiar. It had been so long since she had seen the outside of the palace.

A beautiful noise hit her ears. She turned to look at the fountain, dancing over the sides of a towering ornate column, cheerfully splashing its way down a slight incline and finally disappearing over the wall. Delighted, she walked over to it and held out her hand to enjoy the refreshing splash on her hands. The wind finally caught her veil and it fell right off her head onto the ground, freeing her head totally of cloth. Her black hair shimmered in the moonlight. She smiled and looking up she slowly twirled around just enjoying the vastness of the starry sky above her.

It was only when she bent over to pick up her veil that she noticed him out of the corner of her eye. She froze, surprised to find him sitting on a bench watching her. Unsure of how to react she paused for a moment then slowly stood up, leaving the veil laying where it was. She respectfully lowered her head and walked toward him.

She was a few steps away from him when she stopped. She bowed low as she had been taught, keeping her eyes respectfully averted downward although she longed to look up at him. His feet where huge, she noticed. She could not refrain any longer and the silence was getting quite awkward. She squared her shoulders and began to questioningly raise her face.

"What is your name?"

Startled, Esther looked in the direction the voice came from. A small man sat on a little stool beside the king, a scroll in his lap, pen in hand. Esther remembered Hegai telling her of the king's enjoyment of meticulously detailing every event of his reign. Of course, he would document every encounter.

"Esther of Susa," she replied.

"Who are your people?" The scribe did not even look up at her.

"I am a daughter of Susa," Esther replied. The king turned his head fully to look at her. The scribe looked up from his scroll.

"Who are your people?" he asked again exaggerating the words as if she had not understood the question.

A sudden thought popped into her mind, and she calmly repeated her answer only this time in Egyptian. Now she had the scribe's full attention.

"In Persian please," he was notably rattled. The king's face pulled into a smile, and he chuckled.

"I wish to be known as Esther of Susa," replied Esther in clear Persian. The scribe looked up at Esther long and hard. He then looked over at the king who was smiling, watching Esther with interest.

"Who are your people?" this time the king asked. Esther carefully kept her head reverently bent even as he spoke with her.

"My people are those I find myself surrounded with, my King." Esther replied, her palms beginning to sweat. "This past year has taught me much about who my people are."

"How so?" The king asked uncrossing his legs.

"One's people are those who help a person grow, learn, and succeed, my King. They are not limited only to origin or land."

"Well said," The king stood up. Esther was thankful in that moment Hegai had told her of the king's great height. Esther was tall for a woman, but the king towered. His name, Xerxes the Great was a play on his height as well as his status.

"Esther of Susa," He repeated, looking curiously at Esther who remained standing still, head bowed. He walked around her looking at her with great interest.

"You interest me, "he said bluntly. "You are choosing not to tell me who your people are, and I find this fascinating. I am not used to wondering for long, especially in the presence of a woman."

The king gestured to the scribe who disappeared into a small doorway. Esther was alone with this huge man who looked at her with amused curiosity. Esther understood that very little was ever denied this man. Withholding information from him might be the single most interesting thing that ever occurred to him. She was mildly amused by this simple fact.

The king had still not allowed her to look at him. He offered her his arm silently. She took it. He walked her over to the edge of the garden.

They stood for a long moment looking out over the city, admiring the lights. Esther watched the water from the fountain run as a shimmering river cascading down the side of the terraced palace, plunging down and down into the darkness. The king seemed comfortable in silence, but Esther found herself growing more and more curious about this great man beside her, gently supporting her on his arm.

"My King," she finally gathered the courage to address him, not knowing what to expect.

"Hum," he replied appearing distracted or deep in thought or bored. Esther was not sure of which.

"What was the most interesting thing you saw on your travels during your campaign on Greece?" she asked the question bravely. How else would she get to know anything about him? Esther was a little stumped by his behavior. She had prepared herself for a sexual encounter and nothing more. A brooding man was not what she had anticipated.

The king turned to look down at her.

"Fancy you ask," he said. He looked deeply at her this time as if seeing her for the first time. "The most interesting thing I saw." He looked away, pondering his reply. A slight smile crept over his face as he remembered.

"I think I would have to say it was the darkening of the sun as I advanced toward Greece. It was daylight, with the sun high in the sky and suddenly a dark shadow was noted. The sun became so dark it looked as if it was twilight. The horses where restless, birds unsettled and silent. It lasted a full ten minutes, and then began to move off the sun. It was the strangest phenomenon I have ever seen."

"Of course, I was told, it was the sun setting on the Greek empire as we knew it. It was my sign of sure victory. Or was it?"

"What about the lions of Axius? What does a lion look like?" Esther's curiosity and excitement overtook her, and she let herself be herself. The king looked down at her surprised.

"You are well read," he said obvious admiration in his voice. "The lions, yes, the lions. They looked terrible attacking my camels." Here he chuckled. "One of my men brought me the body of one they killed as I was curious too to study this great animal. It looks like a house cat just much, much, bigger." He held up his hand and reached for Esther's hand.

"I held up his paw against my hand like this," The king lifted Esther's hand up against his. His massive hand dwarfed Esther's delicate hand. The king nodded and looked at Esther. "That is how my hand looked against that lion's paw!"

Esther smiled in delight her face tipping up capturing the king's gaze. He lifted his hand to her chin and turned her face so he could see her.

"Look at me," said the king at last. Esther lifted her eyes up, up his chest, across the royal crest tied around his neck, up his black beard, brushed with grey, up his strong mouth and to his eyes.

"You are indeed beautiful," he admired.

"Thank you, my King," she said a slight blush creeping into her cheek. The king's look changed, and he leaned down toward her. He stopped moments from her face a thought suddenly halting his motion.

"May I kiss you," he asked very gently. Esther met his eyes, black in the moonlight, for a long moment. She was a bit nervous to see his great face so close to hers. As he hesitated to ask her permission, her anxiety dissipated.

"I have spent a year waiting for you to ask me that, your Highness."

A strange courage coursed through her body, giving her strength. "My King may kiss me."

An eyebrow shot up over the king's right eye. He dropped his face and kissed her soft lips long and gently. Esther had to admit to herself it was not the worst thing she had ever experienced. Her body responded and seemed to know what to do.

She was very close to him when he lifted his head.

"I like you, Esther of Susa," he said looking down at her, holding her body tightly, close to his. He seemed surprised even at his own words.

"I am glad I can please my King," Esther responded.

A feeling welled up in her. It was not love. It was a pity almost; a pity for this man who had everything yet was so easily surprised by her. It seemed he had never met someone like her, someone who spoke the truth. Someone who did not lie just to please him.

Suddenly the king picked her up. Esther gasped, surprised. The king stopped and looked at her.

"Did I scare you?" he asked, concerned.

"You surprised me, my King. I am not used to being picked up."

The king threw back his head and laughed at this. He strode across the garden, Esther draped in his arms feeling rather helpless. The king was not only very tall but also strong.

"I like you," he said again, still chuckling at her honest reply. They were moving fast, and the wind suddenly blew. Esther shivered in his arms.

The king stopped and looked down at her.

"Do I scare you?" he asked shocked at the very idea.

"A little, my King," Esther replied. He paused for a long moment.

"I suppose I would," he muttered. He began walking again but then stopped and looked at Esther.

"Would you rather walk?"

"Yes, my King, I would rather walk." Esther responded honestly. The king nodded and gently set her down. He offered her his arm and Esther took it, walking quietly beside him toward the curtained rooms.

"Thank you, my King."

He made no response but did turn to look at her, walking willingly beside him, leaning on his arm. He held up a curtain for her to enter and they walked down a carpeted hallway with flickering lanterns on either side. The hallway emptied into a large bedchamber, surrounded with curtains. Roses were generously tossed on the rich tapestries of the bed.

Thankfully there was not a servant in sight. Esther felt they were quite alone. It was an odd feeling to suddenly be all alone with a man after being only with girls and eunuchs for so long. She had never experienced any of this in her life but spent a year preparing for this one night. She knew he was no stranger to women, yet he seemed mildly awed by her. She just had to trust she would be OK. He had not hurt her and seemed careful not even to scare her.

He was focused now on what he wanted. Esther just let him lead, following his guidance. He was fascinated by her hair and took his time stroking it. It made him smile, watching it shimmer in the light. He was gentle and respectful. Occasionally, he would stop and look deeply at her.

"You are so beautiful," he repeated as if fascinated by it. Esther was surprised. He saw many beautiful women. What was it that he was seeing? She did not know the answer to that. She found herself folded in the great blankets, enjoying the smell of the rose petals around her. She tried to please him as best she could with her inexperienced body.

At last, they lay still and quiet, nothing stirring around them. She lay there not knowing what to do or think when suddenly a noise startled her. The king lay stark naked beside her, his arm draped over her abdomen, fast asleep, snoring softly.

The vulnerability of him sleeping there beside her, without a piece of clothing on his great body, struck a chord in her. Carefully as not to wake him, she pulled a blanket over them both. The king stirred but did not wake. Esther felt tired herself. The night air was cold and fresh. She turned toward his sleeping form, enjoying the warmth radiating off his body. She closed her eyes and thanked God she was unharmed. It was all over, and she hoped she had pleased her king.

It was light out when she awoke. A male servant stood staring at the bed in surprise. Esther jumped a little and pulled at the blanket, very aware she was still naked. Another man servant came in and startled to see the king still sound asleep with Esther beside him.

The servants began backing out of the room but not before the king opened his eyes. He smiled when he saw Esther looking back at him. His arm tightened around her, and he snuggled into her chest, his lips brushing against her skin.

"I'm glad you are still here," he said closing his eyes again.

"My King had not dismissed me," Esther responded. He smiled his eyes still closed. The servants looked greatly uncomfortable and almost tripped over themselves to get out of the room.

Esther thought the king had fallen back to sleep when suddenly his stomach rumbled loudly.

"Esther, my dear," he said. "Have you ever tasted coffee before?"

"No, my King," she admitted. "Shall I serve you some, my King? I have only read about it."

"No no," said the king, his arm tightening around her. "My servant will get some."

As if by magic the man servant materialized beside the bed with a tray and a cup. The king rolled over and finally let go of Esther, sitting up to get his cup of coffee.

"Javad, your manners, get the lady a cup as well." The servant nodded and hurried out. He seemed quite frazzled. The king took a long sip, sitting up against the pillows. He looked over at Esther, curling up as not to let her chest be exposed if the blankets pulled away. The king smiled and held out his cup.

"Try it; I want to see if you like it." He handed her the cup. Esther took the steaming cup looking at the black, frothy liquid. It smelled strongly but good. She put the cup up to her lips and took a small sip, willing herself to enjoy it.

The king leaned over the side of the bed and grabbed a robe off the floor. He turned to Esther.

"Lean forward my dear," he said gently. Esther sat forward as the king gently wrapped his robe around her shoulders.

"Thank you, my King," she said sincerely, enjoying the security of clothing, touched he cared about her discomfort enough to help her.

"Well," he asked watching her face intently.

"I think I like mine with sugar and cream," Esther replied. The king chuckled taking the cup from her.

"I did at first too," he assured her. "It is an acquired taste to be sure."

Javad appeared again with a cup. He seemed to have collected himself a bit, and had both cream and sugar prepared. He carefully mixed them together in the cup of coffee and handed it to Esther.

"Thank you," said Esther as she took the cup from his hand. Javad smiled slightly.

"How did you sleep, Sire?" he asked.

The king smiled and looked over at Esther.

"It was one of the best sleeps I have ever had," he admitted.

Esther returned his gaze in surprise. The stories about the king and his dreams were true. Was it not a dream or apparition that had convinced him to invade Greece to revenge his father's death in the early years of his reign? The king's sleepless nights were well known around the court.

Was it so unusual for the girls to be with the king all night? Esther tried to begin to understand Javad's surprise. Could it be that the king never fell asleep with a woman in his bed? That he would dismiss them long before?

Esther wondered when he would dismiss her. But till he did, she was sitting with the king's under shirt wrapped around her shoulders, sharing his morning coffee with him. Another manservant came in and began to read through the schedule for the day. Esther listened with interest, curious as to how the king would fill his day.

Suddenly the king threw back the covers and rose to his full height, undisturbed by his nudity. His servants seemed use to his behavior as well. Javad helped him into a robe. The king casually wrapped the robe around himself as the servant continued reading the day's planned schedule. The king moved toward the door once the servant was finished.

In the doorway, he suddenly stopped. He turned and looked back at the bed. He handed his cup to Javad waiting beside him so abruptly the servant almost dropped it. He strode across the room and stood beside the bed towering over Esther. He cupped her face in a great hand and bending down, kissed her lips.

"Come back tonight?" he asked softly, looking full into her face.

"I would be honored, my King," Esther responded.

He nodded and kissed her again.

"Good." He hesitated a moment, not wanting to leave her. At last, he stood back up with a slight groan and strode out of the room.

"Javad, bring Esther back tonight," he said as he disappeared out the arched doorway.

Chapter 11
Esther Meets Banu and Shaashgaz

A couple of eunuchs hurried into the room. Esther recognized them as eunuchs of the women's palace by their dress. They assisted her to put on her jeweled slippers. Esther slipped out of the king's undershirt into a day dress brought for her from the court of women. Once she was ready, the eunuchs and Javad escorted her back through the maze of hallways, across a courtyard, to the court of women, the harem, her new home.

Arjana stood just outside the doorway anxiously watching for her mistress's return. Her face lit up as she saw Esther approaching. Javad took a long glance at the delighted maidservant, joyfully watching the return of her mistress.

"I will come for you as the King wishes," he said awkwardly, a blush splashing his neck red. He seemed uncomfortable in Arjana's presence. They stood at the entrance to the women's palace. Armed eunuchs stood at the doorway. No uncut man could enter except the king, not even Javad.

"Thank you, Javad," Esther said softly. "I will be ready."

Javad nodded and hurried off down the hallway.

"Mistress!" Arjana ushered Esther through the entrance, into the palace of women, into a different world, her new life. The great wooden doors closed behind them, and the rasp of the bolt being drawn sounded faintly. Were the doors bolted to keep all in or all out?

Esther gasped as she stepped inside. The floor was glistening white marble with gold veins running through it. The passageway opened into a brightly lit breezeway overlooking a huge common room. Sunlight streamed in the windows; silken curtains fluttered in the breeze. A huge marble fountain stood in the center of the room. Every were she looked, the décor was colorful, romantic, and feminine.

118

Rich ornate decorations covered the walls, some made of gold, others of carved wood painted in bright colors. Women walked about wearing the most beautiful gowns Esther had ever seen. She looked about her in wonder as the maids, all with big smiles, escorted her along the breezeway, down another hall, around a corner, up a flight of stairs and down yet another hallway.

A eunuch stood beside a doorway, watching for her. He smiled and bowed as she approached. His face was scarred, his head shaved bald, and his ears appeared to have been damaged long ago. He smiled widely at Esther, showing a hole where a front tooth had once been.

"Do not be alarmed at my appearance, My Lady," he said with an Egyptian accent. This explained his shaved head.

"Forgive me, I was taken in battle and fought for my freedom before being captured and brought here to serve my King, the Great Xerxes." Esther nodded to him, hearing again the familiar story of war, conquest, and pain. It was a narrative she was getting more and more use to hearing.

"I am Shaashgaz, the King's eunuch who cares for all the women and concubines of our Great King. I am honored to meet you, my Esther. Hegai has sent me explicit instructions ensuring your greatest comfort and continued education. You will find, my Lady, your life here under my care to be most comfortable and instructional. I am at your service. Anything you need, don't hesitate a moment to ask me."

Esther returned his bow with a deep nod and smile. She reached out her hand to Shaashgaz.

"My dear Shaashgaz, I am delighted to meet you. My dear friend, Hegai, has seen to all my comforts. I am deeply grateful and am welcomed. I am encouraged to know I have friends here in the court of women already."

Shaashgaz nodded, his bald head shining in the natural light shifting through the lattice of the open arched windows.

"I have assigned a lesser concubine to you, Esther of Susa. Her name is Banu. I believe you will find her of great comfort and guidance as you transition from candidate to concubine, unless, you have found favor and the King places the crown on your head and makes you his queen wife."

"Master Shaashgaz," she said, relief rushing over her. She let out the breath she did not know she was holding in a rush. "I am so glad for this. The King has asked me to return tonight and I so wanted, I so hoped for, advice. Master

Hegai helped me with everything last night. Now, I'm here with you and I don't know everything I should do."

Shaashgaz's eyes grew large.

"Again? Tonight!" he exclaimed, clasping his hands.

Esther nodded.

"Is that normal?" she almost whispered.

Shaashgaz cast his gaze about suddenly aware of just how public their conversation was in the open breezeway of the women's court. A few of the women were looking their way but most carried on their daily tasks, undisturbed. They were used to the steady stream of new faces, morning after morning.

Shaashgaz ushered Esther into the door of her new apartments.

"You will have a chance to look around later," he assured her. "But for now," he snapped his fingers. "We have work to do! Asked to return to the King's chambers for a second night." Another eunuch hurried over to him who was hovering a slight distance away.

"Quickly now, people. Future bride of our King in the making."

People started rushing around. A tall, beautiful woman with deep brown eyes as dark as the king's coffee and a wealth of thick brown hair, dressed in a beautiful dark green velvety gown was beside Shaashgaz in a flash.

Esther liked her instantly and soon knew her to be Banu, the concubine Shaashgaz had assigned to her. Esther could see a few greying hairs and slight wrinkles around her eyes, especially when she smiled.

'I wonder how long she has lived here?' the thought flashed through her mind. But, as Shaashgaz reminded everyone who was in the main room of her new apartments, there was much to do.

"I will design and create a gown for you, Esther of Susa," Shaashgaz explained to her as he walked about her. "Allow me to take a few measurements if you don't mind." A measuring strip appeared in his hands, and he was already busy. Esther stood quietly and followed his instructions.

A eunuch followed him closely carefully documenting the measurements he called out.

"A theme, I need a theme," Shaashgaz was all business now. His dark eyes lit up and he snapped the fingers of his right hand as he spoke. He looked at Esther's eyes and nodded.

"Tonight, we ask, we demand. We are bold. We have already found favor. Tonight, we wear yellow!"

He smiled then and bowed to Esther.

"I will leave you with Banu and your maids to see to your needs, Esther. I will now go and make you a gown fit for a queen."

Esther nodded, amazed at the man's confidence. She looked at Banu as Shaashgaz swept from the room, a trail of eunuchs behind him.

Banu laughed at the shocked and amaze look on Esther's face.

"Do not worry, dear child," she said. "Shaashgaz is an amazing tailor. He will make a gown unlike anything you have ever seen before. Now, let's get some food into you before you faint away!"

She smiled into Esther's face encouragingly. Her look was so mature and nurturing suddenly emotions overwhelmed Esther. A tear slipped out onto her cheek. Arjana was beside her in a flash.

"Oh Mistress," she groaned.

Esther let out a sob. Banu slipped her arm around Esther's shoulders.

"Hush now!" the older woman soothed. Esther sobbed again confused as to why she even felt this way. Shouldn't she be delighted? Instead, she felt lost and confused, conflicted and helpless.

"Hush my beautiful child," soothed the woman. "It gets easier with time." A note of profound sorrow crept into her voice.

"Is it normal he wants me back again tonight?" The look that passed over Banu's face told Esther it was anything but normal.

"Girls, step out for a moment, could you? I need to talk with your Mistress, alone." The girls hurried out, Arjana looking back over her shoulder questioningly at Esther. Esther nodded and she was left alone with the older woman.

"What is it my child," she asked gently. "Tell me what it is troubling you?"

Again, the tears came.

"I don't know how I feel about him!" Esther burst out. Banu laughed almost bitterly and folded the girl into her arms.

"Of course, you don't," she soothed. "You just do as you're told! Making love to the world's most powerful man doesn't feel much like a choice."

Esther sobbed again.

"That is what I don't understand!" she cried. "He asked me and was kind about it, but I don't know if I love him or not! I always dreamed I would love my husband. This man is not even my husband, yet I am to know him. I don't know how I feel about him."

Banu rocked Esther gently as she sobbed against her. At last, Esther stopped. She sank back, tired. She had not slept well, careful not to move too much, careful not to wake the sleeping man beside her. She was hungry and felt very alone. She wanted to go back but there was no place to go back to. She kept seeing this hugely tall man in her mind's eye, vulnerable and powerful, terrifying, and helpless all in the same look.

What on earth was happening to her? She wanted to protect him in the same moment to never see him again. Yet, she wondered how he was at that very moment? What was love? What did it feel like? Would she ever be able to talk openly with this man? Would she ever feel safe with him? What if she made him angry? Had she pleased him last night?

Banu watched her face, gently stroking her hair.

"You have no idea what you have done, do you?" she asked her suddenly. Esther turned to look at her, confused.

"You have just made the King fall in love with you. Being invited back to his bed before leaving it is a great honor none of us received. It was an honor afforded to his former queen."

Esther sighed and then smiled.

"Very well," she said softly. "I will accept the honor." She looked up at Banu.

"I am assuming you were with him too if you are here in the palace of women." It was a statement not a question. The words hung between the two women for a long moment even as the bees buzzed happily from trumpet to trumpet of the Morning Glories climbing the lattice covering the window.

"Yes," Banu nodded. "I was young; your age and beautiful."

"You still are beautiful!" Esther gasped out. Banu laughed and shrugged.

"Beautiful and unused." She smiled sadly. "It is not just beauty that he is looking for."

Esther nodded her eyes suddenly downcast. She was now used, discardable, vulnerable.

"I only went once, and I never had a child. So here I am, alone and waiting. I have been here now for ten years." A slight sigh escaped the older woman's body like a wish.

122

"It is wonderful. Very comfortable really. But lonely. I am glad you came along and Shaashgaz assigned me to you." Banu's arms tighten around Esther, and she cradled the younger girl's head against her chest for a moment.

"I feel I can do you lots of good. I feel we will be dear friends."

Esther's eyes lit up. She grabbed the older woman's hands in her own.

"My God sent you to me to encourage us both!" She exclaimed the realization making her giddy with delight.

"I made Him a promise as a little girl, and He has led me here. He is the one that has brought us together and I am so glad. Oh Banu! You have gladdened my heart so! I have found friends even in this place, even in this moment. My heart rejoices."

Banu pulled Esther close and hugged her so tight it almost hurt. But a great peace fell over them as they comforted each other, drawn together by similar circumstances. At last, Esther raised her head to investigate Banu's beautiful soft face. A glow had crept into her deep, rich dark eyes and her cheeks had a flush they did not have before. Hope had crept back into her heart.

"Do we have any coffee?" Esther suddenly blurted out and Banu laughed, her eyes dancing.

She is as beautiful as my mother, Esther thought in that moment. *How the Almighty knew I would need a mother now*!

"Let us get you some breakfast," Banu explained and instinctively kissed Esther's forehead. The two parted and Banu opened the door. Arjana and the other maids were all standing there waiting.

"Breakfast!" Banu ordered. "And coffee!" The maids smiled and away they went. Arjana hurried to Esther's side just to be sure.

"I'm OK, Arjana," Esther assured her. "I just need to eat and get some sleep."

The maids, Banu, and Esther all gathered sitting cross-legged around the breakfast spread.

Esther let her eyes wander over the beauty and comfort of her new apartments. She smiled as she saw all the scrolls stacked carefully on a shelf near the window. A breeze laden with the smells of lavender, jasmine and mint rustled and fluttered the white silken curtains. The sound of splashing water from a fountain somewhere in the garden outside mixed with happy voices, floated in. Somewhere a woman was singing a haunting, beautiful tune.

This was the palace of women. This was now her life. She looked back at the pile of scrolls. The great God had brought her this far, He would carry her through!

Sleep called with its gentle caressing fingers. Esther's eyes shut as soon as her head hit the pillow of her new bed. Nothing could keep her awake now, not even racing thoughts and new apartments.

It was later in the afternoon when Esther awoke. The maids were about their chores, laundry, and baths. The apartments were silent and still. Esther felt that the whole world was paused, holding its breath, waiting as she was. Waiting for that moment she would see the king again, see his smile, hear his voice, feel his touch.

Her bare feet were silent on the deep Persian rugs. She wandered across the living room area and through the arched doorway. A covered walkway led out overlooking a small private garden. The fountain stood in the middle splashing merrily as it bubbled over its white sides and playfully spilled into a small pond. She wandered out across the grass, enjoying the unfiltered sunlight on her face. Esther looked up. The great palace walls towered up around her.

An unsettled sensation suddenly flooded into her chest. Was this to be her life? To ready herself at a moment's notice for the whims and lusts of a pagan man, an uncircumcised man, who made no effort to obey the laws of Jehovah? He proclaimed himself a god, knowing no humility or restraint. Her eyes slid shut as shearing guilt and shame tried to burn through her. Her mind cast about trying to find something to cling to, something to anchor itself to, a truth, a hope.

"*Oh, Great God of our Father Abraham!*" the prayer of that helpless hurting child tore again from her heart, her face raised up to the sky, her knees buckling under her. "*Save me! I will be Yours forever. I will be Your servant till the day I die.*"

The fluffy white clouds moved restlessly overhead. The deep blue of the sky gazed down at her as if wishing to impart some great wisdom. Did she, she, the cousin of Mordecai, a daughter of Benjamin, possess the strength to stay the course the great God of Israel had placed her on? Did she have the courage to go again to the king and do all that was asked of her? To what end? Would he really place the crown on her head, choose her above all the other girls, and make her his wife, his queen, his confidant?

Memory stirred Mordecai's words to her, *"No longer shall you be called Hadassah but let us call you Esther. For the Lord our God will guide you as a star in the night sky. You will shine brightly for Him all the days of your life. You will bless all you touch even as you have blessed your cousin's wife, Adinah, and I, more than seven sons."* His voice echoed in her head, his love reverberating in her heart.

"Hadassah!" he spoke her given Hebrew name. *"Obey my voice all the days of your life. You have obeyed me as a father. May our God bless you for your obedience, child. May He protect your going ins and your coming out."*

She set her face and took a deep breath. Her God, the God of Abraham, Isaac, and Jacob, the God of Racheal, Sarah, and Leah the forgotten, had called her, Esther of Susa, to charm the heart of a king, to serve him with her body, to request to be his wife. And she had given Him, the King of the Universe, her life, her body, and her heart. She would be obedient even in this task He laid before her.

A psalm flashed through her mind. *"You have turned from me my hurting into dancing; you have put off my sackcloth and clothed me with gladness, to the end that my glory may sing praise to You and not be silent. O Lord my God, I will give thanks to You forever!"*

King David had penned these words of praise so long ago when the Lord had given him promises that seemed impossible. With God all things where possible, even this. A familiar peace swept into her heart as the breeze played with her curls.

The Almighty had set her on this path that led her to meet Banu just when they both needed each other the most. With every turn, He provided a new friend to help her through. With every overwhelmingly new situation she found herself in, He had already provided a guide, a touch that she would recognize as His hand. How could she be sorrowful if He went before her? Her pathway was illuminated with His love and His hand carried her through. She may be trapped physically, but she was loved deeply.

She could hear her maids coming, laughing, and talking as they hurried back. Arjana burst into the garden, troubled to see her mistress kneeling on the grass. Esther turned and greeted them with a smile even as tears shimmered on her cheeks.

"Come girls!" Esther sang out. "I need to start getting ready for tonight. One must not keep a King waiting."

These words sent the maids into action. A bath was drawn. Arjana was busy pouring and measuring spiced oils and perfumed potions into the water. Esther's apartments smelled of wealth and passion.

Arjana smiled as Esther stepped into the bath.

"You will be irresistible!" she said with a mischievous smile. Esther laughed.

"No one has a maid with your skills, Arjana!" she said. "I am definitely blessed."

Arjana smiled at her mistress's praise.

After Esther's body was oiled and perfumed, her hair shimmering with brushing and care, a knock came at the door. Anatu jumped to open the door and a smiling Banu swept in, followed by a eunuch bearing a beautiful yellow gown draped in his arms. Shaashgaz was right behind him followed by other eunuchs carrying bundles and bags.

Shaashgaz himself assisted Esther expertly into her gown, taking care not to expose her at any moment. The gown fit her like a sleeve, every seam expertly accentuating her beautiful body. Shaashgaz walked around Esther, his hands clasp in front of him, a look of pure delight on his face.

"Yes, yes, yes!" he muttered. "Hegai was right on yellow. Perfect! Absolutely, perfect! Esther, my Lady, look for yourself."

She walked over to the large, polished silver mirror. A reflection stared back at her. The golden yellow gown hugged her body. It streamed off her, accentuating her hips, buttocks, and breasts. It was elegant, modest, yet very, very flattering. It was unlike any article of clothing she had ever seen before. And it was beautiful. There was no denying it. She turned from the mirror and looked at Shaashgaz, tears brightening in her eyes.

"Shaashgaz, you are a genius!" she burst out, walking toward him, and throwing her arms around him. He stiffened, unsure what to do with her outburst of affection. Slowly he softened and awkwardly pattered her shoulders.

"There, there, my Lady," he fluttered. But Esther saw the gleam in his eyes. "You must put on the head dress. Yes, yes. Banu, the headdress."

Esther had to sit down again so Shaashgaz could place the headpiece over her mass of black, shining hair. All in the room stood back and looked at her once he was finished.

Arjana was the first to break the silence with a gasp.

"My Mistress," she said in a reverent whisper. "You look like a queen!"

Esther rose and turned to the mirror. Even she could not recognize herself. Gone was Hadassah. Gone was sweet, innocent Esther. Before her stood a woman, dressed and ready; ready to take the hand of a king and sit down beside him on a throne; a woman ready for a crown and the king's bedchamber.

Esther stood and looked at the image that stared back at her for a long moment. If only Mordecai could see her now. If only Adinah could see her at this moment. What would she say? She had been so adamant that the palace was no place for a daughter of Abraham. What would she say if she saw her this moment, her beautiful body draped for a man not her husband, her hair uncovered, a headpiece on her head fit for a queen, or goddess, or sex slave? What was the difference?

Esther raised her hand and covered the left side of her chest. She could feel her heart beating under the yellow silk. The difference was this. Her heart belonged to the Great God Almighty. A man could touch her body, but no one could touch her heart. She was His and only His. And He had led her here for this very moment.

She turned and faced all those who stood there, watching her with fascinated interest. Here she was surrounded, by a roomful of people who were all supporting her and helping her reach this goal, this moment, and this truth.

"My going ins and my coming out." She repeated Mordecai's last words of encouragement out loud, under her breath in Hebrew. A smile spread across her face, and she sighed.

"I am ready."

Banu and Shaashgaz nodded. Their eyes met for a moment. They had just witnessed a girl become queen. The maids all stood around, unsure of what to say or do.

But no messenger had come from the king, yet. Ready or not, Esther had to wait. To appear before him unsummoned was punishable by death according to Persian law. The room was still as Esther stood waiting, trying to calm her nerves. It was dear Arjana who spoke up. She came and stood beside her mistress.

"Can we pray together before you go, my Lady?" she asked softly. Esther smiled and turned to her. Wordlessly she reached out her hand.

"Arjana, what a wonderful idea."

The maids all gathered beside Esther as they knelt in a line, facing the window, facing Jerusalem. Each girl lifted their faces and prayed for their mistress's protection silently. Banu and Shaashgaz stood and watched in respectful silence.

Chapter 12

A Second Night with the King

As if on cue, a knock came at the door. Shaashgaz himself opened the door and there stood a eunuch.

"The King's man, Javad, comes to summon Esther of Susa to the King's chambers," his eyes widened at the sight of the beautiful girl standing waiting.

Esther moved forward and everyone followed her. As they walked back down the breezeway, Arjana moved up beside Esther. Her hand slipped over and squeezed her mistress's. Esther smiled and squeezed back.

The heavy bolt was pulled back by the armed eunuchs at the entrance of the women's palace. The door glided open, and Esther stepped through with only Shaashgaz and Banu following. The maids waited and watched.

"Good evening, Javad," Esther greeted him with a smile. Javad stood for a long moment almost gaping at the beautiful woman in front of him. He bowed. He did not know what else to do.

"If you please, my Lady," and he turned to lead the way. Esther turned and raised a hand in parting to her maids. Banu moved up beside her and Shaashgaz took her other arm. Together they hurried after Javad's vanishing back, poker straight, the back of his neck flushed.

Esther noted the difference in the reaction of all they passed in the hallways. The guards did not peep curiously at her. They stood in frozen solemn silence, their eyes staring straight ahead. Servants moved to the side and bowed as she passed.

She was grateful they did not pass any free men or nobles or courtiers. She was still only a concubine, a girl who had found favor enough for a second night with the king. She was still to be hidden and covered, only for his eyes, an unspoken, unacknowledged figure of the workings of the palace; obediently meeting the sexual needs of a man denied nothing, a means to create a staggering number of heirs all jostling for the throne.

It was a relief to finally reach the carpeted hallway leading out through the curtains to the open-aired garden that led to the king's bedchambers. Banu gently squeezed her hand as she silently instilled strength into Esther, her eyes willing Esther to succeed. Only Shaashgaz and Javad led her on toward that heavily curtained doorway.

At the door the two men stood to the side, and each lifted a curtain edge. Wordlessly, Esther passed through. Javad melted away, and Shaashgaz moved up beside her.

Together they stepped out into the garden. This time Esther's eyes did not fixate on the fountain. She looked past it and saw her king sitting on the bench. He was looking away, over the side of the balcony, looking out over the city. He looked very relaxed; his face soft and wrinkled in the dancing light from the torches. He looked tired and old, worn, and weathered. His head was bare, and, in his hand, he held a goblet.

Javad materialized beside him and spoke to him. The king turned and looked toward the doorway. He watched the shadowy figure of Shaashgaz and Esther moving silently across the lawn toward him. He did not look at Shaashgaz at all. His gaze was fixed on Esther as she moved toward him.

After a long moment, the two stood before him in the light of the torch. Each bowed. Shaashgaz spoke first, stepping forward and gesturing toward Esther.

"I bring you Esther, oh my King," he said bowing low.

"So I see, Shaashgaz," said the king looking at Esther with interest. "So I see." Esther stood with her head respectfully bowed, suddenly feeling shy. She felt too exposed, too vulnerable, like she was openly asking for something. It was not hidden or subtle.

"Is this one of your gowns, Shaashgaz?" asked the king. Apparently, Shaashgaz was known for his talents.

"It is, my King!" The pride crept through Shaashgaz's voice. Esther smiled even as she remained looking down.

"Look at me, Esther," the king commanded softly. It was not a request. Esther swallowed hard and raised her face. She lifted her eyes and looked right into his. His expression was unreadable. He met her gaze for a long moment. A slight smile crept across his face, and he handed his goblet to Javad.

"Shaashgaz," he slurred his name slightly. "This time you have outdone yourself." Shaashgaz blushed at the king's praise.

"Thank you, my King." His head bobbed up and down in a couple deep bows.

"Now leave us."

Shaashgaz nodded and backed away still smiling. Javad began to back away, but the king snapped his fingers.

"Is it all ready, Javad?"

Javad nodded. "Yes, my King. Ready exactly as you requested."

"Good," said King Xerxes and he stood up.

"Esther," he held out his arm to her. "Come. I have something to show you but first, I must eat." Esther took his arm and allowed herself to be led over behind the fountain. A table was spread out and prepared for a meal. The king led her to a couch and lay down on it. Esther stood for a moment not knowing what she was to do.

"Sit with me, Esther," the king patted the couch in front of him.

Esther sat and looked down at him, waiting for his next request. She remembered his schedule that the servant had read off this morning. He must be hungry and tired after such a day. She bent forward and picked up a plate. It was heavy, made of solid gold with embedded jewels. She began placing a portion on the plate for him, not knowing what he liked or preferred. He watched her every move silently. He did not hide his obvious enjoyment of watching her.

Once Esther was satisfied, she turned back toward him. She moved across the couch closer to him and held the plate. The king's eyes never left Esther's face. He began eating and Esther took note of what he ate and did not eat. She poured him another goblet and held it waiting for him to reach for it.

"I have a surprise to show you," he said at last. Esther smiled. She was unsure of how to proceed. Her mind searched for a clue of what to do. The memories of Adinah speaking with Mordecai when he came home from his work at the king's palace burst into her mind. Did she dare just speak to the king about his day?

"How was your day, my King?" she asked glad he had broken the silence and seemed open to talking. The king stopped eating for a moment.

"My day," He repeated thoughtfully. He seemed surprised by her question. "My day…it was exhausting really. This uprising is proving to be a challenge.

The Egyptians want more grain, and the army wants a pay increase." He looked old and tired again for a long moment. His look changed again, and he appeared surprised he had told her so much.

"But surely you don't want to hear of these matters. Matters of state bore women, do they not?"

Esther met his gaze for a long moment.

"They can." She acknowledged remembering poring over scroll after scroll of the political history of the Persian Empire. "Or a woman can comfort and ease the head and heart of the man of whom she asks the questions."

Again, that right eyebrow shot up.

"Are you such a woman as to attempt to ease the heart and mind of a King?"

"My King," Esther leaned closer to him. "I am here to be such a woman as you have need of."

The king was silent. He seemed thoughtful for a long moment. Then a smile flashed over his face, and he sat up. He stood up off the couch and pulled her up with him. Esther hurried to place the plate on the table.

"Come, I have something to show you." He repeated. He led the way across the garden toward his bedchambers. Esther had to hustle to keep up with him. He held back the curtains for her to enter then led the way to his bedchamber.

There, stretched out on the bed was a huge lion skin. Esther gasped. The king chuckled.

"I had them dry the skin." The king explained. He picked up the paw to show Esther. "Your question last night reminded me of it. I had it brought in to show you." He seemed pleased with himself. It struck Esther that this man never thought of anyone but himself. This was a touching gesture to be sure.

"I thank you, my King!" said Esther sincerely, stepping toward him. "Seeing it does satisfy my curiosity. I can now say I have seen a lion; albeit a dead one."

The king chuckled even as he wrapped his arms around her. He kissed her long and hard.

"You are beautiful tonight, my Esther," he murmured huskily. He was focusing in on her again. But suddenly, he stopped. He seemed confused or unsure of himself.

"What is it, my King," Esther asked. "Do I displease you?" The king shook his head; his hands on her body seemed anything but displeased.

"Esther, how does a man show his affection to a woman?" he asked suddenly. "How does a man court a woman he loves? How does a King ask for the heart of a woman?"

"He could try just asking her," whispered Esther.

The great Xerxes paused for a long moment, his head bowed, his dark, expressionless eyes staring deeply into the turquoise eyes of the girl in his arms.

"Would you, Esther? Would you agree to be my Queen? Would you stay by my side? Would you ask me about my days regardless of how boring and long they are? Would you let this selfish heart try to find room to love you?"

Esther was struck with how vulnerable and boyish his request was. This man had been married before. He knew how to charm a woman, did he not?

No, how could he? His marriage to Vashti was a political move. She was a princess; of course, she would be married to a king. This man had never asked anything of a woman in all the years of his life. And here he was, asking her; asking her if she would be his queen, stand beside him, listen to his days, and love him despite his selfishness. Would she? Could she?

Her eyes gazed into his as he stood over her waiting for her response. This is what she had waited for, was it not? Was she prepared to accept this man as her husband? Was she prepared to serve this man with her life? Was she prepared to obey and honor him as a husband? Was this the life the Lord had planned for her? Mordecai had blessed her. Hegai had told her the king would be a fool not to choose her.

Esther smiled as that deep familiar peace again washed over her.

"Yes, my King," she said gently. "I will be your queen. I will serve you as best I can with all I do. I will stand beside you. I will come when you summon me. I will comfort you with my body and my mind. I will love you."

The king smiled down at her. He seemed touched by her response and just looked at her for a long moment. Then he kissed her.

"Stay with me all night?" he asked his lips brushing hers as he asked.

"Yes, my King." Esther replied.

Next morning Esther awoke, and the king was gone. The bed was empty. She was shocked and hurriedly sat up. She looked over and beside her, on his pillow was a single flower. A ribbon was tied around the stem with a beautiful ring on it. A letter lay under it. She picked it up and eagerly opened the letter.

"My dearest Esther," it read. His writing was not the neatest in the world, Esther noted with a smile. *"Please accept this ring as a symbol of my desire to wed you. I could not sleep for my racing thoughts, but you were so peaceful beside me I had not the heart to disturb you. Sleep well, my princess.*

Your loving,
Xerxes."

Esther closed the letter. She looked at the flower, the ribbon, and the ring. She gave her head a bit of a shake. The king had asked her to be his wife last night. She was now engaged to the king. What had she done? She smiled. The better question was what had God done?

She slipped out of bed and noted a pair of slippers and a robe from her closet carefully placed beside the bed. She smiled again.

She was now the betrothed of the king. She did not want to leave his chambers, quiet and shameful, only a night fling. She chose to put on the exquisite gown she had arrived in, minus the head piece. It was much harder than she anticipated, getting the long row of intricate clasps done up her back but at last she succeeded. Once she was robed and gathered her things, Esther turned to go.

There stood Javad as always, appearing just when needed. This time he bowed even without the king present. Two eunuchs hurried in and quickly picked up Esther's things, taking everything from her hands except the flower, ring, and letter.

"Come, my Lady," said Javad. "I will escort you back to the women's palace."

They were crossing the garden when Xerxes appeared, striding across the lawn toward them. Javad melted away as the king hurried to Esther. He looked down at her hands still holding the flower with the ring tied to the stem with the golden ribbon.

"Does the ring displease you, Esther?" He asked in surprise.

Esther shook her head.

"Not in the least, my King." She said and handed him the flower, with the ribbon and the ring. "I could only take such a treasure directly from the hand who gives it."

At this, the king hesitated a long moment. Esther waited, watching him. Slowly, he untied the ribbon and pulled off the ring. Looking in her eyes he reached for her hand and slowly slipped on the ring. He looked down at the ring, glittering in the morning sun, on her beautiful slender hand.

He looked back up at her, a big smile pulling on his face, his eyes flashing brightly.

"Thank you, Esther of Susa, for agreeing to be my wife," he said sincerely before kissing her deeply and openly. He lingered just looking at her, seeming torn, reluctant to leave but pulled away by invisible strings.

"I won't see you till we wed, my dearest." He groaned a little. He did not touch her, just stared at her, his face only inches away. "One night away from you is too long. I have only just found you. I will call you once all is ready, my dearest, my promised. I will call you to the court and place the crown on your head."

He laid his big hand on her head, her hair shimmering in the morning sunlight.

"From that moment on, you, Esther of Susa, will be my wife, my queen, my love."

Esther smiled into his face at those words. Very gently she laid her ringed hand against the large chest in front of her. She felt his heart beating under his robes, decorated with a golden necklace, jewels sparkling in the morning sunlight as he breathed.

"Go, my Lord, to whatever demands your attention." she said gently. "I will come the moment you call me. I will be ready regardless of the hour. My heart will leap at the voice of my husband."

This gentle promise hung in the morning air, spoken softly, intimately. The king raised his hand to cover Esther's still laid against his chest. He pressed it there as if to hold those words inside for a long moment. At last, he lifted her hand to his lips and kissed the fingers and the ring. He backed away with a slight bow, his eyes holding hers for a long moment.

He turned and strode off. Esther watched him cover the garden with his rapid pace. She noticed a group of robed men looking at her from across the lawn and realized she was no longer an invisible figure in the palace. She was now a pawn in this political chess board. She was the nobody everybody was talking about. Suddenly shy, she turned and hurried toward the doorway, willing Javad to come.

He appeared before her, as if reading her mind. He held the curtain open for her and followed her, guiding her gently with a word or two through the maze of passages. The guards stood at attention as she passed. No longer was she Esther of Susa, an insignificant, concubine girl slave of the king, she was now the Queen-to-be, the king's betrothed, a true princess.

Chapter 13
A Marriage

She breathed a huge sigh of relief as the doors of the court of women came into view. The doors stood wide open, and Arjana practically pulled her into the passage leading into the court of women. She led her down the breezeway at a furious pace.

They burst into her chambers almost breathless from walking so fast. Esther stood there, the flower clutched in her hands, a love letter written in the king's own personal hand clasp against her heart, a ring worth more than anything she had ever seen, on her finger, and her dress halfway undone in the back because she had missed a few clasps. Banu was there with all the maidservants, a smile always playing about her face, her brown eyes dancing with joy.

A huge bouquet of roses, all red, stood on the floor in the big living room. There was no table big enough for it to fit on in Esther's entire apartments, so the eunuchs that delivered it had just placed it on the great Persian rug in the middle of the room.

Esther burst out laughing. There was nothing else she could do. She laughed at the sheer, extravagant, ridiculous, over-the-top, gesture of the king. Of course, he would send her so many roses she could barely get around in her own living room. Banu joined her as did the maids. They all stood and looked at the huge arrangement.

"It took three men to bring it in," Anatu finally blurted out between giggles. "And even with that they barely made it through the doorway."

This set off a new round of giggles. Esther raised her ringed hand to wipe away the tears that squeezed out onto her cheeks for laughing so hard. Her other hand covered her stomach, sore from so much mirth.

"What is that on your hand, Mistress?" nothing escaped Arjana's sharp eyes. All faces were suddenly serious as they all looked at Esther's hand as she stretched it out for all of them to see. Banu inhaled sharply and was the first to drop down, her head bowed.

"No!" cried out Esther moving toward her. "Don't bow to me! Please!" she dropped down onto her knees and threw her arms around the older woman.

Banu slowly embraced her. The maids all dropped onto their knees and looked on, the significance of the ring on Esther's finger beginning to sink in. They were now the maids of the new queen of Persia.

"Your God, Mistress! Your God answered my prayer!" Arjana's deep, dark eyes met Esther's. The bitter conversation that first night so long ago in the palace of women again hovered in the air between them. Over a year later they sat, hugging, a ring on her finger and a crown waiting for her head.

Shaashgaz burst into the room an army of eunuchs with him.

"A wedding gown!" he cried. "A wedding gown for my Esther. Today we dress a queen!" And with those words, Esther's apartments became a crowded cheerful place. The roses had to be moved and finally were pushed out into the covered courtyard of the garden so there was enough room for bolt after bolt of cloth to be laid out, held up to her face, admired and stroked, then piled to the side.

It was later that day that Esther sat down and wrote out a letter to Mordecai. She smiled as Anatu silently took the letter from her hand and carefully placed the blue scarf over her head. There were tear stains on the paper as Esther wrote of her wonderful news, news that sealed her fate with that of the palace.

Once crowned and married, Esther could move about more freely, see who she wanted to see, write to who she wanted to write to. But she must be careful as well to not let it slip who she was. Now everyone would be monitoring her every move. Now more than ever, she must hide so much, hold back her language, people, and faith. She would now mingle with nobles, princes, and advisors. She would become an instrument of influence, someone close enough to the king to request, persuade, and even know things.

A note arrived from Hegai. Esther smiled as she read it. She was so happy Hegai had learned to write in her school of maids. He rejoiced in her appointment, delighted in the king's good taste. And so it began, the love story of a lifetime, the delight of many a household in Susa. A girl no one knew anything about was suddenly the talk of the entire palace.

It was in the silence of the night that Esther slipped off her bed and knelt by the window facing Jerusalem and poured out her heart to her God. Fear gripped her so hard she could only shake and sob quietly in the bath of moonlight shining in.

"Jehovah God," the teenage girl pleaded. "I am but a woman, a girl. I cannot enter that palace, that bedchamber, as the King's wife, unless you come with me. How am I to hold his favor? How am I to love this gentile man?"

Peace flowed through her even as the prayer rolled off her lips.

"Your word is a lamp for my feet, a light on my path. I have taken an oath and confirmed it, that I will follow your righteous laws." (Psalm 119:105, 106).

Rapturous worship filled her as she knelt, her eyes closed, tears slowly streaming down her cheeks. Of one thing was she sure, God had placed her there for His purpose and His purpose alone. Only in His strength could she carry on, day after day, week after week, month after month, year after year, for a lifetime.

The next days passed in a flurry for Esther. She felt as if she was an onlooker, watching things happen to someone else. All her things began to be moved to her new apartments; the apartment's vacant since Queen Vashti left them in shame. In the mist of it all, Mordecai sent her a note.

"My Princess, My Queen," was all it said and that was enough. She treasured it, rolling over the words in her mind, remembering the sound of Mordecai's voice. He used to call her his princess, so long ago, around the warm candlelight of their home on the quiet shaded street of Susa.

The moment arrived. Shaashgaz had performed a brilliant feat and created a gown with a train so long it took three of her maidservants to hold it up. Her veil was a shimmering mass of jewels, sown meticulously into the lace. The dress itself was a rich, mint green, intricately embroidered with gold thread and studded with jewels. Its weight was shocking as it was placed on her body. The veil was also a matching green lace and flowed down the back and over the dress. The embroidered edging was all done in gold and jewels. Esther had never seen anything so beautiful in her life. The maids stood around her exclaiming repeatedly over its beauty while Shaashgaz stood back and beamed his delight.

The color only heightened the turquoise of Esther's eyes. Banu applied the black makeup to her already dark eyelashes. Shaashgaz coached Arjana to also apply a light greenish shadowing on Esther's closed eyelids.

"The Queens of Egypt did this to exaggerate their eyes and heighten their beauty." He explained. The effect was stunning. Crimson paste was added to her lips. Esther was draped in a thick, wide, heavy gold necklace and huge cascading earrings. She looked every inch a queen ready to be presented to her king.

The trumpets blasted at the entrance to the palace of women. The concubines lined the breezeway cheering and tossing flower petals on the white marble floor. Javad and an armed band of the king's own royal guard waited at the palace entrance. It was time. The king was summoning his bride.

Esther turned and smiled at Hegai. Her grip tightened on his arm. Banu and her maids were all dressed in white gowns, tied with green sashes, matching her gown. Shaashgaz was dressed in his best tunic and looked fabulous with the typical group of eunuchs around waiting to do his bidding.

"Are you ready my Lady?" Hegai whispered.

"Thanks to you, Master Hegai, I am."

She needed the strong, gentle arm of the eunuch who had taught and prepared her for this moment.

"Then let us go. The King calls and we must not keep him waiting." Hegai assisted her out the door and moved up beside her. He felt the tremors of her body as they walked. The breezeway was covered in rose petals. They softened the footsteps and crumpled up in the train of her gown.

Javad's face lit up into a smile when the great wooden doors of the court of women swung open. Esther stood, veiled, surrounded by her people, her team. Javad bowed low and the royal guard banged their spear handles on their shields. Esther blushed at the loud show of honor given to her.

Javad led the way, a trumpeter with him. The royal guard fell in beside Esther and her procession forming two lines as they escorted her to the court room of the great King Xerxes. The trumpeter raised his horn and blew loudly. Esther could hear the cheers coming from inside the king's court. The great gates slowly swung open. She lifted her face and looked down the long red carpeted walkway leading to the steps. Up those steps, on a raised platform, stood the throne. Her groom, the king sat on that throne, awaiting his bride.

Everyone instinctively paused and waited for a welcoming gesture from the king. Persian law dictated all who approached the king uninvited would die on the steps leading up to the throne. The hall hushed as all waited. The king rose and smiling, he lifted out his golden scepter, gesturing for his bride to come to him.

The trumpeter sounded with a great blast and Esther stepped on to the carpeted hallway that Mordecai had told her about, so many years ago. Now it was her turn to make that long march to the throne. Hegai's arm was strong. Esther found herself leaning on him for strength.

"Courage, my Queen," he murmured under his breath.

The king watched her every step. She moved gracefully through the space separating her from the steps.

"*May He bless your coming ins and going outs...*" Mordecai's voice played in her mind as she walked forward toward the throne.

"*For you are my rock and my fortress: Therefore, for Your name's sake lead me and guide me...*" David's psalm was the silent prayer of Esther's heart as she continued, step by step.

King Xerxes looked magnificent. His imposing figure was robed in green silk, almost lost in the gold embroidery, jewels and pearls that enriched his tunic. A jeweled knife hung by his side, tucked under the golden belt around his waist. The crown of Persia stood proudly over his great brow, his dark hair in oiled curls, spilling over his broad shoulders. His eyes flashed as he watched his veiled bride make her journey toward his throne.

Courtiers, princes, and noblemen hushed as they sat or stood, watching the veiled woman walk toward the king, on the arm of a eunuch. A few whispered her name as they wondered among each other who she was, whose daughter was she, who where her people, what would be her political preferences?

Esther did not cast her eyes to the left or to the right. She did not seek Mordecai's face from among the scribes. She fixed her eyes on her job, her position. She was to stand beside this great man as his queen or die on the way. That and that alone was her calling, all others had to come second. This is what her God had requested of her to do.

Hegai and Esther reached the stairs. The royal guard stopped and turned inward toward her. She bowed low, her forehead brushing the second stair. Then she looked up, way, way up, into the king's face. He smiled down at her and stood, towering majestically over her. Slowly he raised up his arm and stretched out his scepter. The jeweled tip flashed in the afternoon sun, causing a gasp to ripple over the silent courtroom.

Under the welcoming cover of the scepter, Esther slowly let go of Hegai's arm. She could see his smile flashing at her from the corner of her eye. She kept her eyes on her master, her king.

"Go, my Queen," the soft, deep voice whispered beside her. "May your God bless you, oh favored of women."

Esther lifted the front of her gown. She placed her jeweled slipper on the great marble steps. Gracefully, she stepped up, covered by the king's scepter, between the row of guards that stood on each of the ten steps leading up to the platform the throne sat upon. Each one of those guards stood with drawn swords, glistening in the sunlight, ready to cut down any who dared to approach the king uninvited, even his betrothed.

Time seemed to stand still as the tall, slender, figure ascended the stairs toward the king. At last, Esther neared the top. The king, still smiling, stepped down two stairs in one stride and reached out his hand, supporting his bride as she ascended to the top. She stood before him, smiling behind her veil, her eyes turned up to his face.

Total silence fell over the court room. Every face strained to see what the king would do next. Slowly, he lifted the thick, green veil, glittering with clusters of jewels. The sunlight sparkled around them, rainbows of colors dancing off every surface. The courtroom gasped in wonder. Never had a bride been so beautifully adorned for her husband. The king lifted the veil oh so slowly.

The thick laced cloth fell away from her face. The king lifted it and tossed it theatrically aside, as chuckles and laughter filled the room. Esther waited, her face upturned toward his, her long black hair streaming down her back. Even from behind, all could see that the queen was indeed a most beautiful woman. Without his eyes ever leaving hers, the king reached for the crown, held by an elegantly dressed man on a beautifully embroidered cushion.

The room was so silent, even the scribes held their pens, poised to document the exact moment that crown touched Esther's brow. A true fairy tale was playing out right before their eyes. A romance fit for the empire of the known world; a king's heart stolen by an unknown girl.

Slowly, Xerxes the Great lowered the crown onto Esther's head. His large hands trembled slightly as he carefully placed it onto her brow and over her thick, black curls. His pinkie finger caught in her hair, a shimmering black strand sliding across her face. Esther raised her hand to right herself, but he beat her. Her hand covered his as he gently brushed it away. The crowd erupted in screams and shouts.

Esther smiled, her hand still covering his as he cradled her face in one of his. His face was soft and open making him look young again. His smile widened with the shouts and cheers of all the spectators. He lowered his face and kissed his bride, long and sweetly. Slowly the king straightened. He gently placed his hands on Esther's shoulders and turned her to face his courtroom.

"Behold!" his voice boomed throughout the room. "I present to you, my Queen, Esther of Susa!"

Esther let her eyes wander over the crowd. A sea of faces greeted her, all cheering and throwing flower petals. She looked over at the scribes and a familiar face met hers. Mordecai stood, his hands clasped against his heart, tears of joy and pride streaming down his face unchecked.

Tears filled Esther's eyes and her smile widened. Her body shuttered. Her husband felt her emotions and a strong hand gently supported her lower back. Comforted Esther blinked back her tears and lifted her hand in a greeting. Mordecai raised his back toward her.

The king turned and sat down on his throne, a huge smile on his face. Esther stood till her husband was seated then sat on the throne next to him. As soon as she was seated the king waved his hand. A trumpet blast followed, and a great hush fell over the hall again.

"It pleases me," he said loudly. "To declare this day a holiday in all the provinces of the great empire of Persia. On this day no man, no woman, nor child, or even beast shall be made to work! We shall feast in honor of my Queen, Queen Esther of Persia."

There was a flurry of trumpets. Suddenly, with a great clatter of hooves, the riders galloped out of the waiting courtyard on white stallions bearing the seal of the king. The king's decree was out! His word spreading across the provinces as fast as the fastest horses could run. The hall erupted in cheers. The king reached out his hand toward Esther, smiling; she nodded her crowned head and gave him her hand. He raised it to his lips and kissed it, his beard tickling a little.

Shouts of praise and *"long live King Xerxes, long live Queen Esther"* echoed in the hallway as the couple rose. The king and queen descended the staircase together, hand in hand. The king stopped Esther at the bottom and kissed her dramatically much to the delight of the audience. Esther blushed with his playful display of affection.

The couple walked down the long carpet Esther had previously walked alone. It was a very slow walk as the king greeted everyone of any importance. Esther's head was swimming by the time they made it to the end. She met prince after prince, advisor after advisor, general after general. Name after name floated around her. She was delighted to finally see the faces of all the names she had pored over, evening after evening, in her room in the court of women.

Memucan did stand out to her. She knew who he was. He was the very advisor who had set this whole plan in motion, presenting girl after girl to the king till a new queen was chosen. Esther knew she was not his choice, looking into Memucan's face.

She also met Artabanus, head of the king's security and dear friend to the king. Only slightly shorter than the Great Xerxes, Artabanus was never far from the king's side, a faithful shadow carrying a great sword.

No one could deny the happiness of their king. His face radiated his joy and his long looks at his queen satisfied many that the right choice had been made. This beautiful young woman, standing gracefully by their king's side, dressed like no woman had ever been dressed before, looking every part a queen, seemed the perfect solution. The kingdom had a queen, now a holiday and feast had been declared. Who could be sad on this day?

Somehow Mordecai muscled his way up to the edge of the carpet. Suddenly Esther was looking into his kind grey eyes, shimmering with pride and joy. She gave him her hand and he kissed it, his tears falling freely onto her skin. Esther lifted her fingers and gently brushed away the tears from one of his cheeks. The king stepped forward, noting how this man clung to his wife's hand. His hand covered Esther's and her husband drew her hand away from the man who was her father. Mordecai smiled even as Esther's eyes filled with tears of her own.

"Our God has not forgotten us," Mordecai's words were lost in the noise to all but Esther. Her face split in a huge smile even as her husband wrapped his arm around her, drawing her away from the crowd. Protocol must be followed, always, even by the queen. She must obey her husband. Mordecai's face was soon lost in the sea of jostling people. Esther's eyes never stopped searching for another glimpse.

Once out into the courtyard, the king helped his bride into the royal carriage pulled by four white stallions. The carriage ride through the streets of Susa was a tradition for the citizens to all see their new queen and great king. They cheered and showered the road with flower petals. Blessings were shouted to the royal couple in every language and tongue of the great, sprawling empire.

At long last, the king led his bride down the carpeted hallway, across the garden, toward his bedchamber. Esther was exhausted. She had not eaten or drank much at all. There was food everywhere, but everyone wanted to talk with her and congratulate her. Many touched her hand and kissed her fingers. She found she could not lift a glass to her lips or eat much more than a grape or two before someone else was asking for her attention. The king on the other hand seemed to have no problem finding plenty to eat and drink. She noticed he drank liberally of wine and frequently bellowed out a toast in her honor.

There she stood in the king's bedchamber as his wife. He pulled her close and kissed her. When he lifted his head, Esther looked up at him.

"My Lord," she said gently. "I am so hungry."

The king stopped and looked at her for a long moment. Slowly it seemed to dawn on him that he had not seen his wife eat much at all.

"Oh, my Esther," he said. He backed away from her. "Come with me, let's get you something to eat, my dear." He led her out of the room back to the garden where she had served him his meal. Javad was just finishing laying out a meal.

"Sit, my dear Esther."

Thankfully, Esther sank onto the couch. She watched in awed silence as her husband filled a plate with food and then brought it to her couch, kneeling beside her to watch her eat. Suddenly he shook his head.

"Water, she needs water," he looked up at Javad and nodded sharply. He quickly poured a bit into a small cup and tasted it. He then filled a golden goblet and handed it to the king.

"Thank you, my Lord," said Esther gratefully. She drank her fill and ate enough to curb her hunger.

Then, her husband proceeded to surprise her further.

"What was your favorite part of the day?" he asked, truly interested. Esther smiled. A million moments flashed through her mind but only one stood out to

145

her. She lifted herself up on the couch and slipped her arm around the king's neck.

"Now," she said smiling, leaning so close to him, her forehead touched his. Her husband needed no further encouragement. He lifted her up off the couch and carried her to his bed, his wife, his queen.

So passed a beautiful month as the king delighted in his new bride. He tried hard to please her; usually ending in Esther laughing with delight. This made Xerxes smile, a rare experience for him indeed. His courtiers and servants, princes and advisors all noticed how happy the king was with his new queen and the palace, the city, and the empire rejoiced.

Chapter 14
Esther Learns of Palace Cruelties

Esther stood in front of the huge, polished bronze mirror, framed with gold and jewels creating elaborate designs. It stood on a stand built of oiled cedar in the corner of her dressing room. Today she must look especially beautiful.

Today was the birthday feast for her husband, the great King Xerxes. He loved to gather his extensive family together, enjoying the company of his sons, the princes, all jostling for his attention, his wife, the queen, with his favorite concubines and wives of many of his children all gathered around him in an elaborate and gilded display of his wealth, power, and prowess. This evening was her first as the queen, the favored wife of the king.

"You look stunning, my Queen," Arjana assured her as she finished off the touches to Esther's hair.

Banu floated in from another room, her arms full of fresh cut flowers.

"Was that ever even in question?" she cooed, smiling as she looked at Esther. Their eyes met in the mirror and Esther flashed a quick smile as her cheeks colored slightly. She was dressed in a rich golden, yellow gown. Crimson threads created an eye-catching contrast, embroidering a rich pattern along the hem, sleeves, and neckline a gift from her ever generous husband.

Banu, with her bubbling personality of happiness and her instinctive wisdom had quickly become Esther's palace mother. Daily Esther praised God for sending her Banu to help and guide her through becoming a woman, then wife, queen and finally friend of her husband.

Cheerful chatter filled the queen's apartments as the maids prepared her for the feast. Anatu hurried in.

"Mistress, a eunuch by the name of Hathach is here. He requests to deliver a message from the King to you."

"Send him in."

A tall, very tall lean man with shining dark skin walked in and flashed a row of white teeth. He bowed so low his forehead seemed only to miss the white marble floor by a hair's breadth.

"Oh Queen," he said still smiling. "It is my great pleasure to inform you that the great King Xerxes has sent me to you, to serve your every need as fast as my feet can move. He asks that I embody his generosity and remind you of his continuous thoughts toward you, oh favored Queen."

Esther smiled.

"I welcome you, Hathach."

Hathach bowed again. He drew a silken bag from his satchel secured around his waist with a thick leather belt.

Anatu stepped forward and took the bag from Hathach's hand. She brought it to Esther.

Esther smiled as she took the bag from her maid's hand. She carefully opened it and gasped in wonder. A bracelet made of pure, blood red rubies glittered in the sunlight. It matched the crimson embroidery on her dress.

"Queen, it matches perfectly!" Arjana exclaimed. "I was wondering what you should wear with this gown. This is perfect."

"Thank you Hathach." Esther said. Arjana clasped the bracelet on Esther's right wrist. After a bit of discussion, all other jewelry was removed. Esther wore only the new gown, her bracelet, and the ring the king gave her as promise to be his wife. With a last look in the mirror, Esther nodded. The crown was placed on her head. She rose.

She was ready to meet the king's family as his wife, the queen. Anatu announced that Javad was at the doors with a group of royal guards and eunuchs. The king was asking for his wife to meet him, and enter the dining hall with him, at his side. The familiar wave of nerves coursed through Esther's body as she stepped forward. It still surprised her that the king would request her presence and bestow such favor toward her.

The king was standing just outside his apartments waiting for her. He looked up hearing footsteps coming from the direction of the queen's apartments. He always looked so tired initially then his face softened as he watched the beautiful woman approach him. His eyes took on a sparkle they lacked before as he watched his wife approach.

She met his gaze with a smile then bowed her crowned head to her husband and king. He stepped forward and reached out for her hand. He drew her toward him in a sudden gesture and the servants and guards melted away behind them. He held her at arm's length looking over the dress, the crown, the face.

"Oh, my Queen Esther," he said still just looking at her. "What a sight you are for sore eyes. If only my advisors and ministers looked as beautiful as you do this evening."

"My King," Esther replied her eyes sparkling. "It is your generous gifts that make me so beautiful for you this night."

The king sighed gently and pulled her to him for a kiss.

"Come, let us be marry now." He said. He put his arm around her shoulders and held her close as they walked toward the banquet hall. Just before they entered, he stopped and laid his face against her hair. It was in these silent moments that Esther felt her heart stirred with sheer pity for this man that had everything yet still craved a moment of encouragement. She always wondered what passed in those brooding dark eyes as that tired look flashed over his ageing face. Then he turned to her and smiled at her.

"You give me strength, my queen," he said. And the two walked into the banquet hall together.

All together the banquet hall held about seventy people, all talking and laughing. All the princes rose when the king entered, his queen on his arm. A hearty cheer rose and shook the hall as the sons greeted their father. The king nodded and smiled.

He went up and hugged his eldest son, Crown Prince Darius. Next, he greeted his third son, Prince Artaxerxes. Once the formal greetings were over and the king was settled on his couch, the feasting began in earnest. Through the course of the evening, Esther found herself speaking with Prince Artaxerxes. He was the third son of the former Queen Vashti. He was a young man, full of life. He looked much more like his father than the crown prince.

"Thank you for making my father, the King, so happy again," Prince Artaxerxes spoke out.

Esther was surprised he spoke so frankly. He bowed to her and kissed her hand briefly before moving away into the crowd. Esther instantly felt she could trust him. She did not have the same reaction with Crown Prince Darius, who looked at her briefly. He had an entitled air and treated those around him as lesser than himself. A shiver ran down Esther's spine even as she smiled and greeted him, and he bowed slightly to the crown on her head.

The banquet was a huge success. After supper, the king rose from his couch slightly tipsy from drinking to every toast to his health. Many of the princes had already passed out or had stumbled out of the dining hall, finding beds and women to finish off their evening.

Esther's eyes lifted and met her husband's gaze. She smiled slightly and he nodded. She crossed the hall to him and took his arm. It was a thoughtful jester. In this way, they stabilized each other. Artabanus materialized with a group of armed guards. Javad and several eunuchs were with them. Esther noted Hathach among them, a long dagger hanging from his belt.

"I have a surprise for you, Esther," the king said as the group walked down a hallway.

"But it is your birthday my King," said Esther. "I should have a gift for my king."

"You are my gift," he said simply. "And sharing in your delight when I surprise you is your gift to me."

Esther was now curious. The king's gifts were never that predictable. They walked down a long, gently sloping, walled garden walkway. Esther had never been in this part of the palace before. A sound met her ears, like water lapping against wood.

The roof of cedar ended, and the moon shone down on them bathing the world in silvery light. A few more steps and Esther found herself on a wooden wharf overlooking the river. She turned and the palace towered behind her. She remembered the roadway sloping downward toward the river when she and Mordecai came to the palace of women. He had told her that the palace was built right into the riverbank, allowing river access as well as land.

A boat rocked itself as the small waves rippled under it. Silken curtains waved a greeting and a soft light invited one to enter. Esther gasped as the beauty of the moment struck her.

The king chuckled needing no more encouragement. He strode up to the drawbridge. He turned and extended a hand to help her onto the boat. It took a moment for her body to adjust to the rolling movements of the boat. The king led the way through the curtains her hand still clasped in his.

The world shut off behind them. The silken screen closed behind them. They crossed the boat to the other side. A bed covered in rich crimson silk with golden embroidery looked out onto an unobstructed view of the water, the riverbank, and the rising ridges and mountains off in the distance, all bathed in moonlight. The stars burned in the night sky; the breeze blew away any fatigue. Esther turned from looking out, a smile of sheer delight on her face.

The king had already taken off his crown and outer robe, sighing as he brushed his hands through his hair. His dark eyes lit with desire as he watched her.

"Do you like it, Esther?" his voice took on a husky tone even as he came toward her. She waited for him, letting the question hang in the air.

He came to her and stood right in front of her looking deep into her face. Still, she did not answer. He sighed again and looked up over her shoulder at the view. The noise of the water splashing against the side of the boat was the only music or noise. She could almost hear his heartbeat. Waiting was not what the king did well. She could see the fire growing in him.

He growled a bit and folded his arms around her.

"Tell me you like it," he demanded, playfully squeezing her tightly.

"My King, it is magical." Esther admitted, snuggling into his embrace. She could feel his smile of satisfaction through the muscles of his chest. They stood a long moment clasp tightly in each other's arms.

"Come on, my Queen," the king mumbled into her hair.

Esther struggled to stay awake longer after the king's deep rhythmic breathing joined the gentle splashing of the waves. The night was just so beautiful. It was a magical dream, shimmering back at her from the water, this life she now lived. But every dream is tested, with time and reality.

Esther woke with a start. The rhythmic rocking of the boat and the gentle lapping of the waves against the wooden hull reminded her of the magic of the night before. She sat up smiling. She looked over at the pillow beside her, still indented from the king's head on the shining silken case. But it was empty. The king was already up and slipped out silently as to not arouse his sleeping wife. She gently touched the pillow with her hand, a gentle sigh escaping her body.

A maid Esther had never met before bustled into the room. Her face lit up when she saw Esther awake and sitting up.

"Oh, my Lady!" the maid exclaimed. "You are beautiful. I can see why you were the King's birthday fling."

Esther was shocked. She stopped what she was doing and stared with her mouth gaping for a long moment. The maid was busy about the room and did not even look up.

151

"This reminds me," she continued as she plumped the pillows, her breasts shimmering under her dress so great was her effort. "Queen Vashti was beautiful too, dark, and stunning. She was as cruel as she was beautiful though. A servant girl once made a minor error, forgot to turn the bed or something," the maid shrugged and smoothed the bed out as if she herself was fixing that error.

"Anyways, the queen had her breasts cut off in her very presence. Rumor has it she enjoyed the process. She was a witch all right. No wonder she was so beautiful. Probably bathing in blood or something terrible like that to keep her youth. Wouldn't put it past her. She really had it out for the Jewish girls though."

The maid shuttered at her own story. She was expertly gathering anything she could in her arms. She looked over the room in satisfaction and finally turned to Esther, who had dressed herself, standing dumbstruck in horror, tears sliding slowly down her cheeks.

"What became of the maidservant?" asked Esther, trying to cover her emotions. Was this a reason why Mordecai had forbidden her to reveal her people, her race, and her genetic heritage? He was saving her life, her body, and her dignity.

"Oh, she was thrown to the men to have as they pleased. No one has seen her for a year or two now. Rumor has it she fled the palace, or possibly she fell on the sword of one of her lovers. What does it matter anyway? The world is better off without those Jews around anyway."

At this, Esther's eyes flashed, and her cheeks flushed. She had to grit her teeth to contain her anger and she turned abruptly for the door. If she did not leave at once, she would reveal her secret in her wrath, breaking the promise she had made to Mordecai.

She stumbled out of the boat and onto the wooden dock. The world had lost its magic. The moonlight was gone and replaced with the scalding hot summer rays. The royal guard was gone. Javad was nowhere to be seen, busy beside his king. She seemed alone and forgotten.

She looked up at the huge palace walls towering above her. How was she to find her way back to the court of women, to those wooden doors with bolts and guards, to Arjana and Anatu? How had she been put in this position? Hot tears rushed to her eyes and frustration rose like a fire in her.

Elegantly dressed people wandered along the river's edge. A few paused to look at the woman standing on the docks, unsure of what to do. Most just carried on. A horse or two whinnied to each other and stopped to drink at the river's edge, their grooms chatting happily to each other. A world she did not belong to any more carried on around her, outside of the palace walls. It had been so long since she had just people watched in the streets, curious and unseen.

A tall figure moved quickly catching her eye. He was coming toward her, his long legs carrying his body quickly across the paving stones. Relief coursed through her. Hathach! Her man the king had given to her only hours ago had been standing watching and waiting for his mistress all this time.

She burst into tears of relief and covered her face to keep from showing too much emotion. She felt his presence close to her.

"My Queen," he almost moaned as he knelt to her.

"Oh Hathach, I'm so glad to see you!" Esther exclaimed reaching out her hand to him. "Please take me back to the palace of women. I'm lost and I don't know the way."

"My Queen," Hathach's voice was calm and soothing. "You are never alone and never lost. I am always watching."

The maid came looking for the beautiful girl she had been speaking to. She gasped as she realized that this girl was the new queen, the teen bride of the king.

"My Queen!" the poor girl gasped, falling hard to her knees on the wooden dock and lowering her face to the planks. "Forgive me, your Majesty, I did not recognize you."

Esther turned back to the maid. Many thoughts dashed through her mind. But she paused and chose her words carefully.

"I understand you did not recognize me as the Queen, the King's wife." She said gently. "But spread kindness not hatred and you will never need to be ashamed of yourself in the presence of anyone."

The maid did not even lift her head.

"Yes, my Queen!" she gasped. And turning, Esther left her. Hathach, her man, her eunuch, a few steps behind her, a sword at his side, his gentle voice guiding her skillfully through the passageways and back toward the palace of women and her chambers.

Her mind struggled to understand and digest what she had just heard. Mordecai had told her the history of the Hebrews since her childhood, entering his home as an orphan. She knew her people were hated and persecuted because they were chosen by the Most High God and separated to Him to be His people, but! To hear it, to see the nonchalant way the girl spoke of the horror done to this poor Jewish girl astonished Esther. Was abuse like this continuing to happen in the palace?

Once back at the palace of women, deep in a bath, Esther was free to ask Arjana more about the happenings in the palace around her.

"Arjana," Esther finally spoke fearful of what she would discover. "What does happen around here?"

Arjana looked at her mistress sharply.

"What you see, of course," she replied, a bit too quickly.

"No Arjana," Esther said shaking her head. "I need to know. I need you to tell me."

"There is nothing to tell, Mistress." Arjana insisted trying to look busy, desperately trying to find something to do.

"Arjana!" Esther spoke sharper than usual. Arjana startled. Esther reached up and took the girl by the arm, holding her still.

"Tell me your story, Arjana," Esther begged her softly. "Tell me what has happened to you since you came to the palace."

"I told you of my capture, that day I was taken from the side of the river." Arjana began, realizing Esther would not rest till she was satisfied. "I was taken with a group of other girls to a large house in a city somewhere. We did not know anything. We were totally isolated from all we knew. We were trapped just by ignorance alone of the place we had been taken too. All I know was it was a port city, with lots of noise every time a new ship sailed in."

"There were lots of slaves there, captured from all over the world. The sailors were rough, and many people died on the ship. I remember the smell of rotting flesh blowing through the windows at night making some of us vomit. It was a most dark and horrible time."

"I quickly learned the best way out was just to do a good job. I hid my emotions and tried hard. I spoke the language they forced us to use, and I did all they told me to do. I learned quickly not to be caught in a room alone with men. Bad things happened to those girls. It was sad."

"Overall, I was a lucky one. The African mud made me strong. I never forgot the feeling of that mud between my toes. I knew where I was from, free and proud, living along the riverbanks. It was eunuchs that purchased us from the markets. Hundreds of us. It was a marvelous day once we arrived at the court of women and Hegai took over our care. The sexual abuse stopped as we were surrounded by eunuchs, and we were allowed to work in peace."

"I had been in the palace only a week when you arrived, assigned to my room. I had no idea what to expect from you."

She turned to look at Esther. Esther sat stone still in the bathtub; her arms wrapped around her to protect her even as she listened intently to Arjana.

"But now I have the honor of serving the courtliest of all Queens that ever sat on a throne." The tone of her voice pleaded for Esther to turn and smile and say all was well and good and happy. But Esther turned to look at Arjana, her great eyes blazing with blue-green passion, her lips quivering with emotions.

"This is not right." Her statement sounded like an understatement. "This is the palace of Susa, the greatest empire in the world! There must be better here. There must be better!"

At that moment, Anatu hurried in, her dark blue eyes bright with excitement as she bore a letter for her mistress. She stopped startled at the look of anger and frustration on Esther's face. Arjana looked at her in concerned helplessness.

"What is it," asked Esther, her eyes closing as she struggled to control herself.

"A letter from the man." Anatu said hesitantly. No names where mentioned. Mordecai was only known as "the man" to protect all involved.

No one had seen Esther so upset before. Esther nodded her eyes still closed. She took the letter out of Anatu's hand. She rose quickly from the tub and wrapped herself in a gown not even bothering to dry herself. She did not open the letter, just tapped it impatiently on her other hand.

Both maids were going to just quietly back out of the room but Esther's eye caught Anatu.

"What happened to you, Anatu?" she asked. "Tell me your story!" And one by one, Esther sat and listened to every one of her maids tell her their stories. Hathach was last, having everyone in tears as he described the deep sorrow and pain of losing his manhood, his sense of identity, and the desire to have a wife and children of his own. Each one who shared their story looked up at Esther, a huge burden lifted from their faces and assured her they were now honored to care for her.

"But why," asked Esther in shock. "What is it about me that makes you feel honored to serve me as you all do?"

"Kindness," Hathach was the first to speak it.

"Your kindness," Anatu nodded.

"Your kindness and because your God brought you here." Arjana said softly. "You are not here because you want to be here, you are here because your God sent you here."

"Was the former queen so bad?" Esther asked Hathach. "Was she as cruel as that maid made her out to be?" Hathach was silent. He only nodded.

"And the Hebrews," she almost whispered. "Are they deeply hated?"

Again, Hathach nodded. The maids looked at each other a long moment.

"We have heard chilling tales of the former queen's cruelty to her maids or any in her care that were Hebrews or even a friend of them." Anatu admitted. She had been born in the palace of women and knew no other world.

"It was our only comfort sometimes, the fact that we were not one of them." With this Esther sighed. Her heart ached inside her chest. Her secret burned inside her. How wise Mordecai had been to protect her from this terrible truth all these years by making her promise not to breathe a word of her heritage. No wonder Adinah's face flushed with rage every time she spoke of the palace.

Esther's eyelids slid shut to hide the tears trying to escape at the thought of how, as a happy, innocent child, she had begged for any information about the palace, not knowing how this would have troubled Adinah and Mordecai and even Ruth. How this wonderful family of hers had sheltered her from the horrible truths of their captors.

Suddenly Esther did not feel safe even as queen. A chill ran up her back and the hair on her body stood up. Arjana's sharp eyes saw the color change on her arms, and she hurried to get her a shawl, even as the sunlight streamed in the windows.

"Thank you, Arjana," Esther murmured. She then turned to her maidservant, her dearest and closest friend inside the palace walls. She trusted Arjana, totally.

"You told me your story, Arjana," Esther continued, looking the girl right in the eyes.

"You have been my faithful friend over this year right till this moment. Thank you for sharing all this with me but thank you for waiting till I asked it of you."

Arjana nodded.

A loud knock sounded at the door and Esther jumped visibly. A frown furrowed Hathach's brow even as Anatu hurried to open the door. After a brief conversation, she turned and bowed low to her mistress the Queen.

"The King is requesting you to prepare to dine with him and a few of his sons, my Queen." Anatu always bowed when she addressed Esther as Queen no matter how many times Esther chided her.

This time Esther did not.

"Thank you Anatu," Esther said. She turned to look at her beautiful handmaiden for a long moment. She saw her differently now, knowing her story. Esther let her maids busy about her laying out clothes, and preparing perfumes, jewelry, a crown, her hair, makeup, and jeweled slippers in preparation to appear beside the king for another banquet of wine, laughter, and crude talk.

Stories whirled through Esther's mind as Javad, Hathach, and Banu along with a couple of armed eunuchs accompanied Esther to her dinner with the king. Esther greeted her king with a low bow and a kiss on his hand. The king chuckled and cupping her chin in his hand kissed her shamelessly in front of his guests. Esther felt her cheeks flush slightly, suddenly aware of the eyes on her.

"What is it my dear," asked the king teasingly. He was in a good mood and already smelled of alcohol.

Esther struggled in herself. Right now, she felt repulsed by this man before her, almost sneering at her, openly enjoying her body in front of other men. He was part of the problem was he not? He openly treated women as objects of sexual pleasure, and not much more. How could his sons, his nobles, his advisors, his guards, his servants not but follow suit?

When Esther did not reply, the king's voice changed.

"Are you ill, my dear?" True concern shimmered in his voice.

Her eyes slid shut for a long moment before she opened them and looked up, way up into his face. She smiled up at him sadly trying to reassure him.

"My King," she began softly. He bent down to hear her better. "I have heard a sad story today. It has troubled me deeply. I am thoughtful tonight, my King. I will try to be merry for you, my Husband."

The king took her arm, and they went slowly toward his couch at the head of the table. He sank down and pulled her down with him.

"A sad story has my dearest Esther downcast?" The king sounded genuinely shocked. "Then my dearest," he continued raising his goblet full of red spirits. "I will have to tell you a happy one." With this, he laughed delighted with his cleverness.

He pulled his beautiful wife close, insensitive to the slight stiffening of her body.

"Oh Lord God Jehovah!" the cry tore from Esther's heart even as she placed a smile on her face and kissed her husband. "Give me the strength to honor this man in this moment."

The princes all whistled and clapped as their father kissed and caressed his young queen. The food arrived in heaping platters and the wine flowed. The king lost his interest in Esther for the time once the food arrived.

A man Esther had not met before was sitting cross-legged on the ground beside the king's couch. The two were laughing and chatting like old friends.

Esther found herself sitting near the king's son, Artaxerxes. It was one of the first times they had been seated near each other. Curious, Esther pressed him about the extended family of King Xerxes and his many sons. They spoke together for some time, beginning to genuinely enjoy each other's company. The second son of King Xerxes and Queen Vashti had died during the campaign in Greece. Prince Artaxerxes's eyes and voice betrayed his sorrow as he spoke of his fallen brother. Esther found the prince to be intelligent and genuine. He seemed as intrigued by her as she was of him.

"What of Crown Prince Darius's wives," she asked innocently.

Prince Artaxerxes paused a long moment. He had drank freely of the wine and was in a great mood. But this question made him hesitate even in his jovial state.

"My, that is a story!" he managed but when he looked at the queen, her large eyes were fixed on him.

"Is it now?" She asked. He had only raised her curiosity. He sighed and put down his plate. Against his better judgment he began his story.

"During the march back from Greece, the once grand army of Xerxes was a miserable crumpled company," Artaxerxes began, setting the stage for the tragedy about to unfold as any masterful storyteller would. "Masistes, nephew to King Xerxes, my father, possesses the same explosive temper of our King. I hope you have not had to meet this trait of the King's yet." He smiled dryly his cheeks slightly flushed from drinking.

"A bit drunk from wine, Masistes publicly accused the general of the army as being responsible for the crushing defeat delivered to us at the hands of the Greeks. He called the general's leadership the work of a woman. No offence to your sex intended, my Queen," The prince nodded.

"None taken, my Prince." Acknowledged Esther.

"Enraged and intoxicated, the general pulled his dagger from his belt and lunged at Masistes. The general would have killed the fool were he stood save for the quick actions of a certain man standing nearby watching the events unfold."

"As a trained soldier, he anticipated the general's response and grabbed him by the waist throwing him down to the ground. Masistes's bodyguard stepped in-between the men, sword drawn, and grabbed Masistes's belt to keep him from attacking the fallen general. This action greatly delighted my father the King, of course." Here Artaxerxes shook his head and glanced up at the king.

The king was lounging on his couch greatly entertained by the man, who was now standing, acting out something, his arms flailing around. Esther followed his look for a long moment, watching the king drink heavily from his goblet once again.

"King Xerxes was feasting at Masistes's house at the time of this event, lucky man. Masistes got off with only a mild scolding from the King for insulting his trusted general then trying to kill him. This may have been largely influenced by the fact my father had fallen heavily under the spell of the beautiful wife of his host and nephew. She was present during the feasting as hostess and served the King and his company most graciously."

"I can't even do her the justice of remembering her name. She was fair indeed as memory serves me. I do not know how forward my father was, but she would not be tempted into adultery even by the great King Xerxes, try as he did, I imagine."

"Master manipulator as he is, Xerxes arranged a marriage between Masistes's wife's daughter, Artayntes and Crown Prince Darius. It was a fine enough match, keeping the family ties very close indeed."

"Flattered, the young woman accepted and left with the King for the palace here in Susa. This all happened before you were even brought here to the palace, so, have no fear." Prince Artaxerxes was obviously trying to soften the story for her. He fell silent for a long moment, reluctant to continue.

"Tell me Prince Artaxerxes. Go ahead." Esther encouraged him.

"A relationship sprang up between Xerxes and Artayntes, who did not possess her mother's wisdom in resisting the flatteries and attentions of a King. You see," said Artaxerxes with a small sigh. "My father is denied nothing. Neither did the indiscretion of laying with the wife of his very own son, stop him."

Shocked Esther did not reply. This tale was beginning to disclose more than she had anticipated into the twisted life of palace romances.

"I have no idea if the Crown Prince knew of his wife's indiscretions or of his father's, but my mother, the Queen, was not blind to the King's obvious affections for Artayntes. Queen Vashti was suspicious of all the women of the court. I believe it was her own indiscretions that drove her to be so discontented."

"She, being a very skilled weaver, created a most beautiful robe for my father in her continuous attempts to remain in his favor. King Xerxes was delighted with the gift and immediately put it on. He wore it constantly. I remember him showing it to me that very day in court."

"All may have been fine, but Queen Vashti presented it to him on a day he had pledged to visit Artayntes, in her bedchamber. He arrived, wearing the Queen's, beautiful robe. Foolish Artayntes was infatuated with it. She obviously greatly pleased him that visit."

"Of course, in his delighted passions, he agreed to give her anything she desired. She requested his beautiful robe, woven by the hands of her own mother-in-law. Foolish girl! My father tried to tempt her with anything, a province to govern, even an army to command. Of course, she being a woman had no desire or skills to command an army or rule a province."

Here Artaxerxes laughed dryly.

"You are harsh on our sex, my Prince," Esther said. The prince paused and nodded.

"Yes, I suppose I am, but as the story continues, you may forgive my harsh judgment of her skills. I am forever grateful she did not choose the army, my Lady," he admitted taking a drink from his cup. "I have no idea what more damage she could have done with one."

His face took on a slightly sad look. But he continued his story without request, as there was no turning back now.

"So, Xerxes parted with the robe made by his wife's own hands. Artayntes, made no move to hide the cursed article of clothing. In fact, she almost never took the thing off, so proud was she of it. Appearing with it in public settings, it was only a matter of time before Vashti found out that the very robe she had made as a gift for her husband, was the same robe another woman was wearing. And not just any woman, but her daughter-in-law, wife of her own firstborn, the Crown Prince."

"My mother is beautiful indeed, but she is also extremely spiteful and manipulative, using her good looks and womanly charms to get what she wants, every time. It was only a matter of time before she discovered it was the princess's mother that had first captured her husband's wandering eyes. She focused all of her jealous rage on the beautiful wife of Masistes. This was not the first time a beautiful woman captured her husband's eye, but she wanted blood this time."

"As was yesterday, the King's birthday was a huge feast with every relative invited. Of course, cousin Masistes, was there. For obvious reasons, his wife chose to stay in the villa that night and was not in attendance. As we both know, the King loves to drink and when he drinks, his tongue is loosened."

"As currently is mine," Artaxerxes quirked. Esther flashed a smile even as she reached for the pitcher of wine and refilled his cup.

"Thank you," He acknowledged her service.

"Go on," encouraged Esther. By now, she was totally invested in the tale. He continued in a matter-of-fact voice.

"So, waiting her chance, Vashti charmed the King with her beauty as she always could. She requested something of him publicly at the banquet so all could hear. Curious and foolhardy, he loudly agreed to grant her anything she wished."

"If there is one thing the King, the Great Xerxes, can't bear," continued Artaxerxes. "It is to lose face. And if he is curious, he will promise you anything."

Esther nodded as she had noted this tendency already. Had not her obedience to Mordecai ignited an initial flame of interest in the king when he met her? Had he not been interested the moment she denied information? A bridled tongue did seem to surprise him every time he noted it. With the way this story was weaving out, Esther was beginning to see more and more that the less one spoke, the more powerful the words when spoken.

"So, of course, the King promised her whatever she desired, intrigued with what she could possibly want that she did not already have. Her answer shocked him to his core. She requested Masistes's beautiful wife be given to her to do with as she willed."

"King Xerxes nodded and cracked a joke. Masistes, himself at the table, had no idea what was going on. I can only hope that my father felt guilty for placing my mother, his wife in this very public position of humiliation."

"Either way, Masistes's wife was granted to Vashti by royal decree and signed with the King's signet ring. Vashti left the party, a triumphant smile on her face."

"Xerxes offered one of his daughters to Masistes as a wife. Just put your current wife away privately, he advised and become my brother-in-law. Insulted instead of impressed, Masistes refused the offer. Thinking the King was just grossly drunk, he got up from the dinner table. He was a happily married man. What did he need of another wife? The insult! Masistes hurried home now concerned there was foul play of some sort in the making."

Here Artaxerxes stumbled and again drank from his cup. Esther waited patiently almost scared of what she was to hear.

"Please tell me, Artaxerxes," she asked softly. He looked uncomfortable but drew a deep breath and continued.

"Masistes found his once-beautiful wife marred beyond recognition," he said concluding the matter. But Esther was not satisfied. The story she had heard today spurred her on.

"How exactly was she disfigured?" she pressed.

"Her breasts, ears, lips, nose, and tongue were cut off by the swords of the royal bodyguards," said Artaxerxes turning to look fully at Esther. "These pieces of her body were eaten by the dogs of the household."

Esther felt her stomach turn.

"Heartbroken and enraged, Masistes fled Susa with his sons. He was killed on his way to Sacae along with all his sons by the command of my father. It

162

was hidden under the guise of a rebellion. So ends our sad tale with the King killing his very own nephew along with all his sons over a fling with the Crown Prince Darius's foolish wife." Here Artaxerxes sighed.

"What happened to Artayntes?" whispered Esther. She stared in horror at the prince.

"The Crown Prince moved her to a house of his in another province to keep her away from the King. He keeps most of his wives away from the palace now. Confirms that any son's born are truly his."

Esther choked a little at this. Prince Artaxerxes shrugged. Then he smiled, seeing just how horrified she was.

"It comes with the title." He said. He gestured toward the table surrounded by princes. "Any one of us could try to usurp the throne someday. Just because that man," he nodded his head toward the king half asleep on his couch. "Just because he is our father does not mean we wouldn't try if given the chance. If it is not me, it is another. It is something we all live with every day, especially the King."

Esther was silent. This was the life of the people around her. So different from the quiet, peaceful table of Mordecai and Adinah. There was love, joy, and support. Here, around a table dripping with lavish delicious foods, was strife, discord, envy, and self-promotion.

She remembered how vulnerable her husband could look at moments, how lost. He had been raised in this environment, watching his own father, Darius, constantly watching for his chance to rise to power. How could a king be endearing to his sons, even the crown prince, his chosen successor, knowing his reign would be challenged as he aged, if he did not die gloriously in battle first?

Once crowned, the disgruntled King Xerxes, void of his father's love, had vowed to invade Greece. In attempting to fulfill his father's dream, he had instead lost a great army, many friends, and his own princess wife, Queen Vashti. No wonder life caught up with him at times and a deep sorrow furrowed his brow and greyed his hair. No wonder he distracted himself with luxuries and rose early to avoid his troubled dreams and thoughts.

Esther looked up again at the king, lounging on his couch. He looked tired and old. Her heart felt something for him, not love so much but a loving kindness, gentleness, a pitying sympathy, an urge to comfort him. As if reading her thoughts, he raised his head and their eyes met across the table.

Esther smiled at the king, and he flicked an eyebrow. She was wanted, she knew, and needed.

"Thank you, Prince Artaxerxes, for telling me this story," Esther said as she rose gracefully.

"I look forward to another enlightening conversation with you and I do hope to meet your wife, Laleh, someday soon." He nodded and watched her as she walked gracefully toward the king, her face showing no emotion other than interest in him.

"That is a real woman," said Artaxerxes admiringly to the man beside him. Half-drunk, the man nodded. No one could deny the power this one woman possessed. They had all seen it before, Xerxes in love, but not with a woman like this.

"I hope this one lasts," the prince muttered as he raised his glass in Esther's direction. "I like her."

Chapter 15
Esther Asks for a School

Esther walked over to the king's couch. He rose a little tipsy and after a final toast and roar from his sons and advisors, he took Esther's arm. The man that had been so entertaining earlier was nowhere to be seen. Esther steadied him as they walked down the long-carpeted hallways. She was beginning to know her way around this part of the palace. Javad trailed behind the couple not needing to guide Esther on the way. Artabanus was the ever-present shadow with others of the royal guard.

They walked silently to the king's bedroom. Javad backed out of the room realizing he was not needed as Esther herself helped remove the king's clothes. In this way, Esther ministered to her husband gently.

Afterward, as she lay with his head on her chest, she was unable to sleep. The king seemed restless too. A Babylonian song came to her mind. She sang softly, stroking his hair. The king mumbled softly. It took some time but at last he was asleep, his breathing regular and deep.

This gave Esther time to think, think of her situation, her position, and her possibilities. What was she to do in this palace surrounded by such sorrow, heartache, and wickedness? Historically it was the perversion of the nations around them that caused God to use the Israelites to afflict His righteous judgments on the pagan kingdoms around them. Now, after falling into disobedience, God had allowed His people to be carried into the very heart of this evil empire.

Here she was, lying on a huge bed covered with the finest silken sheets, the head of the world's most powerful man lying on her naked chest. What did God have with her, a Jewish orphan girl, in the bed of the great King Xerxes?

She was beginning to realize the extreme cruelty the people around her were capable of, men and women alike. They did this to each other, cutting off symbols of femininity, marring bodies beyond recognition, destroying lives all because of passion, lust, and envy. How could she, one young woman, stand up against all this cruelty? How could she do this without disobeying Mordecai and acknowledging who she was? She had to find a way.

She searched her memories for what comforted her when she first came to the palace. What was it that held her together through the past years of change and uncertainty? The answers leapt into her mind even as she asked the question.

It was the snippets of Scriptures she had stashed away from Mordecai. It was the Psalms of David she had memorized and sung as the little Hebrew girl Hadassah. It was her faith in the fact God had a plan for her, even her, in the palace, separated from all she loved and trusted.

An idea slowly unfolded in her mind. What if she continued what she had begun? Teaching those around her how to read and write so they might find the Truths on their own. They might read a Scripture or Psalm one day about the God of all gods, the God Jehovah.

Esther snuggled down into the soft silkiness of the bed with a smile on her face. Softly, gently, in Hebrew, she sang a song of David as the stars twinkled down on the great palace of Susa, washing the king's chambers in mystical moonlight.

The next morning the king rose as was his custom. Esther waited till he was happily sipping his coffee trying to clear the cobwebs from his brow. She sat up and crawled over to the king totally unconcerned by who might walk in and see her naked before her husband. Javad was nowhere in sight.

The king noticed Esther staring intently at him and he stopped.

"What is it my wife?" he asked stroking his beard. "Have I grown two heads over night?"

Esther laughed and shook her head, her dark hair shifting, covering her nakedness.

"No, my Lord," Esther responded. She hesitated, trying to find the right words. The king waited, a slight smile on his face, enjoying the moment of wondering. What could his queen want so much that she hesitated so before asking?

"Do you need an army?" the king finally offered. And due to the story, she had just heard Esther burst out.

"No, my Lord! Certainly not! I was more thinking of a school."

"A school?" The king frowned.

"Yes, yes," said Esther nodding, unable to contain her idea any longer. She slipped out of bed to emphasize her point. She paced about trying to contain her excitement.

"Yes, my Lord, a school. A school where people, girls, women, concubines, maids even, can learn to read and write. Much has been taken by the Persian Empire and now it is time the Empire began to give back."

Her last sentence hung in the air a moment as the king was silent, watching his beautiful wife, her eyes sparkling with fervor, challenge him. Here he had led the greatest army in history to failure and a woman, his wife, totally naked, was requesting he start giving back?

He sat back against the pillows. He sipped his coffee. This was proving to be a very interesting way to begin his day.

"How so, my Esther?" he asked.

"Well, my Lord, let me begin with myself. I came here as a nobody, obedient only to my Master's call. I have been blessed with learning. Hegai had a teacher come and help me with my reading and writing the first year as I waited for my turn to come before you. I shared my learning with my fellow contesters and maidservants."

"Their people, culture and language have all been stripped from them. Can we not give back the Persian language? Can we not learn from all the peoples that make up this great empire? Can we not begin to unify the peoples through language, written and spoken?"

Javad came in and backed out instantly, knocking the other servants back as well. The door closed. The king's daily schedule could wait.

The king and Esther looked briefly at the door then back at each other. The king rose without a word. Esther picked up his robe and helped his great body into it. The king put his arm around her and kissed the top of her head.

"Esther, my wife," he spoke softly holding her body close. "You just may be the greatest thing that has ever happened to me."

He moved toward the door to leave but turned back, aware his wife stood waiting.

He nodded, looking at her for a long moment.

"Yes, my wife," he said at last. "A school it is!" At this he turned chuckling shaking his head. "A school!"

He disappeared out the door, his servants ready with his bath and schedule.

Delighted Esther stood a long moment a smile on her face. She turned and grabbed her robe. She called for Hathach. The faithful eunuch always waited for his mistress to be ready for him before he hurried in.

Hathach and the four-armed eunuchs escorted Esther back to her apartments, hurrying to keep up with the queen. The young woman was on a mission this morning. Never mind she had just spent the last evening feasting with the king and his sons, advisors, and generals. She was inattentive to the pandemonium she caused in the hallways as she hurried along, men and servants backing into the wall to let her rush past. Once in the safety of her chambers, with Arjana oiling and combing her hair did she speak of her excitement. Arjana was surprised by Esther's revelation.

"Mistress," Arjana muttered in awe. "You really are going to change things, aren't you?"

Esther laughed.

"I don't know Arjana; how much I can change in this palace, but I am sure going to try!" And with that Esther set to work.

That morning as she knelt facing Jerusalem, she lifted her face and earnestly prayed to Jehovah Jira, the Great I Am. Only He could somehow give her back a relationship, a freedom, to see and work with Mordecai again. Before she rose, she whispered a prayer for her husband, requesting God to cover him with His protective hand, give him wisdom, and discernment in his daily dealing with the rule of this great empire he had inherited.

And so began Esther's evolution of the palace workings. She gathered a group of girls and women around her eager to learn how to read and write. Esther's former teacher was delighted with the invitation to come to the court of women and continue educating the queen and others of the harem. He sat behind a privacy screen, his every moved watched by armed eunuchs, till he left the palace of women, delivering a weekly lecture to the eager pupils gathered in the common room.

The girls delighted in his stories as he vividly described Persian history, philosophy, and religion. Their laughter and chatter filled the entire palace. The group grew and grew till soon they were spilling out into the breezeway overlooking the common area, seated on colorful cushions placed along the railing. This again spurred an idea in Esther's mind. She waited for a moment to present her request.

Eight months had passed. She and the king were dining together at the supper table outside his bedchambers.

"Esther how is your school, my dearest?" asked her husband suddenly. Esther smiled delighted he had remembered.

"We have outgrown the common room, my Lord." Esther admitted. "Which I do believe is a good sign."

"Really!" Exclaimed the king. "My Queen, I must see this. Could I come to your next class?"

Esther rose from her couch and came over to the king's couch. She sank down onto her knees so she could look her husband in the face.

"My King! I would be honored!" she exclaimed.

The king laughed at her delight. "I will have Javad write it in my schedule."

"Husband," Esther breathed kissing his hand. "Your servant is honored."

"My sweet wife, no one delights me as you do."

He kissed her and Esther went back to her couch. She was so excited she could not eat any more. She wondered what the king would think of her group of girls, concubines, wives, maids, guards, eunuchs standing in the background, the teacher sitting on his cushion behind his screen, lecturing some of the hungriest minds he had ever encountered, one being the queen herself. Esther had no time to warn the poor teacher that the king would be visiting his lecture hall. She smiled happily.

"Esther, my dearest," the king was watching her.

"Yes, my Lord," she answered looking up at him.

"Can you sing for me that song again? The one you sang in Babylonian?"

Esther smiled. He had not been too drunk to remember. She also hoped he would enjoy her school enough to grant her request.

"Yes, my Lord," she answered. The musicians changed their tune and Esther sang along with them a haunting Babylonian love song. The king appreciated his wife that evening in a way he delighted in very few women. He enjoyed her voice, noted her carriage, and admired her self-assurance. King Xerxes cherished his own wife for the first time in his lifetime.

The next week Esther woke with a start. Today was the day the king was going to come to her school. She rose quickly. She told no one who was coming although it burned in her to share the news. She kept it to herself, not wanting to make the girls nervous or intimidated.

She personally oversaw the cleaning of the common room, encouraging it to be swept and set in order. She requested food and delicacies be laid out in a beautiful display. She arranged a huge bouquet of flowers to sit beside the professor's screen, putting together the flowers herself. Overall, the palace of women looked amazing. No one knew why the queen was so fussy and distracted this day. She seemed preoccupied but happy.

Arjana brushed the queen's hair as she insisted, she needed to look presentable for school today. Arjana was mystified by her mistress's behaviors but quietly did as she was bid. Esther ensured the girls where all properly veiled as they sat in the hall waiting the teacher's arrival.

The teacher arrived, papers squeezing from his bag. He stopped a moment to admire the hall. It looked very beautiful today, but he was more interested in the homework he had given his pupils. Eager to see how each was advancing in writing the Persian script; he hurried to his screen and requested the queen begin with hers.

Arjana took Esther's papers up to the teacher just as the king and his armed guard entered the palace of women. The teacher was so intent on his mission he did not notice at first. Delighted with Esther's skills, he instructed Arjana to turn and hold up the sheet so all the girls could see the beautiful figures gracing the page.

Pleased with his timing, the king walked quietly up to his wife's couch. She made a move to stand, surprised at his arrival but he covered his mouth with a finger. Esther slid over and the king sat down beside his wife, placing his arm on the back the couch, his great legs stretching out almost hitting the professor's screen.

The girl's twittered and shifted unsure of what they were to do, very distracted by the king's presence.

"Now girls," continued the teacher, his eyes on the piece of paper, Arjana bravely held up. "Look at the forming of these letters; this is how I want you each to aspire to write. This is great work, my Queen, as always..." he turned to look at the queen and was shocked to see the king sitting there quietly beside her, enjoying the quality of his wife's writing.

"Ahhhh! My King!" exclaimed the teacher already pale, paling even more. He bobbed his head from behind the screen not knowing what to do.

"Go on teacher," The king waved his hand impatiently. "I want to hear more of my wife's qualities."

The poor teacher broke into a sweat as he dictated his lecture. The girls were not very tentative, the armed men standing at the back of the room and the great long legs of the king proved to be most distracting. But the teacher made it through. The class stood and applauded once he was finished and diligently wrote down their homework instructions.

The lesson completed, Esther rose. She smiled at her husband and requested him to wait so she could bring the teacher to him for proper introductions. The teacher nodded and mopped his brow. Esther smiled encouragingly at him through her veil and led him over to meet the king.

The teacher bowed low, wondering how he was suddenly honored to meet the Great Xerxes. It was all merely because he agreed to assess and teach a candidate, over a year ago. He stammered out his praise to the king about his wife's brilliant mind, her keen interest in learning and her aptitude for articulating languages.

The king nodded and smiled. He was clearly enjoying this moment. That over, the queen served the king from the delicacies laid out. Esther knew what he liked so he enjoyed his plate very much. The queen served the teacher. The girls devoured the rest, laughing and chatting among themselves.

Once the hall cleared of the girls and wives and concubines, Esther turned to her husband who had not left yet.

"Esther," he said looking around with interest. "You need a bigger school." Esther's smile almost split her face. The teacher nodded and began gathering up his papers.

"Let me see my wife's writing," requested the king. Arjana handed him the papers. The king looked over them, reading Esther's short poem on the beauty of the moon.

"You are a romantic," he smiled down at her. Esther's eyes betrayed her happiness at his praise. He turned to the teacher.

"Today the King is well pleased with you, Teacher. I want you to teach these girls more. More lectures. I will see to it you have a proper school." With that the teacher bowed low. The king kissed his wife's veiled head and turning, left the room with his guards and servants in tow.

"My Queen!" the teacher turned to Esther. Esther smiled at him. The unspoken excitement passed between the two of them.

"I best be off," the teacher gathered his things. Esther thanked him for his time and the man left, sweat on his brow but a smile on his face. He would now have a proper school. The king had decreed it! And in the palace of women of all the places in the entire empire.

True to the king's word, construction began on building a lecture hall, capable of sitting a hundred eager pupils, greatly changing the dynamics of the women's palace. Once construction was complete, classes of all sorts began in the huge hall. Every day singing and dancing, reading, writing, calligraphy, drawing, embroidery, and even cooking commenced in the huge hall.

The women and girls began to share with each other their skills. The hall became a place for anyone and everyone to be something, do something. No longer was the harem a place of idle gossip, back biting, and strife. There was simply too much to do and learn.

One day, Shaashgaz glided in and began what Esther had been begging him to do for weeks. He started to teach how to design and sew clothes to the women. Many of the women who were not interested before were right in there for this class. Esther modeled the stunning dress Shaashgaz had created for her second night with the king. The woman "oooohed!" and "awwwwed!" much to Shaashgaz's delight.

Soon the hall was full of tables heaped with cloths, laces, and threads from across the empire. Arjana created a beautiful dress, complete with a head piece from a colorful cloth woven in Ethiopia, looking every inch the African princess, she was born to be. Esther's eyes stung and her throat swelled even as she beamed at Arjana, proudly displaying her creation to the group of admiring women. Arjana's face blazed with happiness and her smile flashed wide and free. Her dark eyes took on a fierce flash of pride and she held her head up and looked Esther full in the face, as an equal, not as a maidservant.

How Esther wished she could share this moment with Mordecai! He would be so happy to see how all these women bloomed. She could just see him in the corner, his head covered, reverently reading, and teaching the Scriptures, a psalm of David, with a crowd of girls gathered around eager to hear all he had to say, just as she had done, so long ago, as a little girl.

A look must have passed over her face, for Arjana came through the group of women, right up to Esther and the two friends embraced for a long, long moment before the maid turned back to her stitches and the queen back to her smiles.

Slowly, the culture of the court of women began to change with Esther as queen. This was not unnoticed by the palace. At the next monthly gathering of the princes, Prince Artaxerxes sought out Esther and congratulated her on her accomplishments.

"You seem to be raising up an army for yourself, my Queen," he said with a sly smile.

Esther laughed at this and blushed with pride.

"A very industrious one too, so I have heard." He continued. "You greatly improve all you touch, my Lady." This was said softly and in a serious tone.

Esther smiled again.

"Thank you, Prince Artaxerxes," she said. "That is high praise indeed and I am grateful."

"There are too few women like you," he noted. "They do well to respect you. If only all queens brought such honor to their house." This was said with a sad twinge.

"Not all queens are graced with a gracious Lord and Husband," acknowledged Esther.

"Not many women would say that, of your husband, my Queen," said the prince with a raised eyebrow.

Esther smiled as the similarity to the king showed for a moment on his son's face. She nodded her head to acknowledge his statement but chose to say no more on the reputation of her husband. All too well did she know that more virgins were, even at that moment, being gathered in the first court of women under the care of Hegai. Merely because the king had chosen her and crowned her did not close the open invitation to all virgins of the empire to come freely or forcibly, to the palace in hopes of being allotted a night with the king.

The queen had been crowned and married for almost three years now and still, no pregnancy announcement. Although she frequented the king's chambers, Esther did not become pregnant. Month after month passed and there was talk. Esther buried herself in her school or kept to her chambers to rest, avoiding as much as possible the comments that let slip around her. It was hard to ignore as some women came to the class pregnant or with infants at their breasts from their encounters with the king. But here she was, at another formal dinner with her husband, surrounded by his sons, all from different women, some she knew, some she did not, childless.

A king had to have heirs, many heirs. It was used as a guarantee to the stability of the Empire, as a move to maintain political cohesion, and always to gain favor from the Crown. Every nobleman, governor, judge, and king wanted his daughter to be married to the Great King Xerxes. Beautiful women continued to arrive from all over, hoping for their chance to win the king's favor.

It was also noted that Xerxes never visited Esther's apartments. She always came to him, in his chambers regardless of the day or hour. Xerxes was known for his sexual prowess and how he frequently visited the bedchambers of noble women, married or not, that attracted his attention. But his wife was one of the few women that held the honored position of coming to the king in his room. Esther was the only woman the king allowed to sleep in bed with him all night.

"You chase my demons away, my sweet Esther," he murmured often into her dark hair. Esther would smile at this then wait till he was asleep. Gently and softly, so even Javad could not hear, she would whisper a psalm of David as she watched the moon trace its set course in the sky. She knew Jehovah smiled down on her and that He cared for her as He had from the moment she turned a childish, tearstained face upward over the dead, still bodies of her parents so many years ago.

Had not God answered her heart's cry and sent her protector, teacher, and best friend, Mordecai, to rescue her right from the depths of her misery? Now, in a plan of His, He had placed her in the palace, with the king's head on her chest, singing the psalms of David to him in secret, chasing away his nightmares. Had not King Saul requested this very thing from the Psalmist himself?

Chapter 16
Esther Visits Prince Artaxerxes

The next dinner feast, Esther met the man whose company so delighted the king, a man by the name of Haman. He was young, in his thirties, in his prime, sharp, shrewd, and very flattering. He was the very same young man the king had been so interested in the last family banquet when Prince Artaxerxes told Esther of the mad tale of Queen Vashti and her revenge. Esther found his mannerism repulsive, but the king lapped up his praise as he did his wine.

Esther spoke with Prince Artaxerxes that very evening and the two discussed Haman's sudden rise in the king's favor. No one quite knew where he had come from. Somehow, he was there, among the princes that gathered every month for feasts with the king.

Haman had caught the eye of the king during a discussion and the king seemed unusually drawn to him. He spoke well and had a broad range of knowledge. He had traveled extensively in his years and always seemed to have been somewhere or knew something that delighted the king. They spent a lot of time together and the king began to lean increasingly on this quick-witted, silver-tongued man for advice.

At first, Esther thought nothing of it at all. Then one evening as she was sitting on the king's couch with him as he talked, she noticed a bitterness in Haman she could not place. He was speaking of Egypt when suddenly the conversation changed to Israel and Jerusalem. A hard coldness came into Haman's voice with such noted hatred that Esther shivered. The king gently rubbed his wife's arms and Hathach grabbed a shawl for her in his quick quiet way.

That morning, after the king rose from his bed, Esther hurried back to her apartments. She was on a mission. Her spirit was so disturbed by Haman's mannerisms and obvious connection to the king, her husband, she had been unable to sleep. Instead of going to the hall as she usually would have, she chose to call Banu, and her guard, and notify Shaashgaz that she was going out. A litter was called and she and Banu, and Arjana climbed in.

Esther loved to get out, but it was hard. Everywhere she went she made quite the stir in the crowded streets. Her armed eunuchs instantly notified everyone that it was not just an ordinary litter being carried about. Hathach stayed beside the litter, his short sword in his belt. Esther knew he would fight to his last breath for her. He called out the owner's names of the huge mansions as they passed. How he knew all this, Esther did not know.

Esther loved to see the streets as they walked along. She longed for the days she could just blend in and run down the lane to the well unnoticed, undistracted. But those days where long gone, and she knew it.

They passed Haman's house; a huge mansion all gated. He was very wealthy she knew the moment she looked at his estate. Banu was curious as to the queen's sudden interest in the politics of the palace. They also passed Prince Artaxerxes's house. Esther's determination wavered but she shook her head clearing her mind.

"Turn around," she requested. The litter obediently turned and Hathach stood quietly beside the doorway. He helped Arjana step out and accompanied her up to the door of the great house. The prince was home and the news spread quickly through the house. The door flew open, and the prince hurried out with his servants, running to assist the queen.

"My Queen!" He exclaimed delighted to see Esther. He helped her out of the litter then graciously helped Banu out as well.

"What an honor, my Lady!" Artaxerxes offered Esther his arm and the two walked slowly toward the massive stone structure.

"What a beautiful home!" exclaimed Esther enjoying a view other than the palace walls.

Artaxerxes delighted in describing the design to her as they walked down long marble hallways and into an open courtyard in the middle of the house. A fountain splashed with exotic and beautiful flowers, trees, and shrubs from around the empire blooming about it. Esther delighted in the beauty, holding out her hand to feel the drops of water splashing down.

The prince's daughters burst into the room all excited to meet the queen. They stopped when they saw the young, beautiful woman smiling at the garden. Artaxerxes laughed.

They sat down together, food and drinks served to the constant music of the fountain. Finally, he grew more curious.

"What brings you out today, my Queen," He asked. "There must be something on your mind."

"There is," said Esther truthfully glancing at the girls. The prince nodded and the girls all rose and bowed. They thanked Esther for the visit and left the room, laughing and whispering. Esther smiled after them, remembering. Her face grew serious again.

"I am curious about Haman." She admitted. "I want to know all you know about him. Who is he? Who are his people? What is his claim to fame?" She sighed. "I have never so doubted the judgment of my husband. I detest that man after two minutes in his presents, yet the King spends time, too much time with him and continues to promote him. He is now an advisor, on the same level as you, my Prince." She stopped and looked up at Artaxerxes, worry and confusion making her turquoise eyes deep pools of turmoil.

The prince saw the queen's concern through her veil. He heard it in her voice and blunt honesty. Never had he heard her speak so harshly of her husband, the king's behavior. His heart turned for her. She was in a hard position for sure, unable to express her concerns to her husband but intelligent enough to understand the implications of poor decisions. It seemed that the more the king was with Haman the less he was with his wife. No wonder the queen hated him so.

"Well, this is what I know my Lady," he said leaning forward. "I trust your confidence as I tell you this. Your conduct has proven you are a woman who can be trusted."

Esther nodded toward him acknowledging his compliment.

"I came this day to seek your council, Prince. I will not break your confidence. This is not a conversation for a dinner table or over a feast of wine and fruit."

"Well said, my Queen," Prince Artaxerxes noted. "Haman first made a name for himself in war. He is a great worrier and honored his superiors with gifts of booty from his conquests. He promoted quickly and all his friends and superiors speak well of him. With time, he made it to the circle where the King heard his name."

"Artachaees, a huge, massive giant of a man, even taller than my father and dear friend of the King's, introduced the two, I think. I don't really know as I was not there at the time. I only heard bits and pieces of the stories. I imagine it took an exaggerated story or two over a fair quantity of wine, and the Great Xerxes, my father, requested to meet this man."

"When they met, Haman charmed the King as no other man has. An invitation to court followed of course. Now he is included in every major discussion in the King's concerns. If he is not present, my father asks for him to be summoned or for the affair to wait till he can discuss it with his trusted Haman."

"You know as well as I, that the King and Haman appear to have formed a friendship based solely on drinking and laughing together. But Haman is a warrior at heart. He speaks out against an unnamed group of people that must be annihilated from the empire. He claims they refuse to obey the laws of the King."

"He promotes aggression, a stance I hope my father is wise enough to squelch. It is a concern of mine; that Haman convinces Xerxes to do something that will spark a rebellion throughout the empire."

"Many would have your style promoted," here Artaxerxes smiled again. "My Queen, the peace that is descended on the palace of women under your leadership bares testimony to the power of your presentation."

Esther smiled.

"Thank you, Prince Artaxerxes," she responded. "I am grateful I have been allowed to run my school. I have received much help from others along the way. The women love to learn and better themselves. The only way the empire will remain strong, is if peoples are brought together, work for the betterment of each other, and not in causing disunion and resentment based on race, origin, or religion. War has done enough of that."

"Well said, my Queen," the prince nodded. "I did not answer one of your questions though. Haman is an Agagite, of the land that was once called Canaan. It is now Israel with Jerusalem as the capital. Much of his wealth comes from killing and stealing from the pilgrims that return there. His sons lead raids regularly gathering booty and wealth which Haman uses as bribes and gifts." The statement was said in a matter-of-fact tone with little to no emotion on the prince's face.

Esther startled and almost dropped her cup. Prince Artaxerxes instantly realized his mistake.

"Oh, my Lady!" he gasped. "I am sorry! I forget that I speak to a woman."

Esther smiled weakly.

"No, no, Prince," she assured him. "I should be more prepared. Your statement just startled me. I did not expect that."

"I am so sorry my Lady," The prince apologized sincerely. He genuinely enjoyed Esther's company and was deeply upset he had troubled her. Of course, he had no idea why the queen should react so to the killing of Jews. How could he know she was a Jewess?

Esther longed to speak with Mordecai. An Agagite from Canaan! Had not King Saul been assigned to kill them all, men, women, and children because of the greatness of their sin against the Lord God Jehovah? This would explain this man's hatred for the Jews. His bitterness became clearer to Esther. She shivered again realizing just how very close her enemies were, surrounding her like hungry dogs, waiting for a wrong move so they could pounce upon their prey and tear her to pieces. The imagery of what Queen Vashti had done to the maid and Masistes's wife rose uninvited into her vivid imagination.

The prince saw her shiver. He rose quickly and called Banu, requesting a shawl for the queen. Esther rose and walked over to the fountain.

"Could we walk around a little more before I leave," she requested, changing the subject all together.

"Nothing would delight me more, my Lady." The prince offered her his arm and they walked through the long hallways out to the grounds surrounding the mansion once again. Esther breathed deeply of the fresh air laden with the scent of jasmine and orange blossoms. Huge hibiscus flowers fluttered in the breeze.

The estate overlooked the river that plunged down from the great palace walls, enriching the valley below. It was a literal reminder of the great blessings favor from the palace could offer. Along the sides of the river, trees, vineyards, and all kinds of life sprang up. Estates lined the ridge overlooking the river, in full view of the palace walls. Esther smiled, feeling the freest she had in a long time.

"It is a refreshing sight," Artaxerxes agreed with her silent enjoyment.

"It sure is!" sighed Esther breathing deeply of the fresh clean air. "It must be lovely to live here, being able to enjoy this view every day. The palace is beautiful but open space is hard not to miss."

The prince nodded. Esther had seen very little open space for years now. He wondered at it for a moment, never thinking before of what it must be like confined to a section of the palace, unable to leave without permission, always waiting, never free to come and go as one pleased.

"It is why reading, and learning are so important to me," Esther spoke quietly. "When one's body is caged, one's mind does not need to be also. Despair is a terrible prison. It traps both the body and the mind, but there is always hope if one is learning, growing, moving forward."

"Complacency kills both the mind and body. So, we must grow. We must learn. We must stretch for the light as plants do, no matter how little is shining down. Therefore, we study and grow. As we grow in this way it brings us together. We can begin to heal the hurts and the losses in each one of our lives. This great empire has asked us to give much."

She turned and looked at Artaxerxes deeply.

"Thank you, Artaxerxes, for your friendship. It means more than you will ever know to have a friend to confide in, a conversation to look forward to, and a place to visit, a space to enjoy. It is lovely to just be in a home once again."

She glanced at the great stone structure, the fence around it, the graveled roadway running up to the door. She smiled as a face or two peered through the lattice to get one more glimpse of the queen.

"You are blessed with a beautiful family. Treasure that, Prince Artaxerxes. It is the simple things that one can easily miss but mean the most. But alas, I best return to the palace."

She took the prince's arm and they walked back toward the litter, Artaxerxes silently helped her back in. Banu hopped in and the litter bearers lifted the women up. The armed guard fell into position, and they were ready to go, back to the palace and its walls.

"Thank you, my Lady," The prince bowed low. "I am honored by your visit. Do come again. I know my wives would love a visit from the queen at any time."

"Oh, my Prince, I would love to meet your wives! Thank you for answering my questions so openly," said Esther. She smiled down at him. "I look forward to seeing your face again at the palace. And next time, I will only visit for pleasure and not on business."

With that, the curtain fell shut and the litter moved back onto the street. Esther was silent, watching the people as they passed. They passed other litters bearing women, dressed richly. They passed princes, mounted on beautiful horses of every color. Carts loaded with fresh fruits and vegetables, ready for the next day's market. Many carts were headed to the palace kitchen, bulging with every good and lovely thing the empire had to offer.

Esther looked for Mordecai as they passed through the gate. How lovely it would be to see his dear face again. Everyone pressed against the walls to let the litter pass through the narrowed gaits, between the two huge lion statues, with eagle wings spread, ready for flight. It was someone important for sure if there were armed guards. Esther smiled as a few looked and pointed. A little girl waved shyly. They passed by much too quickly and they were in the palace courtyard.

Servants leapt to help Esther step out. Banu followed. She too was silent. Anatu came running a big smile on her face.

"My Queen!" She made a sweeping bow delighted her mistress was once again back to the court of women. Esther laughed.

"Come along," she said. "Let's see what is going on in the hall."

Although her voice was lively, the conversation with Prince Artaxerxes lingered heavily on Esther's mind. She longed for a quiet moment to really think over what she had learned from him. They walked along a covered hallway beside the palace walks to the great gates leading into the women's palace. Once inside they ambled along the breezeway, through the great room and into the long school hall the king had built in only a couple of weeks.

Esther slowly moved up and down the long room, looking at all the women's handy work. The hall was mostly empty, only a few women lingered desperately trying to finish a project or two. It was soon time to bathe. Most of the women would be preparing. One by one they left till it was only Esther left in the hallway, pacing slowly up and down, deep in thought.

Arjana, Anatu and Banu watched her for a while. Banu slipped away to bathe and Arjana and Anatu were left, watching their mistress's every move.

"She has an idea," Arjana said, her eyes never leaving Esther.

"What interesting things did you see on your trip out?" asked Anatu, her eyes momentarily darting to Arjana's face.

"My favorite is the river, winding away from the palace, free to flow, free to follow its own whims along the way."

"You always say that!" Arjana chuckled.

"And you, Anatu, always ask," the maids shared a quick smile.

At last, Esther stopped. She was looking at a painting of a vineyard. It was well done. The artist obviously had seen many in her short lifetime. It was very realistic, spacious, with rolling hills in the background. Esther smiled and nodded. She turned and smiled at Arjana and Anatu.

"I best get going," she said and headed for her chambers. She bathed and dressed, prepared if the king should summon her. When no Javad or other message came, she buried herself in books and scrolls. It was late at night before she finally crawled into bed. Her head was swimming with ideas and the info she had learned from her conversation with Prince Artaxerxes.

But Esther could not sleep. She rose quietly as not to disturb Arjana who always slept close to her bed, so as not to miss anything her mistress may need. Anatu slept with the other maids in another room, but Arjana would not leave Esther alone in the dark for anything. Esther knelt by the window, looking out toward Jerusalem. She struggled to remember every detail Mordecai had ever taught her of the history of the Jewish peoples.

Softly she whispered her heart's prayers, her sadness that her husband not calling for her once again. She knew he was seeing other candidates. It did not surprise or shock her in the least. Yet, it still pained her to think of him with someone else when she was his wife, his queen. If the rumors she heard of Vashti and other noble women about the courts was true, this was not an affliction only given to men. Noble women were known to have visitors to their bed chambers as well.

Esther shook her head. She had no desire to have others in her bed. The idea was repulsive. She must be obedient to her husband as she was to her cousin, Mordecai and to her God. It was the only way she would live her life; it was the only way she wanted to live her life. If her husband did not need her than she would be about her own business, studying and growing, even as she had described to Artaxerxes.

Her mind wandered over all the beautiful sights she had seen that afternoon. The river, winding its way through the valley as far as the eye could see stuck in her mind. She bowed her head and prayed for her husband, that the Lord would give him wisdom that he may sleep this night that he would awake refreshed.

She prayed for Mordecai, that the Lord would bless him and comfort his heart. How lonesome he must be. How she missed him. But she would obey her God; she would wait on Him to bless her. She would hope and trust that He was great enough to thin the stone walls of the palace and that once again, she would be able to be free to embrace, and speak with, Mordecai.

Her heart settled and she turned to go to bed. It was well past midnight. But there was a gentle noise at the door. Esther went to the door herself and opened it quickly as not to have the maids roused. A eunuch stood at the door."The King's man, Javad, is at the entrance to the women's palace." He explained in a soft whisper.Esther grabbed a robe and hurried after him to the entrance of the palace.

"I'm so sorry, my Queen, but…"

"I'm coming Javad." Esther interrupted him.She found her husband standing at the doorway of his bedroom. She smiled up at him and hurried forward. He held out his arms and the two embraced for a long moment.

"I missed you," Esther admitted.

"As did I, my sweet wife, why I waited so long, I don't know!" The king shook his head as if trying to clear it.

"It is OK, my Love, I'm here now," comforted Esther.

"Umm yes, you are," the king picked her up in his arms and carried her to his bed. Esther giggled as he tossed her gently on the thick covers.

The king was nuzzling her when Esther suddenly burst out.

"That is it! I need a garden." The king chuckled.

"A garden you will have, my dearest, in the morning. Till then, you are all mine!"

Chapter 17
Esther Gets Her Garden

The king and queen slept long into the morning. Javad peeked in several times only to be met with soft breathing as the two slept in each other's embrace. He smiled. It had been a week since the king slept well. All felt the relief as his mood improved greatly, with sleep.

Javad stood guard over the doorway, keeping all the princes, servants, and any other intruders out of the king's chambers. Today court could wait. The empire could wait, the world could wait. For today, the king slept in the arms of his wife.

True to his word, the king and Esther discussed a garden plot the women could use to grow things.

"So why would the Queen want a garden? Are there not flowers and such about in the court of women?" The king scratched his head then stroked his beard. "What would you want with the manual work of tending to such a thing?"

"Why my King, to watch them grow. To plant and try new things. It is a labor of love." The king smiled mischievously at this and raised his right eyebrow.

"Besides, I can be a bit useful." Esther continued, smiling as she remembered the garden she loved so much as a child.

The king silently reached for her, and she snuggled up against him. He kissed the top of her head. He sighed slightly.

"I have never found plants to be of much interest." The king observed. "But my grandfather, King Cyrus did. I wonder," he stopped for a long moment.

"Persepolis that is a name I have not spoken in a long time. His gardens were around Persepolis. I wonder what they look like."

The king looked over at his wife. Her eyes were huge as she stared up at him over her coffee mug.

"Persepolis," she breathed the name, and her eyes took on a dreamy look. The king smiled.

"I will take you there." He stated. He sank back against the pillows of the bed. "Someday I will take you there." He looked tired again. The sun had weathered his skin with time. Even the baths and oils could not hide the laughter lines around his eyes, and the creases across his brow. His head was bare, and his dark hair curled rebelliously about, the streaks of grey present around his temples.

These were the moments Esther liked him the most. It almost, almost felt as if she was just sitting on the bed talking with her husband. She treasured these moments. They were wonderful memories between lengthening absences and formal, drunken feasts.

"What has become of Persepolis, city of the kings?" Asked Esther truly curious.

"Ohhhh, war is expensive." King Xerxes admitted. He was looking up at the ceiling, his eyes tracing the strong cedar rafters and billowing curtains. "My father, Darius, totally abandoned building the city as he prepared for the invasion of Greece. I followed right behind him. I threw everything I had at Greece."

"You raised, trained, and led the biggest army in the known world, my King," Esther mentioned gently.

"Yes, but I failed." The king groaned. "That phantom, that hideously beautiful creature," here he sat up. His eyes blazed as Esther had never seen before. Xerxes pointed to the side of the bed he always slept on.

"That vision, either from Anahita, goddess of wisdom or Duzakh, the burning inferno, threatened me night after night mocking my plans of peace and tranquility."

"I had Artabanus dress as me and sit on the throne for court. Then later, he came in and lay down still dressed as me. Sure enough, that horrible phantom appeared to him too and tormented his sleep till he came running to me while I sat waiting."

"The phantom never promised victory, but I thought that obedience would surely appease the gods and they would smile on my endeavors. Anahita

185

instead spurned me and dragged me home humbled and humiliated. The entire campaign nearly cost me my kingdom."

"I lost much, my Queen Esther, I lost much. The Persian people do not need or want a garden in the desert. It would have only been seen as a reckless expense, so I neglected the city of the kings and the great gardens of King Cyrus."

"Has that phantom ever returned, my King?" Esther asked quietly.

The king shook his head.

"No." he admitted. "It never again appeared to me as it did those nights so long ago. But I did have a dream. My advisors and wise men assured me it was a sign of victory. I saw myself crowned with a victor's crown. It sprouted up into a huge tree that filled the entire earth. It was wonderful.'

"Then, suddenly, the crown was violently removed, and I stood alone, with nothing over my head, vulnerable and exposed. This scared me. I was assured it was only a reminder of my immortality, that I was not a god, a warning to keep me humble even as I conquered the world."

Esther was silent for a long moment. She had never heard this story before. The similarities to the dreams of King Nebuchadnezzar of Babylon, which Daniel interpreted accurately, rose to her mind. She sorrowed over the misinformation that had misguided her husband and resulted in so many lives lost."Tell me more of Persepolis," Esther pleaded. "I have only read of the city of the kings. It sounds glorious!"

"Oh! Glorious it is indeed! Cresting the final ridge, looking out over the valley and seeing the great columns of polished marble rising out of the sand; it is a glorious sight indeed. It has been so long since I have seen it."

"I have not traveled down from Susa for the summer months on the Great Plains as King Cyrus and King Darius did. I do remember going down as a boy. It was such a grand affair."

"Mother would wake and dress me and we would mount up on a great camel. It was a glorious adventure. I loved camping in the huge tent and running around with the other boys. We would hide from our duenna and drive her into hysterics."

"She would threaten us with terrible stories of monsters and trolls who ate disobedient boys. But we did not heed her. It only disrupted our sleep and made our dreams more vivid."

He laughed at the memories, his dark eyes flashing.

Esther had never seen him so free. She smiled delighted with the vision of the young prince Xerxes and his mischievous, boyish antics.

"It is a three-day journey down through the mountain passes to the lowlands." He continued, his body naked to the waist, the morning sun running its fingers over his muscular frame. He laughed at a memory.

"I fell off my first horse," he rubbed the left side of his head. "Artabanus had the brilliant idea of stealing two horses from the guards. It was a much better adventure than on the camel with a snoring duenna and other fussing children."

"We tried to blend in as best we could and not be called out. Everything was going great till Artabanus spooked his horse and it took off galloping. He slid off as soon as the horse spun but I was not so cowardly. I hung on for dear life. That horse galloped flat out. All would have been well, but a group of guards came galloping after me. My horse only went faster and then suddenly swerved as they approached, trying to grab the reins. I flew off into the sand."

"Nothing was hurt save my pride. My mother, Queen Atossa, was furious. I had to ride with her on her camel for the rest of the trip so she could personally keep me out of trouble. Of course, Artabanus followed behind on his horse."

"When my father, King Darius heard of it, he immediately took me riding again. I had regular horseback riding lessons after that event."

The king laughed again. He grew serious again and looked at Esther.

"I should take you. We should go this season to escape the summer heats. It would be fun to see the place again and you would enjoy the gardens, if there are any left."

Esther nodded. It sounded like a delightful adventure, and she would get to see more of the countryside.

"My Lord," Esther ventured. "Perchance you could tell me how you met Haman?"

"Haman? I did not take you for the jealous type." The king shot Esther a long look with his eyebrow raised. Esther was almost nervous she had offended him till his beard moved and his great smile flashed through.

Esther returned his smile and snuggled up against him. But her heart did pound in her chest with an intensity she struggled to identify. Was if fear of the king or fear of Haman? If so, why should she fear either?

"Haman, "the king mused. "He will be very angry I am in here speaking with you and not preparing for court." He chuckled as he took a long sip of his coffee.

"I met Haman on the campaign to Greece. He was the personal assistant of my friend, Artachaees."

King Xerxes looked down at Esther snuggled up against him before he continued with a long sigh.

"Speaking of architecture, Artachaees was a genius. If I needed anything built, I turned to him. He was a big man, taller even than me. He stood about eight feet in height. There were few horses big enough for him to ride without his feet dragging on either side."

"Artachaees's final act was to build a canal. He had a huge billowing voice, and he had his men dig that canal at a speed never seen before. It was a marvel to watch him work. But there was a deep, deadly marsh nearby. It was the reason we dug the canal, to drain the marsh so the army could march on. But in that swap were bugs that bite humans and suck their blood. Artachaees fell sick probably from the swarms of these biting insects that would descend every evening on anything that moved man or beast."

"Haman was Artachaees's man. He nursed him as if he were his own son. I had never seen a man so devoted to his superior before. Artachaees died anyway and Haman never left his body till it was buried. Artachaees's loss was a deep blow. I feared Haman would die standing over that mound that held his dead master."

"I invited Haman to come with me and serve me and my kingdom as my friend Artachaees had. He agreed. Since then, I have promoted Haman to a position among my sons. He is now a prince of Persia. No one could make me laugh as Artachaees could. He would tell a joke and the entire dining hall would laugh; his voice carried so. No one makes me laugh as Haman does. He remembers so many of Artachaees's jokes that I never had the privilege to hear."

"That is why, dear wife, I value Haman so. He makes me laugh and we speak of Artachaees often."

Esther nodded. She was glad she had asked. It did her heart good to know why the king and Haman laughed so much together. Now she understood. And in a way, it was through Haman, that King Xerxes had his friend, Artachaees back for a moment. No wonder the king enjoyed his company so. Maybe Haman was not so dangerous after all?

Even as the thought passed through her mind, she shivered. The King's arm tighten around her and he rubbed her arm thinking she was cold. He pulled the tapestry that covered the bed up around her.

"There," he said kindly. Esther thanked him with a smile.

"Where does Haman's wealth come from?" she asked, curiosity making her bold. The king was very open to talking this morning.

The king laughed.

"Does a man look a gift horse in the mouth?" he asked and kissed her hair. "I would assume he is paid well for his services. I do believe he guarded pilgrims along the road. That is how Artachaees met him. 'Haman, my man!' Artachaees would thunder. 'Saved my life, my man did.'"

Xerxes smiled somewhat sadly remembering.

"But I best be off, my love, my wife. And you," He stopped with his legs hanging over the bed and shot her a smile. "Have a garden to tend to."

Javad materialized and King Xerxes rose. He shrugged on his robe. He kissed his wife and still chuckling, strode out of the room for his bath and to dress for court.

Esther smiled till he was out of the room than her face fell. So, it was true! Haman did work as a guard along the highways. Everything Prince Artaxerxes had told her was true. But Haman meant a lot to her husband, the king. She saw that clearly. She also now understood the king saw no guile in Haman. He trusted him. Liked him. Probably even loved him if he was honest with himself.

She would have to pretend to like Haman for her husband's sake. She would have to tolerate him, maybe even trust him at times. She shook her head as she climbed across the king's huge bed and over the side.

Esther, Queen of Persia, wife of King Xerxes could tolerate and like Haman, but Hadassah, the Jewish girl, the hidden one, could never trust this man. He was an Agagite, a vengeful enemy to all children of Israel, a snake dressed as a prince. She must know her enemy and keep him even closer than a friend.

Hathach came to her side when she softly called his name. Other armed eunuchs stepped in behind her as they passed out of the king's bedchambers toward the palace of women.

Esther hoped that she would never have to consider Haman an enemy for any other reason than she was a Jew and him an Agagite. She knew he killed her people and stole all they had. But she was queen. He could not kill her, let alone steal from her. That would be stealing from the very King himself, would it not be? Something Prince Artaxerxes said troubled her even as she smiled at princes and advisors she passed in the hallways.

But Haman is a warrior at heart. He speaks out against a group of people that must be annihilated from the empire. He claims they refuse to obey the laws of the King. What could this mean? Again, she shivered, and her steps hurried. She did not feel safe till she reached the court of women and the large wooden doors closed behind her and the armed guards stepped in front.

It was that very afternoon, a group of eunuchs arrived sent from the king to make a garden for the queen. The king delivered a huge bouquet of flowers and fruit, which delighted the entire palace of women.

It was weeks later that the king summoned Esther to come with him to look at a monument he had just completed. The couple walked through the huge project discussing the designs, the structures, and the plans. The king was struck with how interested his wife really was, in what he was doing and building. Never had the king found himself so awestruck by a woman before, a woman so young and so inexperienced, yet so passionate and curious.

Esther's interest in building and architecture grew. She wandered the palace looking over the columned hallways, the huge cedar beams, the ceilings, and intricate designs. She studied the fountains, the stone walls, and the gardens.

Over the next banquet for the king's sons and princes, the topic was discussed with much laughter and enjoyment. The princes treated Esther with increasing respect and interest. She was not just their father, the king's, latest romance, but an influential figure. Esther began, without really knowing it, to create a place for herself, a following, a station. She became the queen slowly over the following years, her opinion considered by the king, princes, and advisors alike.

True to his word, that summer, the king took his family down out of the mountains to the city of Persepolis. For the last couple hours of the journey, the king rode his horse beside the camel that carried Esther so he could see his wife's reaction as they crested the final ridge. They crested the last ridge and suddenly, the huge city sprawled out before them, rising out of the desert sands with determined beauty.

The gardens of Cyrus were gone, withered away into the scorching heat of the desert. Only the trees closest to the palace lived on, cared for by an aged gardener. He cried and bowed low when he saw King Xerxes and Queen Esther walking about looking at the huge, ancient trees.

"Welcome, my king," he sobbed. "I am so glad to see a son of King Cyrus again at the city with my own eyes. I can now die a happy man!"

Moved with compassion, Esther gave the man a silken napkin to dry his tears. At her prompting, he happily described the old gardens, sprawling across three acres of desert, watered with an intricate aqueduct system, the first of its kind.

"The Great King Cyrus would bring home plants from all over. He planted them here in his gardens. He loved watching them grow. Every evening I found him walking through his gardens, his hands always touching the plants. He smiled at the blooms; he watched the birds nesting in the trees. I even found him, on his hands and knees one day, cleaning out a water ditch that had been plugged with leaves and dirt. There was very little the King loved more than his garden, save his children."

The old man paused, his cloudy eyes shifting over the land, now covered with weeds and sandhills. A few straggled branches were all that remained of the once glorious gardens.

"I remember watching King Cyrus play with Crown Prince Darius on that lawn." He pointed with his knobbed finger, disfigured with age.

"Now it is just a desert, lost to time." The old gardener sighed but he smiled again quickly.

"Time has changed things, my Queen," he admitted. "But I am blessed to have seen your beautiful face, so full of life. I cannot thank you enough for bringing King Xerxes back to the city. His grandfather was so proud of this place."

Esther quizzed the aged man on what King Cyrus was able to grow and the different plants and trees he collected. The gardener was delighted by her curious mind.

"I have a gift for you, my Queen," he said, patting her hand with both of his rough ones. Slowly, as the gardener could not walk fast, he led the party over to his humble house. He disappeared inside, insisting the dwelling was

191

too humble for the king and queen to enter. Plants and shrubs Esther had never seen before surrounded the cottage. The gardener had kept something alive from the great garden.

He reappeared bearing a bag full of seeds. He carefully presented it to Esther with the instructions of how to plant and grow each seed. He begged her to come next year and tell him how her garden was growing.

Esther promised and many evenings found her and Hathach sitting with the gardener. Esther brought parchment and took notes much to the gardener's delight. At Esther's request, Hathach ran a bag of fruits from the king's own table to the gardener's cottage every week they were in the great city so the old gardener could experience the tastes of the fruits from across the empire. Sadly, the next season the royal family arrived, the gardener had passed away in his sleep, a smile on his wrinkled face, and a note left behind for his queen.

Chapter 18
The Plot

Over time, Javad and Arjana fell in love. The two were head over heels for each other. Javad blushed every time he saw Arjana. Once Esther got wind of the budding romance, she would send Arjana to speak with Javad as he waited at the doorway to the palace of women. She always ensured a eunuch or two were present to ensure Arjana's safety. But this gave the couple time to speak with each other.

Javad treated Arjana like the princess she was. Relationships between servants was always hushed and hidden, usually resulting in neglected children or orphans. Many mistresses cast out their handmaids due to any pregnancies or forced abortions on them. Others would steal their maid's child and raise it as their own, especially if the woman was childless.

Arjana came to Esther, trembling despite their deep friendship, and tearfully told her of her love for Javad. Esther's reaction was anything but expected. She laughed with delight and hugged her friend and maidservant. Esther had to get permission from the king for Arjana and Javad to truly be together as a couple. She smiled happily, her mind bursting with ideas.

That evening Javad escorted Esther to the king to join him in the garden for the evening meal. She planned the timing of her request.

"Javad, wait a moment," she commanded softly. She was sitting on the king's couch.

"My husband, it has come to my awareness that Javad has a sweetheart."

The king looked up at his man servant in surprise. He looked at him as if seeing his humanity for the very first time.

"Of course," said the king with a teasing smile. "He is a fine-looking young man! Any woman would be happy to have him."

"But, My Lord," continued Esther gently. "The woman is one of my maidservants." At this, the king's eyebrow raised.

"How do you feel about this, my Esther," he asked finally paying attention.

"I like it." Esther said simply. "I think it is very romantic."

At this, the king laughed with delight.

"You would, my dear!" He kissed her hand even as she smiled. Her face grew serious again quickly.

"You have an idea." The king stopped and looked fully at Esther realizing her sincerity. "Tell me what you desire my dearest wife. Your generosity and kindness do me much good."

"Thank you, my Lord," Esther smiled up at her husband. "I think they should have an apartment together."

Javad waited, holding his breath, admiring the queen's courage to bring up such an issue on his and Arjana's behalf. He barely dared hope that the king might agree to the queen's proposal. It was just not done. It had never been heard of before.

"Humm," the king was deeply thoughtful for a moment, even stroking his beard. He looked at his wife with admiration. "This is not often done."

Esther nodded.

"It is not usual for sure, but I think it will only strengthen the relationship between the king's palace and the court of women. It could reduce frictions and animosity between the King's men and the maidservants of the wives and ladies of the Great King Xerxes."

"You are very persuasive, my dearest," said King Xerxes after a long moment. "You are becoming very good at presenting your requests and laying out the details. I like it. I like the idea. It is a good vision. I am loth to lose my man, though."

"Oh, my Lord," Esther laid a hand on his face. "I don't ask you to lose your man. Only give him the nights off that is all. As I will my maid. There are plenty to serve and I can assist you if I am present."

Javad's face flushed and he slipped back into the shadows. The king smiled as he looked at his beautiful young wife flushed with passion.

"You have brought so much unity to the palace since you arrived. I will let you do as your heart desires. Your instincts are kind and intelligent, your execution effective and well done." He concluded with a nod. "I am also not above admitting defeat."

Esther laughed with delight. The king tucked a strand of shining hair behind her ear. His gazed lingered over her for a long time enjoying her happiness.

Esther shot Javad a triumphant look even as he slipped away, his heart pounding with excitement. The king kissed his wife and carried her off to his chambers.

The next morning, Esther hurried back to her chambers, her mind bursting with excitement, looking forward to sharing her good news with Arjana. It was Arjana who opened her door and bowed her into her rooms.

Anatu stood waiting for her holding a letter in her hand.

Hathach stood at the door looking on.

"A letter!" Esther gasped out.

Anatu stepped forward and handed Esther the letter a big smile on her face.

"I will speak with you, Arjana." Esther said. "Let me just read this letter first." Arjana nodded eager to hear how Esther's conversation with the king had gone.

Esther opened the letter. Her face paled as her eyes quickly followed the writing.

"There is a plot on the King's life." She said in a monotone voice. "Hathach, hurry and get Hegai and Shaashgaz. They will know how to help get news to the King."

Hathach hurried to do as his mistress bid.

"Arjana, hurry. I must get dressed." Quickly the maids had Esther dressed and ready by the time the eunuchs arrived breathlessly in the room, trying to keep up with Hathach.

"Read it aloud, Banu," Esther requested. "We must all be sure we understand exactly what is being said." She turned and looked out the window toward the gate. Banu nodded and took the letter in her two hands.

"*My queen,*" the letter read. "*It has come to my awareness that there is a plot on the life of your husband, the King. I know not how to warn him more effectively than telling you, the keeper of his heart.*

I overheard two eunuchs arguing together at the gate as I sat doing my work. They have become furious with the king and are plotting to kill him. Their names are Bigthan and Teresh. Please, warn the King. And hurry, I

195

heard them mention poison. Don't let the King eat anything before you warn him.

Your Servant,
Mordecai."

Banu looked up. The decidedly Jewish name hung in the air for a long moment. Esther made eye contact with Hegai.

"We must get the queen to the king." Hegai stated. "Oh, Bigthan and Teresh! They are assigned doorkeepers in the palace of the King. I don't know them well, but I have an idea who they are."

"Court has begun." Shaashgaz rang his hands as he always did when he was nervous or anxious. "We only have a few hours till the King will be partaking of his noon meal. Oh, what is the fastest way to get a message to him?"

"Let's get a message to Javad," said Esther. "If Javad tells him I have urgent business to discuss with him, surely, he will call me to him before he eats."

Everyone's head nodded.

"Hathach, give me a moment, my man. Let me write a note for Javad to give to the King. It will please him, and I must gain his favor."

Hathach waited for Esther as she sat down and quickly wrote a note to the king. She carefully folded the parchment and sealed it with a kiss.

Hathach dashed from the room.

"I need to go!" Exclaimed Hegai and he too left the queen's apartments.

Arjana hurried to prepare a perfume for Esther.

"Arjana," Esther grabbed the hand of her faithful friend and maid. "The King said yes to my idea! He said yes!" Arjana's dark eyes sparkled with hope and admiration. She impulsively hugged her mistress then hurried to ensure everything was laid out for her.

Shaashgaz laid out clothes. He was nervous and nothing calmed him like preparing a gown for his queen.

At noon, Esther was dressed in royal robes and ready to come before the king. No one was allowed to appear before him uninvited. It was certain death. So, even with news that could save his life, she had to wait, pacing back and forth in the breezeway, waiting for the notification that Javad had come to summon her to her husband's presence.

She heard footsteps approaching the doors. A guard called out and she heard Javad's voice. The door was unlocked and swung open.

Javad looked up and nodded when he saw her. He quickly bowed and chanced a glance at Arjana. She flashed him a brief smile despite the circumstances. Normally Esther would ensure the two had a chance to speak but today there was no time. She flashed an apologetic look at Arjana.

"The Great King Xerxes wishes for the Queen, Esther, to accompany him at his noon meal." Javad delivered the formal summons and Esther hurried toward the courtroom with Hathach and her armed eunuchs with her.

Javad led them through the columns that lined the court room. Esther always gasped a little when she saw this great room. Even silent and still at noon hour, it was breathtaking in its magnificence.

Her anklets jingled softly alerting the men gathered around the noon spread that the queen had arrived. The king looked up, his golden cup in his hand.

"Esther, my wife," he said happily. Haman sat beside him on his left. The Crown Prince lounged lazily on his right and Artabanus stood guard behind, unaware of the danger hovering over the king.

"My Lord King!" Esther bowed. King Xerxes waved his scepter, his wine sloshing in his cup. He moved to place the cup against his lips. Esther hurried toward him. She knelt before him and lifted her hands to take away the cup.

"My Queen!" exclaimed the king surprised. He suddenly lifted up his goblet.

"Get her a cup, quickly. She is thirsty." The men present burst out laughing but Esther looked up into the face of her husband. The king saw a look he had never seen before on the face of his wife, the queen. He sobered quickly.

"What is it my Queen, that has you so concerned?" He asked.

"My King, it has come to my knowledge that there is a plot against your life. I am afraid for your health, my King, even if the contents of your cup may be deadly!" The king paled notably at his wife's words.

"A plot against the King's life?" His face flushed red and a vein on his forehead began to bulge.

"Who has told you of this? And who dares to threaten the life of King Xerxes?" Artabanus's huge muscular form was suddenly bending over the right shoulder of the king, his hand on the hilt of his sword.

"My King, it is two eunuchs, Bigthan and Teresh that stand as doorkeepers in your place. Please my King, send for them. Mordecai, a scribe who sits at the King's gate, got word to me of this plot. He said he overheard them speak of poison. My King don't drink anything more from your cup. I beg you!"

Artabanus snapped his fingers and four of the royal elite guards disappeared out of the room at a dead run.

The king looked at his golden goblet. He handed it to his cup bearer.

"Check it!" he ordered. The young man poured off some wine into a small, silver cup he held in his hand. He took a quick sip from the silver cup. His knees seemed to shake a little as he tested the wine.

After a long moment with everyone staring at him, the cupbearer shook his head.

"I taste nor feel nothing, my King. I believe the wine in this cup is safe."

The king nodded and took the golden goblet handed back to him. Everyone in the room sighed and the whispering began.

"Did you say the name Mordecai?" asked Haman leaning over to speak quietly to the queen. Esther turned to look at him. What did Haman have to do with Mordecai?

"I did, Prince Haman." Esther spoke lightly. She must pretend Mordecai meant nothing to her after all.

"Uhhhh! The Jew!" scoffed Haman.

Even the king noted the open scorn in Haman's voice.

"Whatever does this man have on you, Haman? Are you not a man of enough honor already?"

Haman's face flushed red with rage or shame; it was unsure.

"That, that!" he almost sputtered spit flying from his mouth and coating his beard. Esther started back.

"That Jew gives me no honor, my King. That is my problem with him. He refuses to honor me at all!"

If Haman's display was supposed to concern the king, the opposite was true. The king laughed at his face.

"Haman, my Haman," said King Xerxes. "One would think you a spiteful and jealous man. Calm your pride, my prince. Honor is only due to him whom the King delights to honor."

Esther smiled at this, dipping her head so her lacy vail would cover her emotions. When she looked back up, her face displayed no emotion.

Inside her heart pounded in her chest to hear the name of her beloved cousin, spit from the mouth of none other than Prince Haman himself. But had not Mordecai been the one to warn of this plot? Now she prayed he was right as his good name with the king now hung on the truth of his accusations.

The room was suddenly filled with noise as the four soldiers marched in with the two eunuchs strung between two of them almost ripping them apart by the arms. They were thrown down before the king, Esther leapt up to get out of the way.

Hathach was beside her in a flash, pulling her away from the king and back behind a few of the princes. Esther's heart thundered in her chest and ears.

"My Queen," Hathach stood beside her, his bare arm protectively in front of her. "This is going to get dramatic, my Queen."

Esther nodded; her mouth suddenly so dry she did not trust herself to speak. The eunuchs held up clenched hands toward the king, loudly pleading for their lives. The four soldiers stood behind them, their arms crossed, waiting for orders.

The king lay on his couch, undisturbed by all the noise about him. He nodded and food was brought. Instead of laying it out in front of the king, the food was laid out before the two eunuchs.

"Eat, gentlemen," the king invited, a slight smile playing about his lips. The two eunuchs went silent, and they cast a glance at each other. One bravely reached out and began to eat slowly.

"Faster," taunted the king. It was now a game. The two eunuchs were on their knees eating as fast as they could.

"Faster," Thundered Artabanus, joining in the game. He stocked about the men, his hand patting his sword hilt. The royal guard thumped their shields on the floor.

"Faster!" the entire room echoed with the noise. Esther gasped, her hand covering her face, scared to watch, her other arm clung to Hathach's strong arm. Her knees felt weak and faint. She felt like she wanted to scream.

The room took on a hostile feel. Princes began to bet loudly on who would die first. For a long moment, it seemed as if nothing would happen. Suddenly one of the men groaned and sat up sharply grabbing at his abdominal area with both hands. He began to vomit violently. Blood gushed from his throat, his breath coming in choking gasps.

The king watched, unaffected by the sight. A smile playing tauntingly about his lips. Prince Haman now stood, his arms crossed, stroking his beard.

"Faster," the king sang out. Never had Esther been so unproud of her husband. He looked boyish in his open pleasure as he watched the eunuch hemorrhaging and writhing in agony. The second eunuch did the same, spreading blood in a large, oozing puddle.

"Hang them on the gallows in the courtyard of the palace!" thundered the king. "This poison is taking too long. Let everyone see what happens when one dares lift a finger against the King of Persia."

The eunuchs were drug out, leaving behind them a bloody trail. Servants jumped to clean up the mess streaking across the cold hard marble floors. The room was silent for a long moment.

"Well, gentlemen, princes, and advisors," the king spoke at last, a hard coldness creeping into his voice. "There is treason in the palace. An attempt has been made on the life of the King."

Prince Haman was the first to move. He swung around and knelt before King Xerxes.

"Let me, my Lord King, let me have the honor of getting to the bottom of this! I promise, my King, I will bring the unfortunate wretch responsible for this treason to you, dead or alive."

The king looked at the prince for a long moment. He nodded and rose quickly.

"Do it and be quick about it, Prince Haman!" he commanded curtly. Artabanus was at the king's side in an instant. The royal guard surrounded him so tightly the group had to shuffle as not to step on each other's feet.

"The King will not leave his chambers till the person responsible for this act of treachery is dead!"

With that the king, Artabanus, and the royal guard swept from the room. Utter silence followed. Then the Crown Prince rose, his bodyguards close beside him. One by one the princes and advisors left the room. Esther stood frozen, clinging to Hathach's arm her face drained of all color.

Prince Haman stood looking at the spot where the eunuchs had been for a long moment. He was the last to leave, casting a glance in the direction of the queen before striding out of the room.

"Hathach," Esther gasped, the tears suddenly spilling from her eyes. She was more horrified than she had ever been in her life. She felt as if the king had shut her out instead of thanking her for saving his life. He could have been lying there, bleeding out, his gut shredded by the deadly poison. Instead, he was now suspicious of everyone, going to hide out in his room, letting Prince Haman hunt down the assassin.

She was just a woman, and she would be wise not to forget it. She was just a woman in the king's eyes. When the king sat on his throne, woe to any who dared to assume they held any power over him. He felt he was a god, enthroned in his entire splendor, invincible, till death stared him in his face.

"My Queen!" the concerned eunuch was more distressed with Esther's tears than he had been with anything else going on around him.

"Take me out of here, Hathach. Get me out of here!" Esther gasped out, her strength leaving her legs. The strong eunuch half carried her, half drug her towards the door.

Prince Artaxerxes appeared in the doorway. He moaned when he saw Esther, her face white, almost fainting, her head nodding against Hathach's chest.

"Oh, she had to see that." He hurried to help Hathach support her as they moved her out of the room.

"Here, give her to me," he instructed and picked Esther up with a sweep of his strong arms. He carried her through the silent court room, past clusters of princes and advisors, huddled and whispering in groups. Alliances were quickly forming. A power struggle had begun. Princes glanced with mild interest at Prince Artaxerxes as he carried the queen past, her face pressed into his chest.

"She saved his life!" He finally gasped out turning angrily toward the whispering groups. "The Queen saved the King's life today!"

A few of the princes nodded. The Crown Prince looked up for a moment. He smiled coldly.

"That she did, Brother that she did." He said slowly walking toward his younger brother his face pulled into a sneering smile. "Be careful Brother, who you align with. How did she know of this plot? Looks like a nice acting job to me! Besides," He shrugged and gestured with his hand. "She looks good on you."

The group of men laughed then turned back to their discussions.

Prince Artaxerxes groaned and rolled his eyes.

"Insanity!" He muttered under his breath. "Come along, Hathach," he called. "Let's get the Queen to safety." The prince carried Esther all the way to the palace of women, following Hathach through the maze of hallways and staircases.

Esther roused herself, aware Prince Artaxerxes was carrying her.

She moaned softly, as the prince soothed her.

"Prince, I can walk." Esther finally spoke clearly. "I can walk now. But tell me, what happened? It got blurry there for a moment."

Prince Artaxerxes gently stood Esther up on her own two feet. He tucked her arm in his to help support her. Esther groped with her other arm and Hathach came up beside her and took it. In this way, the three continued at a slow walk toward the palace of women.

"My Queen," the prince spoke after watching Esther closely to see that she could walk on her own legs unassisted. "What has just happened will set off a palace-wide purge. Do you know who was behind this plot?"

Esther frowned slightly. She shook her head.

"No, Prince Artaxerxes, I don't. The information I was told informed me that it was only the two eunuchs that were angry with the King. The plot was all theirs I do believe. But he gave them no time to confirm this. There is no proof now that both are dead."

She stopped walking and her eyes widened. Her mind began to connect the dots, quickly.

"He thinks," She blinked hard. "He thinks it could be me?" The prince was silent. Esther turned and looked up at him.

The prince sighed and looked back at her, his handsome face sad as he watched the look of agony cross the face of the young queen. Already in his short life he had seen so much, felt so much, knew so much.

"He will suspect everyone." The prince stated bluntly. "Everyone but Haman apparently."

Esther's shoulders sagged a bit.

"Oh!" she groaned. "I feel that was a test I was destined to fail. If I spoke, I am a suspect, if I am silent, I would be a widow this very hour!"

"Politics is not a fair game, my Queen. It never is. All of us are suspects, you, me, the Crown Prince, even Prince Haman if the King has eyes to see it."

"Even if it is just the eunuchs, someone will have to suffer for it. Someone living must take the blame." Esther spoke dully.

"Yes, my Queen, someone has to take the blame." The prince stopped and turning to her, he reached for her hands and pulled her close to him. His voice was low and soft. Esther had to turn her head, her ear close to hear what he said.

"My Queen, you are aware of the rising power of Haman. You know what power can do to a man." He stopped and lowered his voice further.

"You are an exception, my Queen. You have taken any power given to you and shared it with others, bettering those around you, raising all up with you." His eyes smiled even as his voice was serious.

"The same is not so with Haman. He is a powerful man, very intelligent and manipulative. He has the ear of the King like no other man does. They spend lots of time together, more and more and more time as the years pass."

"He is not related to the King by blood, yet the King has raised him up to a position above most of his princes and advisors. If, may the gods prevent it," he lowered his voice as if to try to keep the gods from hearing what he was about to say, "our great King where to need to name a successor tomorrow, the princes are not sure he would choose the Crown Prince over this man, Haman. You can only imagine the tension this causes between the Crown Prince Darius and the King."

"Haman will find someone to accuse, be sure of that. None of us will know just who it is. There are many who have reason to fear Prince Haman."

The doors of the palace of women appeared at the end of a long hallway. The sunlight filtered through the billowing white sheets covering the walkway allowing natural light to illuminate the pathway. The armed guards stood silent. Esther was comforted by their sight.

The prince stopped.

"My Queen," he said and lowered his voice to a whisper. His face leaned in and he spoke quietly for Esther's ears alone. "Let me place a guard or two of mine around your person. It will help me to sleep at night knowing you are safe."

Esther did not move. She paused a long moment. The prince's lips had brushed her ear as he spoke. Was it by accident or did he do it by design? No other man was ever this close to her other than her husband, the king.

Esther did not step back but she moved her face ever so slightly away.

"My Prince, our friendship is no secret, not after today. Don't let the matter of my personal safety concern you at this moment."

With this she moved, putting more distance between her and Prince Artaxerxes so she could look up at him without their lips touching.

"I will rely on the guards I have been assigned from the King's palace. Anything more may be misread."

Again, she stepped toward the doorway of the court of women and the armed eunuchs and away from Prince Artaxerxes and his handsome face.

"If I am to lose favor with the King, let me do it without pulling your name down as well. I have my people, my friends, who I trust. I will be safe enough among them. My reputation is clear."

The prince nodded. His face showed no emotion as he watched Esther move purposely away from him.

"May the gods protect you, my Queen," he said at last. He bowed low and kissed the back of her hand.

"Thank you, Prince Artaxerxes. Again, you have been a true friend. Greet your wife for me. For now, I must stay in the palace of women till the King requests my presence."

With that Esther turned and the guards opened the doors for her. She turned back toward the prince who watched her. He nodded and waited till the doors closed behind her.

He then called for one of his men. A quiet discussion followed, and two armed men blended into the shadows around the columns. They would watch the palace and inform the prince the moment the queen was in any danger.Once inside, Esther let out a ragged breath. Her ear burned where the prince's lips had brushed it. Her heart was pounding in her chest and emotions she had not the time to identify coursed through her body. Arjana met Esther in the breezeway leading to her chambers. She took one look at the queen's face and her smile faded.

The faithful servant took the queen's arm and silently they walked toward her apartments. The happy morning thoughts where long from Esther's mind as she re-entered her apartments. She was shaking visibly. Hathach escorted her to her couch.

"Please, my dear Queen," he said his face creased with a frown of concern. "Let me get a plate of food for you. Let me refresh you with a glass of water."

"Hathach, never mind food and water, can you tell me whatever you know of the relationship between Mordechai and Haman?"

Hathach nodded and sat back onto his feet. His large body was still as he thought for a long moment. Shaashgaz and Hegai were also present in the room waiting to hear how the meeting with the king had gone. Everyone was silent, seeing the queen shaken and pale. The three men glanced at each other before Hathach began.

Arjana stood beside her mistress, desperate to hear what had troubled her so.

"Power corrupts my Queen," Hathach began. "Haman demands the respect of everyone. He insists that he be treated like the King even when the King is not present with him. Haman commands, no demands, that all the King's servant's prostate themselves before him every time he enters or exits the gates, coming and going from the palace, which is twice a day, every single day."

"The man, Mordecai, the scribe that sits at the King's gate, does not bow before Haman. He does not bend his knees. He refuses day after day after day. Haman has threatened him, struck him, and yelled at him but this Mordecai is a strong man."

Esther gasped in horror. Of all the men in the kingdom that Mordecai could make his enemy, it was Prince Haman!"Haman has a personal vendetta against Mordecai for this. He purposely tries to hurt him or belittle him or throw something at him every time he passes through the gates. But Mordecai is faithful. He is always at the gate, waiting for a word of your welfare, waiting for me or on one of the other eunuchs in your service, to bring a word or note. I don't know your hold on that man, but he loves you most dearly, my Queen."

At this, Esther clapped her hands over her mouth. No wonder Haman had offered to take on the task of finding the source of this treason. She had told the king it was Mordecai that had discovered this plot. Unknowingly she had given information, very useful information to Mordecai's enemy, a very powerful enemy indeed.

Fear, like white hot liquid, coursed through her veins, chilling her to the bone. She saved her husband's life this day. She may have also given Haman the information he needed to justify Mordecai's death.

This political dance that she was inadvertently dancing seemed deadly no matter what she did. The world she had lived in for the past six years, secure in the title as queen and wife of King Xerxes, shattered around her. She needed to pray. It was the only place that would bring her any form of peace or security.

"Thank you for telling me all this, Hathach." Esther's voice quivered slightly as she struggled with the emotions raging through her. "I had no idea this was happening or to what extent Haman's pride and power had swelled. I know so little of what happens in the courts or outside those gates." She wiped tears from her cheeks as she spoke.

"Your care to know does you great credit, my Queen." Hegai stated. "You wield more influence than you know." With this, he rose and kissed Esther's hand.

"Thank you Hegai," Esther smiled at her friend and teacher. Shaashgaz called Arjana to get food for Esther.

"The Queen has had a big enough dose of political intrigue for one day." He gave Esther a quick smile. "Rest my Queen. There is nothing to do now but wait. Your maids will care for you." He slipped from her apartments. Esther noticed the guard around her apartments doubled that very hour.

Arjana brought her food and water. Suddenly realizing just how hungry she was, she ate with her maids. Silence folded over the apartments. Esther longed to go and see her husband and comfort him, gently stroking away all the heavy worries. What was it like to live with the ever-present fear of someone trying to kill you for your power and position, someone you had perhaps embraced only hours ago?

She rose and knelt by the window, overlooking the city gates, facing Jerusalem. An odd sense of unrest settled over the palace. Even the city seemed to have paused. She lifted her face and began to pray.

Chapter 19

"If I Perish, I Perish"

The king did not call Esther to him that evening to dine with him. Javad did not come to speak with Hathach or Arjana. It was as if all the ties with the palace, with the king, and with all that were close to him were severed. Esther found herself at a loss. She had done what she knew was right, bringing this plot to the awareness of the king. She thought he would be grateful and reward Mordecai for his bravery. Instead, it seemed to have the opposite effect.

The king had restrained his affections for her for up to a week in the past and then repented the moment he saw her, criticizing himself for not calling on his beautiful queen earlier. After a week passed, she grew restless.

Thoughts whipped through her mind. Had she broken some unspoken rule? Had it upset the king that she had contact with a man outside the palace? What if the king thought she was in love and cheating on him? Maybe she should have sent a servant instead of going herself? Should Hathach have gone in her place? The court was no place for a woman, even the queen.

What plagued Esther the most and made her heart doubt her head was the feeling that coursed through her body when she remembered the prince's lips brushing her ear, the smell of his bathing oils that lingered in her mind. She shook her head, stopping the thoughts but, as doubt always does, thoughts continued to plague her the longer her husband refused her presence.Despite the circumstances, Esther and Arjana found a room attached to a larger room that was not being put to any good use. Esther had the rooms stripped. Arjana chose a cheerful paint to plaster the walls with color. They worked together sewing and collecting cushions, bed coverings, night dresses, and other items a couple would need in their little home. The door was fitted with a lock and two keys were made. Arjana wore one around her neck. They waited to give Javad the second key.

Javad finally slipped away two weeks after Esther had visited the king in his dining hall. Hathach told Esther who instantly requested Javad be brought to her garden so she could speak with him.

"The King is in a frightful state, barely sleeping at night. He is suspicious of everyone and turns most of the princes and advisors away in anger. Only Haman and a few other princes are allowed into his presence. There are rumors swirling around all through the palace. This only makes it all worse! The King will hear one thing one moment and the very opposite only hours later." Javad shook his head sadly.

"Has there been found any connection from the two eunuchs, Bigthan and Teresh to anyone else in the palace to justify any of these rumors?" Asked Esther concern for her husband furrowing her brow.

"No there is nothing. Every person in the palace has been extensively examined. Everyone denies any knowledge of a plot. The King's own cupbearer knew nothing. It would be hard to poison the King if the cupbearer died first."

Javad sighed and shook his head. He cared for his king. He was beside this man day and night, awake or asleep. He heard and saw everything.

"He has just buried himself in his work. He becomes angry and flings his goblet at anyone who dares to interrupt him unless the King needs him. He is bent on creating a masterpiece, a thought so bold, a building so magnificent, a ruling so glamorous that he will be remembered for generations."

"It is like he has been reminded of his humanity and he is struggling to find something to ensure the eternity of his memory. Right now, all he has is his failed invasion of Greece, his greatest accomplishment is leading the world's biggest standing army to epic failure."

"Every night he sends me to Hegai to get a girl from his care. Every midnight I escort her away to the palace of women. My Queen, I have asked him repeatedly to let me bring you to him. But he refuses."

Javad continued his voice husky with concern and exhaustion. "No one can calm him like you can. No one can charm him as you do. No one is as good for him as you are, my Queen. Your courage and grace as you asked him for permission for Arjana and I to love each other will never be forgotten. Your kindness to us both has earned my greatest respect, my Queen."

"I would die for you. I will serve you as best I can, till the day I perish, and human strength fails me."

"Oh Javad," Esther hurried to the young man kneeling to her. She gave him her hand which he kissed softly. She slowly drew him up to a standing position. She laid a hand on his shoulder and beckoned for Arjana to come and join them. The three stood together in a circle, Esther's hands on one of each of the faithful servants' shoulders.

"You both are so good to me." She spoke softly, from her heart. "I don't deserve either of your friendships or pledges of service. I am so grateful for you both. You have helped me so very much and I am so happy for your happiness. Now go, be together." She gave Javad the second key, tied to a string, to hang safely around his neck. He smiled, his usual sparkle returning to his eyes, his fair face flushing red with emotions.

Arjana smiled and kissed Esther's hand and the two lovers left the palace of women, hand in hand. Esther stood for a long moment looking after them, smiling slightly despite the news she had heard about her husband, watching history in the making. Then she turned and headed for the school hall.

She could not rest that night and her hands and mind needed something to do. Anatu stood watching over her mistress, as she had promised Arjana she would, her tired head bobbing occasionally. Hathach stood, blending into the shadows, his sword at his side, his eyes blinking heavily.

Esther buried herself in her projects and garden to speed the passing of this time. She designed and built a large gazebo in the garden. The sides were open. Rose bushes were planted at each column to climb up as they grew, a gift from the old gardener of Persepolis.

The roof was peaked and tiered, very different from the rounded dome-like curves of the palace all around her. She had read about the dramatic palace roof styles of the Far East. Based on pictures and the writer's descriptions, Esther and her builders recreated this style as best they could.

Torches were set all around the gazebo on each column. It was more beautiful at night then during the day, the light of the torches creating a magical air. The white marble fountain with water splashing over its sides, stood nearby, feeding a stream that zigzagged its way through the garden. With no summons from the king, Esther completed the garden to her satisfaction. She enjoyed watching the plants grow and bloom, thriving where they were planted. It reminded her of the lush greenery along the river. She thought of the old gardener often and wished he was alive to hear of how well her garden grew.

Esther was in the school hall, listening to an intense lecture on economics and business planning when the door burst open and Anatu came in almost at a run, straight for Esther. Hathach jumped up and almost ran after her. He recognized her and quickly sheathed his sword. Arjana jumped up ready by Esther's side. The teacher stopped and waited.

Anatu hurried up to Esther and dropped to her knees.

"Mordecai," she gasped out. Esther's face went pale and she stood up quickly.

"Please excuse me, Teacher," she said, nodding to him. Anything regarding Mordecai was no matter to discuss in front of a group of curious women. She hurried over to the end of the hall, Anatu and Arjana right behind her.

Once they were away from the group, Esther turned quickly.

"What is it Anatu?" she asked.

"Mordecai is in sack cloth and covered in ashes!" She burst out in a whisper. "He did not even respond to me when I passed by, ready to speak with him. He just kept crying out and tearing at his chest as if in pain."

If Esther could go any paler, she did. Her beautiful face froze. In all her years, she had never known Mordecai to do anything like this. This extreme behavior was what God commanded of His people when they needed to repent, or they were given terrible news. Something terrible must have happened! Mordecai must have received life-changing news. What could have happened to cause him this great of sorrow?

She needed more information. She sent Arjana to run for Hegai. She hurried from the hall headed toward her chambers. The door burst open and Hathach and Hegai hurried in.

"Is it true, Hegai?" Esther asked the moment she saw him.

"Yes, my Queen, it is!"

"What has happened?" Esther wondered.

"We don't know, my Queen." Hegai admitted. "Here in the palace, we have heard nothing."

"Send me, my Queen," Hathach stepped forward, dropping to his knees. "I will take clothes and food to him. I will encourage him to wash and dress and tell me what the great trouble is."

Esther walked over to her window and looked out toward the gate. The streets seemed oddly emptied. She laid her hands against the lattice covering the windows. How she longed to go herself to Mordecai. It pained her deeply she could not.

"Yes," said Esther, tears gathering in her eyes. "Something has happened, and we must find out. Who knows, maybe I can help him in some way."

Quickly clothes were gathered. Fresh fruit from a bowl, bread, cheese, water, and soap hurriedly put in a leather satchel and slung over Hathach's shoulder.

"Encourage him to wash his face, eat, and drink. This will refresh him as he tells you what has upset him so," Esther said. "Tell him they are from me."

She stood by the window as Hathach hurried out. They all waited there, watching Esther pace about the room struggling to keep her emotions at bay. What news could trouble Mordecai so much that he was in sack cloth and ashes before the king's palace? In all her life, Mordecai had dressed well to go to work, sitting at the king's gate proudly. He did not even crumble in front of Haman's constant taunting. What could cause him so much grief?

Hathach could run. Bless that man, he could run when he needed to. His feet burned with the news Mordecai told him as he dashed past the gate, through the doorway, up flights of stairs, down hallways, and along corridors. He burst back into Esther's apartments, gasping for breath. He needed a short moment to catch his breath then he hurried forward. Esther gave him a glass of water which he gulped down.

"Thank you, my Queen." He panted. "I found Mordecai in the city square."

Esther knew the square well. It was there she and Adinah had run to hear the king's messenger; it is where Adinah had died. She waited for poor Hathach to catch his breath. He was trying to tell her as fast as he could, the poor man.

"He refused the clothes…the food…the water, my Queen. Something terrible has happened! Just this past month, my Queen! It involves Haman and the King."

At this, Esther froze. Fear coursed its way through her, her stomach frozen, her feet and hands going numb with cold. Haman! Haman hated Mordecai. Haman wanted Mordecai dead. What could be worse than that? But what, oh what, had Haman convinced the king, her husband, to do?

211

Hegai and Arjana helped Esther to sit on a couch. She was pale, staring at Hathach, fear, great, great fear swimming in her huge eyes.

"I am so sorry to bring this news to you, my Queen." Hathach was on his knees, tears forming in his eyes. Esther clutched Hegai's hand with chilling strength, her knuckles turning white as she waited.

"Mordecai says that Haman has taken out his hatred on the Jews, all the Jews. He convinced the King there is a people in the land who are planning a rebellion against him. He told the King that they refuse to obey the King's authority. They steal from the King and withhold taxes, instead spreading discord and rebellion around the empire, openly fighting unity. Haman convinced the King that he, Haman, was the only one who could deal with this rebellion. He begged the King for the honor of rooting out this terrible plague of a people, the blight on the great empire of the Persians, cockroaches that must be hunted down and killed, every one of them."

"Without hesitation the King gave Haman his ring, his signet ring, the ring that must seal every law in the Persian Empire and the provinces. Your husband has given him the full authority of the Crown to do whatever must be done to free the great empire of this scourge. The King does not even want to know the name of the people Haman is accusing!"

"Since the treason of Bigthan and Teresh, King Xerxes has been consumed with any potential plots on his life and Haman has fed into this fear, waiting for this, just the right moment, to convince to the King to agree to his horrible plot. Once he had the King's signet ring, Haman gathered a group of scribes and cast the dice. The dice fell to the month of Adar. This year, during the twelfth month, Haman has drafted a decree, signed it with the King's signet ring and distributed it all over the empire that all Jews can be killed; all Jews, in every province of the great Persian Empire."

"Here," Hathach's hand trembled as he handed a crumpled, tear-stained document to Esther. Numbly, Esther took the parchment, but she could not hold it. It fluttered out of her fingers onto the floor.

Hegai picked up the document in his large hands. He held it up so Esther could look at it. She stared at it, as if seeing writing for the first time. Her hand rose, and her finger traced the stamp of the signet ring, stamping this horrible massacre into law. Never to be revoked, never to be denied, never to be broken, the law of the Medes and Persians. The god of the Persians was the ever-abiding, undeniable, unchangeable law.

Just months ago, the empire had gathered to celebrate the twelfth year of the Great Xerxes's reign. She had been there, sitting with him, at times on his couch, at times on her own, surrounded with princes, and counselors, and happy throngs of people. Only five weeks ago she had come before the king to tell him that this man, Mordecai, had overheard a plot on his life. Mordecai had saved the life of the very man that was now ruling his death! Her husband, the king, was authorizing the death of her cousin, her father, her teacher, her mentor, her life!

A scream of agony tore from her body dropping everyone in the room to their knees. Arjana gasped clasping her chest as if in pain just watching her mistress's agony. Not one of the servants yet knew that this edict authorized the death of the very woman they all loved and served.

"I have more," gasped out Hathach, tears now streaming down his face as he labored to say the words. "Mordecai says," he faltered. "Mordecai says…" he was shaking his head. "Mordecai says you must go before the King and plead for our lives!"

At this, Arjana and Hegai leapt to their feet and moved between Esther and Hathach.

"But that is certain death!" Arjana spat out the words, cold hard rage over coming her, her body trembling, dark eyes flashing. She stooped, posturing toward Hathach as if daring him to come any closer to Esther. Hegai stood shaking his head, both hands held out toward Hathach. Hegai was silent for a long moment then turned and fell before Esther onto his knees.

"No, my Queen." He gasped out. "No, no, no! Who is this man, this Mordecai, to you that he dares even ask such a thing of you, my Queen?"

Esther sat silent and pale. She did not move again for a long time, her eyes fixed on the floor. She chewed at her bottom lip, deep in thought, her intelligent mind digesting the events she had just been given.

How his heart must have broken with the idea of asking her to go before the king, risking her life. He knew the risk she took in doing this. He would not ask this of her unless there was no other way. No one knew she was a Jewess. No one knew Mordecai was her one relation on this earth. No one knew. She had told no one. Just as he had told her, she had told no one. This meant Haman did not know either. She was a wild card, a player he never anticipated, a move he didn't see coming. If he had known the queen was a Jewess, he would have been way more subtle than this.

It was time to move. This was not the time for tears, or indecision. She needed Mordecai's help, his guidance, even if it was messages through Hathach. Hathach was the best gift the king had ever given Esther and now Esther was using that very gift, Hathach, to try to save the life of Mordecai and her people.

"He is the fastest of all my runners." The king had said proudly in one of his many love letters. *"May he speed the wishes of my dearest wife. May she not have to wait long for her every wish to come true."*

Did this hold true if her wish, her desire, was for her life and that of her people? For what life did she live, caged in this gilded golden palace, held at arm's length from a man twice her age, unable to move freely, hiding her people, her tongue, her heritage, having only her God to speak to if Mordecai, along with all other Jews of the empire lay dead? How could she live knowing she could have tried to stop his death along with thousands of other lives? How could she live unless she died trying to save him and her people? She finally bent and picked up the document, her own tears falling on the paper and mingling with Mordecai's.

"My faithful Hathach," she began at last, looking deeply at Hegai, then slowly turning her gaze to Hathach. Everyone in the room fell silent. Banu was there, her arms around two maidservants both sobbing. Shaashgaz paced ringing his hands. The guards pressed in, spilling through the doorway to hear her speak. Esther's entire team was there surrounding her, waiting for her.

"Remind Mordecai of this; every man, woman, and child in the palace, in the city of Susa, in the province of Persia and in every one of the hundred and twenty-seven provinces of this great kingdom, knows that anyone who dares to step into the inner court uninvited by the King, is condemned to death by the sword, unless." She paused a moment and swallowed hard.

"Unless the King holds out his golden scepter as they approach, holding back the swords of the King's guard. I have not been called to appear before the King in over thirty days. Even I, as wife and queen, cannot expect to be spared at this moment."

Hathach nodded and rose quickly to do his mistress's bidding. Esther was asking Mordecai for her life. Everyone knew the law.

Hegai and Shaashgaz had both seen it with their very eyes, persons shredded by the sharp swords of the guard, the king looking bored as a human was dismembered in front of him, blood spraying around, the carpet needing to be changed. Could they look on as this happened to their beloved queen, their Esther?

The queen's chambers where silent as they waited. No one moved or said anything. The fountain splashed merrily in the garden. A bee buzzed lazily from flower to flower by the lattice window. The curtains billowed in the playful breeze. The teacher was finished his lectures and the women chattered happily to each other as they went about with their afternoons. All around them, the world carried on as if nothing was wrong, even as Esther had been only an hour ago.

Hathach returned running back into the room. His shirt was saturated in sweat. Everyone pressed close to hear what Mordecai had to say. Anatu handed Hathach a glass of water and he drank thirstily, catching his breath fully before kneeling before Esther to deliver the message.

"Mordecai says," began Hathach in a steady voice. He says, "my Queen, to ask you this. 'Do you think, my Esther, even in the most secret places of your heart, that you can escape this slaughter just because you are in the palace? You will live, even there, in your gilded cage, with a price on your head and a death sentence in your heart.'

'If you remain silent and hold your peace during this time, deliverance will arise from somewhere else as Yahweh will protect His people, but you, my daughter, will surely die. Who knows, my princess, my daughter. Could it be that you came to the great palace of Susa for just such a time as this? Could not this be why God has set you up as queen?'"

Hathach's words hung in the air. Every face was staring at Esther. They all knew. They all now knew that Esther was a Jewess. Her people, the ones closest to her, the ones she trusted the most, now all knew who and what she was. Every one of their lives was now in danger if they hid her identity. It was only a matter of time.

It was only a matter of one slip of the tongue, one thoughtless word or look or comment and the palace would know that a Jewess sat on the queen's throne. What would Haman do then? He would find a way to get her. So deep was his hatred for the Jews, he would die even trying to kill the Queen of Persia.

Hegai crumbled at Esther's feet. His great body shook with sobs as he clung to her feet. Arjana just dropped to her knees, all life draining out of her face. Shaashgaz rang his hands, tears running down his cheeks.

"We love you, Queen!" Banu sobbed out the words everyone else was too shocked to say. Esther looked around at the faces surrounding her. The faces that had prayed with her, laughed with her, cried with her, helped her when she was lonely, when she was scared, when she had no one else.

"I love you all too!" she sobbed out, burying her hands in her face, and sobbing for a long moment. The weight of the decision she must make was crushing. She carried so many lives, so many hearts, with her everywhere she went. Her life was not her own. She was a queen, a servant of the Most High God. He had called her to this place. He had moved the heart of the king to set a crown on her head and to raise her up beside him as queen. Mordecai's words rang in her head.

"Am I placed here for just such a time as this?" She asked herself, speaking out loud in Hebrew freely speaking the tongue of her people, at last. She stood up and walked over to the window facing Jerusalem. She sank down onto her knees.

She remembered Daniel, eunuch and advisor to the kings of old. He had spent a night in the lion's den for his obedience, his faithful habit of prayer. God had not failed him even when he broke the law of the land. King Darius had embraced him like a friend, when, miraculously, he emerged from the pit full of hungry lions, without even a scratch.

Was God really asking her to go before the king and petition for her people? If not her, then who else, who else was so perfectly place? Who else could move through the palace and enter the inner court of the king unnoticed, unstopped, and unsummoned like her? Mordecai was right. She was the best one to do this. She had obeyed Mordecai's voice her entire life. And now, now, he asked her, no, told her to go before the king, her husband and plead for the lives of her people, her cousin and herself. Would she?

The deep strength she had learned to love so well fell over her. Even as fear coursed through her veins so did a Power not her own. A still voice of peace spoke through the fears of her mind. A lamp lit and her path became straight before her.

"*Your word is a lamp unto my feet and light to my path.*" Esther recited the psalm of David, her heart shifting, her voice steady. "*I have sworn and confirmed that I will keep Your righteous judgments.*" Strength poured into her body, her knees, her mind. A smile played about her lips even as tears coursed down her cheeks.

"*I am afflicted very much; revive me, O Lord according to Your word. Accept, I pray, the freewill offering of my mouth, O Lord.*" Her eyes closed and she rocked back and forth, pouring out her life before His Greatness.

"*And teach me Your judgments. My life is continually in my hand, yet I do not forget Your law. The wicked have laid a snare for me! Yet I have not strayed from Your precepts. Your testimonies I have taken as a heritage forever,*" She folded her arms up against herself. "*For they are the rejoicings of my heart. I have inclined my heart to perform Your statutes forever, to the very end.*"

Her head dropped and tears fell silently onto her clasped hands. She had her answer. She was to go. This was her time. This was her call. She wiped the tears from her cheeks.

"Hathach," she called softly. "Come, give this message to Mordecai. Do not fail me, my friend. This message is the most important of all the messages you run today."

She laid her soft hand against the cheek of her faithful servant.

"Tell Mordecai to gather all the Jews of the city of Susa and the surrounding neighborhoods together. Tell him to fast for me. I fasted before I went to the King the first time, and I will fast with all of you, for three days. No food or water will pass over my lips starting this moment. On the morning of the third day, I will go before the King, at this very hour, unsummoned. And if I, a servant of the Almighty God, am to perish, then there on the steps before my husband, I will parish."

"If I succeed in my quest, if God turns the heart of the King and I am granted favor, he will hold out the golden scepter and I will have the chance to beg for my life and for the lives of my people, my friends, and my relations, before I die. This just may be the very reason Jehovah called one of His own servants into this great palace, into this very place, into the heart of a King."

Hathach nodded and his hand covered the hand of his queen, holding it against his cheek for a long moment. Then he rose and ran from the queen's chambers, his legs carrying him faster and faster.

Inside the room, Arjana was the first to move toward Esther. She dropped on her knees beside her. Esther smiled slightly at the girl and reached out her hand to grasp hers.

"Do you really believe God hears you?" Arjana asked tears rolling down her cheeks unchecked.

"He brought us this far, did He not?" whispered Esther. "He gave me you."

Arjana nodded and bowed her head. Her lips moved as she soundlessly poured out her heart. Suddenly she lifted her head and looked back at Esther.

"What is His Name?" She asked in an awed whisper.

"He is the God of Many Names," said Esther quietly looking out the window up at the deep blue of the noon sky. "He is Yahweh, He is the Holy One of Israel, the God of Abraham, Isaac, and Jacob, He is the Rose of Sharron, the Lily of the Valley, and He is the Bright and Morning Star."

"Beautiful!" whispered Arjana.

Wordlessly, each one crying openly, Banu, Anatu and the other maids came to kneel beside Esther. Hegai, sobbing openly stood a long moment before he too, knelt. The guards held their post, though one moved to wipe a tear from his eye. The other glanced over at his companion and his head bent in humble reverence. Shaashgaz summoned eunuchs who silently cleared all food and water from the room. He returned and knelt too, with his queen, in prayer.

Hand in hand, the queen and her maidservants knelt in a line, lifting their faces toward Jerusalem to petition a God none of them knew well, save Esther. They saw Him lived out in the kindness of their queen every day. They saw Him in her smiles, her grace, her calm faith, her gentleness, and her love for each one of them. They saw Him in how she bettered those around her, lifting the suffering, feeding the hungry, educating the simple. They saw Him in how she honored her husband, the king, regardless of age, circumstances, and cultural expectations. They saw Him in her and they loved Him.

Hathach returned and joined the prayer group. He told them Mordecai was moved by Esther's response and promised to gather all the Jew's he could. Esther knew he was a respected man among the Jewish community. She knew his house was probably already full of those gathering for advice and comfort. She knew he would place his prayer shawl over his head and open those precious scrolls. He would read out the Scriptures in his clear, strong voice. How she longed to be there, among that group, at that moment, hearing his voice, hearing those words of David, ringing in her ears and heart.

"Arjana, go to my bedroom and in the very back of the mattress, deep under it, right where my head lays, there is a blue tallit, can you bring this to me?"

Arjana rose quickly and did as she was requested. She brought the tallit to Esther who opened it reverently. There lay the letters Mordecai had written her over the past six years. There lay the Scriptures he had written down for her, the Scriptures she had written down as her memory allowed her to. There lay the necklace and earrings, the blossoming myrtle flowers.

"I go as a daughter of Zion. The myrtle blossom is a symbol of God's promises to His people. In His love and by His promises I will be established, even into the great unknown that I am called to enter into." Esther murmured the words she had spoken to Mordecai so long ago, the day he gave the necklace to her, the day she left for the palace, stepping out into the unknown.

She picked up a letter and read them softly to those in the room, translating the Hebrew into Persian so all could understand. The life-giving words flowed over the hearts of all present.

After a long time, the eunuchs rose and went to their chambers and their duties. Life must go on as usual. No one must know what the queen was doing or who she was for the next three days.

The three days of fasting passed in quietness for Esther and her maids. The time seemed all too short for Esther. Every evening Arjana drew a bath and gave Esther beautifying treatments of oils and perfumes, preparing her just as she had been prepared so many years ago, for her first night with the king.

Hegai and Shaashgaz talked over everything they knew about the king hoping to find some bit of information that could save Esther's life. Shaashgaz sewed, his nimble fingers, flying expertly over the seams. He was building the gown of a lifetime. He was sewing to save the life of his queen, his beloved Esther.

Banu sat by his side and helped with anything he needed. Esther's maids all took turns, sewing around the clock to ensure the gown would be ready by noon of the third day. Many tears mingled with the seams and stitches, many prayers whispered as the needle darted back and forth, back, and forth over the silken panels.

Chapter 20
Esther Goes Before the King

The morning of the third day dawned, bright, beautiful, and full of promise. Sunlight streamed in the windows as Esther rose, feeling weak but determined, prepared, and resigned. She walked out into the garden the king had given her. She walked around the fountain, splashing merrily, not a care in the world. It flowed over its rock basin, collecting in a deep shimmering pool before flowing carelessly through the garden. The hibiscus bloomed, opening wide like great trumpets. Hummingbirds darted swiftly from flower to flower. A bee buzzed lazily by and for one moment, just one moment, the world was perfect.

She looked over her gazebo, standing there in the garden, rose vines winding up its columns. It was beautiful just as she envisioned. She had enjoyed designing its every detail, its peeked roofs, its delicate lattice, its feminine grace.

What a good place for a dinner party, the thought floated by, so ordinary and so fleeting. Her fingers instinctively rose to her neck, and she fingered the necklace there. She had put it on three days ago when she did not need to hide her heritage any more from her servants. She found herself fingering the flowers, reminding herself repeatedly of the faithfulness of her God. She sighed gently then turned. She walked back up the stairs toward her chambers. She needed to prepare. Court would be beginning soon. She needed to arrive before the noon break.

The king was a morning person. He was most cheerful after his coffee. It was her best chance and honestly, she could not live much longer with the weight of what she was about to do hanging over her.

Wordlessly Shaashgaz dressed her in the finest gown he had ever made her. It was yellow, a bright happy yellow. It was trimmed with dark green emeralds that heightened the color of her eyes.

Esther's eyes met those of Shaashgaz in the mirror and they held for a long moment. Esther mouthed the word, *beautiful*! And Shaashgaz broke down and wept shamelessly.

Arjana combed out her hair, tears running down her cheeks as she wordlessly prepared her mistress. Banu sat watching, unable to lighten the mood as she usually did, her dark eyes, still and worried. Anatu stood unsure of what to do, shifting her weight from one foot to the other, then back again.

Hegai knelt by the window, tears running down as he lifted his face toward Heaven.

"Bow down Your ear, O Lord, hear me!" Esther spoke out the psalm of David bravely in Hebrew.

Arjana gently placed the crown upon Esther's head of shining black hair, the very crown placed by King Xerxes himself the day he crowned her queen of Persia. Arjana hooked earrings, shimmering with gemstones, into Esther's earlobes.

"For I am poor and needy."

The words of David's eighty-sixth psalm coursed through Esther's heart and mind. She closed her eyes as they painted her eyelids, lining them with black paint.

"Preserve my life, for I am holy," She whispered out.

They painted her lips with a deep red paint carefully accentuating every curve of her mouth perfectly.

"You are my God; Save Your servant who trusts in You!"

She lifted her feet one by one as Arjana slipped on jeweled slippers.

"Be merciful to me, O Lord, For I cry to You all day long!"

Arjana's gentle hands clasp ankle bracelets on her ankles.

"Rejoice the soul of Your servant, For to You, O Lord, I lift up my soul."

Shaashgaz's hands trembled as he laid a huge necklace about Esther's neck. The intricate details of the design highlighted the dress perfectly, accentuating Esther's blue-green eyes.

"For You, Lord are good, and ready to forgive, and abundant in mercy to all those who call upon You."

They dipped each finger in dye, discoloring the tip, accentuating her long delicate fingers.

"Give ear, O Lord, to my prayer; and attend the voice of my supplications."

Ring after ring slipped on her fingers. First the ring the king gave Esther on her second night with him, the ring that sealed his question of asking her to accept the position of becoming his queen. Others were gifts from him, jewels befitting a queen of Persia.

"*In the day of my trouble I will call upon You, and You will answer me.*" Esther shook her head when they lifted a veil toward her head.

"Today I do not cover my face. Today I will go as I am, free and unhidden."

"*Among the gods, there is none like You, O Lord; Nor are there any works like Your works.*"

The Jewess stood and looked for the first time in the full-length mirror, her maids gathered around her. Had they missed anything? Here she was, crowned the queen of Persia, looking every inch the queen of the most powerful empire on earth, going unsummoned before her king. Surely this was the work of the Almighty!

She turned and smiled at all those around her. Arjana fell in step just a few feet behind her. Hegai took her arm silently, blinking back his tears. Banu, Anatu, Shaashgaz and Hathach fell in behind her. Her guards went before and behind her, all of them silent. In this way, they left the queen's chambers and headed for the inner court of the king.

"*All nations whom You have made shall come and worship before You, O Lord, And shall glorify Your name, for You are great, and do wondrous things; You alone are God.*" Esther whispered the words.

They were passing people in the hallway; servants plastered themselves against the wall, looks of shock and interest on most faces as they passed. There was no doubt the queen was on a mission, her face was set, her gait steady and sure.

They passed down long hallways and climbed steps. They were getting closer and closer.

"*Teach me Your way, O Lord; I will walk in Your truth; Unite my heart to fear Your name.*"

They began to pass princes and counselors in the hallways. Some followed behind, curious. Others just looked on, slowly shaking their heads in wonder. What could possess the queen to come before the king? Had he summoned her, and they missed it?

"*I will praise You, O Lord my God, with all my heart, and I will glorify Your name forevermore.*"

The carpets changed color. They entered the last hallway. The door stood before them. When Esther passed through, she would be standing in the inner court of the king, unhidden. No longer Esther, but Hadassah, coming to beg for her life and those of her people. All would know who the queen was, a Jewess, condemned, a death sentence signed and sealed by her very own husband, hanging over her crowned head.

"For great is Your mercy toward me, And You have delivered my soul from the depths of Sheol."

Esther felt her physical strength falter, that archway, loomed closer and closer. She could hear the hum of voices. It was business as usual in the court room of the Great King Xerxes. Arjana was suddenly beside her; Esther leaned on her shoulder willing her body to keep moving forward.

"O God, the proud have risen against me, and a mob of violent men have sought my life and have not set You before them!"

Wave after wave of nausea washed over her. The color left her face. Her legs felt shaky and rubbery. She leaned heavily on Arjana; her face never moved from its forward position. Anatu came up besides her supporting her on the other side. The guards stopped on the side of the arch way. This was as far as they needed to come.

Hegai, Banu, Shaashgaz and Hathach all stopped and watched her back. Hegai raised a hand as if to try to stop her then let it fall to his side, his face crumbling. Tears flowed unchecked down his cheeks. Never had he seen such a woman. Never had he known such a girl; never had there been such a queen as this in all the history of the great palace of Susa.

"But You, O Lord, are a God full of compassion, and gracious, longsuffering and abundant in mercy and truth." A slight smile played about her lips as she voiced the words.

The three women passed through the archway. They slowly began to descend the steps. Heads began to turn; a hush fell on all as they saw the queen descending the steps. Her anklets jingled softly, alerting those around her that a woman was present. Esther had to look down, concentrating on her body and movements so she would make it down the steps without falling.

Someone was talking in a loud, authoritative voice. Esther did not look up to see who it was. Stair by stair she descended, her breath coming in rapid gasps.

"Oh, turn to me, and have mercy on me!"

A total silence fell on the room. The king had seen her. The last stair was there. She stepped down onto the carpet. Then, she lifted her face and looked up at her husband. He was staring at her, a great frown on his face, his mouth partly open in speech.

"*Give Your strength to Your servant and save the son of Your maidservant!*" She prayed the words. She looked fully at her husband the king, so he could see that it was her, his wife, coming before him. She was drawing closer and closer. She could no longer feel her legs or hands or arms. She felt cold. A loud buzzing began in her ears.

"*Show me a sign for good, that those who hate me may see it and be ashamed, Because You, Lord have helped me and comforted me!*" She pleaded watching his arm, waiting for him to lift the scepter.

The king rose with a swift action. His robe streamed off his body. He was massive, a full seven feet tall! Esther gasped, unable to look away, terror clutching at her heart beyond all control. She felt her strength fade, she did not see him lift the scepter. The room was becoming blurry. She stumbled forward desperate to reach the steps with any strength left in her. The jingle of her jewelry sounded loud to her own ears.

Arjana and Anatu almost threw her forward, as she crumpled in a faint on the steps to the throne, guards standing over her, each one holding a great sharp sword.

Something cold touched her cheek. Someone was holding her head; a hand was stroking her hair. It was familiar but she was unsure. A face was peering into hers, eyes full of concern.

"Get me a glass of wine!" she recognized the voice of her husband. Her vision cleared and she looked up into the king's face. His eyes were brimming with concern, his brow creased in a deep frown.

"Esther, my dearest, Esther," he repeated her name almost in a groan, stroking her cheek with the back of his fingers, gently, tenderly.

"You have fainted, my dearest. What a fright you gave me crumpling down on the steps, looking as pale as death itself. Ohhh my dearest!" someone passed him the glass of wine. He held it up to her lips.

"Drink this; it will steady your nerves." Esther sipped the wine welcoming its sweet richness. Her mouth was so dry she feared she would not be able to speak.

"There! Color is returning to your cheeks now." The room cleared and Esther became aware she was draped in the king's lap, her head cradled against his chest, sitting on the steps leading up to his throne, armed guards standing on either side of them holding their swords. The king had his scepter laid over her as he held her, laid protectively between her and the sharp blades.

Voices began as whispers around her, all the princes and noblemen and advisors watching their king revive his wife.

"She is all right," he looked up. A cheer rose and clapping broke out. The king turned and looked at her, her face cradled against his chest. His eyes softened as he looked deep into the eyes of his queen. He looked for a moment like he would like to kiss her but did not.

Instead, his fingers gently stroked her cheeks as he looked down into her face. Esther noticed wrinkles around his eyes, grey in his beard she had not seen before, a scar on his forehead, just under his crown. He looked old and vulnerable for a moment. Then, curiosity flooded his face. A slight smile pulled at his lips as if teasing her.

"What is your wish, Queen Esther," he asked in a firm voice. "What is your request of me? I will grant you anything even up to half my kingdom to rule over."

Esther swallowed. She struggled to sit up. Strength found her limbs and she half-kneeled, half sat before the king, Arjana still supporting her heavily. The king smiled and held out his scepter toward her. Esther smiled and reaching out, she gently touched the jewel on the top of it. The winged symbolism on both sides of the jewel captured her attention for a moment. They looked to be the wings of the Angel of mercy to her in that long moment.

But the king waited.

What was she to say?

Oh Lord! Cried her heart.

Her gazebo suddenly popped into her mind. Of course!

She lifted her face toward her husband, the king and spoke.

"If I have found favor in your sight, my Lord, my King. And if it pleases the King to hear my request and grant me my heart's desire, please, let the King come to a banquet I will prepare for him. And let Haman, the King's preferred advisor, also attend the banquet I will prepare this evening."

The King smiled and rose to his feet; he turned and looked up at Haman standing beside the throne, watching all this drama unfold.

"She wants us to join her for dinner," he said loudly, a smile breaking over his face. He turned to his wife and reaching down, he helped her to her feet.

"The King and Haman will be there as the Queen asks," he assured her.

"Thank you, my King," Esther bowed low and backed away as the king climbed up the stairs to his throne. He sat down and watched as his wife exited the room, his face unable to hide his curiosity. Had the queen just risked her life to ask him to dinner?

Esther left the court, her heart pounding, a smile almost splitting her face. She passed through the archway and was almost knocked over by Hegai, Shaashgaz, Banu and Hathach.

"Hurry, hurry!" exclaimed Esther. She lifted the front of her gown.

The servants almost ran to keep up with her.

"Well, she has found her strength again!" Hegai huffed. Esther slipped her arm into his and smiled up at him.

"We have work to do, my friends," she said brightly.

In her mind, she was already planning a menu for the king. She would gather food from the garden the palace women had planted. The food must be the best and oh so fresh! Wine must be bought but first, Mordecai must know she had an audience with the king at last!

Esther had her maids and eunuchs running everywhere as she paced back and forth in her room, removing article after article of jewelry, preparing for work. Hathach ran to tell Mordecai then purchased the best wine from the vendors.

The women gathered in the great hall and Esther told them of her dinner date with the king. Many clamored to help and soon the gazebo was covered with decorations. A table was moved in. Three couches placed around the table. A tablecloth woven by one of the women, embroidered with strands of gold, graced the table. Huge flower arrangements stood at the base of each column. The curtains were pulled back with golden cords, allowing the evening breezes to float through. The fountain splashed merrily. The air was laden with the smell of flower blossoms. The torches were lit, and Esther stood, dressed in her new gown, the crown on her head, the jewels of Persia around her neck, waiting for the king to arrive.

He was quite distracted the rest of the day and could not concentrate. He found himself excited. This woman fascinated him. Never had she done something so bold and so endearing. He dismissed court early, telling Haman to hurry home to prepare for dinner.

The two men arrive together, the king dressed in his royal robes, a smile on his face, Haman dressed in his finest beside him. Esther was struck again with how much the king delighted in mystery. A man that held everything at the tip of his fingers, delighted in the unknown, the anticipation, the waiting. She watched as the two most powerful men in the world, descended the steps from the palace of women toward her garden gazebo. She bowed low as they approached, her eyes humbly averted.

"Rise, my Queen," The king spoke, and she took the hand offered her. The king looked around, impressed.

"I am glad I granted your request for a garden," he said. He looked a long moment at the gazebo roof.

"What gave you the ideas for the pointed roofs stacked in such a fashion instead of rounded domes?" he asked interested.

"Something I saw at Persepolis. The old gardener told me it was built after the constructions of palaces in the Far East," Esther replied enjoying the conversation with her husband, grateful it was not strained or forced. It had been over a month that the two had been together.

The food was served, and the wine flowed. Esther rose often to serve her husband and guest personally. Haman seemed to be enjoying himself immensely. He was in fine form that evening and had the king laughing with his relentless trivia and jokes. The wine goblets were never empty under Esther's watchful eye, and she smiled as her guests grew quite marry.

At last, the king sat up on his couch and looked over at Esther across the table. Esther rose and came to his side. The king pulled her down onto his couch as he was custom to do. He had his hands around her, holding her close. He laid his head in her lap for a moment.

"I have missed you," he murmured.

"As I have you, my Lord," Esther gently stroked his cheek again noting the wrinkles and the greying hairs about his temple. She lingered with the king then rose to refill the goblets of her guests.

"What is it my dearest?" The king begged, sitting up on his couch. "Free me of my pain! What is your request? What does your heart desire? I will grant it even up to half of my kingdom."

Esther turned from the table; she had his full attention now. Was now the time? Could the evening go from laughing to her pleading for her life in a moment? The breeze was gentle and warm, inviting, persuasive.

"*No*," was the clear message. "*Wait*."

The Lord God Jehovah had more work to do in this great drama unfolding in the palace, behind closed doors. Haman was watching Esther intently. Esther dropped down to her knees before the king's couch. She smiled, composing herself quickly.

"My wish and my desire is this." She smiled into the king's eyes. "Come again, you and Haman, join me tomorrow night, for a banquet I will prepare for you."

"Then, My King, I will tell you what lays heavy on my heart. I have enjoyed the evening so very much; I can't ruin it now with what my request is. It is not yet the time."

The king sighed dramatically. He lifted the bejeweled hand of his queen and pressed it to his lips.

"I take it you don't want half the kingdom then." Esther shook her head. "My king must have his kingdom." She said and gently stroked his hand that still held hers. He laced her fingers into his, looking deep into her eyes. He sighed again.

"Thank you, my dearest Queen," he said stifling a yawn. "I best go now as it is late; it has been a long day. I will be sure to come to your table again tomorrow. There is no table I prefer more."

"What say you Haman?" the king tore his eyes away from his wife's face and looked over at his trusted prince. "Shall we join the Queen again tomorrow?"

"It is an honor to dine with the Queen." Haman smiled. His face showed only delight, his cheeks blushed slightly with the wine the queen so generously served.

With this, the King rose. Haman rose as well. The king moved to leave then stopped. He turned and kissed his wife, unashamedly. Then he and Haman ascended the stairs and left the court of women.

No sooner had they left then Arjana, Anatu, Banu, and Hathach tumbled down the stairs in their eagerness. Esther smiled watching them hurry toward her, questions all over their faces.

"Well?" Arjana was not so discrete, and the question burst from her despite herself.

Esther shook her head.

"It went very well but it was not the right time. They have agreed to return tomorrow for a second meal. Then, I must ask. But for now, I will be satisfied with our success."

Arjana and Banu looked over the gazebo.

"It is a beautiful place!" Banu explained.

They all joined in the work and soon the table was cleared, any leftover food put away. The flowers remained for another evening. Esther climbed the stairs slowly, Arjana, Anatu, Banu, Hathach and the others following her. They were all exhausted. They had gone from such fear and trembling this very morning to a successful banquet with the king and his promise to return for another tomorrow evening.

"I must thank you both," Esther said softly, placing a hand on each of her maidservants and friends' shoulders once they reached the top of the stairs. "I could not have done it without you. You both risked your lives to come with me. I could not have made it without you."

With that, she stooped and placed a kiss on each cheek of the girls. Anatu and Arjana looked at her their eyes shining.

"Our promise holds true," Arjana said, looking steadily up at Esther. "We will lay down our lives for you, our Queen."

"I am a blessed woman," said Esther. "Come, let's sleep. We will have a busy day again tomorrow."

Esther dropped her tired body into bed, breathing praise to God for sparing her life and those of her maids. Her eyes closed and sleep with its blissful silence overcame her, and she slept deeply. But, in his bedchamber, her husband, the king, was not given the same pleasure.

Unable to sleep, he kept seeing his beautiful wife's form fainting before him. Why would she come to the court, risking her very life, simply to ask him to a dinner? Then, when he asked her, she only asked him to attend yet another dinner?

Women could be exasperating but this, this was something else! He had wanted to ask her to come to stay with him tonight. He wished she was there in his arms. Maybe then she would tell him what it was, in the privacy of his chambers, in the lock of his embrace? Why had he not called for her sooner?

Why had he been separated from her for these last weeks? As his mind drifted, searching for the answer to his questions the thought suddenly burst into his memory. Was she not the one who had warned him of the plot on his life?

He sat up with a jolt.

"Chronicles!" he called out, knowing Javad was waiting within earshot. A steady voice began reading from behind the curtains.

"Last month's entries," instructed the king. He closed his eyes as the voice read out the entries one by one. Suddenly he stopped and listened closely.

The Queen was invited to the King's luncheon at noon hour as she had urgent business to discuss with him. She told him of the plot between the two eunuchs to kill the King. Mordecai, a Jew that sits at the King's gate as a scribe, was the one who informed the Queen of the plot.

The voice continued to read but the king's mind stayed on the name, *Mordecai*, rolling it over and over in his mind.

Early in the morning the king threw back the covers and rose. As Javad poured his coffee, the king looked through the chronicles himself. Nothing was recorded that was done to honor Mordecai. Odd! How could he have missed this?

"My King," Javad came, bearing his cup. "I passed Haman waiting to see you."

"Perfect!" exclaimed the king reaching for his cup. "Bring him in I want to talk with him. Serve him a cup too. Mine is the finest coffee."

Javad hurried to do as the king bid, surprised by the king's cheerful mood. Haman came in quickly and bowed low. The king was thoughtfully sipping his coffee still staring at the pages of the book of the chronicles. Haman made a move to speak but the king lifted his hand.

"Tell me, Haman," the king began. "You are a wise and insightful man. What should be done to the man the King wishes to honor?"

"Well," Haman took a long sip of his cup, thinking.

"How about this, my King; let a horse that the King has ridden in public during one of the parades be brought out, tacked in all its finery. Let a robe that the King has worn in public, at one of your generous feasts, be placed on the man. And then, let the very crown that sits on the King's brow be, for a time, placed on that man's head. Let one of the esteemed princes walk this man, the very man the King delights to honor, mounted on the King's horse, wearing the King's crown, through all the streets of the great city of Susa, proclaiming as he goes, 'Such is done to the man whom the King delights to honor!'"

The king turned to look at Haman a smile in his eyes.

"You have vision my man!" he exclaimed. "This is why I have elevated you so. That is perfect. Go and do this very thing, everything you have just described to me. Do it to Mordecai, the Jew. He sits at my gate every day as a scribe."

The king turned and was on his way out the door. He did not see the shock that descended onto Haman's face.

"Mordecai?" Haman spat out the word. His coffee cup banged onto the nearest table spilling over.

Undisturbed, the king nodded and removed his crown. He handed it to Javad.

"Yes, Mordecai the Jew. He was the one who sounded the alarm on this whole plot on my life. You would approve, would you not? You are personally seeing to the details of this. You are the perfect man for the job. Tell me all about it this evening. Remember, we have dinner with the Queen. Don't be late!"

And with that the king swept out of the room.

Chapter 21
Esther's Request

Esther was awake, kneeling beside her window. She had finished praying and, resting her chin on her hands, she watched the people below, moving freely in and out of the gate. She saw a man, dressed as one of the noble princes, leading the king's horse. She recognized the royal crest on its bridle at once. The horse was covered in a silken purple blanket with golden tassels at all four corners, its leather tack sparkling in the morning sun. It arched its noble neck proudly, its silken mane fluttering in the breeze.

But the man riding the horse was not the king. It was…!

She blinked and shook her head. At this point she was standing, straining against the screen to see well. The man looked up at her window for a long moment, his hand raised to keep the crown from falling off his head.

Esther's heart leapt with joy! Hope flooded her being with a warm embrace.

"God has heard our prayers!" she exclaimed. "He has heard us!"

Arjana and Anatu ran into the room. Hathach was right behind them. They stared at Esther, overcome with joy, tears streaming down her face, pointing wordlessly at the window. They rushed over to look but it was too late. The horse and rider, led by the prince, had passed. A voice floated in the window, strained, and forced.

"Such is done to the man the King delights to honor!"

Esther clasped her hand over her mouth and dropped to the floor, her body wracked with sobs. Arjana fell beside her, scared to touch her, desperate to comfort her.

"My Queen!" Hathach was deeply troubled.

"She looks happy," said Anatu thoughtfully. Anatu was still at the window straining to see what Esther had seen.

Esther nodded.

"Hathach!" she gasped out. "Follow them! See if it is true. Maybe I have gone mad, but I just saw Haman leading the King's horse with Mordecai crowned and dressed in the King's robe riding out the gate!"

Hathach needed no more instructions. His jaw dropped for one moment and he turned and ran from the apartments, his feet pounding on the cold tile floor of the breezeway as he ran from the palace of women.

Esther placed her arm around Arjana and the two women rocked back and forth for a long time.

"He heard me," Esther kept repeating, smiling around her tears. Arjana stroked Esther's hair her tears mingled with the shimmering strands. Oh, to be heard and answered by the Almighty God, was there anything better?

Anatu and Banu joined Esther and Arjana on the floor. The women held hands and Esther lifted her face and led them in a psalm of praise.

"Oh, clap your hands, all you peoples! Shout to God with the voice of triumph! For the Lord Most High is awesome; He is the great King over all the earth. He will subdue the peoples under us, and the nations under our feet. He will choose our inheritance for us, the excellence of Jacob whom He loves."

"God has gone up with a shout, the Lord with the sound of a trumpet. Sing praises to God, sing praises! Sing praise to our King, sing praises! For God is the King of all the earth; sing praises with understanding. God reigns over the nations; God sits on His holy throne. The princes of the people have gathered together, the people of the God of Abraham. For the shields of the earth belong to God; He is greatly exalted. The psalm forty-seven by King David."

Esther smiled joyfully through her tears; the psalm echoing off the walls of that great stone palace. It echoed through the chambers of the queen of Persia. It filled the hearts of the women with unspeakable joy. They stayed on the floor, drenched in joy, faces uplifted in unashamed, open worship to the Almighty God who had heard their prayers and saved the life of Esther their beloved queen.

They were interrupted by the sound of running feet and the door flew open.

"It's true!" gasped out Hathach not even waiting to catch his breath. "It's true, my Queen! The great Prince Haman leads the King's horse, prepared as if for a grand parade and Mordecai, the Jew, sits upon the horse, dressed in a robe the King has worn, with the crown on his head! Haman is calling out, 'such is to be done to the man whom the King delights to honor'!"

He shook his head looking at Esther.

"In all my life I have never seen a more fascinating sight! Your God, my Queen, has heard our prayers!" Joy, hope, and wonder simmered in his voice. Esther smile widely.

"Now is our time, my friends," she said excitedly, rising to her feet. "Now is the time. Let us prepare for a dinner unlike any this empire has ever seen before. God is on our side. The Almighty is with us. We will not fail in our request. The King will grant us life today!"

The women's hallway was abuzz with activity. Esther tasted everything to make sure it was the best. The women and girls helped as best they could. At times, they simply ran out of room because of everyone who crowded in, wanting to help. But the result was quite perfect.

Esther smiled contentedly, her mind turning over every detail, as she soaked in her bath of lavender and jasmine. Never had she thought her gazebo would be such a blessing in disguise. It was set to stage one of the most dramatic conversations of her lifetime.

Candles floated in the fountain. A couple of the women had embraced candle making developing a recipe for candles that could float on water. The effect was stunning, and Esther could hardly wait to see them lit this evening. She hoped the king would find them enjoyable too.

The table was covered with a dark blue cloth, with golden threads embroidered through it. It reminded Esther of what some of the cloths of the temple may have looked like. She had never seen it. She had never seen her homeland; it was always a distant place, a dream but this cloth seemed a timely testament to her heritage. Banners of deep blue graced the ceiling and a huge chandelier decorated with cut crystals simmered above the table. This evening it was dinner fit for a king.

Esther cut an arrangement of orchids, rich in deep blues, purples, and bright yellows for the table. The flower arrangements from the evening before where enriched with ferns, hibiscus, and other bright flowers. It was all ready. There was nothing more she could do except dress and wait.

Esther chose to wear a deep blue gown. It was trimmed with a gold lace. She chose only to wear the string of golden myrtle flowers Mordecai had given her before she entered the palace. They looked so simple and plain compared to what the queen of Persia usually wore. The royal crown was placed on her flowing hair reminding all that, although simply and elegantly dressed this evening, she was indeed, the queen.

The king arrived alone, and Esther greeted him. The two walked down the steps together. They admired the fountain with the floating candles. Esther told him of how the women worked till they discovered a recipe that allowed the candles to float. The king seemed touched with the intimate and ordinary details of Esther's life.

Hathach and a couple other eunuchs hurried to the house of Haman for he was nowhere to be found in the palace. It was not good to be late to a meal the queen had invited one to, by name!

Haman hurried down the palace steps toward the garden, almost an hour later. The queen welcomed him graciously and bid him enter. Esther was very calm and still. She was prepared. He was starting the evening off on the wrong foot. Judging by his expression and the occurrence of the day, Haman's entire day was way off.

This evening Esther did most of the talking. She described what the women were doing and making together in their school. They discussed the school and library outside the palace that Esther had established for women and girls.

Haman listened in silent shock. He was seeing a very different side of the queen than he imagined. Not only was she beautiful, but she was also kind, intelligent, and motivated. This was a far cry from the bejeweled sex slave he had dismissed her as in the past. He was feeling quite uncomfortable. The day's events had really shocked him. He was not able to play the king like the puppet he had imagined. He drank heavily from his wine glass hoping it would help.

The queen was quick to keep it full, serving the wine and supper personally, again. No servants helped unless she beckoned. The king seemed to be enjoying every moment with his wife. He pulled her down onto his couch as she served.

"Stay with me a while," he demanded merrily. The king was drunk with delight not with wine. He was fascinated by this woman even more this evening then the last.

The king had had a wonderful day. He was in a great mood. All day he had looked forward to his wife's banquet. The beautiful garden and her handiwork made him all the happier. He was not the least disturbed his companion was unusually quiet. The opposite may have been the truth, as instead of discussing politics or laughing, the king carried on a conversation with his wife, learning of her projects and enjoying her tastes.

"So, Esther, my queen," the king said with a smile on his face. Darkness had fallen. The torches cast a shifting warm light over the table. The crystals of the chandelier reflected the light all over the gazebo in tantalizing rainbows of fractured light. His queen looked like a goddess she was so beautiful. He loved this part.

"I ask you again, what is it that you desire, what is your request? My offer still stands! Name it and up to half of my kingdom is yours. Ask it of me and I would be delighted to grant it to you."

Esther rose. Now was the time! Now was her chance to lay out her petition and request her life. She dropped to her knees before the king. Her countenance changed and her eyes filled with unshed tears. She lifted her hands clenched together in a gesture of pleading. Her beautiful face fell away. It was suddenly replaced by a face creased with pain and suffering. The king rose up on one elbow in surprise.

"If I have found favor in your sight, O my King, and if it pleases you to grant me my request. The petition I lay before you is that my life be spared! My request is that the lives of my people be saved by your generosity, Oh King!"

"My Lord, I have been sold to be slaughtered, both me and my people. If it was just to be slaves, I would have held my tongue. This action will be a scar to your reign, a blight on your name from generation to generation, Great King."

"No king of Persia or Babylon or even Greece, has sold his own wife and her people for annihilation. No compensation promised to you by the enemy could even begin to truly justify such an act of abomination. What good is ten thousand pounds of silver if your kingdom lies in ruin before you?"

No longer was the king lounging playfully on his couch. He was sitting bolt upright, staring at the face of his queen. He could not doubt her sincerity for one moment. Had she not risked her very life to ask him for her life?

"Who has done this? What man is capable of even entertaining the thought of endangering the life of my Queen and destroying the reputation of the Great King Xerxes?"

The king was now standing, towering up in his rage, his hands clenching by his sides. His knuckles white around his wine goblet. He spit out his words, his great body shaking with wrath.

Esther looked up into his face. She pointed, then looked right at Haman.

"This man, my King, this wicked and deceitful man, Haman. He is your enemy and the greatest threat to my King's reputation." Her face was pale, but her accusing arm was strong. She did not falter in her quest.

The king looked at Haman. The man was cowering on his couch, terrified. The goblet whistled past his head mere inches from his temple and clanged hard onto the stone steps of the gazebo. The king followed the goblet out. The dark night swallowed him from sight. Esther looked after her husband, her heart breaking with how acutely he must be feeling Haman's deceptiveness.

Her part was over. She had done it. She hoped the king could save them. She rose slowly to her feet and sat down on the couch the king had been laying on only moments ago. She felt very tired as the adrenaline slowly left her body. She closed her eyes drawing in a long breath.

When she opened her eyes again, Haman was standing over her. She startled and let out a scream.

"Oh, my Queen," exclaimed Haman dropping to his knees before her, just as she had moments ago, knelt before her husband. "Spare my life! I never meant you any harm. I did not know you were a Jew! How could I?"

The man was half-crazed with fear. He knew his life hung on a very fine thread. He buried his head in the trails of Esther's gown, clutching at her legs. In his dramatic pleading, he looked and felt to be struggling to lift her gown.

"I have children, my Queen, spare me!"

At that moment, Esther looked up. Her husband was running up the stairs into the gazebo. He had heard her startled scream and was hurrying to her side. He saw the man Haman half kneeling half lying on the couch his head between his wife's legs, his hands struggling at her gown. In one great step, he was over beside the couch. He grabbed a handful of Haman's hair and threw the man away from his wife.

"How dare you assault my wife? With me still in the room, in my very own house!" He thundered. Haman's body flew across the table. His head and back struck a column, knocking over a flower arrangement. Blood sprayed from his nose. Esther gasped and the king came to her. He scooped her up in his arms shielding her from seeing any more.

Royal guards rushed to restrain Haman; one quickly covered his face with his cloak. Hathach ran to his queen's side. Arjana, Anatu, Banu and others were right behind him. The once peaceful garden was suddenly full of people, soldiers, princes, scribes, and advisors. Artabanus stood behind the king's couch, his sword drawn beside him. The king sat on the couch cradling the queen in his arms.

"Did he hurt you, my dear?" He panted.

Esther shook her head. "No, my Lord, I am safe. I am well."

"I am sorry I left your side at all, my Queen. I was so angry by the betrayal of a man I trusted, even with my own life. He dared to lift a hand against my wife. A man is nothing if he can't even protect his wife from assault in his own home!"

One of the king's eunuchs stepped forward toward the king.

"Speak, Harbonah," the king growled. Harbonah bowed then spoke.

"When I ran to collect Haman from his house to bring him to the banquet the Queen had prepared, I saw great gallows in the courtyard of his house. Word has it, my King; he meant to hang Mordecai, the Jew, his personal enemy, from them this very morning!"

"The gods denied you sleep, Lord King, enabling you to discover the truth of what Mordecai had done to save your life. Haman was in your chambers early this morning to ask for your permission to hang Mordecai before he came to this supper the Queen so graciously prepared, so his victory could be complete."

Esther could not have been more shocked. Mordecai had been that close to death this very morning?! The very morning the king told Haman to lead him about and proclaim that this is what is done to the man whom the king delights to honor? How great was her God!

"Hang Haman on the gallows he made! Let his own handiwork be his place of death!" The king thundered; spit flinging from his mouth as he roared out the orders.

"No! No! Noooooo!" cried out the poor wretched man. "My sons! What of my sons?" The guards drug him away writhing and screaming. Esther buried her head in her husband's chest, her eyes shut tightly.

"Are you not coming, my Lord?" One of the princes turned back to look at the king. The king looked down at Esther then shook his head.

"I have much better things to do," he said.

The prince nodded. They hurried off into the night, justice to be served at the king's command.

There was silence for a long moment. Esther could only hear her husband's heavy breathing and the deep comforting sound of his heart pounding in his chest. It took a long time for it to slow down.

"Who are your people?" his voice cut through the silence.

Esther lifted her head, tear stains on her cheeks. Her eyes widened as she studied his face for a long moment. A smile spread across her face as she recognized the question the king had asked of her so long ago.

"I am Hadassah of the tribe of Benjamin, the last living descendent of my father. The Jews are my people. I proudly reveal to you my heritage, Oh my Husband."

"Hadassah," the king whispered the name foreign to his lips.

"After all that, I married a Jewess." He said, almost to himself. Esther nodded watching his face carefully.

"Yes, my Lord, you did."

"Why did you hide it from me?" asked the king.

"Mordecai, the Jew, the man whom the King delights to honor is my cousin and guardian. He saved my life, so many years ago as an unwanted orphan in the slums of Susa."

"He saved me from a life of poverty, slavery, and ignorance. He took me in, an orphan girl with nothing, no hope, no relatives, and no other options. He gave me a home, an education, and a family. I lacked nothing in his house."

"But one of the greatest things he taught me was obedience. He told me the day I came to the palace to never reveal my heritage, or my people, to hide my language and my name. I left it all behind to become Esther of Susa."

The king nodded.

"He was wise to advise you such. My former wife, Queen Vashti hated the Jews and took great pleasure in torturing any in her care. To be honest, you would have been treated differently if your heritage was known."

Esther nodded.

"Above all odds, out of hundreds of other women, you chose me, my Lord King. My God, the God of Abraham, Isaac, and Jacob, turned your heart, my husband, and gave me favor in your sight. You chose me and loved me. You married me and crowned me, a nobody. I stayed silent all these years in obedience to my promise to Mordecai."

"I have obeyed you and honored you as I would him, my Lord King. Please know the power of my love for you, revealed in the obedience to my cousin. My God set a great plan in motion, so many years ago, so I would find favor in your sight this very night and be able to kneel for my people and beg for the lives of my countrymen. If I had not stepped forward and appeared before you, their deliverance would have come from somewhere else but I, I would have surely perished in shame."

"Esther, my dearest," the king cradled Esther's face in his hands. He wiped away the tears from her cheeks with his thumbs. "Or should I say, Hadassah, my angel. You, you are the strength of my reign. It will be because of you, my Queen, that peoples from generation to generation will remember my name. It is you that will mark my kingship. It is you that will bless my days. This day will be forever recorded in the chronicles of the Kings of the Medes and Persians."

He pulled her face toward him and kissed her forehead, a single tear sliding out of his tightly shut eye. It dropped on Esther's hands.

"My Lord?" she raised her hands to wipe it away, but the king captured her hand in his.

"No, my Queen," he said shaking his head. "The Great Xerxes would do well to cry more tears. I have been so foolish, my dearest. I have been so easily swayed with bribery, sweet speech, and flattery. You are a much better Queen than I am King."

"No! My Lord," Esther's brow furrowed in a frown for a moment. "My King needs better councilors and advisors around him. Ones who do not flatter with their tongues yet stab him in the back."

"My Lord if I may suggest. Meet my cousin Mordecai. He is a wise man, and it would do the King well to hear him. He came to the gate daily to seek my welfare. Don't doubt his love or devotion for you one moment. He would lay down his life for you, my King. Has he not already saved the life of my Lord the King?"

"I want to meet this man." The king said. Esther's face lit up in a smile. She quickly rose to her feet in excitement.

"Hathach, run and bring Mordecai to the King. Tell him Esther waits to see him. It will warm his heart." Esther breathed out the words, excitement dancing in her voice.

Hathach nodded and ran to do his queen's bidding. This was the best news he had borne in a long time and joy gave his feet wings.

Chapter 22
Esther Sees Mordecai Again

Esther paced about, filled with excitement at meeting her beloved cousin again after years apart. They need not hide their relationship with each other any longer. It seemed to be taking so long! Oh, how her heart rejoiced in this moment.

Esther's mind ran through the passageways and out the gate, down the cobblestone streets, across the square, up the small winding road lined with houses on either side. Then there, on the right, a familiar door stood. Hathach would knock loudly on the door stating that he came in the name of the Great King Xerxes.

The hour was late. Mordechai would be reading Scriptures. He would hurry to the doorway; his prayer shawl covering his head as he would not take the time to take it off. His face would fill with joy, and he would hurry to come, hurrying to see his Esther again and meet his king.

The king chuckled as he watched her excitement.

"The success of your school has inspired me," the king said after a long pause. "I think I want to build more of them. They are a good idea. They could bring unity to the empire and provide enrichment to my citizens."

Esther turned toward him.

"The crown needs more structures to use as these schools." She said seriously. "A school could be built in all the major cities across all the provinces. This will cost money for sure, but once the schools are up and running, the goal can be to make them as self-sufficient as possible. The school in the city has been able to cover its own costs and even make an income selling household wears in the marketplace of Susa."

"Wise insight. One would think you have considered this already."

"I have my Lord," the queen admitted. The king nodded. He glanced around.

"I threw my goblet." He noted.

Esther laughed as the excitement and shock of the evening wore off.

"Use my goblet my Lord," she said filling it with wine and carrying it over to him.

"Thank you," said the king. He patted his couch and Esther sat down beside him.

"My Queen, as a gift to you, in hopes it will bring you great enjoyment and happiness, I am gifting you the estate of Haman, the Agagite. I know he had great wealth. In your generous and wise hands, that wealth could have no better manager."

"Oh my Lord!" exclaimed Esther. Her eyes shimmered with delight as she remembered the beautiful estates along each side of the river, the wide openness of the countryside, the beauty of the river view flowing through the valley.

The king smiled at how her face lit up with joy. None of his other wives had enjoyed gifts as much as Esther. He wondered what she would do with it. He was curious. How he would enjoy hearing her tell him of all she did with her land and wealth.

"Thank you, my Husband, my King," she said.

They were talking softly with each other when Hathach and Mordecai arrived.

Mordecai's eyes glistened with tears as he saw his dear Hadassah seated beside her king, looking every inch a queen, healthy, alive, and oh so beautiful, the necklace he had given her gracing her neck.

"Mordecai, my King and Queen," Hathach announced and both men bowed. Esther rose and walked toward Mordecai, her face trembling with emotion. She walked up to the man who had rescued her, raised her, and loved her as a father. Their hands met and he squeezed hers. Tears fell unchecked from his eyes.

"Oh, my Hadassah, how I have missed your dear countenance," Mordecai's voice trembled with emotions. He spoke softly in Hebrew.

"My dearest Cousin and father," Esther whispered, the Hebrew a welcomed familiarity to her tongue. "Yahweh is good, my Cousin, my father, Yahweh is good. He has heard the cries of His people and spared my life."

"My Queen," Mordecai said switching to Persian so the king could understand. "Your courage and obedience will be remembered for as long as stories are told."

The king rose and Esther smiled again, a slight blush dusting her cheeks at Mordecai's praise.

"Meet my husband, the Great Xerxes." Esther walked beside Mordecai toward her husband, holding his hand in hers.

She moved beside the king, lifting Mordecai's hand toward him.

"My King, if it pleases you, meet my Cousin, Mordecai, the man who raised me like a father when I had no other place to go. This," she smiled up into Xerxes's face. "Is the man in whom the King delights to honor."

The king looked at Mordecai long and hard. Slowly, he reached out his hand and the two men greeted each other almost as equals. The unshed tears shimmering in Esther's eyes finally slid unashamed down her cheeks.

Never in all her life had she dared imagine this moment. Here she was, unhidden, freed from her vow of silence, standing before the two men that ruled her heart and commanded her obedience. Her God surely did hear her prayers. He had answered the one request she had prayed from the very first night she had arrived at the palace and, every night since over the years; to see her beloved Mordecai face to face once again; hear his rich voice speaking over her in Hebrew, touch his hands and feel his love.

God was good. He was oh so good to His people! He had heard and answered the cries of her little orphaned heart, answering in ways past her understanding. Now here she stood, introducing Mordecai to her husband, the king of Persia.

The king sat down on his couch and Esther directed Mordecai to the couch she had sat on. No one wanted to go to the couch Haman had vacated in such disgrace only an hour before. Esther stood and waited to see what her husband would say next.

He looked up at her standing there waiting for him.

"Come Esther, my wife, sit with me," he said. Esther came and sat down on the couch with him. The king pulled off his signet ring. He looked at it for a long moment. It had been pulled from Haman's disgraced hand; the sting of his deception still burned in the king's heart.

"I want to give this to another who is more worthy of its power. Another who manages the interest of the Crown of whose authority it represents with greater care and honor than the last man it was entrusted to did."

"Let it be recorded in the chronicles of the Medes and Persians that the position of Haman is stripped from him and is given instead to one more worthy of it. Mordecai, the Jew, cousin of the Queen, is this man." The scratch of the scribes' pens sounded as they scrambled to record this order.

"I know Mordecai is worthy of this position. The great wisdom he has instilled in my wife, the Queen, is testament enough. His council has preserved her life and influenced the course of history this day. My wife kept her identity and her people hidden as instructed, revealing it only to petition me for her life and the lives of her people. If the Queen recommends this man to me, I do well to heed her advice."

"In light of this evening's events, I declare that the Queen is ever welcomed in the court of the Great King Xerxes. Her presence in court shall never again involve her risking her life. The King will be honored to hear his Queen's opinion among those of his most trusted advisors and princes."

Esther looked over at her husband sharply. Did he truly mean this? He looked back at her, his face set in calm authority. She smiled slightly looking deeply into his eyes, a light shining there that the king had never noticed before. It was pride. His wife was proud of him.

Mordecai approached the king and queen. He bowed low and humbly received the ring.

"I am deeply honored to receive this position and to serve you all the days of my life, my King, and my Queen. I will serve you, King Xerxes as Daniel faithfully served the King Darius of Babylon, till his death."

The king nodded his crowned head at the respected name of King Darius the Mede, the brilliant general of King Cyrus, who conquered the unconquerable city without a fight.

Esther broke the silence after a glance at the king.

"My cousin and father, and now regent second only to the King Xerxes; Mordecai, in a glorious twist of fate, due to the power of the God of Heaven and Earth, I place the estate of Haman the Agagite, once your enemy, in your capable hands. It will be a home fitting a man of your position and a better steward a Queen could not find, though she searched the entire empire."

Mordecai's face beamed with joy and gratitude. He bowed. Esther reached out her hand toward him, asking him not to bow to her, his daughter. Mordecai took her hand and gently kissed it.

"My Queen and my daughter," he said. "You have blessed me more than seven sons this day and every day you grace this earth."

A single tear slid down her cheek as she remembered the praises of Adinah, the dearest mother who was not there with them in this happy moment. But her smile did not falter nor did the praise in her heart.

The king rose and the evening was over. Esther smiled at Mordecai as she moved to escort the king out. The king bent and kissed Esther gently.

"Thank you, my Queen, for the banquet," he said graciously. "It was most illuminating, and the entertainment was unrepeatable."

Esther laughed. The king began descending the stairs. She stopped, waiting.

"Stay with me?" she asked so quietly, so softly, he almost missed it. He stopped and turned, looking up for one of the few times in his life, to his queen.

He smiled a slow wide smile.

"I have waited for years for you to ask me that," he said with a chuckle. He reached out his hand. She took his and gracefully skipped down the stairs. Esther cast a smile back at her dear Mordecai, standing in respect for his king and queen. She would see him again in the morning. Arm and arm, the king and queen ascended the steps and disappeared into the queen's chambers.

Next morning, Arjana hummed softly as she opened the queen's curtains. She knew Esther enjoyed waking up to the light streaming into her apartments. Anatu came in bearing a tray with coffee on it.

"I wonder what we will be up to today." Anatu wondered out loud. "Now that the crisis is over, what will the Queen be up to now?"

Another maidservant arrived with a bouquet of fresh flowers placing them on the small table in the sitting area. The queen always loved fresh flowers.

Arjana walked into the bedroom. From the sounds of the breathing, the queen was still fast asleep. She grabbed a side of the bed curtain and pulled it back, tying it up in a neat little bow. She quietly walked around to the other side of the bed. As she lifted the curtain she looked into the bed and gasped. There lay the king, sleeping peacefully, his head on Esther's chest. By the looks of it, they were both naked. Her eyes widened as she noted the clothes piled on the floor.

Arjana froze totally unsure of what to do. Anatu heard her sharp intake of breath. Curious she walked into the bed chamber only to freeze, seeing the king in the bed and Arjana still holding back the bed curtains.

Arjana looked up at Anatu unsure of what to do. Anatu motioned for her to let go of the curtains, but it was too late. The king stirred and woke up with a groan. Terrified Arjana ran from the room dragging Anatu with her.

Esther's eyes popped open.

"I just gave your maid a terrible fright," said the king his voice a soft morning growl. Esther looked at the open curtain on one side of the bed.

"I do believe you are right." She said with a sleepy smile.

The king snuggled in close.

"Why is your bed so much more comfortable than mine?" he asked.

"Do you really want to know the secret?" Esther asked hope lighting up her face.

"Well of course, you are in the habit of telling me a few!"

At this, Esther laughed aloud.

"Well," she said rolling over onto her stomach. She pushed back the covered to show the sheets.

"These sheets are made with silk spun by our very own silkworm caterpillars. I wove the cloth myself. You can see here," she pulled back the covers more. "I made a little mistake and there is a bubble of extra fibers there."

The king watched her in fascination; the joy on her face as she told him about what she had made, the slight pride in her voice when she spoke of '*us*' or '*we*'.

"And," she added oblivious to his fascination. "I sewed the comforter and stuffed it with the softest goose down. It makes it so warm and so cool at the same time. It is my beauty secret so don't you spread it around."

Esther slipped out of bed and grabbed her robe. She wrapped it around her and then looked at the king. He lay there watching her intently, a very odd expression on his face.

"There seems to be great satisfaction in the making of things," he said still staring at her.

"What have I made?" He looked at his hands as he held them up in front of himself, a frown creasing his brow.

Esther sat down on the bed and reached out her hand to stroke back his hair making him look up at her not his hands.

"You, my Lord, have made an empire. With those two hands, you need to preserve it and rule it wisely. At a flick of these fingers," gently she traced them with her long fingers. "Lives are spared, men have order, and peoples hope. Don't discredit what these hands have done, my King."

The king looked at her for a long moment.

"I want a pair of these sheets for my bed too." He said with a smile. At this, Esther laughed with delight, shaking her head.

"I would be honored to dress the King's bed."

The king rolled out of the bed. Esther held his robe for him and helped him slide it onto his broad shoulders.

"Does this place come with coffee too?" he asked turning to his wife.

"Of course," said Esther. She stood on her tiptoes and dropped a gentle kiss on his lips. The king was startled. Never had anyone given affection to him without him initiating it. He smiled as the kiss lingered on his lips.

"That is for saving me last night," Esther moved toward the door, throwing a glance at him over her shoulder.

The king followed her, intrigued. He had been to the queen's chambers many times in the past. But Esther had changed them. They were different. The spirit of the place was so peaceful and gentle. He found himself wanting to stay, feeling like he was a guest here.

They walked out into the living area. Esther was already headed to the small round table that held the coffee tray. Two cups were on the tray with not a maid in sight. Esther smiled as she poured a cup and handed it to her husband. She poured herself a cup and walked, by habit, to the window.

The king came and stood beside her for a long moment, looking out on a view he almost never saw. At last, he kissed his wife then left to dress and prepare for his day. The moment he left with Javad, Artabanus and his royal guard, Arjana materialized and stood staring at Esther. Anatu and Banu appeared, as did all the maids.

Esther laughed at their curious faces.

"He is my husband you know!" she exclaimed defending herself.

"Ya!" exclaimed Banu. "Not once in these six years has, he come here!"

Esther smiled and looked down at her coffee cup a moment.

"Much has changed, Banu." She said seriously. "Much has changed. And I need to get dressed. I have much to do today."

Anatu clapped her hands and ran for the clothes closet. Much discussion on dresses and hair styles commenced and Shaashgaz showed up as if summoned. The apartments were again filled with laughter, love and celebration, a stark contrast to the tears, prayers and terrified whispers of the past four days.

Esther could not wait to see Mordecai in person again. Hathach ran to find him.

"I will meet him in the hallway just outside the palace of women." Esther told Hathach. "We have so much to discuss."

Esther walked swiftly from her chambers once dressed and ready. There he was, standing across from the guarded doors, watching for her. She broke into a run; just as a little girl would run to her father.

Mordecai's great laugh bellowed out and he threw open his arms. Esther embraced him in a long embrace.

"Oh my child!" he exclaimed dropping kisses onto her head. "The joy of this moment, oh my girl!"

They parted for a moment so he could look at her.

"If only Adinah lived to see this day! Her heart would sing." They embraced again and Esther placed a kiss on Mordecai's wrinkling cheek.

"Yes," said Esther, looking over her cousin, dressed in robes of royal blue, white and purple, a gold chain gracing his neck, a heavily jeweled belt around his waist.

"So, what of the law, Esther?" asked Mordecai suddenly becoming serious. They turned and began walking toward the inner court of the king, arm in arm.

"I forgot in the joy of the moment," said Esther. "We must ask him to revoke the edict. It is the only way to save our people!"

"Yes, you are right, my Dear One!" said Mordecai firmly. "You have had to do so much on your own already. I am blessed to accompany you on this, the completion of your plea to save the Jewish people, to save both our lives."

Esther nodded. Arm and arm the two walked toward the inner court of the king. She paused at the doorway and looked at Mordecai as if to reassure herself he was still there. Mordecai met her gaze.

"My daughter, you have changed much with your obedience. You have gained the respect of the King as no one ever has before. This day, you write history. Let us go and complete our task. Save your life and those of your people, my Queen."

Boldly the two stepped through the doorway. The guards stood solemnly on either side of the entrance. They descended the steps together and began the long walk up the carpeted approach to the marble steps that led to the throne of Persia. The king looked up and saw his queen approaching on the arm of her cousin, Mordecai. He broke into a smile and watched as they approached.

Crown Prince Darius stood beside his father, where Haman had stood. Prince Artaxerxes rose and nodded his head toward Esther as she approached. Much had changed overnight in the court of the great empire of the Medes and Persians.

Esther came forward to the base of the stairs, this time her eyes filling with tears even as she approached. The guards with drawn swords stood on each stair step, ready to strike down anyone who dared approach the throne without permission.

Esther sobbed. She dropped to her knees before the stairs and lowered her face into her hands. Her body shook with the force of her emotions. The king rose, startled, his smile evaporating from his lips. He held out his golden scepter over the stairway, inviting her to approach.

"My Queen! Esther, my wife, what troubles you?" He asked. "Have no fear, approach, and tell me what troubles you?"

Esther obediently rose and climbed up the stairs at his bidding, protected under the outstretched scepter. She approached the throne and reaching out, she gently touched the cold hard jewel, set in a casket of gold.

She stood before her husband the king, tears standing in her eyes leaving trails as they streamed down her cheeks.

"My Lord King, I implore you to undo the death sentence that hangs over me and my people. My King, you are the only one who can save us. We still have the law, sealed by your order, authorizing the death of all the Jews in your kingdom. I have not completed my quest nor fulfilled my calling till I have been able to turn this tide of destruction and prevent the annihilation of my people."

"My life may be spared under your protection but how am I to live with the destruction of my people perpetually before me? How am I to live, my Lord? Am I worth ten thousand talents of silver to you, my Lord? Are my people to be slaughtered for the royal treasury to receive silver?"

Esther had fallen to her knees during her pleading. She looked up at the king seated on his throne, her hands clasped in front of her, outstretched, pleading.

The king grew thoughtful. His countenance clouded. Esther feared for a long moment that she may have failed in her petition. The princes looked startled at the queen's outburst. Many brows furrowed. Utter silence filled the courtroom as the princes, advisors, generals, and noblemen realized the queen was a Jewess. Then the king spoke.

"I have halted former Prince Haman's vendetta against the Queen and her family by hanging Haman on the very gallows he intended for Mordecai. I have also given Haman's estate and property, with all its wealth, to my wife the Queen. But no Persian law can be revoked, once written, and sealed with the King's signet ring. It is our law that law itself can't be undone."

The princes and advisors of the king nodded. It was law that no law could be revoked once written. How was the king to save the life of his queen and her people?

"But you, my Queen Esther," continued the king his voice, steady with authority. "With the help of Mordecai, regent of the King, who now holds the signet ring; I give you the task of devising a law to save your own people. Even I, the King Xerxes of Persia, cannot undo the law, now written and sealed. But you can change the parameters of the law, even though it is written. I know not more capable persons to do this task nor more passionate ambassadors for the Jewish people and their preservation."

Esther smiled and bowed low to her king her forehead touching his feet.

"Does this satisfy your heart, my Queen?" asked the king softly, bending forward to touch his wife's head.

"My Lord King has put my heart to rest. I thank you my King! You have answered my request and granted my petition. I will go and do as you have instructed. I will bring honor to your reign and compliments to your character, my King, and my husband."

The king smiled and held out his scepter to her again.

"I am well pleased with you, my Queen," he said. "May my favor forever rest over you."

"My King has made his servant's heart delighted." replied Esther. She rose to descend the steps, but the king's next statement stopped her in her tracks.

"You still owe me a pair of sheets." He said with a soft chuckle, and then leaning forward so only she could hear. "Can you invite me over for dinner again soon?"

Esther smiled. She paused there on the steps leading up to the throne. Turning she stepped forward and extended her hand toward him.

"My King and my husband is always welcomed at my table," she said kneeling before him again. He took her soft hand in his and kissed it, their eyes meeting for a long moment as the married couple flirted openly with each other in the presence of the entire court of Persia.

Esther's smile lingered as she stood up and backed away from her king. The king watched her as she gracefully descended the steps. Suddenly he stood up and lifted his scepter.

"The Queen of Persia, long may she grace this court!" His voice was loud. It echoed off the thick tapestries and reverberated through the room. The princes, nobles, councilors and even the scribes laid aside their pens to applaud the queen as she walked down the long carpet and left the inner court.

How different was she than her forerunner, Queen Vashti. Honor and respect for her king and her husband reverberated in all she did. This woman had great political power and the story that had just played out before their very eyes, proved it true. Every nobleman, prince, advisor, and general who had watched the queen come before the king only days earlier, risking her life to make a request and petition of him, now stood watching her leave with a triumphant tribute from the king, wondered of their own wives and daughters. What powers could they hold? What potentials, if allowed, could they produce? What courage could drive them?

Mordecai took Esther's arm and the two left the courtroom together, Esther's eyes shining with excitement.

"You did it, my girl!" Mordecai said proudly once they were out of the courtroom and in the hallway once more and could hear each other speak. "Yahweh could not have provided someone better than you for such a time as this."

Esther embraced him quickly.

"Thank you, my dear Cousin," she said. "I am so thankful I can complete this task with you by my side."

Together Esther and Mordecai drafted up a law. They could not reverse the allowance of their enemies to gather and attack but they could give the Jews permission to fight back. This new law allowed the Jews to arm themselves and mount a defensive against the attackers. It also warned the attackers that this was no longer a passive act of aggression but a war. The Jews had the legal right from the king himself to defend themselves, their wives, and their children. And fight they would.

Esther and Mordecai read the edict over again and again. Once they were completely satisfied, Mordecai called the king's scribes together. He read out the decree before hundreds of scratching pens, the words of life and redemption for a condemned people. These words spared an entire race from genocide, raising them from death to life, from hopelessness to hope. Esther sat and watched the process, tears standing in her eyes as the sound of hundreds of pens scratched out words of life for her people.

Mordecai stamped each of the documents with the king's seal making them official Persian law, unable to be contradicted or denounced. The letters were given to the king's riders, mounted on the fastest horses. They galloped out of the palace gates carrying the news as fast as possible. All one hundred and twenty-seven provinces of the empire of Persia, sprawling across the world from India all the way to Ethiopia must be reached in time. Each letter was written in the language of each region of each province.

The edict went out to the city of Susa that very day. Other letters took more time as translations needed to be checked and double checked. Esther was so grateful for every moment she had studied language in the years leading up to this point. She and Mordecai worked tirelessly, stopping only when Arjana and Anatu, escorted by Hathach and Hegai, begged them to stop for the food they brought.

Arjana and Anatu watched in amazement, all those pens working simultaneously as scribes from every corner of the Persian Empire labored to write down the letter Mordecai drafted, word for word, letter for letter, life for life. Wave after wave of horse and riders galloped out the king's gate at breakneck speed, carrying the happy news farther and farther out over the empire.

Gladness and joy erupted in every town and city the letters reached. The city of Susa was in a glorious uproar most of the night, people shouting the king's praises loudly in the streets. Citizens shared food and gifts with their neighbors, delighted there was not to be genocide in their city. The first decree had been met with confusion and anger, rage, sorrow, and discord. This decree was met with relief and gladness, dancing, singing, and shouting. No people wanted to live with the reality of extermination looming over their heads at a whim of the king.

A couple days later the king called for Esther and Mordecai to join him for the taking of the evening meal. Esther smiled to see her dearest cousin dressed so royally in a long robe of fine linen, white underneath and blue overtop, layered in the fashion of the court of Persia, signifying his status. He wore a crown of gold embedded with jewels.

Arm in arm, Mordecai and Esther crossed over the grass lawn, past the fountain, toward the king's apartments.

The king was not sitting at his bench. He was standing looking out over the city, watching the light from torches dancing in the streets as the city continued to rejoice.

Mordecai stopped by the bench and Esther approached her husband alone. The king was silent for a long moment, the breeze playing with his hair. He sighed finally and reached an arm around Esther's shoulders.

"You make a better politician than I, my Queen," he said smiling slightly. He pointed to the open courtyard. "Look at how happy they are, all because of you."

He turned then and looked at her.

"My Queen, you look tired," he said concerned.

Esther lifted her hand to caress his face.

"Politics comes with its hardships," she said. The king nodded and kissed her.

"You are a sight for sore eyes, my Queen." He admitted. "Let us eat. Mordecai came as well?"

"Yes, my King. We arrived together."

"Good."

The three lay around the table spread with food. The atmosphere was so different from the meals Esther had shared with the king and Haman. The conversation around the table was serious but light, hopeful, and charged with energy. Mordecai, a well-spoken man, use to leading others, entertained the king with his insightful analysis of situations around the kingdom.

The king was very interested in the status of the letters and how their delivery to every province was progressing. Time was closing in. They had six months to complete the translations and get the letters delivered before the attack of the Jews occurred on the thirteenth day of the twelfth month, the month of Adar.

"The Almighty God controls even the casting of the lots," said Mordecai. "He has seen fit to give us time, just enough time to get the last letter to the farthest reaches of the provinces."

"How right you are, Cousin," Esther nodded. "Even fate is controlled by God."

The king listened as the two spoke affectionately with each other, discussing day's events as a family would over the evening meal. Esther held up a piece of bread. A sudden memory made her laugh out loud.

"The first time I ground flour for Ruth, she told me it was fine enough, fit for the King of Persia. And now," she smiled at her husband. "I dine with him."

The right eyebrow shot up at this.

"You grinding flour?" The king stared at her, openly horrified.

"Yes, my Lord. It is satisfying." Mordecai smiled, remembering the moment.

The king shook his head a little.

"I can't picture it, my dear Queen." He concluded. "But there is much I did not foresee."

"But God can," continued Esther with a smile at the king. "We must pray for good weather, Cousin, to ensure the last of the riders make it to Ethiopia."

It was a long ride across Asia all the way to Ethiopia. It took the riders months to cover this much land and the task was dangerous. The roads held many dangers. Weather in a mountain pass or crossing wide rivers could delay a rider for a week if not longer. That edict must reach every single Jew and Gentile, in their own native tongue, across the great sprawling empire of Persia.

"I have done enough killing in my day," admitted the king. "I see how my lovely wife has created so much harmony and good in the years she has worked in the women's palace. I want to spend the rest of my days building. I want to make things with my two hands, things that last. Although," He moved a bit and patted his couch inviting his wife to join him. "No matter what I build, this woman here will be the true testament to my memory."

Esther rose and crossing the short distance she sat down beside the king. She shared a lingering smile with him.

"So my King finds pleasure with his wife," she said.

"Yes, he most certainly does," replied the king. "A man my age needs to begin to truly enjoy the pleasures of life, the real ones."

Mordecai smiled at the two, obviously respectful and loving of each other. Esther had gained her husband's deepest respect through her brave and desperate actions for the sake of her people. Her grace and kindness made her a pleasure to be around. She served him as best she could with all she did and said. She truly built up this man, deserving or not. She made him a better king, and a better man.

Mordecai left later that night. The king and Esther walked arm and arm toward his bed chambers.

"My offer of half of the kingdom does still stand," he teased her. Esther stopped and looked up at him. She lifted both of her hands up to cradle his aging face.

"My Lord King, do you really want to know what this woman's heart desires."

The king moved closer as if to kiss her.

"You know I do." He said, waiting.

"It is this, my King." She looked deep into his dark eyes. "I desire your heart, all of it. My King is blessed with many sons. There are hundreds of women even now, gathered in the court of women under Hegai's care. Send them home, my King. Free them. The palace is a cage to an unwed woman. You have concubines enough to satisfy you if I am unable." The king's gaze did not yield.

"Let me be enough. Let me be truly the Queen of your heart." Esther boldly spoke out her request, the cry of her heart, the desire of her soul.

The king struggled to hold eye contact with this beautiful young woman in front of him. She was asking him to release custom, to swallow pride, to do what few noble men and no king did. That was to love one woman and one woman well.

"Esther, my wife," he said after a long moment. "I will need your help. I am a worldly man use to every pleasure imaginable."

"I understand my Lord King," Esther answered him. "I have lived here for these six years in your great palace. One as a candidate waiting to be brought before you, and five as your wife, the Queen of Persia. I know my husband's heart and habits, but does he know of mine? Cannot my life and dreams and passions capture his imagination and hold his interest? Can we not work at projects and build together with these four hands a lifetime of memories?"

She let go of his face and reaching down she found his hands. Palm to palm, they stood, her looking up into his face, him looking back down at her. Slowly his fingers laced into hers. He sighed gently and lowering his face he kissed her long and slowly. His body moved closer to hers. Esther caressed him; longing to fill his every void, every desire.

Slowly they parted.

"I will send them away. For you, my wife, I will send them away." And he scooped her up in his arms so quickly she squealed in surprise. This delighted him.

"You still owe me sheets," he said and gently tossed her on the bed.

Chapter 23

The Feast of Purim Is Declared

Three weeks later, all the letters were completed. The last of the riders galloped from the city, bound for the very edges of the Persian Empire. Esther was sitting in a room between the palace of women and the king's palace. She and Mordecai had found the perfect meeting place between their two worlds, still separated by traditions and rules. Esther was grateful she was free to move freely between the court of women and the palace. Most of the women in the court had no freedom to leave or move around even in the palace of the king unless escorted and with specific permission.

Here they met and discussed their days together. Here they prayed together, hand in hand. Here Mordecai read the Scriptures to Esther just as in the days past. She sat with closed eyes drinking deeply of the psalms of David, hearing again those words that had comforted her through the long, lonely nights and hallways of the palace. And here, in this room, they began to dream. Esther was the one who captured the vision first.

"Cousin," she asked. She had just finished telling him of the school in the court of women. Mordecai enjoyed hearing about what the teacher was doing and of all the skills the women were learning.

"My estate, that you now manage, what do you think about making it into a shelter?"

"A shelter?" Mordecai burst out. Esther hurried to explain.

"It is outside the palace, so rules and protocols need not exist. What of these girls who need to run from their mistresses due to horrendous mistreatment? I have heard terrible stories of mutilations and even deaths of slave girls that enrage their mistresses. At best, they are severely marred at worst, cast out to a fate worse than death."

"Stories of the former queen's abuses make one's blood run cold! How many terrible situations must play themselves out all over Susa and the surrounding cities of this province? There is so much injustice merely because one human owns another. There is no place for these poor girls to go to be safe or find any mercy."

"What if we made my estate just such a place? They could come for refuge. Depending on their physical limitations or abilities they could work the land, paint, weave, and learn any other skill to earn an income. They can learn to read and write. They can be given a new life."

Her eyes were shining, and her hands had clasped over her chest. She paced back and forth, unable to sit down with the excitement of her idea. Mordecai sat back watching her, love, and joy on his face.

"My daughter," he shook his head slowly. "You have the energy of seven sons!" Esther laughed and spun around her arms outstretched. Suddenly she stopped.

"Oh!" she said placing a hand on her stomach. "I feel quite ill suddenly! Please excuse me for a moment." She hurried over and poured herself a glass of water. Never far away, Arjana was by her side in a flash, a cool cloth laid on her forehead. Arjana guided her mistress to a seat, her own abdomen swollen with the new life in her.

"Thank you, Arjana," Esther said weakly. The feeling passed as quickly as it came. She was about to jump out of her seat and begin on her ideas again when the look on Mordecai's face stopped her. He sat smiling just watching her.

"The Lord God has blessed your obedience and your faithfulness. He has waited till now to bless your union with your husband and King. Esther, my daughter, you are with child."

Esther's mouth gaped open. Slowly the math sunk into her consciousness. *Yes, yes, she was late, very late.* Her hand instantly covered her abdomen. Tears swelled in her eyes, and she looked at Mordecai smiling across the room at her.

"To think I have lived to see this day." He said happily.

"Our children are only going to be months apart in age, Arjana!" Esther cried in delight. "And to think the Lord God waited till the baby could be held and blessed by its grandfather." Tears of joy spilled over Esther's cheeks as Mordecai crossed the distance and embraced his daughter.

Esther sent Hathach to Javad with a letter for the king's hand only once he was done court. The king's face lit up with delight when Javad handed him the letter. No explanation was needed as to who it was from, the king recognizing the beautiful bold handwriting of his wife. He opened the letter with an air of anticipation. He closed it again with a smile. She invited him to her apartments to dine with her, if she found favor in his sight, as she had good news, she wanted to share with him.

The king found himself excited to go and see his wife. The boredom of his countenance fell away and he hurried to wrap up court for the day so he could prepare.

He arrived at the palace of women, to a dinner laid out for him in the garden gazebo of the queen. No trace of the earlier drama remained. The queen herself served him, no servants hovering too closely by. She tasted the food herself, dish by dish before she served it ensuring quality and the absence of added poison. The king lay back, watching her every move, enjoying the silence and peace of the moment. She placed a plate before him, satisfied it was fit for a King. She poured off a small taste of the wine. She nodded as she rolled the fluid around in her mouth. All was as it should be.

She watched him eat, enjoying him enjoy the food and drink. When he was satisfied, she approached his couch and knelt by him.

"My King," she said reaching for his hand. "I have news for you, my King, that I hope will delight your heart as it does mine." She pulled his hand, placing it over her stomach. "My God has opened my womb, my Lord. The God I serve has blessed us both with a child."

The king froze for a moment looking at her. Slowly his hand relaxed and spread over her lower abdomen.

"A child? My Queen, my wife, is with child?" He sat up, interested. Esther nodded, smiling.

"Great is your God indeed, my dear; to bless this King with a child even in his aging years." He smiled broadly and pulled her close to him in an embrace.

"It must be the magic of your sheets," he jested before kissing her.

Six months later, on the thirteenth day of Adar, Mordecai and Esther held their breath and paced about, waiting for news. Today was the day the lot had fallen for Haman. Today was the day the Jews had been sold to be annihilated but today was the day they had prepared for over the last months.

They gathered themselves together, armed, and prepared for the attacks. Once news of Mordecai's rise to power spread, an unexpected turn of events occurred. The city officials, the heads of state and the rulers of the provinces began to help the Jews prepare for the attack.

They feared and respected Mordecai, now regent to the king, and direct relative of the queen of Persia. The shock rippled through the entire city of Susa that the queen, married to their king, was a Jewess and had risked her very own life to go before the king to plead for the life of herself and her people, triggering a series of events that ended up in the public hanging of the former Prince Haman and Mordecai, the Jew, rising to power in his place over night.

With this unexpected support, the Jews mounted a formidable force. Many of their enemies gave up without a fight. Respect and fear fell hard all over the empire for the Jewish people, dispelling the former hate and contempt. Haman was dead. It was his ten sons who continued, stirring up anger and bitterness, vowing to avenge their father's unlawful death.

Those foolish enough to fight the chosen people of God, found themselves dead. As the day wore on and the afternoon sun burned low on the horizon, the shouting and fighting ceased in the streets surrounding the palace. By torchlight, the bodies were laid out and numbered. Mordecai left to walk the streets to see for himself and meet with the Jewish elders for an update.

Esther was left in her apartments alone, pacing and praying. Suddenly a knock sounded. Arjana entered and told Esther Javad was present. Javad entered and requested on behalf of the king that Esther be ready to meet him in his palace as soon as court was finished. Esther nodded and smiled, welcoming the distraction. The king would have an accurate update for her. She longed to know of the happenings beyond the great stone walls of the palace.

She hurried to prepare and when Javad arrived to escort her, she was ready. They hurried along the passageways, Javad knowing how anxious Esther was for news. The hallway opened into the garden. Esther moved toward the fountain. The king's great form could be seen sitting on the bench, watching for her. He smiled and patted the seat beside him. She approached eagerly.

"Sit my Queen," the king was the first to speak. She sat down beside him. He took one of her hands in his and raised it to his lips to kiss her fingers. She watched him, waiting for news. His face was serious, unreadable.

"Five hundred men have fallen in the city of Susa alone, my Queen."

Esther gasped and covered her growing abdomen in surprise. That many, that many men had hated their Jewish neighbor enough to rise, arm themselves, and try to kill them? Murder all, men, women, and children, to erase them entirely from the surface of the earth. The king continued.

"What the Jews have done in the surrounding areas and other provinces is yet to be known. The ten sons of your enemy Haman are all dead and accounted for. Your revenge on the evil man is completed. Or," He turned to look at her. "Is there more that your heart desires? What more can I do to ensure you are satisfied with the turn of events? Is there more that I can do to prove my love and delight in you, my Esther?"

This was indeed a turn of events. Now the king himself was asking her if she was satisfied. Was she? Would all this hatred and animosity really end in one day?

She stood and walked around the fountain, thinking. She had not been prepared for a request such as this from the king. His interest in satisfying her fully touched her. The impact of her coming before him to plead for her life and the lives of her people would never be fully clear to her, of this, she was sure. She had challenged him, changed him, and gained his respect in a way she never imagined possible. He was totally committed to seeing her fully satisfied in this matter.

A thought came to her mind. Esther knew the thought was set there by the Almighty, to protect His people and satisfy His anger against this wickedness. She walked back to the king and gave him both her hands. She looked at him, their foreheads almost touching.

"As I have found favor in your sight, my King, and your affections rest on me, grant the Jews of the city of Susa a second day, tomorrow, to again defend themselves against their enemies. This will ensure the animosity is truly past and, once over, peace can again dwell in this city, the city of the King."

"Also, my Lord King, let the bodies of Haman's ten sons be set up this very evening on crosses beside the roadway to warn all who pass of what happens when a person rises in hatred to annihilate a people. Five bodies on one side of the road and five on the other so there is no looking away or missing the sight. These men terrorize the highways of the great King Xerxes long enough. Pilgrims will know they are safe at last to return to their homeland."

The king's eyebrows flew up at the queen's direct reference to his very actions. During the march on Greece, a man had upset the king greatly. The king had ordered the man's eldest son cut in two. He marched the entirety of his army between the two halves of the young man as a warning to all who dared to displease the king.

"How very Persian of you, my Jewish Queen," said the king, something very close to respect shining in his eyes.

"Thank you, my King, for granting me this request and hearing my petition on this matter." Esther kissed each hand of the king to accentuate her gratitude. She smiled and continued; her gaze raising up toward the twilight sky stretching out above them.

"Our forefather, Abraham was promised by God that his descendants would be as the stars in the night sky, innumerable in number. Abraham was without child at the time yet, he believed the Word of the Lord God Almighty. That night, fire passed between the halves of the sacrifice Abraham laid out before God, solidifying His promise to our father Abraham."

"True to His Word, the descendants of Abraham are numerous today. This day the Lord has protected His people. Our God is faithful in all He promises. May the enemies of God see what is done to those who come against Him and His people."

The king called to Javad, his eyes holding Esther's.

"Javad, call Artabanus. I have orders that must be carried out this very night." Javad disappeared in a flash.

"It is a pleasure to hear of your people at last, my Queen. It only took you five years to answer the question I asked you the first night you came before me. You are a keeper of secrets, my wife, and my Queen. I thank you for sharing these thoughts of your heart with me." With this, the king lifted the fingers of Esther's right hand to his lips.

Artabanus arrived in a hurry. He had been training with new recruits and had not even stopped to wash but hurried to his king.

"My King," the huge muscular man bowed before the Great King Xerxes. "You summoned me."

"Yes, Artabanus," the king nodded to his faithful guard and friend. "Send a group of soldiers you trust to stake up the ten sons of Haman, five on each side of the highway leading from the city of Susa toward the river. My Queen wishes this, and it shall be done for her to triumph over her enemy this day."

Artabanus nodded his head. He flashed a look at the queen and nodded his respects to her. He was quick to leave the presence of the king and hurried to do as he was bid.

By the time, Esther and the king sat down to their evening meal, all was set in motion as Esther had requested. The riders of the royal palace had ridden out to announce a second day of contention in the city of Susa. Although she had eaten very little that day, food was not appealing to Esther at this moment. There was joy in triumphing over one's enemies, but the shedding of blood held little happiness.

The king noted her disinterest and tried as best he could to distract her. He called for music and dancing. Esther tried to smile and enjoy herself for his sake. At last, the king stood up and holding out his arms, he asked his queen to dance with him. A true smile reached Esther's eyes as she followed her husband's lead through a series of twirling Persian dances. It was the first time they had ever danced together.

"Stay with me tonight?" he asked, holding her close.

"I was so hoping you would ask," she whispered back. "Of all the nights, tonight is not one I want to spend alone."

"Alone you will not be," said the king holding her closer.

"Thank you, my King." Esther whispered, brushing his ear with her lips. The king almost shivered with delight and the evening was over. The king carried his queen to his bedchambers without a backward glance. She would be safe in his arms, guarded by the most elite soldiers of the known world.

Great stars hung in the sky. The moon washed the world in beautiful, silvery light. The city held its breath, waiting, waiting for the next day, waiting for the next wave of aggression and fighting.

As promised, the morning dawned upon the bodies of Haman's sons, displayed along the highway as Esther had requested. Three hundred angered peoples banded together and came again against the Jews of the city. All were killed.

Once the fighting was over, the Jewish fighters quietly and efficiently cleaned the city of all signs of altercations, the streets swept and cleaned, bodies delivered to their families to be buried, the marketplace righted. The fighters took none of the property of their fallen enemies. Any money, jewels, or treasures found on the bodies of the fallen were untouched, everything was returned to their families. All was left to the children and widows of the fallen.

The city was righted as if nothing had ever happened. Wails of mourning were only heard in the homes of those who had fought and lost.

It was Mordecai himself that told Esther about the second day's events. The redemption of Haman's evil act was totally completed. What was meant to be a day of total annihilation and genocide of the Jewish people in the Persian capital was instead two days of triumph. All because one woman, one girl, had the courage to take her life into her hands and, after fasting for three days, she risked her own life, breaking the law of the land to appear unsummoned before the king.

The fifteenth of Adar brought on a day of resting, rejoicing, and feasting for all the Jews in the capital city. The streets were alive with dancing and songs of victory. Gifts were given in the streets to all who would receive them. All the Jews of the city of Susa gathered eagerly to hear Mordecai speak.

"Men of Israel, today, the sun was to rise over a city, an empire, a land that had no Jewish people left. It was to be a day of great loss and bloodshed. Instead, the Lord God rose for us a deliverer. A woman, my kinsmen, exalted through obedience to a position to plead for the life of her people. Through her bravery, the plot of Haman was halted and instead, great victory was awarded the Jews of the Persian Empire."

"I purpose that from this day forward, the children of Israel set aside the fourteenth and fifteenth days of Adar as feast days. Let us give gifts and rejoice in the victory the Lord God has given us. Let us remember, always remember, the courage of Esther, our Hadassah. Let us remember the deliverance of the Jews from the hands of their enemies. Let us remember and rejoice!"

The Jews and their Persian neighbors who had gathered to hear Mordecai the Jew, speak, threw up their hands and cheered loudly. The verdict was forged. Letters were sent out to all the Jews of the great land of Persia. The tradition was set to celebrate year after year, remembered by generation after generation. The feast of Purim is celebrated to this very day in remembrance of the mercy of God displayed in saving His people.

Esther's eyes misted and she smiled through her tears as Mordecai told her of the feast of Purim declared in her honor. The feast of the casting of the lots. The feast of courage and hope. A feast that would light in every little girl's heart the courage to trust her God and save her people.

Chapter 24
The King Is Dead

Months later, the king paced the hallway leading to the queen's chambers. It was two in the morning, and no one was sleeping. The queen was giving birth. The king had many children born to him but this, this was his beloved Esther. What if something happened to her? What if the physicians were unable to save her? Women died in childbirth.

Arjana's delivery had gone smoothly, much to Esther's delight. Esther's heart had swollen with love at first sight of the little baby boy's wrinkled face. His dark eyes flickered open for a moment as the queen held him, gently rocking him, singing a Hebrew lullaby.

Javad was smitten. His eyes swelled with tears as he held his little son close, swaddled in a blanket spun by his mother's hand. Anatu's eyes were large, and her face blanched quite pale. Banu wisely requested warm water at that moment to give the poor girl something to do. Even Hathach hovered in the background behind curtains and tapestries in case he was needed to run for something. Esther had insisted her tub be filled and that Arjana's tired body rest in a soothing bath. This took quite a bit of insistence on Esther's part but at last Arjana yielded and enjoy the luxurious moment.

Now it was her turn, only three months later. Arjana was at her side, coaching her through. She told her of the king's agony waiting in the hallway. Javad had given up trying to calm him and stood watching him sympathetically as he paced. Scribes, princes, and advisors stood or sat on standby in rooms waiting for the news. If the queen birthed a son, a contender to the crown, the political landscape would shift and contort to meet this new rival prince. If the queen birthed a girl, all would rejoice and tomorrow would be an ordinary day.

Hathach wisely ran to wake Mordecai and bring him to the palace. Anatu had suggested the idea the moment it was clear a child would be born that night. Hathach was relieved to be able to do something for his beloved mistress. Mordecai was grateful to be called regardless of the hour and readied in a flash. The two men hurried on foot to the palace as few litters where about at that hour and neither man wanted to wait for one.

Mordecai arrived to find the king pacing the hallway before the court of women. He kept silent watching the king agonize away a half hour. Then he spoke.

"My King, if I may speak."

The king nodded and stopped his pacing for a moment.

"Joining me in a prayer may help calm your nerves, my Lord."

"Me? Pray?" It was a foreign thought to Xerxes. "Yes, yes," he nodded. "The temple, of course." He turned to go but Mordecai stopped him.

"No, my Lord King. No temple is needed to pray to the Almighty God. He will hear the prayers of His people no matter where they are. He has heard my prayers at your gates, Oh my King. He has answered the prayers of the Queen from these very hallways."

"If it pleases you, my King, I will pray with you."

The king nodded. The two men stood, united in their love for Esther. Mordecai prayed as the king bowed his crowned head and reverently, respectfully, closed his eyes. Once finished, the king nodded and walked the length of the hallway. There was the sharp cry of an infant muffled by the closed doors.

The king turned to look at Mordecai, his eyes wide with hope and fear. He moved toward the doorway. The door opened shortly. Anatu emerged her eyes shining. She bowed and moved aside from the door.

"The Queen is asking for you, my King." Xerxes nodded and stepped through the doorway, ducking a little as he did. He walked swiftly through the breezeway and into his wife's chambers. The curtains were drawn back from the bed, and he met her eyes from across the room. He was relieved to see her alive and well. He hurried to her bedside.

"Are you well, my wife," he asked dropping to one knee beside the bed to be closer to her face.

"I am, my husband," Esther smiled weakly. "Tired and sore but I am well." Her eyes moved to the bundle beside her.

"Meet your daughter, my Lord King." The king looked at the bundle then at Esther. She nodded and his huge hands, crusted in rings and gems, lifted that tiny body. He looked into the little red wrinkled face. The infant opened her eyes. She had her mother's eyes. They looked huge in her little face. They tried to focus on her father, but they were too young yet. She gurgled contentedly and his heart melted. He held the little bundle to his chest. His eyes closed for a long moment and his heart truly opened. He now understood how a father could love a daughter, how powerful the eyes of a little girl could be.

Esther smiled as she watched them together.

"What do you want to name her?" she asked softly.

He looked from his wife to the little infant cradled in his huge arms.

"Hadassah," he said simply looking down into his daughter's face. "Her mother will always be Esther to me, but my daughter should bare her mother's true name. May she always remember her people and may she be even half as brave as her mother."

Esther smiled even as tears stung her eyes. The little Hadassah cried hungrily. The king handed the little squirming bundle back to his wife. He bent and kissed the shiny black hair on the head of his queen. He left the room but not without first turning to see his wife and daughter, surrounded by loving servants, safe, healthy, and happy. He had some praying to do on his way back to his chambers. He struggled to sleep as a little wrinkled face with huge blue-green eyes danced in his dreams.

Esther and Mordecai worked tirelessly to convert Haman's mansion, once a place of wealth, prestige, and excess into a home for runaway women who had no were else to go. Under Mordecai's watchful care, more and more women and girls came to Esther's house to seek refuge and a new life. Esther enjoyed bringing little Hadassah with her to the estate. The garden exploded under the care of the women and flowers bloomed all around the house. The great lawn was dotted with fruit trees. Grape vines grew along the great stone fence.

At any moment, the house was abuzz with laughter. The girls learned to cook and clean, not because someone told them to but because they wanted to. They enjoyed the taste of their own cooking. They lived in a tidy home, surrounded with other girls, all healing from physical and emotional wounds. Children ran and played as many of the girls arrived pregnant and alone.

Hadassah and Abdiel, Arjana's little son, crawled about and played with the other children, delighted to have the room to roam freely. Esther told the king what she did with the place, but he never visited as it would disrupt the women greatly to see the king arrive. Every evening Mordecai read the Scriptures out loud to the ever-growing group of women around the table. The children learned to read and write Hebrew as well as Persian.

There was discord at times. There were tears, fights, yelling, and sobs, but there was also growth, hope, learning, forgiveness, and time. Time changed things. Time healed. Time separated the pain from the present and gave the future hope. Time marched on.

True to his word, the king did send many of the virgins away. Some refused to leave, desiring instead to stay. Many others took up the king's offer and traveled all over the provinces of Persia, meeting and marrying men of status and wealth. These men received the women as a treasured gift from the king. Feray, Esther's friend from the court of women, wrote to Esther. She was now married to a general and traveling all over her beloved mountains. Esther delighted in receiving her letters full of adventure and beauty.

Although warned by Hegai their life may be wasted with waiting, some insisted they wanted to stay and wait for a chance to go to the king. Esther spoke with Hegai and ensured lessons were set up for the women so they could learn to sew, spin, weave, and make pottery as well as learn to read and write. This way, they could find uses to fill their days.

Much to Esther's delight she gave birth to another girl, Adinah, named after her own dear mother figure. The king threw himself into building. With Mordecai and Esther's help, the king funded schools and other structures to be built and used for the betterment of the lives of the people of Susa and the rest of the empire.

Persepolis became a family destination year after year. The king and Esther picked up where King Darius, Xerxes's father, had stopped. The huge library was completed, housing a book collection from all over the empire for storage and preservation. King Xerxes continued funding the hallway of a hundred columns started by his father and grandfather. Of course, the gardener's cottage was cared for and upgraded, the remnants of the great gardens of King Cyrus clinging to its stone walls.

Prince Artaxerxes strode up to Esther one summer evening as the extensive family dined in the garden of Persepolis. He dropped to one knee and kissed the queen's hand.

"My Prince!" Esther was surprised by the submissive act.

"Thank you, my Queen, for giving me back a family to be proud of."

No further words were needed. The prince and Esther looked across the lawn at the group of children running and laughing together, maids and eunuchs hurrying about trying to keep order to the happy herd.

The wives of the princes mingled together and spoke with each other. Esther herself formed a dear friendship with most of Prince Artaxerxes's wives. His first wife, the beautiful, slender intelligent woman, Laleh, and Esther spent many hours together during the summers at Persepolis. They formed a deep friendship and enjoyed each other's company greatly.

The city was very pristine and secure. Only the royal guard was about. Other than that, the citizens of the city did not feel the need for a standing army. The gates were monitored by doorkeepers that was all. It was a destination of the rich and wealthy and visited by envoys from all over the kingdom to deliver treasures and taxes to the king. Even curious travelers from Greece ventured the journey to behold the pleasant city of Persepolis.

Tents spread for miles all around the city as Persians migrated about to feed their ever-hungry herds and to visit their king at the city of kings. Tribes from all over the land, came, clad in their best dress to deliver their taxes in baskets heaped with fleeces, fruits and vegetables, jewels, and all kinds of treasures from the farthest reaches of the provinces.

Arjana served faithfully by Esther's side despite her family. She and Javad lived happily in their apartment, each serving the king and queen, coming together at night to enjoy life as a family. Esther sat with the king in court regularly as he valued her council and company. So passed years of rich blessing, productivity, and prosperity, for Esther, Mordecai, and most in the great empire of Persia.

Esther had King Xerxes in her garden gazebo at the palace of Susa for the last meal of the day. It was an evening in late Elul. The royal family was back from the city of Persepolis, settled in the palace for the cooler winter months. They enjoyed each other's company greatly. The king did not stay that night with the queen although she asked. He had business he wanted to tend to in the morning and he chose to sleep alone in his chambers. They parted company on the steps, kissing affectionately for a long moment.

It was after midnight when Esther was suddenly awoken with shouting and hurried footsteps running in the corridors. Esther leapt out of bed running to the bedchamber of her two daughters. The two girls slept peacefully unaware of the tumult around them. Esther watched over them, her heart pounding.

Anatu and Hathach were there, she could hear their breathing. Hathach had his short sword drawn. Esther knew it would only be moments before they would hear Arjana's pounding feet coming at a run, carrying little Abdiel close to her bosom.

"The King is dead! The King is dead!" someone was screaming in a loud voice. Esther gasped. Her husband!?! Could he be dead? Fear coursed through her veins. She had to get the children out, now. They had to get out of the palace. The door burst open, with Arjana whispering her name loudly. Hathach hurried to shut the door behind her.

Abdiel struggled in her arms. He was getting almost too big to carry. The maids and eunuchs looked at Esther. Banu hurried in as did other maids and eunuchs. They could hear guards running in the hallways.

She turned to Arjana holding Abdiel, Anatu beside her. She had to make a decision so hard it hurt more than risking her own life. She had to part with her children. She would only be a target and draw any assassin to her girls.

"Take the children." Esther spoke. "Take the children. Arjana don't fail me now my dearest friend. Take the children. Get out of the palace. Go through the servant's gates. Get out and go to Mordecai. He will hide you. I know you will be safe there in the estate outside the palace, at least, till morning." Esther picked up Hadassah, waking her. She kissed the little girl's forehead and handed her over to Banu, wrapping the girl in her blanket.

Banu rocked the sleepy child and hushed her soothingly. Adinah was lifted in the same manner. Her mother blinked back tears and gulped down a sob. She looked into the sweet face a long moment before handing the child to Anatu.

"Now go!" She burst out. "Go before I change my mind in a moment of weakness." She opened the door.

"Guards!" she called out quietly. Two shadowy forms appeared eerily silent.

"Your Queen demands you go with the persons I treasure more than my own life." She said, pushing them toward the group.

"Go!" Arjana kissed Esther's cheek and the group of women, guards, and eunuchs ran down the breezeway and disappeared into the dusky darkness of the palace of women.

They were headed outside, across the lawn and through to the servant's quarters. They would find a doorway that led out into the outer courts of the palace. They would be out on the streets in no time, a group of people with children, hurrying about, nothing to raise anyone's alarm or suspicion. It would only be the royal guards and the fine clothes of the maids that would indicate any attachment to royalty. Once in the large gates of Esther's mansion, they would be safe, and no one would know were Esther's daughters were.

Hathach stood quietly beside Esther as she struggled against the sobs wracking her body.

"If there is indeed treason in the palace, they may come for you next, my Queen." Hathach spoke softly. Shaashgaz hurried in, his eyes wide with fright.

"My Queen!" He said relief filling his voice. An idea popped into her head. It was wild and foolish but in the moment with adrenaline coursing through her and a wild courage in her heart she spoke.

"I will take Hathach with me. I must find out if it is true that my husband is dead. But you, Shaashgaz, get blankets and pillows and make it look as if I am still in my bed. If anyone enters, they will think I am there, sleeping. I will not tell you anymore, faithful man, so you will not have to die hiding my location." She kissed the dear eunuch on the cheek.

Hathach grabbed a woolen overgarment dark in color.

He silently handed it to Esther who slipped it on as the two hurried out of her chambers. Shaashgaz watched her disappear with Hathach by her side. He did not like the idea at all, but he did not have time to try to dissuade her. He sighed even as he turned quickly to do all she told him, knowing full well he could not change her mind even if he tried.

Hathach led the way silently. They ran down the stairs, across the common area, and toward the bathing area. Esther followed without question, knowing Hathach would know of easier, lesser known, well-hidden exits from the court of women. Exits that would not be known to anyone except those very familiar with the palace. They hurried through twisting hallways and passageways, up and down steps and behind the latrine area. Esther had to pinch her nose against the terrible smell, her breath coming in sharp gasps.

"Not much further, my Queen," whispered Hathach encouragingly. "Very few know of this way and fewer are brave or foolish enough to attempt it."

Esther's eyes stung, the smells were so intense. Yes, this was not a well-used way of entering the court of women!

Hathach held open a tapestry and suddenly they were in a wide hallway, the roof covered with billowing white canvas and flickering torches giving little light. The two stuck to the shadows and moved swiftly. The room Mordecai and Esther used to meet was behind them. A great tapestry hung against the wall then a huge cedar column supporting the roof, cast a large shadow. From there, they could see the entrance to the palace across the large open courtyard. Guards and servants were running this way and that.

Suddenly a group of armed men ran out of the king's palace swinging swords and torches. Blood flashed on the drawn blades. They were dragging a body behind them, blood leaving a gruesome trail. Esther gasped, recognizing the great frame of her husband the king. Xerxes was dead indeed. Tears filled her eyes.

Suddenly a hand grabbed her around the waist from behind and another clapped over her mouth stifling her scream. Fear coursed through her. She was terrified for her life and her hands tore at the strong hand that covered her mouth. The man was dragging her behind the tapestry breathing hard. *Where was Hathach? Had they killed him already?*

"My Queen," a familiar voice whispered in her ear. Esther struggled to place it in her terror. "It is I, Prince Artaxerxes! Don't scream my Queen. I will uncover your mouth, but don't make a sound. Your husband is dead. I don't know how many will die tonight but I have come to keep you safe. Hurry, we must get you out of here!"

"Artaxerxes!" relief poured through Esther. She was shaking uncontrollably. It was a mixture of shock and terror. Seeing her dead husband lying in the open courtyard, blood pooling around his body, weakened her legs. She looked at his huge body, then at Prince Artaxerxes. She could hear someone sobbing but did not know where the sound came from. She did not realize it was her own sobs.

"My Queen!" whispered Artaxerxes shaking his head, his hand tightening on her arm. "Think of how dangerous it is to go to him now. They will kill you if you go to the king now, or worse. I don't know who is responsible for this. The coup is still too young. All will be clear in the morning."

Esther could not move. She stood frozen, staring. Prince Artaxerxes grabbed her arm. He nodded to Hathach who grabbed her other arm and together the two men half carried half drug the sobbing queen between them.

A loud shout told them they had been spotted. It was only a small group of armed men with the prince. People were chasing them, shouting, and waving torches. Terror engulfed Esther. She was suddenly a child again, running,

running from the groping hands and terrible red eyes. Prince Artaxerxes called to Hathach and the two turned suddenly, pulling Esther with them. They dashed out a side door.

Horses waited for them tossing their heads, their nostrils flared with the smell of blood. More shouting was heard. The prince mounted up in one leap and two men lifted Esther up onto his horse.

"Ride with me, my Queen," he said. Esther clung to him; her head buried in his robes. The prince flipped his cloak around her, covering her as best he could. Esther instantly felt safe, buried in his robes, remembering the way Mordecai had covered her so many years ago. For a second time in her young life, she was being carried away from the very clutches of death.

"Hold on, my Lady," he instructed. "Tonight, we ride fast and hard."

They galloped from the courtyard in a clatter of hooves. The guards surrounded them, their horses bumping up against their legs at times they rode so closely. They rode out the gate and down the cobblestone streets, everyone scrambling to get out of the way.

Esther's head banged against Artaxerxes's muscular chest with every stride the horse took. She sobbed for her husband, remembering his great lifeless form oozing blood, lying on the cold stone floor. So was the death of the Great Xerxes, by the hand of one close to him. She shuttered to think of what would have happened that night if he had been in her bed. What if they had turned on the children too?

She began to pray quietly. She was glad now she had sent the children and maids away. Her own home would now be their refuge. She knew her daughters would be safe. They were no threat to the throne. How grateful she was to Yahweh she had daughters, not sons.

Artaxerxes's arm was firm around her back. How grateful she was for him. Gratitude surged through her as she snuggled against him, struggling to keep warm. Over the years as their friendship flourished, she admired his courage and firm stance for righteousness. He had just risked his own life to save hers. It was a bold move. He was a threat to whoever was behind this regime change. The prince was now a contender for the vacant throne of the great Persian Empire.

The saddle dug into her. She was acutely aware of how uncomfortable she was and how very cold the night air had become. The horses came to a quick halt. They were at the gates to Prince Artaxerxes's mansion.

"It is I, Prince Artaxerxes," the prince called out, showing his face in the flickering torchlight.

"Welcome, Master!" the guards called out. The large gate swung open, and the horses galloped up toward the house. The gates slammed shut behind them, guarded by a small army of heavily armed men, trumpets in hand to sound the alarm if the walls were breached by invaders.

Strong arms helped her off the horse. Artaxerxes quickly dismounted and picked her up. He carried her into the house, Hathach right behind him. Gently he laid her on a couch. He took off his cloak and covered her with his own clothing. Then he knelt beside the couch looking at her in concern.

"My lady," he said. "Are you alright, are you injured, is anything broken or bleeding?"

Esther shook her head, her teeth chattering. She was shaking with shock and cold. The prince frowned to see her in such a condition. Tearstains marked her pale cheeks, her eyes a startling turquoise in the flickering torchlight.

"You have earned my highest respect over the years." The prince spoke. "I have now had the honor of saving your life. You will always be the Queen of Persia to me."

"Will you use your position and title to help me? I don't know who has done this to my father yet. I have my suspicions, but only time will tell. If we can survive this night, will you use your status to help me avenge my father's death? Will you stand by me during these turbulent times? The people will crave a familiar face; a calming reassurance that all is well in the palace despite the blood shed this night."

Esther paused for a long moment.

"I know this is hard for you, my Queen," he spoke again as she was silent. "You just saw the body of your husband." He would have continued but she raised her hand.

Slowly she stood, pulling his cloak around her. Like it or not, she was now a political instrument. She would have a sway, potentially, in who would sit on the throne her late husband had just vacated due to his untimely death at the hand of a treacherous coup. She slowly paced the room, strength and feeling slowly returning to her numb legs. She turned to Artaxerxes, still kneeling on one knee by the couch watching her.

"Do you have any idea who has done this?" she asked.

The prince sighed and frowned.

"It could be Crown Prince Darius, but he would gain little by doing this. He is entitled to the throne anyway. He did not let on, last time we spoke, that he had any ill intention towards the King."

"Right now, I have no idea, no proof. I mean to find out as soon as I can," the prince said firmly. "I have my people. They will help me. They will tell me all they know of what has transpired this night. Till then I know not what to do, except, keep you safe, my Queen, and see what comes of all this. I would prefer to keep the knives and swords out of my back as well."

The queen flashed a weak smile. She nodded.

"Artaxerxes," she said. "You have been my friend when I had very few friends indeed. I would be happy to stand beside you and help you gain your father's throne, if indeed that is what tomorrow brings. I realize I am not powerless although my husband lies dead and this very morning, I must don a widow's dress."

The prince smiled. Esther walked to the kneeling man and held out a hand of friendship. The young man took her hand and kissed it tenderly.

"Thank you, my Queen." He said gently. "There is no other woman I would rather have by my side in this venture than you, my Lady." Esther smiled at him through her tears.

She nodded unable to speak for a long moment. Her life as she knew it was now over. Despite his faults, his impulsiveness, his cruelty, and his worldliness, King Xerxes had been her husband, her lover, and the father of her children. She would miss him. She would miss making him laugh, making him curious, making him happy. She would miss him.

"What of Mordecai?" Esther asked slowly pacing the room again, thinking out loud.

"I thought of him. I think he is safe, out of harm's way. The King had his signet ring so there is no need for them to come after him. Thankfully he is removed from the palace. I sent a guard over to stand at the gates of your estate just to be sure."

"Thank you," said Esther nodding her head. Unknowingly she had sent her children to the safest place possible.

"Where are your daughters, my Queen?" ask the prince suddenly. His eyes widened as he realized he had not even given the queen time to get her children.

Esther smiled. "They are hidden in plain sight with people I would trust with my own life, never mind theirs," she said evasively. Her girls would blend in with all the children of her house. "Anyone searching for them will find it very hard indeed to track them down now."The prince nodded. His thoughts turned to his own children, safe upstairs in their beds.

Hathach came into the room bearing a steaming cup in his hands. He bowed then looked up at Esther raising the cup.

"Oh, thank you Hathach, you faithful man!" she exclaimed. He hurried over to her. In a show of his loyalty to her, he poured out a little from her cup into a smaller cup he held and sipped it before handing it over to her. Esther smiled as he showed her this gesture of respect.

"Thank you," she said again, taking the cup he handed her. Hathach bowed and disappeared. He reappeared shortly and repeated the procedure then handed Prince Artaxerxes a cup.

Then he came up to Esther and bowed.

"What is it Hathach?" asked Esther.

"Let me go, my Queen. Let me return to the palace to find out what I can. You are safe here with Prince Artaxerxes, my Lady. I can get in and out of the palace with no one even knowing I was there. Let me be your eyes and ears."

Esther looked from her faithful man to Prince Artaxerxes. The prince nodded slightly.

"Take one of my men with you, Hathach." The prince encouraged. "We can use any information you can find out. Don't, upon your life, don't disclose where the Queen is. But I need not press you. I can see from your eyes and your courage this night; you would die for her."

Hathach bowed to the prince. He glanced at Esther.

"God go with thee, Hathach," she said softly.

Hathach flashed her a rare smile, then he was gone, his feet silent on the stone floor.

Restless Esther began to pray softly in Hebrew as she paced. The familiar words comforted her as she let the prayers of David wash over her, flowing over her tongue, words David had penned even as he ran for his life, his own son, Prince Absalom, out to kill him.

She longed to go and find her children. She longed for Mordecai's warm embrace. But she was reliant on Prince Artaxerxes's hospitality. She knew she was safest with him at this moment for he had an army at his command. She only had her faithful guards. It was best she stayed with the prince, assisting him as needed till more information was theirs.

Prince Artaxerxes watched her silently from the couch she would not sit on. His admiration for this woman only grew watching her faith even as she grieved the loss of her husband, the loss of her surety as queen, the loss of her position and power.

"Why don't you try rest, my Queen?" he asked gently. "I will wait for news and rouse you the moment I know more."

Esther shook her head.

"Let me wait with you, my Prince," she asked walking up to him. "I can't sleep yet till I know more. I would just lie and wonder."

She laid a hand on his arm.

"Thank you, my prince, for taking me from the palace." She did not trust herself to look at him. Her voice was thick with emotions. They both knew where her thoughts were. They both knew of a fate worse than death that she could face even now.

The prince lay a hand over hers and gently squeezed it. He did not trust himself to speak at that moment. They stayed in this position for a long moment, each lost in thought, comforted by each other's understanding and presence.

At last dawn broke. The dark night cleared and slowly, oh so slowly the sun peered over the horizon. The city of Susa awoke to the gallop of horses and the shouts of messengers. A letter was delivered by mounted messenger to the gate of Prince Artaxerxes's mansion. A guard ran the letter from the gates to the door of the mansion.

"My Prince," he hurried into the room were Esther and the prince waited. Artaxerxes took the letter from his hand and read it quickly.

He looked up at Esther after a long moment.

"It is Artabanus," he said. Esther stared at him a long moment.

"Artabanus?" she cried out, shocked. She looked over at the prince even as tears gathered in her eyes. "He would never have seen it coming! I hope the King did not know at whose hand he died. It would have broken his heart!"

Tears spilled down her cheeks as she remembered the muscular form, always near Xerxes, his hand on his sword hilt, ever protective of his king.

"There is more," said the prince gravely. "Our new king openly accuses Crown Prince Darius of the assassination. I am requested to attend court today." Sarcasm dripped from his voice as he called the assassin 'our new king'.

278

"Oh Prince!" Esther drew a shaky breath. Even if the family of the king was power hungry and self-centered, now was it to turn on itself, brother against brother? Today was to be a hard day for the prince. He had lost his father and now would have to stand in the trial of his own brother.

Their eyes met and held.

"I will go, but you must stay here, my Queen." He spoke, his voice trembling a bit so great was his emotions. "Stay here. No one knows you are here, save my men who I trust. Hathach is a master of discretion and will be our eyes and ears in the palace. His presence there is more than valuable."

"My guards will stay at the gate of your estate. Mordecai will be safe. I know not where you have hidden your daughters. They will hold little interest to Artabanus anyway. You, on the other hand my Queen, had best stay hidden for now. I will not disclose your location, you know that. A palace purge is coming, and it is best to stay away till all the pieces fall into place."

Esther nodded at his words knowing he was correct.

"Thank you, Artaxerxes," she said softly. "And remember, Prince, all may not be as it seems in this moment. Never underestimate the element of surprise."

The prince nodded. A frown furrowed his brow even as his dark eyes flashed angrily.

Esther watched his handsome form hurry from the room. He stopped suddenly in the doorway and turning to her, he covered his chest, covering his heart with his hand.

"Do not leave me, my Queen. Do not leave me. This heart cannot handle the thought of losing you too."

With that he was gone. Her only hope was that he would be safe, him, second to the throne, second and last son of Xerxes and Queen Vashti.

Chapter 25
A New King Is Crowned

The prince readied himself for the day in court. Servants showed Esther to a spacious room and laid out clothes for her. She dressed herself in clothes made for Laleh, as she was still wearing only her night clothes, the woolen over robe Hathach had given her in haste, then draped in the riding cloak of Prince Artaxerxes.

Esther hurried down to the door of the mansion. She wanted to be sure to bid Prince Artaxerxes farewell. She hoped she would see him return. It was a dangerous game he now played.

The prince smiled when he saw her waiting.

"My Prince," she said holding out her hand to him.

"My Queen," he replied and kissed her hand. He looked up into her eyes for a long moment. She knew he wanted to kiss more than her hand. Ever the gentleman, he then turned and left. She could hear his horse's hooves on the roadway as he galloped off toward the palace, his guard riding with him.

Unable to rest, Esther went out into the gardens she had enjoyed so much her first visit to Artaxerxes's estate. She watched the sun rising, red, yellow, and pink, bathing the world in light and beauty. She sighed as she contemplated all this day would bring. She knew in her heart that her God would see her through, even as He had seen her through all the other trials life had thrown at her.

At least she was safe. She knew her daughters would be safe. She knew her servants would protect those two beautiful girls with the great blue-green eyes with their own lives. She remembered her own harrowing journey through the markets and streets so many years ago, concealed under the robe of Mordecai. It was relatively easy to hide children when need be.

She would stand by the prince during this time. She preferred the throne of her husband honored by a kind, gentle man such as Artaxerxes over the arrogant, violent, drunkenness of the Crown Prince Darius. Most knew the Crown Prince for his love of wine and women, like his father, of course. But had it really been the Crown Prince who was behind this terrible deed? Why was Artabanus so quick to accuse Darius? All Prince Darius had to do was wait and the crown was his. Why rush it? It seemed against his nature to configure something so labor intensive as a murder and coup.

Again, she sighed for the women, trapped in the palace, waiting their fate. She was glad her husband had released many. The ones who had been wise and insightful enough to leave had escaped the terrible intrigue of the gilded cage of the palace. Anything that was Xerxes was now open to another, any other, who wanted it. She pulled her arms around her chest, grateful she was safe, gratitude for Prince Artaxerxes and his honor coursing through her body and mind. Somewhere, a rooster began crowing loudly. Another joined him. Esther smiled as the familiar sound comforted her. It had been years since she had heard something as simple as a crowing rooster. There were no roosters in the palace, only the noisy peacock in the women's quarters she had been in the first year.

A sudden thought made her laugh despite tears gathering again in her tired eyes. Her husband was so impulsive he would probably kill a rooster in a fit of rage for waking him. She sighed, remembering. And now he was gone, forever gone. She remembered their final moments together in the garden, the kiss on the steps. She would never see him again.

Someone moved in the garden beside her. She jumped a little and looked over quickly. Relief flooded her as Hathach and Anatu approached. Esther smiled and hurried toward them. Anatu broke into a run upon seeing her. The faithful maid clutched Esther's hand. Esther searched her face.

"Tell me," she gasped. "How are Hadassah and Adinah? Tell me they are safe! Arjana and Abdiel? Javad?"

"All are safe, my Queen," Anatu hurried to tell her. "They are all safe at your house with Mordecai." Esther grabbed the maid into a hug, tears squeezing out despite her best efforts as relief flooded her body.

"Mordecai desperately wanted to come and see you, my Queen. But we convinced him to not disclose your location in any way. He would be recognized if he came here. I insisted Hathach bring me to you so I can care for you."

"But how did you meet up with Hathach, Anatu? I sent him to the palace."

Anatu smiled and reached into her bosom. She pulled out a silken bag on a string around her neck. She drew out the ring King Xerxes had given Esther on their second night together. Esther's eyes filled with tears as she saw it. She sighed as she reached out for that fateful piece of jewelry.

"Anatu," she said as she slid it onto her finger. "You dear girl!"

Anatu smiled and reached back into the bag. She pulled out Esther's crown, the symbol of her position in the great Persian Empire. Esther gasped as the jewels sparkled in the early morning sun.

"You will need this, my Queen," Anatu said gently.

"You crazy girl!" gasped Esther, understanding dawning on her face. Anatu had returned to the palace, to the queen's chambers to collect these precious articles that had been left in the hasty flight in the middle of the night. It was there Anatu had met Hathach, having the same thoughts in mind.

"Oh!" Esther gasped out as it sunk into her tired mind.

"Did you see him?" Esther asked softly. "Did you see the King or Artabanus?"

Anatu shook her head.

"No men came to the palace of women," she said understanding what Esther feared to ask.

Esther nodded and swallowed hard.

"Come, my Queen," said Anatu. "You have been up all night and now you must rest. All you hold dear are safe. There is nothing more you can do at this moment but rest." Esther nodded. Hathach walked with them to Esther's room.

"I will be right here at the door," he said. He had a long knife tucked in his belt. "No one will cross this threshold unless I let them or die first."

Esther laid her hand on his broad shoulder.

"I thank you, Hathach." He nodded and kissed her hand gently.

"You are my Queen," he said. "I will lay down my life to defend yours."

Esther went in and Anatu shut the door. Esther sat in numb silence watching Anatu lay out bedclothes and turn back the bed. As Anatu fluffed the pillow, Esther roused herself.

"Anatu, can you see to it that Hathach has a blanket and pillow too?" she asked tiredly. The night was catching up with her. Her eyes burned from crying and lack of sleep and her speech was thick and clumsy. "He has been up all night too."

Anatu smiled and nodded.

"Yes, my Queen," she said softly. "I will see to it that he is cared for once you are comfortable."

Esther climbed into bed but when she closed her eyes the sight of her husband, dead and bleeding flashed before her eyes.

"God is our refuge and strength, a very present help in trouble. Therefore, we will not fear, even though the earth be removed. And though the mountains be carried into the midst of the sea; though its waters roar and be troubled, though mountains shake with its swelling."

"There is a river whose streams shall make glad the city of God, the holy place of the tabernacle of the Most High. God is in the midst of her, she shall not be moved; God shall help her, just at the break of dawn."

"The nations rage, the kingdoms were moved; He uttered His voice, the earth melted. The Lord of hosts is with us; The God of Jacob is our refuge. Come, behold the works of the Lord, who has made desolations in the earth. He makes wars cease to the end of the earth; He breaks the bow and cuts the spear in two; He burns the chariot in the fire. Be still and know that I am God; I will be exalted among the nations, I will be exalted in the earth! The Lord of hosts is with us, the God of Jacob is our refuge. Selah, Psalm forty-six a psalm of David, servant of the Lord."

The psalm comforted her even as she quoted it. Her eyelids slid shut and she fell into a deep slumber, her mind filled with the promises of Scriptures. Her God held this kingdom in His hands. He had done the impossible and elevated her to be queen of Persia. He would now use her to help place a new king on that throne.

Esther awoke with a start. The events of the night came tumbling back into her mind and she sat up quickly. Anatu lay on the rug beside the bed, still sleeping. Her movement woke her maid, and she rose quickly.

"Anatu," Esther smiled at her. "I am so glad you are here!"

Anatu returned her smile. "Me too, my Queen." She admitted sincerely. She hurried to prepare Esther's clothes. Esther marveled at all that the maid had been able to smuggle out of the palace in that silk pouch around her neck. Once Esther was dressed and her hair done to Anatu's satisfaction, the two women opened the door. There was Hathach, already standing ready, waiting for his mistress.

The three descended the stairs and joined the household who received them with open arms. Laleh rushed to her friend and pulled her into a long embrace. The women held each other, sobbing.

"You brave, brave woman," Laleh kept repeating even as tears stood in her deep dark eyes.

"Thank you, my lovely Laleh," Esther responded tears standing in her own. "Thank you for welcoming me into your home!"

"Oh!" Laleh exclaimed. "I am honored to house the Queen of Persia as long as she has need to stay here! I am proud of my husband for going to the palace to get you."

"You are too generous, Laleh," murmured Esther and the two women exchanged a long knowing look. Laleh knew her husband, Prince Artaxerxes, loved Esther. They both knew it.

"Come, let us get you fed, my Queen," said Laleh taking Esther's arm and leading her to the dining room. "My husband will return with news when he can."

It was late that evening that Artaxerxes returned. He shook his head sadly as he described the day's events.

"Artabanus is sitting on the throne, claiming to be acting in the place of King Xerxes, keeping the crown of my father on his lap. The evidence against Crown Prince Darius, for staging this treason and killing the King, was staggering. They even found a bloody sword in the prince's bed, wrapped in a sack. In the presence of the entire court, advisors, and princes, Prince Darius was executed, right there in the courtyard. There was nothing I could do. Of course, my brother faced his death as a Persian prince, his face set and his head held high right to the end."

Esther stared in horror at Prince Artaxerxes as he described the terrible events. They were alone in a room, Hathach standing guard at the door, the princes' wives respectful of the need for the two to speak in relative privacy. Even Laleh left so they could speak together.

"It is very convenient for Artabanus that the Crown Prince is now dead, the named successor of King Xerxes. It is too convenient. I saw the sword with my own eyes. It is a sword belonging to the royal guard, not Prince Darius's sword. And why would he leave the sword still covered in blood in his own bed? I fear a set up."

"I will avenge my father's death," he promised turning to look at Esther. "I just need to be sure I know who exactly it is who killed him. There is still much to find out."

"I have no doubt you will, Prince Artaxerxes," said Esther softly. "It is the pride of a Persian son to do so. It was the pride and downfall of your late father to march on Greece to avenge his father's death. Just be sure the same fate does not await you. Do be careful, my Prince."

The prince nodded. "I will be wise about it, my Lady, I assure you."

"Good," said Esther. "My heart does not want to bear the loss of another I love."

She was dressed in a rich black gown. A small black lace veil covered her hair. On her finger glittered the ring King Xerxes had given her when he asked her to be his queen.

At the word *love*, the prince glanced at her sharply. His eyes noted the ring on her finger. He smiled thoughtfully, remembering.

"I thought my father was insane for crowning you queen over all the other noblewomen he could have chosen," he said. "And now, here I am, a prince of Persia, asking for your help in avenging my father's death and taking over his throne which is now rightfully mine. Have I ever told you what a remarkable woman you are, my Queen?"

Esther smiled a bit sadly.

"Your actions have said so, my Prince," she said.

Esther hid in the prince's house for forty-five long days. Prince Artaxerxes was gone almost constantly. He was bent on seeking out the truth behind his father's sudden death. He often left the mansion before daylight and returned about midnight, dressed in all manner of disguises.

He burst into the house one afternoon, his sword drawn and bloodied. He knelt before Esther and laid his sword at her feet.

"The death of your husband, King Xerxes the Great, and my father, has been avenged," he said with a flourish. "Behold the blood of his killer, Aspamitres, a eunuch who served my father. I impaled him with my own hand!"

Esther's face paled a bit, but relief washed over her.

"Well done, my Prince!" she exclaimed. "And what of Artabanus?"

"I ran him through with this very sword as well." The prince admitted proudly. "Once I found out that Aspamitres had killed my father, I demanded he tell me who he had plotted with. It was no surprise when he told me it was Artabanus. In a final act of service to the Great King Xerxes, the very man who killed the King told me the entirety of the plot before I ran him through with my sword."

"Filled with a wrath I cannot describe; I entered the courtroom at a dead run. My guards pushed all opposition out of the way, and I made it up the steps to the throne. Artabanus knew his time had come. He grabbed at his sword, but he was too slow. I impaled him right there on the throne of my father in the presence of the entire court of Persia. I took this," The prince reached into his robes and pulled out the great crown of Persia, "from his lap as he lay dying in his own blood."

"Well done, my Prince," Esther stammered. Her knees suddenly felt weak, and she was grateful to sit on the couch. "I accept your vengeance. May my husband and your father, the Great King Xerxes, rest in peace with his ancestors at last."

The prince handed the crown to Esther. She held it in her hands, looking at it, remembering it on her husband's brow.

"I will only accept this crown from your hands, my Queen," said the prince softly. "You are the one to crown me King, in court, in front of all."

Esther nodded. "I would be honored, my Prince, honored to do so." She smiled despite tears shimmering in her eyes.

The prince rose and kissed her hand. He carefully wiped his sword and placed it in its sheath. He moved to leave the room but stopped. He turned and came back to where Esther still sat, the crown in her lap.

He stood before her, his head bowed for a long moment, looking so much like his father Esther felt her heart burn in her. She waited. Something weighed heavily on his mind. Impulsively, he knelt on one knee and reached for her hand.

"Would you marry me and be my Queen?" he asked so softly, so timidly, Esther almost missed it. Her head snapped up to look at him.

"Are you serious, Artaxerxes, or do you jest?" she demanded pulling her hand away from his.

His eyes told her he was serious. Esther sighed. She shook her head. Deep in her heart, she had known he would ask her this very question someday if he ever had the chance.

"My Prince," she said firmly, her hands playing with the jewels embedded around the rim of the crown in her lap. "I came from nothing, and I desire nothing. A quiet life with my cousin and my daughters is all this heart now craves. I have no love left for a man, even a man such as you, a Prince, a King, whom I admire greatly. Let me help you aspire to the throne then let me go. Let me live as a noble woman who was once the queen, the wife of Xerxes the Great. Let me be remembered as his wife, nothing more."

The prince nodded.

"I figured you would refuse me, but I had to ask anyway." He said softly, sadly. He sighed. A look, the look that often crossed King Xerxes' face, passed over the face of his son. Esther's heart broke a little upon seeing it. She reached out her hand and gently lifted the prince's chin, so he looked into her eyes.

"Your wife, Laleh, is your Queen. Give her any love and respect you feel for me. Let her be your confidence, your advisor, your friend, and your lover. She will not let you down. She is the bride of your youth. Don't shun her now. Crown her as your Queen, my Prince, and you will share the throne with a wise and good woman."

Prince Artaxerxes stared back into Esther's eyes for a long moment. He nodded. "Yes, my Queen," he said quietly. "I would do well to heed your words." He rose and smiled. He reached out a hand and helped Esther to her feet.

"Come, my Queen," he said. "Let us prepare for a new day in the Persian empire."

An hour later, Prince Artaxerxes mounted up on his horse. A litter carried Esther and Laleh. Surrounded by guards, they left the mansion behind. People cheered and bowed as they passed by in the streets. Women hurried to throw flowers before them as they headed to the palace. Esther smiled and waved from her litter. She was dressed as the queen, in her royal robes, her crown on her head, the coveted crown of Persia beside her.

Laleh was dressed in one of Esther's gowns. There wasn't time for Shaashgaz to make her a gown yet. Esther wanted her friend to look every inch a queen from the moment she arrived at the palace.

They entered at the main palace gate. The guards stood at attention, and they passed through unchallenged. They rode right up to the main courtyard; the very place Esther had last seen her husband's body. Artaxerxes dismounted from his horse. He was dressed as the royal Prince of Persia he was, his robes of shimmering blue and purple, jewels glittering every time he moved. He hurried to help Queen Esther descend from the litter. Esther thanked him. He would have turned to escort her to the court room, but she stopped him.

"The Queen of your heart, my Prince." She said directly. To his credit the prince colored a little. He turned and helped his wife, Laleh, as she struggled to dismount from the litter as well. Esther stood by with a slight smile on her face.

Together, with the crowned queen on one arm and his wife on the other, the prince turned toward the palace entrance. Generals, advisors, and princes gathered quickly at the doorway having heard the cheering crowds. Mordecai was there, dressed as regent; ready to receive the new king. Esther smiled and handed him the crown. It was quickly set on a silken pillow and carried by Mordecai toward the courtroom.

Esther walked with Prince Artaxerxes into the palace. They walked through the grand hallways into the inner court room, down the long-carpeted hallway Esther had walked alone so many years ago. Together, the three ascended the ten great marble steps leading up to the platform on which the thrones of Persia stood, vacant.

The three turned toward the crowd, the prince stepping forward and raising his arms for silence. A great hush fell over the courtroom, everyone eagerly awaiting what the prince had to say.

"As you all saw earlier today, I, Prince Artaxerxes, the last remaining son of the Great King Xerxes and his Queen Vashti, avenged with my own hand, the treasonous murderer of my father. Artabanus is dead. The crown is retrieved."

"As the symbol of my right to the throne of my father, I request that his Queen, Queen Esther, in whom he bestowed great power and confidence, crown me, Prince Artaxerxes, today in the presence of all gathered here, as the rightful King of Persia."

"If anyone has a better claim to this throne than I, let him step forward and challenge me. If not, let all contenders be forever silent on the matter. I will command loyalty and I will win your confidence and respect by my actions."

His speech completed, the prince turned and with a sweep of his cloak, he sat down on his father's throne.

The courtroom erupted in cheers. Mordecai held out the cushion with the crown toward Esther. She smiled at him as she took it in both her hands. Esther looked at the coveted headpiece, remembering the last time she had seen it on her husband's brow.

Esther lifted the crown with both her hands, holding it up for all to see.

"Today, I crown Prince Artaxerxes, as King Artaxerxes the first, son of Xerxes the Great, the new King of Persia!" The crowd held its breath as the queen closed her eyes for a long moment and her lips moved silently. The prince sat on the throne, his bare head waiting.

Esther smiled as she finished whispering the Aaronic blessing in Hebrew over that crown and the head of the waiting prince. Slowly, she lowered it and placed it on the prince's head. Esther reached out her hand toward him to signal him to rise. He took her hand in his, kissed it, then rose. He stood before the court.

"Long live King Artaxerxes!" Cried Esther.

The shout went up. People cheered and clapped. Mordecai smiled as he watched his dear Hadassah standing beside the new king, smiling. Her eyes shone with unshed tears even as she smiled and clapped for the new king.

At last, the cheers began to die down. King Artaxerxes glanced at Esther, who raised up both her hands and lifted the crown off her head. The king stopped surprised. Esther winked at him and looked at Laleh.

The king shook his head slightly, but Esther nodded.

"Are you sure?" he said softly. "There is time to reconsider."

"I am sure," said Esther and she handed the crown to King Artaxerxes. The king looked at it a long moment then he looked at his wife, Laleh, standing behind them, a wide smile on her beautiful face.

"My first act as King Artaxerxes of Persia shall be this," he raised up the crown Esther had given him. He turned toward Laleh.

Esther reached for her friend's arm, pulling her forward, so she stood beside her husband.

"I crown my wife, Laleh, as my Queen, Queen of Persia. Long may be her reign." With this, he lowered the crown onto his wife's head. The tears in her beautiful dark eyes, as she looked up at her husband, said it all.

Esther moved over to stand beside Mordecai.

"Well done, my daughter," he whispered, their shoulders touching. The courtroom erupted in cheers and shouts. The guards beat their shields with their swords. The new king and queen descended the stairs from the thrones, and slowly began the long walk through the courtroom. The royal carriage was waiting outside to parade them through the streets of Susa. There would be feasting and celebrations long into the night.

Esther walked the hallways toward her quarters for the last time. She slept in her bed; her night troubled with memories of her husband lying beside her. She woke with a start, looking at the empty space beside her, no indent on the pillow.

Esther rose. She dressed in her wedding gown and tucked the jeweled veil under her arm. She gathered a large handful of flowers from her garden, the very garden where she and the king had enjoyed many an evening together, laughing and talking in the gazebo, watching their daughters play.

Banu had a carriage waiting. Esther climbed in with Mordecai and Banu. Hathach insisted he would walk beside. The small company left the city, toward the valley of the great tombs of the kings. After a couple hour carriage ride, they finally arrived. Hathach helped Esther from the carriage and waited for her.

She walked quietly and soberly to the tomb where he was laid to rest at last. In her hiding, Esther had missed the funeral of her husband, now entombed in the valley of the dead kings. Esther went into the tomb alone. They all knew she needed to do this alone. She needed to say a final goodbye to her husband, taken too soon from this earth.

It was silent and dark in the grave carved out for him. She paused, waiting for her eyes to adjust to the dim light.

"It is I, Esther, your wife," she spoke softly into the darkness. It only felt right to introduce herself before she approached. She laid the bouquet of flowers on the folded hands of the great sarcophagus, carved in his likeness that encased her husband's body. Her tears fell on the cold stone as she traced the lines of his face carved into the stone.

"My husband," she whispered. "You are missed." She bent down and kissed the cold hard forehead one last time.

"May God give rest to your soul." With that, she slowly removed the ring from her finger. She looked at it one more time remembering.

"I will leave this with you, my King, my husband," she said, laying down the symbol of his favor on his coffin. "I will tell our daughters of you so they will know their father." She spread her wedding veil over the sarcophagus and laid the flowers on his chest.

With that, she turned and walked back out into the warm sunlight, leaving behind her old life, encased in the stone with the body of her husband, the king. She smiled at Mordecai as Hathach helped her back into the carriage. She looked back at the entrance to the tomb and silently raised her hand as the carriage bore her away. She knew she would never return.

King Artaxerxes stood on the steps to the palace, smiling at the beautiful picture playing out before him. The carriage pulled up and Esther's two daughters ran to meet her, carrying flowers. Arjana, Banu, and Anatu behind them. Javad stood, holding Abdiel in his arms. Esther laughed and held out her arms to greet her excited children. She bent down and hugged them both, pressing kisses onto their soft, round cheeks. Looking up she saw the king watching her. She spoke to the children and the girls ran back to Mordecai.

Esther left the group and walked up the steps to bid the king farewell.

"Are you sure?" he said, emotions playing over his face, holding her hand in his. "My offer still stands, my Queen."

"I am, King Artaxerxes," said Esther with a smile. "I am free. Remember the Lord God Jehovah and His chosen people and your reign will be long and prosperous."

The king bowed slightly to the beautiful bareheaded woman with the exotic blue-green eyes standing in front of him. Laleh hurried across the courtyard eager to bid her friend goodbye as well. The king looked at his wife, rushing toward them, her brown eyes sparkling and her cheeks flushed.

"Goodbye, my friend!" the two women embraced for a long moment.

"Do come visit me!" invited Laleh. "You know the way and you are always welcome, my friend, my Queen."

The women embraced again. Esther turned to the king. He lifted her hand to his lips. He let her hand go.

"I will do all I can in my power to help your people." He promised. He moved over closer to his wife.

With that, Esther bowed and descended the steps, a huge smile on her face. She joined Mordecai and her two daughters waiting at the bottom of the steps watching with wide eyes. Esther turned and waved. King Artaxerxes had his arm protectively around his wife, her head resting against his shoulder.

Hegai stood with tears flowing down his face, watching his queen leave. Shaashgaz wrung his hands; his only consolation was that Esther looked as beautiful in her wedding gown as she did the day he had made it for her.

Esther blew them each a kiss, the goodbyes having already been said, the promises to write made. Arjana and Javad stood beside her, Abdiel safely in Javad's arms. Anatu and Banu stood close by.

The little group turned and Esther left the palace of Susa, wearing her wedding gown, looking every inch a queen. A little girl holding each of her hands, Mordecai beside her, her faithful maidservants with her, she was at last free.

They passed through the gate and Esther looked up, way up, at the window that faced Jerusalem. Out of that window, she had watched so much of life move freely around her and now, now she was moving freely once again. She smiled down at Hadassah then at Adinah.

"Let's go home," she said.

The little group walked slowly for the children's sake down the cobblestone street, across the square and along the road beside the river. The gates stood open in welcome. Women stood waiting for their mistress to arrive.

Esther smiled as the sun warmed her skin and the breeze blew past her. She was free at last, free to live, free to go, and free to move. Hadassah and Abdiel laughed and skipped ahead, leaving little Adinah running to keep up.

"God sure does hear and answer prayers," said Arjana, watching with Esther as their children ran through the gate toward the great house.

Esther nodded.

"He surely does!" she said. "He hears even the prayers our hearts dare not utter. God is the God of answered prayers. He is the God of Israel, the God of Abraham, Isaac, and Jacob, the King of all kings and the Lord of all lords."

And so, finishes the story of a brave young woman who faced her fears and changed the course of history. King Xerxes is forever remembered as being the husband of Queen Esther.

Esther lived out the rest of her days a free and happy woman. King Artaxerxes listened to the wise council given to him by his queen Laleh. He granted Nehemiah, his cupbearer, all he needed to rebuild the gates and walls of Jerusalem years later. His reign was long and blessed, spanning forty-one years of peace and prosperity.

Thus finishes our tale, set long ago in a time when kingdoms rose and fell at a moment's notice and the obedience of one girl saved her entire race and forever changed the course of history.

Unable to sleep, the king demands the chronicles be read to him. He hears the name Mordicai, the man who saved his life by telling the queen of the plot on the king's life.

The purifying baths in the court of women as the candidates prepared for their night with the king.

Javad and Arjana-history in the making.

The common area in the palace of women.

Printed in the USA
CPSIA information can be obtained
at www.ICGtesting.com
LVHW022054261223
767427LV00003B/112